BETTS' BEST

Gary D. Hillard

Black Rose Writing | Texas

©2019 by Gary D. Hillard
All rights reserved. No part of this book may be reproduced, stored in a retrieval system or transmitted in any form or by any means without the prior written permission of the publishers, except by a reviewer who may quote brief passages in a review to be printed in a newspaper, magazine or journal.

The author grants the final approval for this literary material.

First printing

This is a work of fiction. Names, characters, businesses, places, events, and incidents are either the products of the author's imagination or used in a fictitious manner. Any resemblance to actual persons, living or dead, or actual events is purely coincidental.

ISBN: 978-1-68433-404-9
PUBLISHED BY BLACK ROSE WRITING
www.blackrosewriting.com

Printed in the United States of America
Suggested Retail Price (SRP) $19.95

Betts' Best is printed in Calluna

*As a planet-friendly publisher, Black Rose Writing does its best to eliminate unnecessary waste to reduce paper usage and energy costs, while never compromising the reading experience. As a result, the final word count vs. page count may not meet common expectations.

Mr. Hillard would like to thank the children and adults, whose bravery and resilience provided such inspiration, and hope, and the dedicated readers who loved Betts as much as he did.

BETTS' BEST

CHAPTER ONE

The First Visit

Betts first came to the cabin, all of a sudden, when she was seven. Tina had slid her Chevy up the dirt road, throwing gravel from side to side, and taken the sharp turn to her brother's cabin at speed. Betts, unbuckled of course, flew back and forth in the back seat, padded a bit by the black plastic trash bag of her belongings that her mother had packed just before the impromptu trip, as well as the Taco Bell bags, plastic cups and plastic bottles, all the loose detritus flowing back and forth in the car like trash caught in a whirlpool. She had tried hanging on to the back of her mother's seat, but her tiny fingers could never get enough of a grip. When the car finally slid to a stop, Betts was surprised to discover that she made the whole wild ride without even a hint of her usual carsickness. Perhaps terror is a good preventative for nausea.

Tina was twenty-six years old on this particular June morning, and Ames, her younger brother, who was now standing in the doorway of the tiny cabin, holding a book in one hand and a cup of hot tea in the other, was twenty-three. Both were tall and thin, with dark hair, and both had a look of wary damage about them. Betts was dark and thin as well, seven years old, but only about as tall as a five-year-old might be. Even as small as she was, she had outgrown her pants, which ended several inches above her sneakers. She climbed out of the car, clutching her trash bag, and stood beside her mother, looking out from behind her hip, taking in her uncle and his tiny cabin on the side of the mountain.

Her mother spoke. "Betts needs you to take her for a few days," she said. Betts said nothing, but her look at her mother told Ames that this plan came as a surprise to her as well. Ames thought about the cabin. The lack of plumbing, his total lack of experience with either caring for children or really ever having been a child, his diagnosis of PTSD after two tours in the Sand Wars, and finally the fact that he had never even met this little girl before, in spite of the fact that Tina lived about sixteen miles away. Ames said nothing, and Betts moved a bit to better take in the place. Tina said nothing as well, waiting for her brother to agree to the plan.

Betts looked up at Ames, and then at the book in his hand. "I brought a book along, too," she said.

Ames looked from his sister, who had tossed her cigarette butt onto the ground, and was busy lighting another, to the little girl at her side. She looked back at him. "OK," he said.

Tina paused just a bit. "Her stuff is in the bag," she said. She looked down at her daughter. "Mind yourself," she said and turned to put her hand on the car door. She got in, slammed the door so that it would latch, and then looked out the window at the child. "And don't run your mouth." She backed the car up against the brush, then drove back onto the trail, spinning the tires a bit, and disappearing down the dirt road.

Ames watched her go and then turned to the child. "Would you like some tea?" he asked.

"Sure," she said. "Do you have a bathroom?"

Ames was picking up the cigarette butt, which he crushed out and put in his pocket. He pointed over to the outhouse. "Sort of," he said. "It's in there."

Betts looked at the tiny wooden structure down the gravel path. "Really?" she asked. Ames said nothing, and Betts walked down the path, hurrying a bit. She found the door on the other side, and he heard the door open, and then close. Ames set his book on the saw table, and leaned on his elbows, looking down the valley, thinking about this new turn of events. "How do you flush?" came Betts' voice from inside the outhouse.

Ames grinned a bit, for the first time that day, and said, "You don't," and sipped his tea.

Betts exited the outhouse, picked up her trash bag of belongings, and turned to her uncle. "Where do I put my stuff?"

"I don't know," he answered. He saw Betts's face shift a bit, and then added, "Let's go find out."

CHAPTER TWO

The Little Green Stove

Maybe the best way to see the cabin for the first time would be to look at the drawings that Betts made during her first week there. Betts drew much of the time, on napkins while waiting for her parents to finish at McDonald's, on envelopes, and pages from the school. She drew at school as well, where her drawing was both a source of trouble ("Betts! Pay attention, and put that away!") and a source of wonder to the adults who found that the silent little girl had so much that she could say with a pencil or crayons. Betts brought drawings home to her mother, who looked at them, and then laid them on the counter. "Nice."

Betts drew a bit that first day, after the decision to set up her stuff under the ladder to the loft where Ames slept, and that she would sleep on the couch, long and comfortable, and worn at the edges. Betts had sipped at the tea, found it lacking in sugar, and set it back on the table in front of the couch. Ames had said nothing, aware that his silence was making the little girl nervous, maybe, but simply having no idea of what to say.

Ames sat in the chair by the window, and Betts sat on the couch, her hands in her lap, looking around the small room. "Can I look around?" she asked.

"Sure," said Ames, and Betts wandered around the room, finding the kitchen area with its small propane stove, a plastic bucket of fresh water, an old white sink set into a plywood counter, which she later learned drained to the outside, some salvaged cabinets hung over the counter, and some shelves built below them. The green teapot that now sat steaming on the table was thrown on a wheel by someone unknown, except by the initials "GD" on the base. The pot had thick, even walls, and the shape was almost a perfect sphere, just the tiniest bit squat. The glaze was a dark green, almost black at the base, lightening to a deep green, a lighter green, a green with bits of yellow, like the leaves in the spring, then a lighter blue, like the sky, and finally the darkest blue, like the night sky and space beyond. The handle was set into the pot, an old and dark stained bamboo stick that ran across the top, arched like a rainbow.

Betts studied the pot, not touching it, but walking around it to see. "This is pretty. It looks like the world," she said.

Ames thought about that for a bit. "Yeah," he said. "I guess it does."

The cabin was about twelve feet deep and maybe eighteen feet long. Some of the windows were different sizes, spotless clean and salvaged, showing the green-tinted light of the early summer day, and, to the south, the view all the way down the mountain, across the White River Valley, the curve of the river visible at some points, and the clusters of small towns that led off into the distance. Rochester Mountain stood some twenty-five miles away, and beyond that, Killington and Pico stood, grey-blue in the distance, some eighty miles or more away. The windows gave a view worth a million dollars, as the realtors would say, and Betts was in awe, staring silently for what seemed to Ames like a very long time. She walked to the main window and put her hands on the smooth sill, her nose almost touching the glass. Ames sipped his tea and opened his book.

Bookshelves lined the walls where there were no windows, and books of all kinds stood in neat rows. Betts could see more bookshelves in the loft where the ladder led, in the shadows up above the windows. "You have a lot of books," she said.

"Yeah," replied Ames. "I guess."

"Can I look at them?" she asked.

"Sure," said Ames.

And she did, pulling a few out, then putting them back in place, tipping her head sideways to read the covers as she worked her way across the room. She stopped about midway and pulled a book out. "Can I read this?" she asked.

"Sure," said Ames. "What is it?"

"*The Wind in the Willows*," she replied. "They had this at school."

Ames thought about the book for a moment and remembered gathering a set of books from the table outside the library down in town, extras which were being sold for fifty cents each. He had liked that book, hardcover with the tight library binding, and the pictures that captured the mood of the stories so well. "Can you read that?" he asked.

"Sure," said Betts. "I read good."

"OK," said Ames.

Betts put the book on the table in front of the couch, and then picked up her tea and took a sip. She looked at Ames. "Do you like this?" she asked.

"Yep," he answered.

She took another sip, and then another, and then set the cup down. She went to the little green stove, set on a swept brick hearth to the left side of the cabin, a black stovepipe rising up and then disappearing through the wall. The stove was a dark green, shiny, and threw enough heat that Betts could feel it on her face from several feet away. The stove had long, thin legs, and each side showed a big, fluffy-tailed squirrel with impossibly long ears, eating an acorn, with a wreath of oak leaves all around him. Betts stood transfixed. "Why is the stove so pretty?"

Ames thought about the question for a bit. "I don't know," he started. "I never thought about that. It's a good stove. It's made in Denmark, across the ocean, and it's made really well. People there have winter almost all year long, and everybody has a woodstove. Even the rich folks heat with wood because they know wood heat is the best you can get. And they all burn birch, the prettiest wood on the planet, and the best smelling, too. The guy that had this cabin put it in, so I don't know where he got it." Ames thought for a bit.

"I really like that stove," Betts said. "It's on."

"Yeah, it's still a little chilly, and I like running the stove anyway. We'll probably run it for a few more weeks."

Betts hovered on the word "we'll," looking at this man she just met. "Can I draw it?" she asked.

"Sure," Ames said. "Paper is in the box under the table, and there should be pens and pencils in there, too."

Betts looked under the table and drew out an old cigar box from the lower shelf. It was just large enough to hold full-sized sheets of paper, and about four inches deep, made of straight-grained wood, with dovetailed joints and a dull brass latch and hinges held with tiny nails. "King's Coronas" was written on the front, and the side said "Corona Size," in smaller letters. Betts opened the catch, and lifted the lid, seeing a stack of paper and envelopes, cards, and on top, wooden pencils, a brass sharpener, and old pens, ballpoints, but a couple of fountain pens were there, too. A cellophane envelope held stamps, and a small pair of scissors lay there as well. There might have been the faintest smell of tobacco, but mostly the box smelled of correspondence.

"This is so cool," she said. "Can I really use this?"

"Sure," said Ames, turning back to his book. He was reading about the impact of beavers on wildlife and agriculture in North America.

Betts selected a few sheets of typing paper and two wooden pencils, one of which was dark blue wood, with a fancy ring at the top. She held it up. "This is a real drawing pencil!" she said. Ames said nothing and kept reading. She settled by the little green stove and began to draw. Betts was quiet, with only the sound of her making the occasional "mmmmmmmm" sound as she worked, shifting where she sat from time to time. "This is a great stove!" she said, looking at Ames. Ames said nothing. "That squirrel is really neat!" and Ames said nothing.

Finally, he looked up. "Doing OK?" he asked.

"Mmmmmmm," said Betts. Ames went back to reading, and Betts continued to draw the little green stove.

Betts had a woodstove at her mother's house, of course. Wood heat was the heat of the poor in Vermont and the back-up heat for anyone familiar enough with Vermont winters to not trust to oil and gas. That woodstove was an old sheet metal Ashley, a cabinet stove, with a thin metal cabinet around a heavier sheet metal stove inside. It was brown, and gold and a little bit rusty, and had a slotted lid that was perfect for drying mittens and socks in a matter of minutes.

Any woodstove is a thing of love and fascination if you are a young child, living in a cold and drafty trailer, with cracked and cardboarded windows, a gap at the door sill, and icy winds and even tiny drifts of snow finding their way in on the long winter nights and days. Betts had been drawn to the stove, of course, in spite of the slapped hands and the sharp "NO!" that often came when she was near it. She would toast herself, first one side, and then the other, and then her back, and then turn and face the stove, and feel the heat on her face, fighting the chill of winter that always seemed to win in the drafty trailer.

She was entranced by the searing view of coals and flames when the thick steel door was opened, and a log or two tossed in, and for a moment, the awesome power of fire was seen there inside, dancing and twisting, leaping and flickering, even puffing out a few clouds of eye-stinging smoke into the room. It was a reminder of how the stove managed to keep the thin line between containment and disaster, keeping the fire just a fraction of an inch from consuming the house, and the family with it.

Winter in Vermont, for those who tried to live on the minimum wage, was a terror to behold. Coming as it did every year, it breaks cars, slicks roads, kills kittens, freezes feet, fingers and cheeks. Leaving the honey out on the kitchen table makes it too thick to pour, the pipes freeze, and the shower curtain gets stiff like dried leather in the morning. Winter, though, is pretty sweet if your house is large and warm and the heating bills are paid without worry. And your car sits in a garage. And it helps if you have a season ski pass, cross country skis, and new studded tires on your Subaru. And good winter clothing from L.L. Bean. And a fellow down the road to plow your drive and shovel your walk. Some folks in Vermont have that kind of winter every year. But not Betts and her family. Their winter was hard and long.

But winter had its beauty, like so many deadly things. Betts loved the snow, the sound under her boots, the drifts up against the house. The wonderful way the snow covered up all that was ugly, the dog poop, the abandoned things in the yard, the cans and bottle, the bare and failed flowers and brush of the fall. All was wiped white, soft and silent, with only the thin hiss of the blowing flakes against the faded metal siding of the trailer. Numbness was an acceptable price to pay for this insulating blindness to the hurts and brokenness of the world, a price Betts willingly paid with the snow, and her own muffled existence.

"A woodstove lets you keep a fire in the house, without the house burning down, if you do it right," said Ames, introducing Betts to the little green stove in the cabin. "Do it wrong, and you might set the house on fire." Betts nodded, knowing exactly how that worked. "Do it right," he said, "and you have something magic, pulling the heat of the summer sun out of the last year's wood, shining the sun's warmth into the room, heating up a kettle for tea or for washing up, drying your socks and mittens, leaving birch smoke drifting up from the stovepipe, and a bucket of ashes to bring back to the garden to feed the soil."

The little green woodstove was magic, with its slim, long legs, a lip beneath the door to catch the straying coal or ash, a spinner to let the fresh air whistle in to feed a hungry fire, and twisted down to whisper while the stove burned slow and low through the night. A thing of beauty, with the well-fed squirrel cast in deep relief on each side. A machined plate on the top, perfect for the kettle, or, taken off, a perfect spot for a heavy cast iron pot to sit right over the flames.

Her uncle loved the stove, tending it constantly in the winter, and keeping it dusted and ready in the brief summer months. The stove is the heart of the home, he had said, and she could see that that was true. Tending the woodstove was a careful process in the cabin on the mountain. One step followed another, with the knowledge that if each step were done correctly, the result would be a good fire and a warm home.

Betts loved that. Do it all carefully, do it right, and you could count on things working out well. She had watched her uncle while he tended the fire, cleaning out the ash, and coaxing a fire from the hidden coals at the back of the stove. Waking up to cold air, cold floors and shivering goosebumps on her arms, Betts would hear her uncle already up and started in the morning. Keeping the cabin warm was his first task of the day, and one he enjoyed. The little green woodstove ran "on a single match," as Ames liked to say, from the middle of October through April.

Ames worked differently than the other adults Betts had observed. Ames never swore, or threatened, or complained. He seemed to love his work, or at least accept it, whatever the work was, and leaned close in to see what he was doing. His hands stayed on the job, and his temper was steady and he seemed satisfied with the work at hand. Ames had said, "You can't control much, but you have control over how you respond to what happens, and even if a job goes hard, if you handle yourself well, then that's good work."

Betts had watched her uncle care for the stove those cool mornings when she first moved to the cabin. Shy and cold, Betts had stayed under the covers, peeking out from beneath the pair of quilts and the down comforter that Ames had brought down from the loft for her makeshift bed on the couch. The air had a nip in the mornings, right on her nose, and her breath sometimes made quick clouds that hung for a moment, damping her eyelashes, then fading into the cabin air.

Betts had seen the black stovepipe rising four feet from the little stove, take a turn and disappear into the wall. She soon went outside to see where the pipe went, and found that on the outside wall of the cabin the pipe emerged, took another turn, and rose straight beside the cedar cabin wall, braced twice as it rose some twelve more feet above the roofline of the cabin, topped at last with a pointed hat made of tin. She watched the grey smoke curl out of the pipe, swirling a bit at first, then collecting into a thin stream that drifted a bit in the breeze but rose above the trees, moving off with the wind, scenting the air on the mountain with the sharp smell of birch.

That first morning, Betts had watched her uncle as he squatted beside the little green stove, his wool socks on the smooth plywood floor, his jeans loose and baggy, his shirt untucked, and his eye close upon the dark ashes inside the stove. A tin bucket stood beside him, with the lid of the bucket upturned beneath the open door to the stove. Propped against the stove was a poker, formed from steel about the thickness of a pencil, bent with a hoop for your hand, and with a two-inch hook on the other end. Ames held a small tin shovel, folded from a single sheet of galvanized steel, folded in such a way as to make a hollow round handle, and a flat scoop, ridged with the accordion folds of the steel.

Ames shoveled out the ash from the front half of the stove, tipping each scoop into the tin bucket. He moved slowly, for the ash was both hot and very light, and would move into the air if given half a chance. When Ames had the front half of the stove empty of ash, down to the iron, he leaned the shovel against the stove and took the poker in his hand. He raked through the ash in the back of the stove, finding glowing red coals the size of grapes or plums, which glowed brightly in the sudden fresh air. He moved these coals to a neat pile in the front of the stove, then, setting the poker against the side of the stove, took the little shovel, and scooped the remaining ash from the back of the stove, setting each scoop into the pail. A few more coals were discovered this way, and they were added to the red pile glowing in the front of the stove. When the last ash was removed, he took a small broom and swept the bit of ash on the shelf on the front of the stove into the pail, then pressed the lid on, and set the pail back in its place behind the stove.

He then took three splits of birch, cut the year before and well-seasoned, and laid the first on, and then the second beside it, on top of the bed of coals. The third he laid at a bit of an angle across the two below, leaving room for the air, and the flames to come, to work its way around and between the splits of birch. The white papery bark caught quickly with a burst of yellow flame, and a grey smoke that rushed up the stovepipe but scented the air in the cabin as well. He eyed the flames and the splits, shifted the top split just a bit to one side, and the closed the cast iron door, dropping the latch into place, and opening the spinner, letting in a rush of fresh air to feed the hungry fire. Betts listened to the whistle of the air rushing into the stove, and heard the pop and crackle of the birch as the wood beneath the paperbark began to catch and burn.

Ames squatted beside the stove, listening, and then, after a few minutes, spun the spinner down about three turns, quieting the rushing air to a softer whisper. The iron of the stove ticked a bit as it heated up, and Betts could feel the warmth began to fill the room. Ames went to the counter and filled the kettle from the bucket of spring water on the floor. He set the kettle on the stove, where it rocked back and forth a bit from the shifting water inside. He turned to see Betts watching from beneath the covers on her couch bed, and smiled.

"Good morning," he said. "Stove's going to get hot, so be careful. I'm going outside for a bit. You know where the outhouse is."

Betts lay in her makeshift bed and thought. She had never had a day start like this one. At home, whatever craziness was running around the house was quick to find her, and latch on. It seemed that at least one of the adults in her house had always been angry, and often, it was both of them. Betts had found only temporary shelter in her bed, because the adult anger was like a wildfire, flickering this way and that, hungry for fuel. It was just a matter of time until that flame found her. Betts lay on her couch bed here in the cabin on the mountain, warm beneath the quilts and covers, feeling the air in the cabin warm-up, with the crackle of the stove quieting down as the wood began to burn in earnest.

The kettle began to show just a bit of steam, and Betts was worried that she would get in trouble for touching it or perhaps get in trouble for letting it boil. Just then, Ames came in the door, his face a bit red from the cold morning, slipped off his shoes, and took the steaming kettle off the stove. He set it on the plywood counter beside the sink and took the teapot off the shelf. Betts already loved the teapot, full and round and looking like the earth herself. Ames set a screen cup into the mouth of the teapot, and then took a mason jar of black tea, labeled "Earl Grey," opened the jar and spooned in two heaping spoons full of tea into the strainer. He capped the jar and put it back in its place on the shelf. He took the kettle, lifted it over the teapot, and poured the steaming water through the leaves and screen, filing the pot. He rested the teapot lid over the screen, keeping most of the steam in, and set the kettle back on the counter beside the sink.

He turned to find Betts watching him. "Tea will be ready in a bit. Would you like some?" Betts nodded.

While the tea steeped, Ames slipped his shoes back on and went outside. He returned with an armload of split birch, laying the splits in a stack at the back of the stove. Ames stooped by the little green woodstove, and lifted the latch on the door, peering inside. Betts could see the glow on his face as he studied the fire. He took the poker, shifted the burning splits just a bit, then latched the door, and tightened the spinner down until just a whisper of air could be heard feeding the stove. The cabin was warm now, and Ames had poured a cup of tea for Betts, and another for himself, and set both of them on the table. Ames sat in one of the two chairs, and took up his tea, blowing across the cup.

She saw the steam around his face, and the steam rising from the other cup, the cup that had been set out for her. "That must be my place," she thought, with a slow smile.

The sun was up in the sky, and only a few words had been spoken. The stove had been cared for, a new fire laid, and a pot of tea was ready. In the silence, and in the quiet order of small things done well, Betts could feel the tightness around her heart open just a bit.

Tea, it turned out, was more like hot water than it was like soda, and the brown color and earthy smell was unlike anything that Betts had had before. Coffee she was used to, drinking the bits left in cups at home, cold, and sugared to the point of being a bit like Coke. Tea in the cabin was hot, steaming, fresh from the pot, and poured out just for her. Ames had offered Betts her choice of cups on the first full day, and she had chosen one with a huge moose head on it, the antlers wrapping all the way around the cup and the words "Maine. How Life Should Be" on it.

"I love this!" said Betts.

Ames used a cup that was dark green, with a dark brown strip near the top, and a small chip near the handle. Betts rose from the couch, still dressed in yesterday's clothes, and made her way to the table, taking the empty chair across from Ames, and taking the hot cup in her hands.

She sat, looking deep into the tea as if to find her fortune there, while Ames sipped his in silence. The fire was quiet, the cabin warm, and Ames seemed content with the silence. Betts was nervous. This kind of quiet was something new to her, and it made her uneasy. She was torn between waiting him out, and saying nothing until he spoke, and talking a blue streak, filling the uncomfortable space with busy words, chattering to keep her own thoughts quiet. While Betts was debating this with herself, Ames spoke up.

"Would you like some eggs, toast, cereal? I don't know what you have for breakfast."

Betts didn't answer the question. She rarely had breakfast and had a question of her own. "Where did you go this morning?" she asked. "I didn't hear the truck."

Ames looked like he was still stuck on the breakfast question, but then answered. "Up to the top rock. It's a piece of slate, big enough to stretch out on, that sits up at the top of this slope. You can see pretty much forever from up there. I go up first thing in the morning after I tend to the fire. You can see the cabin from up there, and the smoke from the woodstove. It takes a while for the stove to catch, and I can see from the smoke how it's doing. I like to get up where you can see for a ways. Having my eyes focused way out seems to be good for my head, somehow." He stopped, aware that this might sound odd.

Betts asked, "Can I come up there, too, sometime?"

"Sure," Ames said. "Maybe tomorrow, if you're up."

Betts thought about this. She had wanted things before, but it seemed like a long time since she had asked for something. She had learned to want things in a secret way, wishing for a book bag she had seen in town, or wishing she had a dog or a cat. Wishing that her mother and father would stop fighting. Asking, though, just opened you up for disappointment, ridicule, or worse. "Don't ask" was one of the rules that Betts had come up with for herself, hoping to bring some order and control into her life, a life that seemed to have precious little of either. "Don't ask" was a part of the broader set of rules about not calling attention to yourself. These included "Don't make noise," "Don't show you're upset," "It's not your business," and the most important one, "Don't fight back."

These rules helped Betts to feel a little more in control of her life, although they did little to reduce the amount of lightning that seemed to seek her out to strike. Her parents had had rules as well, including "Do what you're told," and the big one, "Don't run your mouth." But Betts still found herself the target of adult wrath, regardless of how hard she tried to follow the rules. Because it really wasn't about the rules. She had finally understood this.

She sipped her tea, and Ames got up to cook some eggs. It was different here. She wondered what the rules would be. She thought about the top rock and then looked around the cabin. Neat as a pin. She looked at the couch with her covers and pillow, and she got up, and folded the quilts, laying them on the floor to do so, and then the down comforter, and stacked them all beside the couch, and set the pillow neatly on top. Keeping things neat seemed to be a rule here. Betts liked that.

CHAPTER THREE

Settling In, and Leaving

Ames was so different than anyone Betts had ever encountered before. She had heard Ames referred to as her mother's "crazy brother" during the fights at home, although nothing she had seen so far seemed crazy. Just really different. Ames moved slowly, often sitting reading, or sometimes, sitting without doing anything at all, looking out the window, or at the little green stove. Much of what he did during the day was tidying up the already tidy cabin, making simple meals, eating, and then washing up after. He spent time tending to the stove, both bringing in wood, building a fire, and tending to it throughout the day.

Ames read a lot, too. Books were all over the cabin, thick and thin, from the library, from the thrift store, or from garage sales he drove past, and magazines and newspapers, some of which were delivered to the cabin. He read slowly and seemed to go over the same page a number of times, sometimes mouthing the words so that Betts could almost guess at what he was reading. Sometimes he would close his eyes and hold his face in his hands, quietly breathing for a bit. He cut wood for himself and for the neighbors, and he would deliver the wood he sold in the old blue truck, stacking it as perfectly for them as he did for himself. Neighbors called when a tree went down, and Ames had a reputation for being able to tackle a tree that others found too dangerous to work on. Ames did a wonderful job and was offered more work than he chose to take.

Betts was on her own much of the time that summer, while Ames read, tended to the cabin or cut wood. She took advantage of this time to explore the land around the cabin, the top rock, where she often accompanied Ames first thing in the morning and the wildlands within calling distance from the cabin. The spring was a favorite place of hers. The spring was above the cabin, a dark red tile some two feet in diameter, placed long ago to collect and protect the waters that poured up from inside the mountain. A black plastic pipe let the water spill a few feet onto a flat slab of slate, from which it ran and gurgled into clean gravel, and finally, a tiny stream, that worked its way down the side of the mountain, joining other small streams to form the creek that ran along the twisty road, flowing into the White River down in town, and from there to the Connecticut River, and from there, on to the sea.

Checking the spring was a weekly task, and Ames tended to the spring with the same care and reverence he showed the little green woodstove. Betts watched while Ames shifted the heavy steel lid off the tile, exposing the pool of water inside the spring. He brought with him a small screen net on a long pole and dipped out any of the things that might have found their way into the spring, including bugs, leaves, twigs, and once, a tiny green frog. He checked the water level, slipping the wooden handle of the net down into the water until it reached the gravel bed, then pulled it up, noting the wet mark on the wood, which was notched with inches like a yard stick. Ames would then slide the heavy steel lid back into place, and check the cement plug where the black plastic pipe brought the water out from the spring.

Water from the spring was hauled down to the house in a five-gallon plastic bucket, fitted with a tight, green lid. He would bring the empty bucket from the cabin, pry off the lid, and set the bucket beneath the running spring water. Betts like to listen to the sound change as the water filled the bucket. The filled bucket was returned to the cabin, and placed on the floor beneath the counter, right beside the sink. A metal ladle drew the water out, and Ames filled the kettle for tea, for washing up, or took a bit of cold water for a drink. Showers were accomplished with a metal spray tank, filled with a mix of hot water from the kettle and enough cold water from the bucket to make it nice and warm, with the tank then pumped up and carried to the square of bricks set beside the porch, with a real shower curtain that could be pulled for privacy. Two gallons made a nice shower.

The outhouse was a short walk down from the cabin, on a gravel path. It was made from grey barn wood, sided inside and out with fresh cedar, roofed with salvaged tin, and entered by a full-sized wooden door, set with a half window, which both let in the light in the daytime, and showed the beautiful view down the valley while you sat. The wood inside was sanded smooth, and the seat was an old oak seat and lid, with greenish brass hinges, salvaged from a real toilet. A black pipe rose in the corner, exiting a few feet above the roof, carrying all the air from the pit below, leaving the inside smelling like cedar and shade and little else. Betts was leery at first but soon found herself loving the walk, the privacy and the lovely view way better than the stained and smelly bathrooms she had used before.

Ames told Betts about the spring. He put his hand into the cold water that spilled from the black plastic pipe onto the splash rock, a large slab of slate they were both standing on. "This water comes from the snow and rain that fall on the mountain. Bear Mountain was made when the rocks way down deep pushed hard against each other, and the rock layers that used to lie flat, like these here," he said, holding a small piece of slate up for her to see the layers in the rock. "These layers were flat because this rock was made at the bottom of a big ocean that covered up this land a long, long time ago. When the big rocks way deep pushed against each other, this rock buckled and broke, and came up to make these mountains, and the rocks stayed pushed up at angles under the ground." He showed her a chunk of ledge, slate that tipped up from the ground, the bane of farmers in Vermont, but one of the things that makes Vermont so pretty, and a part of what makes the Vermont springs flow.

"When the snow on the mountain melts, and when the rain falls, some of the water runs off, and some of it soaks in, soaking in through the soil, and down into the rocks. Sometimes the water that flows in between these rock layers comes out at the surface, where the rock comes out a piece of ledge, like here, where the spring is. That water might have been seeping through the mountain for ten years, or fifty, or a hundred, filtered all super clean, and cooled down by living inside the mountain, way deep, where it's always cool."

Betts put her hand into the water, and drew it back with a little shriek because the water was so cold. Then she put her hand back in again, and stood with one foot in the pool, her hand in the icy water, and her other hand pointing up to the sky. "You mean that this water was rain or snow that fell on the top of the mountain, like, years ago, and it's now coming out for us to drink?"

Ames nodded. "And the water that we don't drink will run down this little tiny stream here, and then find that other little stream that comes

When her three-week assessment was done, she was transferred to the Children's Retreat, a long-term residential facility with locked doors that could keep children for up to a year. That year was about up, and Betts remained unchanged. If anything, she was worse, with the medication steadily increased until she was bloated and semi-conscious much of the day.

Zoey had returned to visit Betts again, after seeing the children's unit at the state hospital. Betts was in the dayroom, a locked and stuffy place, where seven or eight children gathered around a TV, which was enclosed in a Plexiglas cage, half watching what seemed to be "101 Dalmatians." The smell of burned microwave popcorn filled the air, smothering the weaker smell of urine and dirty socks. Two staff sat behind the children, scrolling on their phones. The TV was turned up to compete with one of the boys who made a constant sound like a goat bleating, and another girl who rocked back and forth and said, "No!" over and over.

Zoey found Betts again away from the TV, standing beside a greasy Plexiglas window, looking out onto the parking lot below. Her hand was on the plastic, and she looked out at the world outside. Zoey squatted beside her, and Betts drew back a bit, looking at Zoey, and then recognizing her as the woman who had visited a few times before. Betts attention went back to the window, and Zoey sat down on the door and stewed to herself. Where could this odd little girl go?

There are advantages to experience in any field, but there are also some great gifts in being wet behind the ears - green if you will. Zoey was green in every good way, green like the new growth in the spring, bright green and full of life and energy, and not yet beaten dull by the astonishing world of child protection and placement. Zoey had been the kid that the other kids went to for help, and she had known that this would be her work since she first had the concept. She had been employed by the county for almost two months, following her supervisor around on cases. Zoey was blessed with a kind supervisor, who worried about her young hire, but respected her as well.

Zoey sat on the floor beside Betts and looked at the drifting, confused child who stood beside her. "Betts?" she wondered. "Short for Betsey? Rebecca? Maybe Bets, like the lottery?" Most of the kids on Zoey's caseload were clear-cut protection cases, kids with belt marks, bruises, cigarette burns and rope marks, even, kids who found themselves in the State of Vermont's custody to avoid further abuse.

But Betts case was so different. Into custody, like the others, with the marks of abuse, but then so many problems. Five foster homes blown, three of them treatment level homes, all because of Betts sudden violence. Her medication list was four pages long, with meds tried, increased, crossed off, new meds tried, increased, and then new meds added. It was clear from reading the record that Betts had taken almost every pill, and several shots, that the doctors had available.

Her current diagnosis list included PTSD, ADHD, Reactive Attachment Disorder, Bipolar illness, with schizoaffective disorder, and even childhood schizophrenia under consideration. There were frequent mentions of the reclusive uncle, as evidence of a family history of mental illness. Notes from the staff showed Betts to be nobody's favorite, with complaints of assault, uncooperative behavior, isolation, refusals, and ongoing struggle with the ADLs, the activities of daily living. Baths and showers seemed to be a source of trouble. And the night shift reported as many conflicts as the day shift.

She made no friends, refused, or was unable to participate in the activities of the day, and when left alone, wandered to the nearest window and stared outside. She had tried to push her way past the locked doors on several occasions and had been restrained six times as a result. Zoey had found Betts in restraints once, lying flat on a stripped bed in the hallway, right outside the nurse's station, her hand and feet stretched toward the grey metal bed corners by long grey flannel bands. Zoey had first seen the slight smile on Betts' face, and then her swollen, purpled hands, and feet. She felt a flush of anger, then asked a passing nurse about the swelling, and the nurse took a quick look. "These might be a little too tight," the nurse admitted, loosening them just a bit. "But she has to learn to not push out the door."

Zoey read all the material she could find on Betts, who, for such a tiny child, had generated over 180 pages of clinical notes so far. There were no school notes in the record, though, and Zoey wondered why there was no evidence of Betts prior to her involvement in the system.

Zoey had a favorite professor in the social work department out in Colorado, Mrs. Cleary, grey-haired and patient, who had always stressed this very point. "Don't make up your mind on what you see after. Find them before; look for the good days, the strengths, the interests, the working person before they became broken. That shows you who they were, and who they can become again." She told her young students, "Use a calendar, look for patterns, check the good days and the bad days, and see where the trouble began. Who likes your client? Who doesn't? Why? Remember, doctors and their staff will always try to build a case for care, and that's a case for illness. Your client needs at least one person willing to see their strengths, this history, and to have faith in their ability to be well."

Zoey loved this so well she wrote it into her notes, and now copied "The Cleary page" into her planner each year as a reminder of the kind of work she wanted to do. Zoey had been in love with the work, back when she was in school, and thank goodness, for Betts' sake, that Zoey still had that love driving her.

Zoey had been instructed to find a long-term placement for Betts, something with "security," meaning locked doors and staff trained in restraints. The only secure, long-term facility in Vermont was the children's floor at the State Hospital, or a semi-private facility down in Brattleboro, a large facility that, with a Medicaid waiver, might consider an admission that seemed to require their "level of care." Zoey had heard horror stories about both places, stories of neglect and abuse, and had yet to hear anything positive, except their ability to hold clients for long periods of time with no need for further placement work. This fact made them a favorite for workers who were ready to "put a case on ice," but Zoey was not one of those.

Her supervisor had been clear that she would not permit Betts access to another agency foster home, for fear of further burning out this precious commodity. Tina and Peter had done nothing to help Betts return to their home, seeming relieved to have her gone. Kinship placements were a dead end as well, with Peter's family known to be unsafe with kids, and Tina's family limited to a dying mother in a nursing home up in Burlington, and the crazy brother who lived up in the mountains.

Zoey was at the end of her very limited options and found herself sitting once again on the floor of the day room, close to her young client, even if she were not able to be in conversation with her. While Betts stared out the window, Zoey stared at Betts, and wondered, out loud, for some sweet reason, "Well, Betts, where can you go to live?"

Zoey was shocked to see Betts turn to her, her eyes struggling to focus, and her dry lips that had been cracked and stuck together, slowly open. "I want to go back and live with Uncle Ames. In the cabin, with the little green woodstove. Where the spring is." Betts's vague smile disappeared, and her eyes suddenly glistened with tears. As one tear made its way down her cheek, Betts said, "I want to go back." Zoey stared, and as she did, Betts slipped away, her smile vague and her hands clutching at the greasy window. Only a tear remained on Betts's cheek, and Zoey reached out, slowly so as to not spook the girl, and wiped the tear away.

And so, it came to be that in April of 2013, about a year and a half after Tina had picked up Betts, that another car drove up the twisty road to Ames' cabin. An early spring had left much of the snow melted and flowing down the mountain, and bits of new growth could be seen in a red blush on the maples. Willows had some light green, and the sound of water had returned to Bear Mountain. Ames was much as we had left him, still going through the day, keeping the cabin neat, the machinery cared for, cutting firewood and clearing out down trees.

Betts shoes remained on the porch, however, and he picked them up every day as he swept, and in spite of his last comment so long ago, Ames was not really how he was before. He saw his life a bit through the eyes of Betts now, and was excited to see a new bird, a new plant, tracks in the mud near the spring. He sometimes said, "Betts would like that." Her interest in the great world around her had caught him up just a bit, and now his library choices had led him deeper into a study of the natural world. Her moose cup was washed but put back on the table, not the shelf, and as sad as he was that Betts was gone, there was a bit of her still about the place, and he liked that.

This April morning, with much of the snow gone, but the ice still very much in the ground, we find Ames having his tea up on the top rock, the little green woodstove fed and happily kicking the sunlight out of some nice birch splits, and the scent of birch smoke in the air. Ames had followed some snowshoe hare tracks a bit earlier in the morning and was pleased to see them disappear into a brush pile he had built a few years before. The woods were not a very safe place for a hare, and he was glad to have provided some shelter. Ames heard the car make the turn into his drive, a rare enough event that his curiosity was up, and he walked down from the top rock, expecting to find a neighbor wanting some springtime tree work done.

Instead, he found a young woman getting out of a four-wheel-drive minivan, shod with all-season tires. Ames was impressed that she had made it up the hill. And he noticed that she was pretty, too. Zoey took in the tiny cabin, the wild-looking man standing beside the rough table, holding the steaming mug, and tried to picture what little she knew about Betts and her time with her uncle. Zoey Simmons smiled, but she felt unsure and a bit vulnerable this cold spring morning. The drive up had been a bit iffy, and she made a note to herself to ask about getting some better tires for the van. She carried a clipboard and glanced at it before she introduced herself. She asked for Ames Bennet by name, and Ames replied that that was who he was. Zoey glanced around at the tiny cabin, the outhouse, and the wood lot, kept clear of snow over the winter, with a set of rounds beside the splitter. Ames' truck, an old four-wheel-drive Ford, had the kind of tires she wished had been on the van.

There was a pause, as Zoey seemed to consider whether she should go on with the conversation, or turn around and go back down the road. Ames was surprised to find himself attempting a smile and then inviting the young woman into the cabin for a cup of tea. And Zoey was surprised to find herself not only accepting the invitation, but also pleased to have been invited. Ames led the way to the porch and held the door as Zoey entered. She noted him taking off his boots, and slipped her shoes off as well, setting them on the swept floor beside a pair of child-sized hiking shoes.

Ames motioned for Zoey to find a seat, and she sat at the table in the chair that Ames usually sat in, and picked up the mug with the moose on it. "That's nice," she said. "The way life should be. I like that."

Ames brought her another cup, filled with tea, and set it down in front of her. "Me, too," he said. She sat at the table and took in the small space. Neat, clean and tidy, the windows spotless and showing the great valley that fell below the cabin, with the trees and woodlot, and an outhouse perhaps, then the towns along the river, and the great green and blue mountains in the far distance.

The sky was the clear light blue of early spring, and white clouds drifted across from the west. The table, chairs, couch, and counters were all wood, worn, but sanded smooth, and oiled, maybe, giving them a fine luster. Bookcases filled the free space, between the windows, below the windows, behind the ladder to the loft, filled with books of all kinds. There were some drawings tacked to the walls in the kitchen area, a child's drawings, but good ones. One showed the little green woodstove, with its wild squirrels on the sides, and its long, thin legs. Zoey looked at the stove, set on a pad of red bricks, with splits of paper barked wood behind, and a whisper of air running in to feed the fire. She felt the warmth on her face, and she thought of how Betts had mentioned the stove and had drawn it. There were rocks, and some shells, and a cocoon or two and some dried leaves and flowers on the windowsill, put there by Betts, perhaps. She tried to imagine Betts living here, waking up to this odd man, in this quiet and orderly world, with the whole valley laid out below.

There was a pause, and then Zoey started in. She introduced herself as a worker with the Orange County Children's Services and noted that she was visiting Ames to see if he might be a possible placement option for a young girl in her care. Even as she said this, all that she had heard about Ames from her supervisor, including his PTSD, his isolation and his inability to get on with his life after the war echoed in her mind. Ames looked at her, polite, but confused. She went on, sipping the hot tea.

"Thank you so much. This tea is really good," she said nervously. "She has some serious problems and is set for discharge from the Children's Retreat. She's been there a year and was hospitalized before that, after being assaultive to the foster parents she was placed with. She's less aggressive now, but she's on quite a bit of medication, and she might be more difficult if the medication were reduced ... " Zoey trailed off, trying to describe Betts in a better way. She could see that this odd man, living alone in a cabin, with his own PTSD, had little to offer a girl as needy as this one was.

She tried again. "She has PTSD and might have some thought disorders as well. She doesn't talk much and doesn't seem to be better since she came into custody almost sixteen months ago. We can't try another foster home, and she might have to go into long term care at the state hospital." Ames looked at her, confused. "We thought of you," Zoey paused, and tried again. "I thought you might be an option, because you're her uncle, and she was here before, for the summer, in 2011? Betts? She said that this is where she wants to live. Here, in the cabin, with you. She lived here before?"

Zoey ground to a halt, because the case she made sounded so weak to her that she regretted having come up here at all, and Ames seemed to have been punched. "What? Betts? Are you talking about Betts?" Zoey nodded. "Please," said Ames. "I thought she was with her mother."

Zoey went back over what she knew of Betts' case, starting with Betts first coming into care in December of 2011, her failed foster homes, the first hospital, and then the second. Zoey was looking at her notes as she talked, and when she looked up, she saw Ames sitting with his mouth slightly open, and tears on his cheeks. She realized that Ames was hearing this for the first time. "I'm sorry!" she said. "I thought you knew. Betts has had a rough time since she left you." She paused, but Ames said nothing, and held his face in his hands for a moment, drawing his fingers across his eyes to wipe away the tears. He looked like someone who had been told of a loved one's death.

Zoey sat in the tidy little cabin, across from a man who now looked a lot like the man her supervisor had warned her about and realized that if Betts did not have a future here, she might not have much of a future at all. Zoey tried to imagine Betts living here, with everything in its place, swept and dusted, the plants watered, a fresh stack of wood behind the little green stove. The kettle had been put to boil when they came in. As the kettle began to steam, Ames took it off the stove.

Zoey took up her tea and held the warm cup in both hands. "I saw Betts yesterday, and all she could say was that she wanted to live with you, here, in the cabin." Ames nodded. Zoey asked, "Can you tell me about Betts when she was here? Maybe ten things that are true about Betts?" She reached for her pad and took up her pen.

Ames looked at her, and put down his tea and said, "Betts likes to be outside, even when it's wet or cold. Betts is interested in plants and animals, not to just know their names, but how they live and eat, and how things work, like the weather and stuff. Betts didn't sleep good when she first came here, and woke up with nightmares a couple times every night, yelling "No!" and swinging her arms and stuff. That settled down after she had been here for six weeks or so. Betts is patient, and waits for things to come at their own time: birds to come to the feeder, the laundry to be done, her burger to come from the kitchen at the diner. Betts gets cold pretty easy but gets her own sweater or coat or blanket, rather than asking me for it. She likes her tea black after she got used to it. Betts worries about her mom, and wonders if she is OK. Her mom is Tina, my sister. Betts wants to be helpful and will try to do stuff like stack the wood or help with the dishes, without being asked to. Betts likes to ride in the truck into town and likes to help with our shopping or delivering a load of wood. I think that's nine. Betts did good while she was here, getting over the nightmares and stuff, and she'd do good, again, if you let her come back. I want her back here, living with me, again."

Zoey sat with her teacup in her hand, the ten perfect things still rolling around in her head. Mrs. Cleary would have been impressed, too. Ames had knocked it out of the park. And this after just three months in the home, followed by eighteen months with Betts away and having no contact since. Zoey decided at that moment that she would see Betts placed with Ames, in the cabin with the little green woodstove and all the rest, come hell or high water, regardless what her supervisor thought she knew about Ames. Zoey stopped for a moment, realizing that she was roaring about this case, and saw that as a warning sign of getting sucked in. "Screw it," she thought. "I am sucked in. And so what? Betts needs this."

Zoey had been quiet for so long after Ames finished talking that he asked, "Is that OK, the stuff I thought of? There's more than ten if you need it." Zoey looked at Ames, taking in for the first time his kind face, his eyes, full of concern, and lost a bit more of her professional reserve.

"You did great, Ames. Now, all we need to do is get Betts back here. Tell me about the toilet and the plumbing."

CHAPTER FIVE

Swimming Uphill

"Well, that's not going to happen," her supervisor told her when Zoey returned to the office the next day. "If she can't make it in a treatment foster home, with trained parents and all the support, and she can't be maintained in a hospital without going into restraints on a regular basis, how could she make it living in a one-room cabin up on the mountain, off the grid, with a half-crazy vet with PTSD?"

Zoey felt her anger rise for some reason at this description of Ames. "Do you know him?" Zoey asked, trying to keep her tongue civil.

"Sure, he's Tina's brother," her supervisor replied. "Did OK in high school, went off to Afghanistan, and came back with PTSD. He lives up in the cabin, no running water, no friends, and lives off his disability check and some spare change from cutting wood. He can't even work. He must be at least as messed up as Tina is. I don't even know why you went up there."

Zoey was stunned. She sat silently, trying to quell the anger inside. Her supervisor noticed that Zoey was upset, and sat quietly as well, looking at the young woman who had so recently been hired. Both could feel the tension, and the supervisor regretted the tone she had taken, dismissive and the classic "full cup" that she hated in supervisors. She was also aware that somehow this case had become very personal for Zoey Simmons. She started out, "I'm sorry I spoke that way. It's a very sad case, and I know you are new to a lot of this ... " She stopped, aware that now she sounded condescending, rather than apologetic.

Zoey interrupted. "I'm going to place Betts with her Uncle Ames. She wants that, and she's been there before. I visited his home," she said, "and it's clean and safe, and wonderful." She stopped, aware that she sounded almost as angry and defensive as she was. She tried again, but the anger was still there. "I've spoken with him. He isn't crazy, at all. He loves Betts, knows all about her, and did a great job when she was with him for the summer." Zoey tried to rein in her anger. "And if we put her in Waterbury, we might as well just kill her and be done with it."

Both women sat in silence, thinking about the remarkable things that had just been said. Red flags were all around. Zoey's tone was aggressive and showed her to be over-involved in the case. Being rude to your supervisor was not advised for new hires just out of school. Zoey felt torn between the need to apologize, and her inability to take back anything she had said. It was all true, after all. And Zoey still cared about what was true.

Her supervisor handled her pen, looking at Zoey, and trying to make sense of the exchange. She tried to picture Ames, and saw him as a handsome enough man, and wondered if Zoey was off-track because of that. She thought of Betts, whom she had never seen, and wondered if there was something in the child that could push Zoey to this place. And she remembered herself when she had first come into the field, twenty-three years old, filled with passion and a desire to bring justice to the poor and oppressed. She felt a pang of grief as she realized how much of that young idealist had died, and how pragmatic she had become. She missed that girl that she had once been. Maybe the best thing about supervising Zoey would be the chance to remember why she came into this terrible field in the first place. She checked her ego and was pleased to find that being contradicted by someone so young and unaware didn't really hit her one way or the other. Her initial anger at the challenge was accepted and set aside. Placement decisions were too important to let personal feelings run the show. And Zoey had the case, after all. She took a deep breath, and then another. Some supervisors are so much better than others, and Zoey was blessed with a good one.

"Well," she said, "you know what needs to be in place for a foster home license. You have a little wiggle room, just a little, since this would be a kinship placement, and since Betts has stayed there before without any problems that we know of, yet." She paused. "But it needs to be done right. Lots of people will not like this placement at all, and you have to be ready to defend it. If anything goes wrong, we'll all be in for it." She paused again. "Laura is the expert at foster home development, and I'll ask her to work with you on this. I'll let her know you're in a rush, and that she can put her other projects off while the two of you get this done, if it's doable." She paused again. "You seem really sure about this," she said. "Can you tell me why?"

Zoey had a flash of love for the older women, knowing that her own tone had been aggressive and rude. "When I was in school, I had a teacher, Mrs. Cleary, whom I just loved. She said to check a relationship by asking one person for ten true things about the other person. I did that with Ames, and he just knows Betts so well. And he loves her, too." Zoey brought out her notes and read the things that Ames had said about Betts.

Her supervisor thought for a bit. "That doesn't sound at all like the little girl in the hospital," she said.

Zoey thought, and replied, "Ames knew Betts at his cabin. She was safe, comfortable, and able to open up and grow. That's the girl we want her to be again. When she went back to her mother's house, something happened, something bad enough to change how she was. And then they buried her under all that medication and kept her locked away with a bunch of strangers who didn't love her at all, and they just sat and watched her get worse and worse. And they tied her up." Zoey felt tears of anger come to her eyes. "I think it's the girl that Ames knew, before something happened and before we made her worse." The words hung in the air. True and awful.

Her supervisor sighed. "Maybe. You better go see Laura. Betts is set for discharge next Tuesday, and they think she's going to the state hospital. Folks are not going to be happy about this. You only have a few days to make this happen. Keep me filled in." She smiled as Zoey got up. "And Zoey, good luck. I'm glad Betts has you on her side."

Laura had an office at the end of the hall, past the file room, and pretty much isolated from the rest of the staff. Laura liked it this way and had picked "the dungeon," as she called it, as her space years before. Laura had held her LCSW for some thirty years, taking her Master's at Smith, moved to Vermont with the rest of the flower children, and had at one time or another filled all of the positions at the agency. She had been offered the director's position at the agency and had declined, requesting instead to be put out to semi pasture developing foster homes. It was the kind of job often done by people with a BSW degree, like Zoey, and resulted in a pay cut that left the rest of the agency in wonder.

Laura knew what she was doing. She had been taking on bits and pieces of all the heartache and despair of the work for thirty years, caring too much about her clients to not, and growing angry and bitter with the trauma she saw. When the development job came open, Laura leapt at it and refused to work anywhere else in the agency, threatening to quit unless she got the job. She got it and had been reasonably happy ever since. She was insulated from the kids and was able to spend her days working with the very specific facts of licensure, where the rules were clearly laid out, and the homes would either pass or not. She knew the 123 pages of state guidelines by heart and could walk into a home, take a five-minute tour, and know exactly what was needed. Her prospective parent interviews were extensive and probing, and she had yet to license a family that proved to be unsafe around kids. She kept perfect records of all the thirty-two homes the agency currently licensed and equally good records on each of the fifty-six licensed foster parents who worked for the agency. She had no assistants, did all of her own paperwork, and was never behind, or at a loss. Laura might well have been the most successful employee in the agency if success was measured by the quality of your work, and the satisfaction you got from doing it right. Zoey was lucky to have Laura as a resource because getting Ames and his cabin licensed in five days would take a miracle.

By the time Zoey had made her way down the hall, squeezed past the copier, and knocked on Laura's door, she found Laura just hanging up the phone. Zoey understood that her supervisor had called Laura as soon as Zoey had left her office.

"Go get your coat, Zoey," Laura said, standing up and putting her own coat on. "We might as well get started." Zoey turned and followed Laura back down the hall, past her supervisor, who sat behind her desk, giving Zoey a thumbs up.

Laura drove, with Zoey riding shotgun. "So. Tell me about this guy," Laura said, as they pulled out of the parking lot. "And tell me about Betts, too." The county office was on the south end of Randolph, and Laura drove north on Route 12, past the gas stations and the cafe, on out into the country, a wide valley carved out by a small river that meandered across it. Beaver dams made bright pools edged in cattails, and red-winged blackbirds worked the marsh. As they moved north, the river narrowed, and small dairy farms began to appear. Hip roofed barns, small houses and farm machinery, and of course, cattle: Brown Swiss and Jerseys, and the larger black and white Holsteins. The cattle were out now, with the younger ones kicking it up and playing with each other after spending the winter in the barns. The cattle looked happy to have some green grass and sunshine, after the long confinement and only silage to eat.

Laura interrupted Zoey's description of the cabin, pointing at a farm they were passing. "That's where Tina and Ames grew up. There used to be an old single wide parked off to the side, back when the Butterfields owned the farm. Their parents worked the cows for them and had that trailer as part of their job. Hard life, especially for the kids. Parents working fourteen hours a day, and everything smelling like cow shit."

She looked out the window and then said, "You know, there was a sister, the middle kid, Clair, who got killed when she was nine. Her dad backed the tractor up onto her there in the barnyard. Ames was there to see it. The whole family just broke down after that. Clair was the favorite, pretty and kind, and always trying to make it better at home, and at school. I don't think that Tina ever got over it. She ran wild, and her folks were too beat up to do much about it. Ames worked the other farms and did OK, but I think he went off to the Army to get away from that place."

Zoey watched the farm receding in her rear-view mirror, and tried to picture the life there fifteen years before. She thought of Tina, struggling with her life in the trailer, the death of her sister, and the life she had after, no doubt a string of boys and men taking advantage of her, and then having Betts so young. Tina had developed some depth, and was no longer just another bad mom. And she thought about Ames, seeing his sister die beneath the tractor.

"I'm about as old as dirt," said Laura, "and I've lived in this town for about forever. Every family has a story, and there's not a thing that goes on that doesn't have a reason behind it. Most days I feel sorry for just about everybody, you and me included." Zoey started to offer directions to the cabin, but she saw that Laura knew the road, and took the turn up to Bear Hill without any hesitation. She drove quickly, her eyes darting along the road in front of her, and then checking the mirrors. She drifted the van over the gravel from time to time, at first giving Zoey a scare, but as Zoey saw the smooth confidence Laura had, she relaxed a bit. "They call it "Bear Hill" because Randolph used to keep a dump up here, and the bears would come for the garbage." She corrected for a bit of a drift around a corner, and then accelerated again. "I know that cabin, too. I used to know the guy that lived up there. A shaky vet who served in Vietnam. He had Ames work for him from time to time, doing trees, so he was up there, as a kid. It's a beautiful spot," she said.

The road up Bear Hill was a good example of why people love, and hate, Vermont. There are four miles between the paved road, down by the cemetery, and the turn off to Ames' cabin, and those four miles climb a little over eleven hundred feet of elevation, twisting back and forth over and around a small, quick stream. The trees that line the road on either side are old for the most part; some are over three feet in diameter at breast height, mostly maples, but a smattering of white birch, yellow birch, ash, and cherry provide some diversity. Maple is the money tree in this state, both for sugar and for lumber and firewood, and the great maples are so common because they have meant money to the hungry farmers in the state. These trees seek the sun, struggling to get to the dinner plate of sunshine, and the road itself provides a winding gap in the canopy that the trees are quick to close. This means that the trees lean in over the road, from either side, creating a bower of deep leafy shade in the summer, and a fine filter of bare branches for the thin winter sun. The road becomes a tunnel and a magical place to drive.

The sky flickered above as Zoey and Laura drove up the hill, bits of sunlight filtering down and flashing by, but for the most part, the road was cool and shady all through the summer. In the early spring, like on this beautiful day, the shade kept the ice in the ground, and while the road looks a lot like dirt, there was a slick surface underneath. Laura gunned the agency van up the hill, sliding through the corners, gravel spraying out to first one side and then the other. Laura picked a careful line, trying to stay on the high spots, and out of the deep ruts that had begun to show the paths of the milk truck and the school bus.

Zoey found herself gripping the door handle with one hand, and trying to find a purchase on the dash, and looked to find Laura with only one hand on the wheel, the other holding a half-full cup of coffee, which she sipped from time to time. "Quite the road up here, isn't it?" Laura commented. The van slipped several feet to the left, and Laura turned into the skid, without taking her foot off the gas. "Sorry about that. You have to pretty much gun it in these little vans, or you'll never make the top."

Zoey held on and wondered at the woman driving the van. Laura pulled the van into the tracks that led to the cabin, and moved up that trail, pulling a bit off to one side near Ames' truck, then shifted and turned, backing the van in a half slide to face nose down the trail, for an easier exit. "That should do it," Laura said. "It stays pretty icy up here. Watch your step."

Zoey got out, and Laura followed, holding a canvas pouch of papers and forms, a tape measure, and a small camera. They walked up the trail to the cabin, and Laura said, "It never looked this good before. Ames has done a good job with this place." Ames was working at the bench in the woodlot, with a small metal toolbox and his chain saw in front of him. He wore a wool vest against the cold and had a wool cap pulled down over his ears.

He waved to Zoey, and then his smile brightened as he saw Laura. "Laura Woods! Are you still working? I thought you would have retired by now. I am so glad to see you!"

He stood awkwardly in front of her, and she said, "So? Give me a hug."

Ames fell forward and hugged the old woman, then got shy. "Laura was a big help to me back when I was a kid," he said.

Zoey smiled at Ames, happy to see him. "Laura is here to help with getting your foster care license in place. She needs to check out your home and help you know what needs to happen to get it in shape for foster care, so we can get Betts back up here."

"Show me the water system, and the toilet, first," said Laura. "Then we need to go inside and do the measurements, lead tests, and fire safety checks." As Ames gave Laura a tour of the spring, explaining how it was maintained, Zoey sat on the bench in front of the cabin. She had worried that Ames might be uncomfortable around a stranger, but clearly, they knew each other, and he was happy to see her. She thought about the conversation in the van and realized that Laura must have been a part of the team supporting Ames' family after the death of his sister. He had mentioned the death once, in response to her questions about his family, and Zoey heard some grief still in his voice as he told her about Clair. Zoey thought that Ames could have given her ten true things about Clair as well, and realized that what she wanted was ten true things about Ames, himself. Zoey felt her face color just a bit, maybe from the cold, and wondered if Ames had missed her.

Ames and Laura had seen the spring and now went to the outhouse. Zoey pictured how surprised Laura would be at how nice it was. She watched Laura go in and come back out again. They walked up the path, Ames explaining things with his hands, and pointing at the land. Zoey followed them in and found Laura making some notes on the kitchen. Laura smiled at Zoey as she came in and then turned back to Ames. "There's a lot of work to do to get this place up to official snuff, but if we get just a few things done first, like the fire safety stuff and having the water tested, we can open under a provisional license, and catch up the rest of the requirements in the next sixty days. Tuesday is five days away, and two of those days are the weekend, so we really have tomorrow, Friday, and then Monday to get it done.

"Take a water sample into the health department in Montpelier today, and they should have it ready by Monday. You'll have to re-test every six months after that if you want to keep using the spring. Keep the results in your notebook. I've never approved an outhouse before, but the regs only specify that the plumbing be in compliance with existing code, and since Brookfield codes permit outhouses, I guess you're fine on that. We might need an engineer to write a statement of support at some point, but for now, I think we're OK. Fire safety includes detectors, extinguishers, exit windows and doors, and a plan. This sheet has all of that described in detail, so follow the instructions, and have it all ready for me by Friday afternoon. Betts can have the loft until you get the porch turned into a bedroom for her, but I wouldn't go too slow on that, say, maybe three weeks at the most. Remember, her room has to be sixty square feet, with an exit window, and traffic can't go through the room. And she needs a door. That might be tough with the loft. Figure it out. If you have questions, give me a call before you do something wrong, and have to do it all over again."

She turned to Zoey. "You need to get him through the initial training, which should be twenty hours, and he needs to cover the material well enough that he can pass the subject tests. Record your class time. The medicine stuff will be important. I suspect Betts is coming out fully loaded. She needs to stay on the medication as prescribed until you get her to see another doctor, who can modify the existing medication orders. I would suggest Ken B., down in Randolph. He's good with trauma kids, and will probably help you get the meds reduced."

Zoey saw Ames making notes on the paper he had in front of him. This man who had seemed almost nonverbal, and so drawn into himself, now organized and committed to making this thing happen. Laura got up and said to Zoey, "I need to get back to the rest of my day. The two of you have a lot of work to do, too." She turned to Ames. "I've enjoyed seeing you all grown up. I think you're going to do a great job with Betts. Don't be slow to ask for help. She's going to be a really different kid from the one you knew before, at least for a while." She took the keys to the van from her pocket. "Can you give Zoey a ride back into town when the two of you are done?"

Ames nodded and said, "Thank you, Laura. And thank you for all the help you were back before. You made a big difference."

Laura smiled and then turned to Zoey. "You OK with being left here?" she asked with a smile. Zoey said yes, blushing just a bit, and Laura headed out the door.

When Ames dropped Zoey off at the agency late in the day, they were well on their way to having Ames as a trained foster parent. Zoey noted that he seemed to have no difficulty with any of the foster parent regulations. He explained, "I just want to do it right. I want it to work. And I don't know anything about being a parent anyway."

Laura was in her office, working on training records when Zoey found her and walked through the door. Laura stopped and pulled a bag of chocolates out of her desk. Miniature Snickers. She shoved the bag across the desk to Zoey. Zoey took three pieces of candy and shoved the bag back with a grin. "Thank you so much for helping us," she began.

Laura shook her head. "No problem. It was nice to be back up on the mountain, and nice to see Ames walking around in his big boy body. He grew into a nice looking man." She looked at Zoey. "So. Do you like him? Like, *like* like him?" Laura had a wicked smile on her face, and Zoey colored up a bit.

Zoey drew in a breath and answered, "Yes. I like him, a lot, and maybe I *like* like him, too." She smiled, relaxing. "This feels so much like junior high. I should be careful, with it being work and all."

She looked at Laura, who said, "Careful is always good. Ames was always a really nice kid." She took another piece of chocolate. "He really made that cabin shine. I think maybe I'll get myself a place like that some time. Pretty, quiet, great views. The nicest little outhouse I have ever seen. I remember the old one up there. Full of spiders, and stinky."

Laura looked sad, and Zoey asked, "How was it for you, being back up there?"

"It was a little hard," said Laura. "I have such good memories of being up there with Todd. Todd Lundgrin was his name. A little like Ames, in a way. Tall. Kind. Handsome. And carrying some real damage from the war. I miss him." Laura looked out the window, and Zoey said nothing.

"Well," said Laura, "this is going to be a tricky case. Betts is going to need a lot, therapy, med management, help with school, and all the rest. Ames thinks she's going to be like she was before, and she won't. Stuff must have happened since she left, and if she starts to trust Ames, it will probably come out. That's going to mean legal stuff. Tina hasn't done anything to get her kid back, but that doesn't mean she won't. And Betts is going to be hurt either way. If Tina shows up for Betts, Ames is going to have to say no, since there's only supervised visitation for her here at the agency. Not that she's showed up for any of that."

Laura shook her head. "And lots of folks are not going to like this placement, with her being up on the mountain alone with a disabled soldier, miles from anywhere, with no running water." She looked at Zoey, who had a bit of fire in her eyes. "I know. You and I like that placement just fine. But not everybody will. Ellen Jensen is the social worker for Betts at the hospital. Ellen worked here once, briefly, and she doesn't like me much. And I'm sure she has already scored a bed at Waterbury for Betts."

She looked at Zoey. "Relax. The discharge planning is a team effort, and the discharge meeting takes place on Tuesday. And you have the final say since Betts is legally yours at this point. But Ellen's nasty, and she might make a stink. And Tina may decide she doesn't want her brother to have her, either. Cross your T's and dot your I's," Laura said. "And calm down. We're going to do just fine with this thing, so put a smile on." Zoey tried to smile and took one more piece of candy. "And Zoey. You should go call Ellen, and let her know what the plan is. I'd hate to have Betts already gone when we get there."

CHAPTER SIX

Some Social Workers Are Not Nice

Ellen Jensen was not happy. She looked at the notes in Betts' file, including her own recent discharge plan, and thought again about the call she had had from Zoey Simmons. Zoey, some brand new hire straight out of college that thought this schizophrenic girl could be placed with her crazy uncle up in the wilderness. Ellen thought about letting it slide. After all, when it didn't work out, they would just do a readmit and then set up the plan for Waterbury. And the readmit would be easy since she could just cut and paste from the first admission. Ellen thought about just going back to the Candy Crush game on her phone. But then she remembered having her work questioned by Laura Woods, and set her teeth in an odd sort of a smile. "Bring it on!" she thought. This one would be like shooting fish in a barrel.

Ellen was tired of the disrespect, the people that came to work with their heart on their sleeve, people that thought that their caring would somehow fix mental illness. Ellen thought back on all the times she had been disrespected at work, the jobs taken away from her, the embarrassment of cleaning out her desk under the laughing eyes of the saps who stayed behind. Bitterness filled Ellen, crowding out any desire to play Candy Crush. So far, she had not taken a stand here on the Children's Unit, partially because the work was so much easier than she was used to, and partially because she had so little interest in the pathetic, ill-behaved, messy and runny-nosed children who were her clients. Betts was nothing special, maybe worse than most. Smaller, but a biter, with that hollow, empty look on her face. Who would want a girl like that, anyway? Probably some psycho up in a cabin who couldn't find a real girlfriend, anyway.

All the same, things were going well so far on this job, and Ellen hated to stir things up at this point. Ellen looked at the game on her phone, which was also going pretty well at this point. She could always decide this later in the day. She wrote "Bets" on a yellow Post-It note, stuck it to her computer screen, and picking up her phone, clicked back onto the game.

Ames had drawn a water sample from the spring and brought it down to the health department in Montpelier. They had looked at the Mason jar he brought, and sent him back out the door with the required plastic bottle and a set of instructions, all sealed in a bag. On the way back home, he opened the Mason jar and took a drink of the still cold water. He set the jar between his legs, screwed the cap back on, and kept on driving home. It was almost 4:30 when he returned with the proper sample, and he was relieved to get in the door before it was locked. He left the sample, and a check for the fees and they locked the door behind him as he left. He stopped at the hardware store and took out the list from his back pocket. He picked up a tall, red fire extinguisher, about the size he had seen strapped on near the door of logging trucks, and three smoke detectors. He stopped at the lumber desk, and put in an order for the materials he would need to build Betts a bedroom on the porch, including an exit window, a new door, all the two by stock for framing the wall, and enough cedar siding to make the new wall match the rest of the porch. Cedar had gotten expensive, but Ames could not bring himself to put sheet rock up in the cabin. He helped load the materials into his truck, just about filling the bed and roped the load in securely.

The cedar would look nice, and smell nice, too, he thought, as he drove back home. Betts would like that smell, always so sharp when the wood was new. He had put off a tree job down the hill until the next week and figured he could get the room all done before Betts came home on Tuesday. He pulled his truck up next to the porch and took a tarp out and spread it over the materials. Rain was forecast for the night. He roped the tarp in place and headed inside. He put the kettle on to boil, and contented himself with hanging the fire extinguisher just inside the cabin door, then mounting the smoke detectors, one on the porch, one in the loft, and one over the window, away from the little green stove. He poured the steaming water over the tea leaves and set the lid on the pot to steep. He went back out to the porch, looked at the space for a bit, and drew some lines for the new wall and window.

He poured a cup of tea, and sat down in his reading chair, looking out at the black night, and the faint lights of Randolph, and the even fainter lights of Bethel, far in the distance. He thought about Betts coming home on Tuesday and smiled. He opened the door on the little green woodstove, and slid two more splits of birch onto the coals already starting to grey over, and left the door open just a crack, and sipped his tea while the air whistled through the door, and over the coals, bringing the bright red back, and setting the new birch to flames.

Ames thought about the fire. The little green stove had been made by Morso, in Norway, across the ocean and way up north, a country that knew something about heating with wood. It was made from thick plates of cast iron, new iron, and cast to not only be precise enough to make the joints between the plates airtight, but to be beautiful as well. While most cast iron stoves relied on stove cement and fiberglass gaskets to seal them against the air, the Morso was cast so well that the pieces fit together without a gap, and needed only a few bolts tightened up to make the stove so airtight that, if he wanted, he could extinguish the fire by simply closing the spinner all the way down. The stove was a thing of beauty and joy.

The air from the room, full of oxygen, wanted in, since the heat of the stove drove the air inside the stove up the pipe and into the air outside. Nature abhors a vacuum, and so when the door was cracked, or the spinner opened just a bit, air from the room rushed in, whistling or whispering, pushing against the dull coals and bringing them to life, and setting the fire to the wood above. Ames loved the stove, which could run all day with only a little care, and give back so much.

The birch splits that he had added moments before were fully on fire, the first crackle of the white paper bark now settled into a quieter pop and creak as the wood gave itself up to the flames. The iron in the stove clicked a bit as well, and the castings expanded with the rise in heat. These birch splits were doing a magic of sorts, a magic that never ceased to amaze Ames. He knew the birch tree he had felled might have been ten inches in diameter at his chest height, tapering off in the forest canopy toward the light, branches, twigs, and leaves reaching higher, seeking the sun, 93,000,000 miles away. That great ball of fire tended to all life on Earth, warming us in the summer and feeding the trees and other plants, and laying in the stocks of carbon to heat and feed us through the long, cold winter, year after year.

Those leaves, and millions like them that the tree had grown out of thin air, gathered the energy from the Vermont sunlight, using that energy to break enough carbon off the CO_2 in the air to build a tree, roots, trunk, limbs, twigs, leaves and all. Breaking that carbon free from the air required a lot of energy, energy from the sun, and freed the oxygen back into the world, where it might be of use to Ames, and Betts, and Zoey as well as all the other animals on the planet, or in the sea. And when oxygen-breathing Ames ate an apple, as he often did, the carbon in that apple met the oxygen in his breath, and as it slowly burned inside him, Ames found the heat to keep his body warm, and the energy to cut more wood. And the energy to think, sitting here in his chair, sipping tea.

This is why he tended the little green stove and the spring with such reverence, as if he were a priest allowed to bring the bread and wine forth to become the Body and the Blood. *Holy* was the word that Ames would have used to describe this act, this act he was blessed to be able to do throughout the day, until the Vermont sun rose at last, high enough in the sky to again heat the land, and keep the cabin warm, and feed the trees as they reached out new leaves for their gift. And while Ames missed tending the fire on these too brief summer days, he basked in the heat of the sun herself and knew that this light was feeding the trees and himself for yet another long winter.

The beauty of this system, and the water in the spring, which was magic as well, gave Ames his faith, his awe and his ability to survive all the ugliness and horror he had seen and done. These systems showed Ames that there was a magnificent and comprehensible beauty and kindness in the world, and he prayed a simple prayer throughout the day: "Thank you." Ames sat in the chair, sipping his hot cup of tea, and feeling the warmth of a hundred years of kind summer days spill out this night in his cabin, and he felt filled with the Grace of the world. Ames had read something of the Navajos, who seek to walk in beauty, and felt that he had found that path here, in the little cabin on the mountain. Ames felt blessed.

And while Ellen was playing Candy Crush, and trying to decide how much effort to put in to Betts' discharge plans, and while Ames sat beside the little green woodstove, aware that he was blessed, and excited to have Betts back at home, Betts herself wandered back to the dayroom, after watching her supper for the past twenty minutes. Her days and nights were spent in pajamas, a striped robe tied around her puffy waist, and socks with a rubber tread hanging loosely on her feet. The staff had given up on getting her dressed, deciding instead of having a fight to simply dock her five points each day for failing her ADLs. She shuffled to the chair by the window, where the light had slowly leaked out of the sky, taking almost all the colors with it, leaving only a deep blue that moved to black, where the mountains rose, the sickly yellow pools from the sodium lights in the parking lot, and the streams of white and red light from the cars on the highway below. This third-floor window provided a view of sorts, through the greasy, thick Plexiglas pane, of the parking lot, the other buildings downtown, and, in the distance, thankfully, the mountains of Vermont.

The room was scented with chemicals and urine, hospital air where windows could not be opened and filled with the thin noise of the TV locked behind the plastic pane, and the noises of the children, and the staff, who had them in their care. It was an artificial world, made of the hard industrial carpet, the vinyl chairs and couches, the tubs of plastic toys, the doors closed and locked, the keys that jingled on the belts of staff, the rolling trays of medication, the dry-wipe charts of meals and meds and discharge and admission, of points given for compliance, and the well-meaning or predatory adults who came to work in shifts marked on yet another dry-wipe board.

This was the world that Betts found her body locked in, and she pressed against the greasy plastic window, her hand on the pane, and a weak smile on her face, as she looked out into the night, seeing perhaps the cabin, and the spring, and the little green stove, and the great loving open world of green and blue, of air and water free of ducts and pipes, the trees, tall and graceful in the sun and wind, or the splits of birch, so carefully laid up and holding their warmth for the winter. Betts had the company, from time to time, of a girl named Rebekah, a girl none of the staff could see, a girl who had first come to Betts in her time of need, and who had stayed with her for the past year and a half. Betts kept Rebekah a secret. While Betts was at the window, she somehow knew the comfort and magic of the woods and the spring, and the little green woodstove, the beauty of the mountain, and the soft voice of her uncle as he went about his day. The thick and steady push of the medication in her blood was the only aspect of this place that was inside her, while Betts, and sometimes, Rebekah, were somewhere else.

The spring flowed, and the small stream rushed quickly down the cuts it had made in the thin soil of the mountain, carrying tiny bits of leaves and soil, shifting first one way, and then the other as it ran into rocks and roots not easily washed away. Betts and Rebekah were at the spring, one foot in the tiny creek by the splash rock, one hand in the ice-cold water from the pipe, and her other hand open to the sky, where rain and snow had brought this flow to the mountain, and to the spring, and to Betts. Sunlight filtered through the new leaves, shifting in the light breeze, and laying patterns of light and shade across the ground. Betts felt the water and the land, the air and the sun, and gave a little prayer she had learned on the mountain. "Thank you."

CHAPTER SEVEN

Just Another Discharge Meeting

Ames had started the day early, even earlier than he might usually be up on a Saturday, tended the little green woodstove, set the kettle on to boil, sat for a bit on the high rock, and come back down the trail when he saw the smoke shift to a cleaner grey. He arrived as the kettle was starting to boil, and poured his first pot of tea for the day. When it had brewed, took his green mug out to the yard, and stared at the truck. The tarp had done a good job keeping the lumber dry, and with the sun just showing on a clear sky, Ames undid the ropes, and folded the tarp, putting them both back behind the seat in the old Ford truck.

He unloaded the door and window, leaning them against the side of the cabin, and then stacked the lumber beside the porch, setting the boards into neat piles of similar length and size. He took his tape measure, a framing square, a handsaw, and two hammers from the porch as well, and went inside for a pencil. He sharpened the pencil with his pocketknife, and took the pad of paper, opened to a sketch he had done the night before. He cleared everything from the porch, then measured and marked along the floor, laying in where the wall would go and marking out the new window on the far wall as well. Ames took notes as he worked, and when he went outside, he cut boards to the lengths needed. Within two hours, he had built the wall marking off Betts' new bedroom and begun to side the wall with the fragrant cedar. He trimmed in the door with more cedar, and then packed the hollow wall with fiberglass insulation, tacking the sheets in place. He then worked his way from the bottom up, siding the inside of the wall with cedar as well.

Ames set the door into the rough opening, shimming it and nailing it into place once it was level and plumb, swinging the door to check the fit, then trimmed in the inside with cedar as well. He worked out the latch with a drill and a chisel, and tested them, finding them a bit tight, and re-worked them some, finally pleased when the door clicked into place just as it closed. No wiggle. No tightness. Just right. He looked at the material pile in front of the cabin and saw that the scraps remaining were sufficient for what was needed to set the window in and trim it in cedar as well. Almost no waste. Pine kindling was the last thing he needed to buy.

Ames took a break for lunch, after about six hours of slow and solid work. He was pleased with the work so far and looked forward to setting in the window. Betts would have a nice view to the east and have a face full of morning sun to greet the day. He went in and made a sandwich, cold turkey from the fridge, with lettuce and mayonnaise and some mustard, clamped inside two thick slices of homemade wheat bread he had baked two days before. He added an apple to the plate, and filled his teacup again, then walked to the table by the fire pit, and set up his meal, where he could face the cabin and think about Betts coming back to live there.

He had not seen Betts since her mother had come and taken her away, more than a year ago. Zoey said that Betts had had a hard time since, coming into the State's custody due to physical abuse in November. Zoey had not said what that meant, and Ames had not asked, but he wondered who might have felt the need to beat on such a quiet and willing child. Zoey went on to describe Betts then attacking the foster parents, and getting bounced from home to home, ending up in the children's psychiatric unit at the local hospital in Montpelier, then tossed in for a year at the big psychiatric hospital down in Rutland, where she was this Saturday. He remembered the way Zoey had described Betts was coming out of the fog and saying that she wanted to go and live with Uncle Ames, in the cabin with the little green woodstove, where the spring is. He wondered at that. He always thought of the cabin that way and was pleased to hear that Betts remembered it in that way, too.

Ames thought of Betts in a hospital for a whole year and tried to imagine what such a place must be like. What would you do in a hospital for a whole year, when you weren't even injured? Just thinking about it made him sad and angry.

He thought about how little he knew about raising children, having been the youngest, never babysitting for cousins or neighbors, never dating a woman with children, and never having any parenting that he could remember when he was a kid. Not much to go on, there. But Betts had felt good about being with him, and he had only been himself while she was here, not knowing who else to be. And Zoey seemed to think that he would be a good choice for Betts, somehow. Although Zoey looked young to know much about that sort of thing unless she had studied it in college. And what good could that be?

Being at the cabin with the little green woodstove and the spring had helped to heal him up when he came from the Sand Wars. Something about the magic in the place, and the peace, and quiet, and the steady work of the day had smoothed over the frayed nerves, moved him just a bit toward forgiveness, and let him keep rising each day to try again. Maybe it worked that way for Betts as well. Betts had felt good when she was here, and she would feel good this next time as well. If he needed to learn how to do something different to help her, he could learn that and do it. And maybe, with time at the cabin, time in the woods, waking early to the routine of the day, the woodstove, the spring, the tea, and the firewood, maybe Betts could get better, and become the active, curious, and eager little girl she had been that summer before.

His lunch finished, and his thoughts somewhat settled, Ames returned his plate and his table knife to the cabin, washing them out in the sink with some still hot water from the kettle, and setting them in the wooden rack to dry. He put the mayonnaise and the mustard and the lettuce back in the old fridge, and returned to his current project. He took out his pencil and the tape measure, and his sheet of notes, and went to mark in where the window would go.

Zoey had come on Sunday, for tea and training, as she said. She was astonished by the beauty and feel of the tiny room Ames had made for Betts, meeting the legal requirements for a foster care room, but somehow feeling more like the cabin of a wooden sailboat on the seas, sturdy and tightly planked, so different from the rooms she was used to.

Ames could have shared his concerns with her at that time, but he was afraid to sound uncertain, and instead, he just worked through the material she had brought for him. Lots of good sense, basically, but oh, so different from the way he and Tina had been raised. These were rules for being a foster parent, of course, and as Zoey pointed out, the State of Vermont was the real parent, and you were just the nanny, working 24/7, trying to follow the State's expectations.

"Lots of folks struggle with this," Zoey had said, "and get upset when they are reminded that a foster placement is not permanent and that the big decisions are made in team meetings. Lots of parents drop out because of that. Maybe the hardest thing about being a foster parent isn't the work of raising the child, but of having to share that raising with a committee of people who sometimes don't even know the child."

Ames thought about that. "I don't know anything about raising a child," he said. "I want to do a good job, but I'll have to ask for help along the way. But a committee of strangers sounds pretty unhelpful."

"Sometimes it is," said Zoey. "Mostly it will just be me and you, and I think you do a pretty good job with Betts. She's an odd girl, and somehow, she got just what she needed when she was here before. I think it'll be OK."

Ellen started that Tuesday morning with a trip to Hardy's, picking up her breakfast, and putting the cup of coffee in the holder in her Jeep. She was oddly excited to get to work this morning, and she looked forward to the discharge meeting on that little girl with the fish hands, whom she expected to discharge to the State Hospital, right in the face of that young know-nothing that had come to her unit. Ellen had read the diagnosis sheet, and made a copy of it, which she planned to read at the meeting, painting a dramatic picture of this little disaster that couldn't even make it on the Children's Unit, with all of the programming, the trained staff, and people like Ellen herself, with a Master's degree, there for support. She had tried to find a picture of the bite mark, but since it was in the incident report, she couldn't get a copy. She had, however, called the nurse aide and told her to come in for the meeting and show her hand.

How anyone could think of placing a kid like that with some PTSD guy up in a cabin in the mountains was beyond her. She sipped some of her coffee at the light. Four sugars, and four creamers. Just right. The light had changed, and the car behind her tapped the horn. Ellen glared in the rear-view mirror, and kept her brake on, trapping the young woman behind her. She slowly, ever so slowly, put her coffee back in the holder, and edged the Jeep forward, at a walking pace, watching the distressed face of the woman behind her. Finally, she flipped the woman off and smiled, speeding up. "Don't honk at me, you little bitch," she said into the mirror.

Zoey had come to work early, with the plan of Ames cabin, the water test results, and a more professional version of the notes from her conversation with Ames about Betts. As Zoey arrived at the agency, she found Laura perched on the edge of her desk, a thermos of coffee in her hand, and a smile on her face. "Do you mind if I go along on this one? I haven't seen Ellen in a coon's age."

"That would be wonderful," said Zoey. "This will be my first discharge meeting, and I would love some backup."

Laura nodded. "It might be a doozy. I heard that Ellen called here, trying to find out information on Ames' home study, which she did not get. She seems to have a dog in this fight, for some reason. I never knew her to be interested in any of her clients before."

"I asked Betts about her," said Zoey, "but she didn't remember her. There is a contact note for every week in Betts's chart, but they don't really say anything except what the nursing notes already said."

"Sounds like Ellen," Laura said with a thin smile. "Let's go do it."

Zoey picked up the keys to one of the agency vans, and Laura took shotgun. Laura sipped her coffee as they rode, and Zoey talked about the cabin, with Betts' room finished and oiled, the bed in place, a small dresser and a comfortable chair.

Laura asked about the training, and Zoey told her that Ames had topped the subject tests, and seemed to be a quick student. "Guess we're all set," said Laura, as they pulled into the hospital parking lot. They parked in the patient visitor section and walked up to the main entrance. Laura led the way to the third floor, buzzing at the locked door until a nurse came and let them in.

They walked down a hallway, empty of children or staff, and then signed in on a clipboard at the nursing station. A few kids were in the dayroom, and Betts was back in her vinyl chair beside the window, her hands moving slowly as if they were in the water, a faint smile on her face. Zoey walked over to her and touched her hand. Betts startled and drew back. "Sorry, Betts. I didn't mean to surprise you. I visited your uncle Ames yesterday, and he said to say hi. He misses you."

Betts worked this information over, and said, "Say hi to him, back. I want to see him." Betts looked at Zoey, confused and worried, and Zoey said, "I'll tell him." Zoey rose and went to Laura, and the two of them were led into the conference room. Ellen Jensen watched from the nursing pod, her phone in her hand, and a thin smile on her face. She gathered some papers up and headed to the conference room as well.

The conference room was about twenty feet square, with a set of four tables pushed together in the center, and a set of upholstered office chairs placed around it. There was a dry-wipe board on one wall, with Betts' name printed on it, and the words "Discharge Planning" written below it, as well as the time of 8:30, which the clock said as well. There was an old school TV, mounted on a rolling cart, used perhaps for training videos, and an attendance sheet on a clipboard, with a pen attached by a long string. There was a coffee machine on the counter in one corner, but no one had made coffee, and the staff came in with their own cups already filled.

Laura and Zoey sat together, and the five nursing staff filtered in and sat down, chatting with each other, and introducing themselves as they sat. Ellen came in last, and closed the door behind her, and sat down on the empty side of the table, by herself. She laid her papers out in front of her, neatening up the pages and looking at Zoey and Laura defiantly. She seemed upset to find Laura in the meeting and ruffled a bit by that fact. Betts remained outside, in spite of the technical right she had to be involved in decisions regarding her care. The staff had long ago discovered that meetings were easier and faster without the kids involved, and Laura had cautioned Zoey against having Betts in the meeting, for fear she might be disruptive and hurt her own cause.

The charge nurse opened the meeting, asking that everybody introduce themselves and their role, and did so herself, to give an example. The staff followed around the table, enjoying, it seemed this ritual. Ellen introduced herself as Ellen Jensen, MSW, and defined herself as the person responsible for discharge planning. Zoey introduced herself by her first name and her job as the child placement worker for Betts' local agency.

When Laura introduced herself, Ellen cut in, and said, "I'm surprised to find you here. I thought you did development these days."

Laura smiled and said, "Oh, I do most anything that needs doing. You should know that, Ellen." Ellen colored, and the rest of the room was left to wonder what the history was between these two. Certainly not friendship.

The charge nurse picked up Betts' chart from the table, and read the data off the face sheet, giving Betts' date of birth, town of residence, height, weight, health issues, and then a list of diagnoses, including, by now, bipolar illness, attention deficit disorder, reactive attachment disorder, possible childhood psychosis, with aggressive behavior. She then read the incident list, which included several assaults on staff, five incidents of bruising and swelling on her face and arms of unknown origin ("We suspect she was hitting herself," the nurse said), and seven uses of physical restraints, two for periods of time longer than eight hours.

The Physical Therapist offered that Betts had been invited to both the Friendship group and the Crafting Our Feelings group, but had been unwilling or unable to participate in any of the group sessions since her admission exactly a year ago on this date. A nurse aide appeared, who, at Ellen's direction, showed the faint scar on her right hand, just above the thumb, and said that Betts had indeed bitten her there while she was trying to help her with her ADLs.

Ellen then took the stage, choosing to stand, and laying out the papers in front of her. She read a selection of nursing notes she had copied, all describing conflicts between Betts and the staff, re-read the diagnostic sheet, reviewed the number of restraints and finished with a dramatic account of the bite wound the nurse aide had suffered. She then produced glossy brochures from the State Hospital, describing the high level of care available there for the severely mentally ill child ("Which this child certainly is!" added Ellen). She listed the medications that Betts was currently on, including Lithium, two adult anti-psychotics, and a blood pressure suppressor. This combination of meds was so common for children in Betts' situation, it was known as "the foster kid cocktail." Ellen pointed through the solid wall toward the day room. "She's out there, now, sitting by the window, moving her hands back and forth, completely out of it, even with all the support and medication she has had on this unit. I heard that someone had considered placing that child with a mentally ill uncle, who lives by himself up on a shack in the woods. I can't imagine that that might be true."

As Ellen sat down, Zoey found herself taking an increasingly rapid number of short, angry breaths, her hands clenched at the edge of the table, and her eyes on Ellen like gun sights on a target. Just as Zoey was starting to stand, Laura stood, using Zoey's shoulder as a support, helping Zoey back into her seat. "Thanks," she said to Zoey. "I'm a little stiff these days, and sometimes I have a hard time getting up." She smiled at the people at the table. "I want to thank you for all the work you have done on behalf of our client," she said, and then turned to Ellen. "And especially you, Ellen. I've never known you to make that kind of effort before." She turned back to the rest of the staff. "I'm sure that most of you have done all you could to help Betts. We know that some kids do better in the hospital, responding well to the environment, the therapies, the medication, and the support and structure. The progress those kids make is a confirmation, perhaps, that the placement was a good choice, and that the hospital was what they needed at that point in their lives. Some children do less well in that environment, and I think Betts must be one of those."

"My, the hospital is such a special place," she continued. "So different from what might be outside these doors. Betts has been in a hospital environment for well over a year, a year here, as of today, and three weeks at the children's unit at Central Vermont. If anything, we have only seen her get worse. And worse. We looked at the data on how Betts functioned before these hospitalizations before she was removed from her home and placed into custody with the State. She did well before and was seen as bright, cooperative, and social. She spent a summer with her uncle, a decorated war hero, who has suffered from PTSD, but who has gone on to help other Vets at the outreach center in Randolph, and who maintains a spotless home on the side of Bear Hill." Laura smiled and looked straight at Ellen. "You might be careful what you say about the people who have given so much for us." She went on to the rest of the group. "Betts remembers that summer well, as does her uncle. She thrived there, and she will again."

"We have approved her uncle as a foster parent, licensed by the State of Vermont, and have decided to make a kin-care placement with him as of today. We appreciate all that you have done for Betts, and we thank you, as I'm sure she would if she were able to. Rather than coming back up here, I would like for you to get Betts ready to leave now, and we will take her back with us. I'll ask Zoey to stay with Betts in the dayroom and have her sign off on the discharge, as Betts' legal guardian. I'll help gather Betts' things. We're in a bit of a hurry." Laura smiled and took Zoey's hand and led her from the conference room.

Laura moved Zoey out the door, into the hallway. "Done," said Laura. "Ellen will still be Ellen tomorrow and the next day. Nothing you can do about that. Betts is where your energy needs to go today." Laura gestured toward Betts, by the window. "I want the three of us out of here in less than two minutes. Before Ellen thinks to get a doctor involved or a screener." Laura moved off toward Betts' room, and Zoey sat on the floor beside Betts, her heart pounding, and her breath still ragged. Laura returned with a black plastic trash bag filled with the clothing that Betts had arrived with a year earlier, followed by a red-faced Ellen, who was looking like she might take Laura by the shoulder, but not quite daring to.

Zoey put her hand cautiously on Betts' arm, and said softly, "We need to go now, to your uncle's cabin. With the little green woodstove, and the spring." Betts looked up, confused, and then smiled, and unsteadily rose, and walked with Zoey and Laura down the hallway, through the locked door, and out into the world beyond.

Laura drove, and Zoey sat in the back seat, next to Betts. When they arrived at the cabin, Betts was the first one out, stumbling on the grass. She promptly sat down, taking off her hospital socks and moving her bare feet on the wet grass, a real smile on her face for the first time in over a year.

Laura waved to Ames, and then went to the back of the van, and took out a large, blue duffle bag that the agency prepared for children going into long term foster care. Ames came down from the porch, unable to hide the shock on his face as he looked at the girl in the grass. He found himself staring at this puffy, dazed girl, still in her hospital pajamas, who had somehow taken the place of the skinny-tough girl who had been so aware of what was around her. He saw Betts loving the grass, and his heart broke, as he recognized the girl inside. "Hey, Betts," he said.

She looked for the voice, and found him; her eyes squinted against the sun behind her uncle. He squatted down in front of her. "Hi, Ames," she said. "I missed you."

"I missed you, too," said Ames.

CHAPTER EIGHT

Back Home

Betts stopped as she entered the porch, her eyes focusing on the new wall and door. "That's different," she said, and moved on into the cabin. Ames followed trying to explain about the new room, but Betts was headed to her couch. "Can I have some tea?" she asked.

"I just put some on," said Ames. "Ready in a minute." Zoey sat on the couch beside Betts and looked at Ames, who now just looked so happy to have Betts in the cabin again. Laura brought in the duffle bag and set it on the floor in front of Betts.

"This is some stuff for you. Clothes and things," Zoey said. Betts ignored the bag, and looked around the room, first at the stove, throwing out a little heat on the cool day, and then out the windows, seeing the mountains in the distance, and the sunshine on the trees in front.

Ames brought the tea and served it around, with Betts' Moose cup set in front of her. She looked at the cup and smiled, sipped the tea and said, "Oooh, it's hot!" Ames brought out some ginger snaps to make it more of a party. After her first cup of tea was gone, Betts rummaged in the duffel. She pulled out the clothing, some books, and two stuffed animals, and laid them out neatly on the couch. She carried the clothing into her new room, putting them into the small dresser, and set the stuffed animals on the bed. She put the books on the table in front of the couch, and looked through them a bit, selecting a Nancy Drew Mystery, *The Hidden Staircase*, and settled in to read.

Betts went to bed that first night in her new room, the room on the porch, going to bed there because she was tired and heavy, and because Ames had asked her to. But she soon woke up, and wandered back into the main room, and lay back down on the couch. She lay there for a bit, remembering the nights she had slept on this couch that first summer she came, and then she went back into her new porch bedroom and gathered up what she needed, dragging her pillow, a comforter and a stuffed dog with her, and setting herself back up on the couch.

When Ames came down from the loft in the morning, he found Betts still asleep, curled up on the couch, her book laid out over her chest, the new pillow under her head, and the new comforter gathered around her against the cool morning air. He thought about the rules for the new bedroom, and then smiled. He had built the room, it was for Betts, and the room met the requirements that Zoey had laid out. And it was a good room, but no one had said that Betts had to sleep there. Ames went to the stove, and squatted down beside it, opened the door, and began to shovel the ash out from the front of the stove, putting shovel after shovel into the tin pail. He was raking the small red coals out from the back of the stove to the front when he heard Betts behind him.

"Hi."

He turned and saw her sitting up on the couch, the comforter bunched around her, the stuffed dog in her lap. He saw a bit of the old focus in her eyes. "Good morning," he said. "Would you like some tea?"

She nodded. "I'll set up the tea while you get the stove going. It's cold in here." Betts went to the counter and got the Earl Grey jar down, and the teapot, and the strainer, then filled the kettle from the plastic bucket of cold spring water. Ames watched her work through the old morning ritual and was happy to see that she still knew how things worked here at the cabin.

When the stove was whistling and starting to snap and pop, Ames went to the paper bag full of medication from the hospital. He knew that the first dose of pills was to be given in the morning. He looked inside the bag at the pile of plastic pill bottles, all with Betts' name on them. He looked at Betts. "These are your pills from the hospital," he said. "They sent them home with you, and I'm supposed to keep giving them to you here until we get to see a doctor. Then maybe we can get them changed." Betts said nothing and started to tidy up the couch, folding the comforter, and bringing the comforter, the pillow and the stuffed dog back to her "porch room" as she called it, setting them on the bed. When she walked back into the cabin, Ames asked her, " Do you think these pills help you somehow?"

She looked at the bag. "I don't know. I don't think so. They give it to me every morning, before breakfast, then again after lunch, then after dinner. Sometimes if I get angry, they give me a shot. The shot makes me feel like I'm empty inside. I don't like the pills," she said.

Ames thought about that. "Let's keep them in the bag for now, then." He said, twisting the top of the bag over and over, making a tight knot on the top of the brown paper bag, and setting it up high on top of the shelf over the counter.

When the tea was poured, and Betts and Ames sat down at the table over some toast and eggs, Betts spoke up. "I like my room," she said. "I just didn't want to sleep there, 'cause when I was up at the hospital, I kept thinking about being here, and you, and the stove, and the spring, and sleeping on the couch at night. And when I got here, I wanted it to be the way I had remembered it. I like the room you made. You did a good job." She paused, not sure of where to go. Ames heard the worry in her voice and thought that she might be so eager to do the right thing that she wouldn't tell him what she needed to be happy here. Like sleeping on the couch, maybe.

He put his tea down and looked at her. "Betts. I want you to have what you need here. And I don't have much of an idea what that is, because I've never taken care of a kid before. I want you, and Zoey, to be the experts on this. Zoey will know what we need to do to be approved as a foster home for you, and you will know what needs to happen so that you feel happy and safe. You need to be honest with me and tell me what you need, so I can help with that. If you want to sleep on the couch, that's fine. If Zoey approves, you can sleep there every night. I just want you to feel OK. I've never been a ... a parent, before," he added. He struggled with the parent word, having first come up with "dad," but shying away from that, and now even the word parent seemed too much. Betts had parents, and maybe she wouldn't want him to think he was a parent to her.

He looked confused, and Betts answered him. "I don't know either. My mom was usually thinking about other stuff, and the guy I thought was my dad isn't, 'cause if he was, he would have done dad stuff with me, instead. I liked being here that summer, and what you did was fine. I like talking, and not talking, and working, and hiking, and going out by myself, and coming back here and reading, and making tea and being with you. That's what I want to do."

Ames looked at her. "OK," he said.

Zoey found Ames and Betts clearing the breakfast dishes from the table, and beginning to wash up with some hot water left in the kettle after making tea. She already saw a different Betts that the one she had dropped off the day before. "You're looking good this morning, Betts," she said. "Did you sleep well?" Ames explained about Betts sleeping on the couch, and Betts looked at the floor. Zoey thought about this and took a sip of her tea. "Laura licensed Ames as a foster parent and this cabin as a foster home. She did that because she believed that Ames and the cabin would be a good foster home for you, Betts. I think it's pretty much up to the two of you to figure out what works, and what doesn't. And I guess I'm here to help you guys with that when you need it. That, and the tea, of course." She smiled, and Betts did, too.

Ames asked Zoey "What about the medication? Does she have to take that?"

Zoey followed Ames eyes up to the brown paper bag on the top shelf, with the top twisted shut. "You're supposed to give Betts whatever medication is prescribed for her. If you think her medication needs to be changed, you need to take her to a doctor and have her change the order." She thought for a bit. "That's the rules. But you could take her in to see Dr. B., maybe even get her in today. Dr. B. is nice," she said, looking at Betts, "and he's pretty comfortable with kids trying it without medication. I have his number on my phone. Do you want me to call and see if Betts can get in today?"

She looked through the numbers on her phone and then selected one. Soon a voice came on the other line, and Zoey asked about a medication consultation visit today, with a foster child just discharged from the hospital. She waited a bit, and then said, "Thank you!" and put the phone back in her pocket. "You need to be there at 1:00 this afternoon. His office is the little blue and white house, just this side of the park, near the hospital." Ames knew the house. Betts looked worried, and Zoey reached out to her, patting the couch next to where Betts was sitting. "You'll like him. Dr. B. is a real sweetie." Zoey turned to Ames. "Take that bag of meds in with you. He'll want to see what you're dealing with."

"Can we go outside?" asked Betts. She still seemed nervous about seeing the doctor. They moved through the porch out into the yard, slipping their shoes on, and grabbing a light jacket from the hooks on the wall. It was still cold outside, but the sun was stronger than it had been a few weeks before, and the sound of water, soft, but constant, was everywhere. The snow had begun to melt a month ago, only a few hours a day at first, freezing up solid every night, then melting a bit more, but finally, most of it was gone. The water had soaked the still-frozen soil, and runoff in thousands of tiny streams that marked the land, gathering into pools and small creeks, flowing ever downward, finding the river at the foot of the mountain and running there on to the sea. The sound of the water, and the moisture in the air, so fresh and alive after the dry silence of the long winter, told the story that the world, so quiet and cold for so long, was alive and kicking, after all, shedding the snow and ice of winter like kicking off the wool blankets after a long sleep.

Betts pulled on her dark green rubber mud boots, kept in the porch these past sixteen months, finding them a bit small, and still caked with mud from when she had worn them her first summer so long ago. "Still fits," she said, lying just a bit. Ames slipped on a similar pair, about four times as big, and the three of them went out the door and down the steps, Zoey stepping carefully in her work shoes. Ames saw this and found himself guessing at her shoe size, so he could surprise her with a pair of barn boots at her next visit.

Betts led the way to the spring, washing her boots off with the water on the splash rock, and then washing the splash rock off with her hands. She held her hand under the water, smiled, and then put both hands into the icy water. "I love being here. Finally." Betts smiled.

Zoey looked at Betts, and saw the way she stood, and the way her hands splashed in the water and understood that the odd way Betts had moved by the window in the day room was an echo of her being here, at the spring. And Zoey understood why Betts stayed beside the window, and moved her hands with that odd smile on her puffy face. "Is this the place you thought of when you were by the window in the hospital?" Zoey asked.

Betts clouded over. Her voice became still and dead. "In the hospital, none of the windows would open. At all. There was no way to open a window, and they wouldn't let you go out of the doors. And if you tried, they would grab you, and tie you down in the hallway. It hurt." Betts was starting to breathe quickly, and her hands had come out of the water and pushed against someone or something that Zoey couldn't see. She began to rock back and forth, crying, twisting away from unseen hands. "Leave me alone!" she cried out. "I don't want it! I don't want it!" Ames put his hand on Zoey's shoulder, but Zoey moved toward Betts, squatting down beside her and taking her arm. Betts jerked away, a flash of rage in her eyes, and she hissed at Zoey, "Don't touch me! Don't touch me, you bastard!" She spit the words out and faced Zoey, her hands drawn back, and her teeth bared.

Zoey found herself suddenly afraid of this tiny, fifty-pound girl, who looked so much like a terrible animal caught in a trap. Zoey stumbled backward, and Ames moved between her and Betts, saying nothing, but backing up, giving Betts a little more space. When he had moved himself, and Zoey, about eight feet away, he sat on the ground, his hands at his side, and said quietly, "Shhhhhh. It's OK, Betts. You're safe." He spoke like someone might calm a horse, soft and slow, over and over, and Betts seemed to come back a bit. Slowly the wild look left her eyes, and her hands began to open up. Her breathing slowed, and her eyes lost some of the brittle fire that had scared Zoey.

Betts looked at her uncle, and saw him, sitting a little way away, still speaking so softly she could barely hear him. Betts began to cry, folding onto herself, rocking back and forth and moaning, "I'm sorry. I'm sorry," over and over again.

Zoey moved to comfort her, but Ames put out his arm, holding her back. "Give her a little time. She won't want you up close yet," he said. "That's OK, Betts," he said, "you just got upset is all. You're OK." Zoey watched the two of them, so different, and yet, so alike, thin and dark and broken somehow, but still strong. She was again struck by the deep understanding that Ames had for Betts and her troubles.

Betts cried softly now, still rocking a bit, but the racking sobs had stopped, and her breathing was slow and steady. She looked around, at Ames, at Zoey, and at the woods and the spring. She relaxed some, and then said, "I'm not even there anymore, but I'm still there, somehow." She looked so sad and hopeless. "Can we go back in now?" she asked.

"Sure," said her uncle. "We'll make a pot of tea." As they walked up to the cabin, Betts leaned against her uncle and held his hand. Zoey walked behind and thought this might be the first time she had seen Betts reach out to touch her uncle.

Betts again moved as if there was a weight upon her shoulders, and they made their way back to the cabin. Betts went to the couch, and took up one of the stuffed animals, burying her face in her hands, and Ames went to the counter, drew up a pitcher of spring water from the plastic bucket, and filled the kettle. He put the kettle on the old gas stove, opened a valve, and lit the gas with a blue-tipped wooden match. He set the kettle on the blue flame, and carried the match, still lit, to the little green woodstove, opened the door a crack, and tossed the match in.

Ames moved to a row of mason jars on the shelf, each filled with tea of some sort, and selected the one marked Earl Grey. He opened the jar and took a heaping teaspoon of the black tea, and tipped it into the strainer cup he had placed in the green teapot. There were two more teapots on the shelf, a small white one, and another large one, black, and made of iron, with a fine crosshatch pattern cast in, round and squat. The green teapot was their everyday pot, and Betts loved it. She saw the world in the pot, which must have been the same thing the potter had seen, and had laid her hand on it countless times, or touched the handle when the pot itself was too hot. Ames set the pot in front of Betts, and her hand came up, touching the hot-fired clay, and then touching the bamboo with the tips of her fingers. Ames set the moose cup in front of Betts as well, and then set his chipped green cup at his place, and asked Zoey to come and pick a cup. Zoey came to the counter, and Ames showed her the cups. Nothing special, all cups chosen from the thrift store down in town, probably.

Somehow being asked to choose her cup felt significant to Zoey, and she took her time with the choice. She settled on a tall brown mug with a green glaze on the inside. She brought it back to the table, and Betts looked at the mug. She smiled. "It's just like Ames' mug, only the other way around. His is green on the outside, with a brown glaze on the inside. You guys are twins, sort of," she said, with a grin. Zoey looked at the mug, and at the mug in front of Ames. She felt a little embarrassed, somehow, and sipped at her tea.

Zoey asked for sugar, and Ames said that they didn't have any, and offered to get some for her next visit. "We have honey," he said, getting up and going toward the counter. He came back with a small clay honey pot, brown glazed, with a finger-sized handle on each side. The lid had a slot on one side, and a wooden stick with a nob came up from inside the pot.

Zoey looked at the pot, and Betts leaned over, lifting the lid with one hand, and the stick with her other. "You just twist the honey up on the stick," she said, doing just that, and bringing a slow liquid glob of gold onto the base of the stick, where wooden disks caught up and held the honey. Betts puts the stick back into the pot and replaced the lid. "You try," she said.

Zoey did as instructed, and was rewarded with a similar glob of honey, which she moved over her mug before the strands of honey began to fall. "Just twist it again when you have enough," said Betts. "Ames showed me how when we had pancakes that first summer. It's way nicer than a spoon." Zoey guessed how much honey she had in her mug, and twisted the stick again, and the honey rolled back into the slotted ball, and she put the honey stick back into the pot and replaced the lid. "Honey is better for you than sugar," said Betts. "And it can't go bad, ever. They found honey in the Pharaohs' tombs in Egypt, and it was still good; they ate it, after like a bazillion years or something." Betts seemed to be getting back to her old self. "We might get bees up here. Ames was talking about it. Back when I was here before." Betts looked at Ames. "Are we still going to get bees?" she asked.

Ames looked over at her and said, "Yeah. I think so. We have to order the hives and stuff. Yeah. Let's do that." He smiled, and so did Betts.

Zoey watched them. She looked at the moose mug in Betts's hands. "Did you go to Maine?" she asked.

No," said Betts. "We got that one at the thrift store, too."

After tea, and after the washing up, Zoey drove her Subaru back to the rest of her caseload, and Ames and Betts headed down the hill to see Dr. B.. Ames had tossed the brown bag of medicine into the back of the truck, a move that Betts thought a little odd since there was plenty of room in the cab. He opened his door, and Betts slid in first, sliding across the worn bench seat, and finding her seat belt. Ames got in, closed his door, and started up the old truck. They backed off to the side, then headed out the path to the dirt road, took a right, and headed down toward town, Ames driving slowly over the rough and slippery spring-washed road. Betts loved these rides under the great canopy of trees, the old Ford moving surely, Ames picking out the best line, avoiding ruts and rocks and sheets of ice that still surfaced in the road as spring slowly pushed winter back.

Betts had watched Ames' hand on the smooth grey ball on the shift stick, marked in faint red with the lines of the gears, and saw his foot move the clutch in and out between his shifts. "Can I shift some, too?" she asked.

Ames thought about it for a bit. "Yeah. Put your hand on the knob, and I'll show you how to move it, then you can try it yourself. He dropped the truck into second gear and then had Betts put her hand on the knob. He put his hand over hers and brought the truck up to speed for the shift into third gear. Suddenly, Betts pulled her hand away, filled with a panic she didn't understand. Ames looked at her, then back to the road, and made the shift up to third gear. "We can try it later, maybe," he said.

"OK," said Betts.

Dr. B. had his office in a small, blue and white Victorian house, just off of Main Street, out toward the south end of town. Ames pulled into a small parking lot, eased the truck into a marked place, and turned off the engine, leaving the truck in gear. He opened his door and got out, holding the door as Betts slid across the seat and climbed down as well. Ames took the paper bag of medications from the truck bed. Betts was nervous, her eyes looking quick and scared as they entered the door. Ames walked toward the desk, where a middle-aged woman in jeans sat working at a computer. She smiled as they came in.

Betts went first to a plastic toy box, stared into it for a bit, and found nothing of interest. She then went to a fish tank on a stand against the far wall, a good-sized tank filled with clear water, some rocks and a few drifting plants and a single huge goldfish, moving slowly between the plants. On one side, the goldfish had lost all of his scales and wore only a tight white skin, showing the muscles beneath his slow movements. Gold scales on one side, and only skin on the other. Betts approached the woman at the desk, and waited a bit, not wanting to interrupt.

"What happened to your fish?" she asked.

The woman smiled at her. "Someone left the lid on the tank open, a few years ago. I came in on a Monday morning and found him dry and stiff on the carpet, where I guess he had been all weekend, from where he jumped out. I thought he was dead, but for some reason, I just picked him up and tossed him back into the tank. I looked up a few hours later, remembering that I had to get rid of the fish, and found him swimming around in the water, coming up to the top, looking for food. He was alive, after all, but he lost all the scales on the side that got dried up. Now he's kind of funny looking."

Betts looked back at the fish, and then at the woman behind the desk. "I think he's beautiful and brave," she said. "And way more interesting than a regular goldfish. Why don't you have any other fish with him?" she asked.

"He eats them," the woman said.

"Oh," said Betts, and she returned to the tank, watching the big fish swim back and forth.

Dr. B. came in after a few minutes, after Ames had dug through the magazines, and found one on sailboats. Dr. B. wore blue jeans as well, and a flannel shirt with the sleeves rolled up, a stethoscope around his neck, the end tucked into his shirt pocket. He had glasses, and looked a little like an elf, Betts thought. He approached Betts, first, but she declined his handshake, giving him a nervous smile instead. Ames introduced himself, and Dr. B. led them out of the waiting room, down a short hallway, and into a small office on the right.

The office must have been the kitchen in the house originally, with the sink and shelves still in place, an exam table near the window at one side, where flowered curtains blew a bit in the breeze from the open window. "If it's cold, I'll shut the window," Dr. B. said.

Betts shook her head. "I like 'em open," she said, and sat down on one of the chairs beside the wall. Ames sat beside her, and Dr. B. sat on the edge of his desk and began.

Looking at Betts, he said, "What can I do for you?"

Betts looked back at him and said, "I don't know. I just got out of the hospital, and now I live with my uncle, and they sent a bag full of medication they want me to take." She ended and looked out the window.

Dr. B. said, "Oh. Ok," and asked Ames for the bag. He untwisted the top, taking some time, and then took out one bottle after another, setting them beside each other on the desk beside him. When all the bottles were out, in a row, Betts looked at them, and then at Dr. B..

Ames said, "Betts just came to live with me yesterday. She's been in the hospital for a long time, over a year, and they sent that stuff home with her, and she doesn't like it. I don't like it, either. I guess she has to take it unless there's a doctor who could say something else." Ames finished up awkwardly, feeling that somehow, he had said too much.

Dr. B. smiled just a bit. He looked back to Betts and said, "I need to ask you a few questions." Betts nodded. "Can you tell me about the nicest place you have ever been?"

The question was so odd that Betts thought she must have misunderstood. "What?" she asked, confused.

"Tell me about the best place you have ever been. The place you liked the best. Where you were really happy."

Betts had heard the question right; it was just a weird question. She wondered if this was a trap, somehow, and tried to see how the wrong answer might make her look crazy. She finally gave up, and said, "Ames lives in a cabin up on the side of Bear Mountain. Way up high, all by himself. You can see all the way down the valley, all the way to the ski mountains. There's a spring where you get water, and a woodstove, and lots of books and tea. That's my favorite place ever," she finished. Then she added, "I live there with him, now."

Dr. B. looked out the window, trying to see the cabin in the woods. "That sounds beautiful," he said. "Ok. Let's try another question. Describe the best day you have had."

Betts thought about this for a while and then said, "When I came up the first summer, Ames and I cut a lot of wood. A good day would be when we both worked pretty much all day and then went for ice cream cones after, or maybe a swim down at the floating bridge. We had a lot of days like that. Those were my best days. So far," she added.

"That sounds nice," said Dr. B.. "OK. Tell me five things you really like, and five things you don't like at all."

Betts thought, and offered, "I like being at the cabin, sitting on the couch, reading and having tea. I like the little green woodstove at the cabin. I like the spring a lot. The water is super cold and comes all the way from inside the mountain. And it goes to the sea. And I like working with Ames, doing tree work. And I like going to the library, and checking out books and bringing them back home. That's five."

She thought a bit more and felt a little less comfortable with these five. "I don't like the hospital, at all. You can't go outside, or even open a window, and everything is plastic and smells bad. I don't like nights in the hospital. Ever." She paused and gathered herself together a bit. "I don't like my mom's husband." She thought. "I don't like questions like that." She finished up. She looked at Dr. B., who looked out the window.

"Well, that's four out of five, a good strong B, and you got an A+ on the first five, so that's pretty good."

Dr. B. looked at Betts. "Here's a few quick questions. Do you sleep through the night, and wake up feeling rested?"

"Usually, at the cabin I do," answered Betts.

"Do you have nightmares?"

"Sometimes."

"Do you ever get angry or scared, even though nothing is happening to you that is scary or bad?"

Betts looked at the floor. "Yes. Today I thought about being in the hospital, and got scared, and yelled at Zoey, even though she was just trying to help. I called her a bad word. And I think she was scared of me."

"OK," said Dr. B.. "What helps you feel better when that happens?"

"Ames talks to me, quiet like, and I calm down after a while. That's what happened today."

"Fair enough," said Dr. B.. "Last one. Do you want to try not taking the medication for a while, and see how you feel?"

"Yes," answered Betts. "I don't think the medication helps me not feel angry or afraid. It just makes it so my feelings don't show as much on the outside."

Dr. B. went back to looking out the window and didn't say anything for a little while. When he looked back, he looked sad. "Well, we are going to order a month without any of these medications, and see how that works for you. I want you, Betts, to spend a little time every evening and think about the day you had, and what was good in it, and what was a problem, and write that down, maybe on the calendar. I want Ames to do the same thing, so we have a record of how things are going without the medication on board." He wrote for a minute, sitting at the desk, then looked up. "Ask Jenny at the front desk to give you an appointment in about a month." He stood up and again offered to shake Betts' hand.

She took his hand and said, "That's it? You don't have to look at me or anything?"

Dr. B. shook his head. "You look fine to me," he said. "When you're due for a physical, you can come back. You take care of yourself, now," he said, as he walked them back to the waiting room.

On the way out to the truck, Betts said, "I like Dr. B.."

"So do I," said Ames.

After leaving Dr. B.'s office, Betts saw Zoey leaning up against her rusty Subaru, parked beside the old Ford truck. She smiled as she saw Ames and Betts coming into the little parking lot. "How'd it go?" she asked.

"Good," said Ames. "No meds for a month. And we need to take notes on how it goes. I think it's going to be fine."

"Dr. B. has a fish that fell out of the tank and laid there on the carpet for the whole weekend, and dried out stiff as a board, and lost all the scales on the side that was up, but he didn't die," said Betts.

"Really?" asked Zoey.

"Yeah. He's regular gold scales on one side, and all-white skin on the other. And he ate all the other fish in the tank."

"Wow," said Zoey.

Ames suggested that they all go for ice cream at the little creamy stand at the edge of town, by the railroad tracks. He and Betts had done this a few times when she had lived with him over the first summer. Ames was smiling and felt excited and happy.

Betts said to Ames, "You're all perky."

Ames grinned. "Yeah, I guess. I don't know. I just think things are going to work out." They pulled up at the ice cream stand, a small cinder block building that might have once been a storage building for the railroad, with only a front window, shaded by a striped awning, with three wooden picnic tables out in front, with umbrellas standing over each table. As they approached the window, Ames announced, "I'm going to have a triple."

Betts looked at him as if he had grown a second head, and then sensing something in the air, asked, "Can I have a triple, too?"

"Sure," said Ames.

Zoey said, "Me too. A triple Moose Tracks. Then I guess I can skip dinner."

They got their cones, tall and heavy, and took them to a table. They sat in silence, happy, trying to eat the cones before they melted into trouble. Zoey licked quickly at her cone, but Betts took bites, gasping from her teeth freezing from time to time, and then biting into the ice cream again. "Arrggh!" Betts said. "My teeth are freezing!" Ames worked at his cone, keeping the edges smooth, and the drips gone as soon as they appeared.

Suddenly, Ames handed his cone to Betts, saying, "Hold this," and leapt up from the table, sprinting toward the railroad tracks. Zoey and Betts looked on in horror as Ames arrived at the tracks just as a train came into sight around a bend, its whistle shrieking a warning and the rumble of the steel wheels shaking the ground. Ames fished coins out of his pocket, and carefully laid them on the rail, ignoring the thundering train. He stepped back just as the train roared past, the engineer visible in the little window, shaking his head as he went by.

Ames grinned and climbed back up to the creamy stand, and took his cone from Betts. "Now you can go down there and try to find the coins. Three quarters, three dimes, two nickels, and maybe four or five pennies. They get knocked off, but they'll be around where I put them." Ames grinned at Zoey, who was staring at him as if a stranger had taken the place of the quiet, steady man she had come to know. "How's your ice cream?" he grinned at her.

"Betts is right," she said. "You're all perky today!"

Betts walked along the tracks, bending over and sometimes picking something up from the cinders and grass. She came back up the hill, a big smile on her face. "Five pennies," she announced. "And they're all squished flat as paper." She laid them out on the picnic table, and sure enough, the dimes were now the size of quarters, and the quarters the size of a silver dollar. The image and the words on each coin was smeared a bit, stretched and faded in places, but still visible.

Betts was delighted. She saw that each of them got a quarter, a dime, and gave Ames and Zoey each a nickel, "so you can have a complete set," she explained. She took a single penny and gave Ames and Zoey two each. They thanked her, and after looking at the coins, pocketed them. They sat at the table, trying to finish the huge ice cream cones.

"I don't know," said Ames. "I just feel better than I have in about forever."

"Me, too," said Betts. "This will go on my 'best day' list."

Zoey looked down the tracks, where, far in the distance, the two rails joined into one. "Me, too," she said.

CHAPTER NINE

Starting School

Betts had taken up a book, a favorite she had read many times over that first summer, and settled onto the couch. She had first poured herself a cup of tea in her Maine Moose Mug and set it steaming on the table beside the couch, where she could reach it once it had cooled just a bit. She looked at the mug. "The Way Life Should Be." "Yep," she thought. "This is it."

She had put her flattened coins on the shelf by the window, where her collection of rocks and shells and dried leaves and flowers had grown to the point of looking a little crowded. Betts thought about the day and decided that a triple cone was probably not such a good idea after all. She thought about Dr. B. and smiled. And she thought about Zoey, who seemed to fit in so well with Ames and herself.

Ames had fed the little green woodstove when the three of them returned to the cabin. Betts had brought in three splits of birch, and Ames had stirred the coals a bit and then laid on the wood, one piece at a time. The teapot sat on a tile on the front of the little green stove, where it would keep warm, and Ames and Zoey each had a cup of tea.

Zoey had watched Ames and Betts with the stove, and making the tea, careful, slow, and working together without a word spoken. She thought of how quiet the cabin was, without the sound of traffic, television, and without much talk. There was a radio on the shelf, but Zoey had not heard it played. She thought of how Ames had found the cabin such a place of healing after he returned from the war, and then she thought of Betts' outburst earlier in the day, the giddy girl eating the towering ice cream cone, and now the quiet girl who had made herself such a cozy spot to read on the couch. She thought of how Betts had first come into custody, and the time the little girl had spent in the hospital. She felt tears in her eyes and brushed them away with the back of her hand.

Zoey turned to Ames and said, "Betts tells me there's a high rock here where you can see all the way down the valley. Could you show it to me?"

Betts looked up from her book and seemed to try to hide the smile on her face behind her book. Ames looked surprised but nodded. "Sure. It's just up the hill. It's real pretty up there. You'll want a sweater."

Ames led Zoey up the hill, behind the cabin, past the spring, and up the little trail that led to a piece of rock ledge that jutted out from the cool, mossy ground. Most of the mountain was made of this soft black, layered rock, and this piece showed seams of white quartz layered through it. At the foot of the ledge, a flat piece of slate, about the size of a large dining room table lay on the ground, swept clean. They sat down on the rock and looked out over the broad valley, across the hay fields, the patches of woods, the bits of twisting road visible here and there, and large patches of snow, still white, where the shade had kept the snow from the searching warmth of the sun. They sat without speaking, side by side, seeing the world stretch out of sight, the green to blue to grey mountains becoming indistinct in the distance.

After some time, Ames said, "That thing this morning, at the spring, where Betts got scared? That was like me when I came back. The other guys at the VA were like that, too. You get that way when you're trapped somewhere horrible with something you can't get away from." He paused, and Zoey heard the anger deep in his voice. "She didn't have that when she came up the first summer. Something must have happened after she left, either with Peter and Tina or in the foster homes or the hospitals. Somebody's hurt her. A lot." She could hear Ames voice raggedy and filled with menace, and she felt a little bit afraid.

Ames took some slow breaths and then said, "I don't want her going back there. Ever. I want her to stay with me." Zoey looked at Ames and saw his loose body, his breathing steady, but she realized that this calm was the result of great effort. She thought of the spotless cabin, the well-tended woodstove, the slow ritual of making tea, the quiet and calm of Ames' life in the cabin was built and maintained with great effort, and she thought of what might lie below this surface.

Zoey thought of the visit she had made to Tina's house, the trash spilling out of the kitchen can, the sink and counter piled with unwashed dishes, and even the yard filled with things broken and discarded. Tina had caught Zoey's eyes taking in the chaos and had said, "Try raising a kid. They make a mess of everything." But Zoey knew Betts was a child of order, as well. She thought of the rocks and dried flowers placed in order on the shelf, with room made by rearranging the collection. "Something's going to have to go," Betts had said. "The shelf is getting too full."

What must it be like for Betts to come and find herself in a place like this, quiet and neat and safe from the world? Out loud, she said, "You're right. Something happened. Betts changed from when she was here that first summer. She may tell us about it when she feels safer. Or maybe she won't." She looked at Ames, breathing steady and looking out on the valley down below. "I don't want her anywhere but with you."

They sat for a bit, and then Zoey said, "I'm worried about school. We need to get her started, this next week, and the school is going to be expecting trouble after her being in the hospital so long. And if she throws one of those fits at school like she did at the spring, everyone is going to want to ship her back to the hospital."

"She can't help it when it happens," said Ames. "It just takes over. You're back in whatever it was, and you can't even see the real world anymore. All she can do is to try to stay safe from whatever makes her scared." He waited. "School might be real hard for her. Some of the kids are bullies, and some of the teachers are, too. I went there, and it was OK, but I kind of kept to myself." They sat on the top rock, the beautiful world spread out before them, and they worried about Betts, who lay on the couch down below, reading about a pig saved from disaster by his friends in the barnyard, sipping her tea and feeling the safety of the cabin all around her.

The East Street School had about fifty students, in Kindergarten through sixth grade, children from the village and farms of Brookfield. The school was a newer building, a long single-story, with a gym and cafeteria at one end, and four classrooms stretching down the hall in the other direction. The small number of kids required that the school combine the classes, and so there was a K-1, a 2-3, a 4-5 and a single grade 6. Each classroom had a teacher, a classroom aid, and there was a principal, his secretary, and a full-time maintenance man, an old dairy farmer who no longer had a farm, who now worked to keep the school clean and repaired. There were two part-time lunch ladies, who worked together in the morning, putting out breakfast for the kids who came early to eat, and making lunch from the frozen boxes of government-supplied food. Art, music, and PE were taught by traveling teachers, who would come for half a day each week, then move on to other small schools in the district.

Outside the building, there was a giant wooden play structure, built in the shape of a pirate ship, complete with wheel and rigging, portholes, rope bridges, and a series of slides and ladders, sitting in a sea of wood chips. It was a wonderful play structure, although the dark interior of the ship was a terror to the younger kids, so far away from the distracted eyes of the teachers on playground duty. Betts had known as a first-grader to stay outside the ship.

Betts had loved the school, finding it a haven of peace and order when she first came at age five, which should tell you something about the life she had at home. Betts was quiet and cooperative, smart, and did her best to stay away from the bullies and out of trouble. Her school record for those first two years listed no problems with behavior, just ongoing reports of head lice, poor hygiene (not her fault, when the water was shut off in the trailer), forgotten lunches and unpaid school and lunch fees. Betts was a part of the crowd who could not afford to participate in many of the school activities. She was not in the band, and never went on the overnight field trips that charged a fee, or ordered books from the Scholastic Book Club, a monthly ordeal during which the class sat in silence while the kids with money received their book orders, and the kids without money sat and watched.

Betts had company in this regard. Brookfield, like much of Vermont, was a mix of the very poor, a few middle-class families, and the very wealthy. It was an uncomfortable mix of the rural native families who had lived on the land as best they could, or worked in the factories and quarries, and the people from out of state, New York, Massachusetts, Connecticut, and the like, who came to Vermont for the beauty of the land and the "lifestyle" of living in a restored farmhouse on a hundred acres. The school was pretty much the only place these two very different populations would meet. The nearest private school was in Burlington, some sixty miles away, and that was a Waldorf school, anyway, so the school ended up with all the children in town who were not homeschooled.

Betts' success in Kindergarten and first grade was not enough of a success to overcome the worries some people now had about a student who had been in a psychiatric setting for over a year. Sadly, Mrs. Eddy was both an officer in the large Congregational church down in Randolph, where Ellen Jensen chose to appear every Sunday, beside most of the other moneyed families in the town, and the mother of an unpleasant little boy named Heath, who was in Betts' class. Ellen had not wasted time or details in spreading the concerns she had about this dangerous child being placed in the community, and Mrs. Eddy had listened, having a son in the Brookfield school. Mrs. Eddy, having grown up with privilege, money and good looks, wasted no time in calling the school to share her concerns, in her self-appointed roll as community leader. And Mr. Bowman, having ascended to the dizzying heights of principalship through his careful study of how to keep those in power happy, wasted no time in barring the door against Betts' admission to the school.

He had already made inquiries about moving Betts to the alternative school up in Montpelier, where she could be transported by the short bus, having a half-day of education to help compensate for the two-hour bus ride. He looked up Betts' records in the school and found nothing useful for justifying this transfer, with her two years at the school uneventful, without incident, with the exception of several lice infestations, and some concerns expressed by the school nurse about suspicious bruises, and possible neglect and abuse, that had never been investigated. Mr. Bowman remembered Betts mother, not an unattractive young woman, but really just one of the lice mothers who could do little to help advance a career in education.

This explains why Betts' file was still on Mr. Bowman's desk when Betts and Ames arrived at the school that Thursday morning. Mr. Bowman's secretary had brought them in, and Mr. Bowman's first thought was concern at the young man accompanying the child. He looked rather serious and not easily discouraged. Ames extended his hand and introduced himself and Betts. Betts remembered Mr. Bowman only vaguely since Mr. Bowman left his secretary to deal with most of the younger children, preferring to spend what time he must with the older children. Mr. Bowman took the lead. "You must be here to see what school might work best for Betts, with her special needs."

Ames stopped and looked at Mr. Bowman. "No. We're here to get Betts enrolled in school. She should be in the 3rd grade. She'd like to start as soon as she can."

Mr. Bowman looked flustered. "Well," he said, "that won't be possible. East Side School has very limited special education services, and we won't be able to safely meet Betts' needs here. I've made arrangements for her to be enrolled at the Alternative School up in Montpelier. It won't be any problem for you since a special bus will pick her up every day, and then bring her back home." He beamed down at Betts, his red face contorted by his attempt at a smile. "Won't that be nice? Having your own bus every day?"

Betts would have been afraid if Ames had not been standing between her and this unpleasant man. Betts looked right back at him and said, "No. I want to go back to this school. And I don't have any special education needs. I always got 100's, and finished my work early."

Ames had shifted from confused to starting to get angry and was doing his best to breath and stay calm. "Like Betts said, we're here to get her started in school. This school. We'd like her to start tomorrow." He leaned in a bit toward Mr. Bowman, and said, "Betts doesn't have any special needs. She was here before. Don't you have her records from then?" Ames looked at Mr. Bowman's desk and saw Betts' records lying right there.

Mr. Bowman stood up from his desk and moved back just a little. "I'm sorry you don't understand. I'll have a letter sent out to you tomorrow explaining the school's position. If you have concerns after that, you can call and ask for a meeting here. For now, I'd ask that you both leave." He looked at Ames, and pulled Betts' record back out of reach as if worried that Ames might pick up the folder.

Betts felt the tension in the room and began to be afraid. She moved toward the door, holding Ames' hand and trying to bring him with her. Ames stood rooted for a moment, staring at Mr. Bowman, then turned and followed Betts out of the office, and out of the building. Ames went to the truck and opened the door. Betts, in her school clothes, climbed in and fished for her seat belt, and Ames got in after her. They drove back toward the cabin for a bit, then Ames pulled off into a driveway, turned the truck, and headed back to town. Betts was worried, and Ames told her, "We're going to go and talk with Zoey about this. She can help us fix it." Betts relaxed a little and looked out the window at the green fields moving past.

Zoey was in, at her desk, working through some papers, when Ames and Betts came in. Ames explained the situation, and Zoey got stiff and red-faced as well. Betts panicked that she was causing problems again and said, "I'm sorry."

Zoey looked at her and pulled her own emotions back into control. "Betts, you're doing just fine, and so are we. Getting upset when something isn't right isn't a problem. We just need to get this fixed. I'll ask Laura for some advice, then we can go in tomorrow and make it right." She turned to Ames. "Have you guys had lunch yet? I was just about the head out, and I'd love to treat you guys. And we can pull Laura out of her office and have her come along, too. She'd like that. And she's a good problem solver."

The four of them met over pizza and spent a few minutes working out what Laura and Zoey would do at the school the next morning. Foster kids have some specific educational protections in Vermont, and Laura was well aware of these. She thought that calling the school out for refusing to provide an education to a child in foster care, and for suggesting special education interventions without the required meetings and findings would be a good place to start. She then planned to remind the school of the privacy concerns from the HIPPA act, since somehow the school had suddenly had concerns with no legitimate source of information regarding where Betts had been for the past year. Laura suspected Ellen Jensen, of course.

Once in, Betts would likely be able to stay in, because her good behavior and lack of trouble would make it harder every day for the school to argue that she didn't belong there. Laura suggested that she and Zoey hit the school first thing in the morning, and decided to request a meeting at 9:00 a.m. Laura turned to Betts and Ames. "We'll call you and let you know how things go," she said. "Maybe we can get you in on Monday. The important thing is to keep your time at school as perfect as possible, at least at first. Bowman will be waiting for a slip-up some sort, and even you getting mad in self-defense might give him something he could use. I know it's not fair," she said.

Betts looked worried, but she said, "Ames says the Fair only happens in the fall, at Tunbridge, or in Rutland." She grinned a bit. "And school is over by 2:30, anyway."

Ames smiled at her. "Pizza's ready," he said. "Want to come up with me and help carry?"

After the pizza, Ames, and Betts took the old Ford back up the road to the cabin, their mood a little lighter, and carrying a few slices of cold pizza to enjoy later. But the two of them rode back to the cabin with a bit of a shadow over them. The new green leaves overhead went unnoticed, and the eager new spill of water by the road went unheard. When Ames parked the truck and got out, Betts slid across the seat and climbed out, too. He rolled up the window, and closed the truck door, and said, "I guess it can't all be easy. Zoey and Laura will get it fixed up tomorrow. They're good at that kind of stuff."

Betts started with, "I'm sorry," again, but Ames cut her off. "Not your fault, Betts. Not your fault at all. You're a good kid, and that school should feel lucky to have you. If that guy thought he was in the right, he wouldn't have looked so shifty. Zoey will straighten it out. Let's go get some tea."

Betts grabbed her book and headed to the couch, and Ames put the kettle on and took his chair by the window. Parenting. A whole new world for Ames, having never experienced a whole lot of it himself, either growing up or as an adult. His childhood in the trailer, on the dairy farm, was still pretty clear to him, but he couldn't remember much that seemed like parenting. His folks had worked hard every day and kept a roof over their heads, and food on the table. He was grateful for that and knew there were a lot of kids, here in Vermont, too, that never had that much. But he couldn't remember any talk at the table, or afterward, and he couldn't remember ever going to his parents with a problem. He tried to do well at school, trying to keep his folks from having any problems with him, especially after the death of his sister, Clair. Ames listened for the kettle to come to a boil.

He wanted everything to be good for Betts. He wanted her to be happy, and for the people around her to see her through his eyes, as smart and strong and kind and interested in the world around her. He was frustrated, as he realized that there were so many battles in Betts' life that he could never fight for her, and that often the best he would be able to do would be to try and not fly off the handle and have his own anger make her scared. He wanted to be an anchor, a steady rock for her, not have her worrying that he was upset because of her. He had enough of that feeling when he was growing up. He heard the water go to boil, and took the kettle off the stove. "Earl Grey?" he asked.

She nodded, not looking up from her book, the book she held in front of her face, with the pages that had not been turned since she came in the door. Betts was worried, too, worried, he was sure, about that piece that Laura had said, about Bowman waiting for a slip-up. What if Betts got grabbed or shoved by some kid, and had another of those spells like she had had up at the spring? She knew she couldn't control that stuff. And he didn't have any answers for her.

Ames tried to remember if he had had an anchor when he was growing up. He had always turned to himself when he was troubled, and he could hear his father's voice in the background, somewhere, saying you had to count on yourself because everyone else would fail you. That seemed like a terrible message, and he thought of Zoey and Laura down at the pizza shop, eager to help, and committed to seeing him and Betts through this thing.

When there were fights between his parents, and fights between Tina and his folks, and anger and frustration when the farm machinery broke down, or the trail roof leaked, or the pump failed, he remembered his dad turning in on himself, never asking for help, never turning to anyone to try and make it easier. His mother had been the same way. And then Clair died.

He remembered that bits of it as clear as if it had happened yesterday. She was wearing blue jeans, patched on one knee with a dark green iron-on patch shaped like a clover, and a purple tee-shirt, purple with a couple of green and blue fish on the front. Maybe from "The Little Mermaid." She had brushed her hair that morning, and tied it back with a high ponytail, a plastic jewel of some sort glued on to the hair tie. His dad was on the tractor, wearing the grey Dickie's coveralls, and the dirty blue Ford hat, his glasses fogged from the barn, probably, and was getting ready to move the manure out from the pile where the gutter cleaners moved it out of the barn, over to the lagoon, the cement lined pool where the manure stayed, reeking, until it was time to suck it into the spreader tank and spray it on the fields. Ames remembered the smell of the manure and the diesel tractor.

His dad did this every morning, after the first milking, and after the cows were sent back. And he and Tina and Clair were waiting for the bus, at the end of the driveway, and Clair had run back to tell her dad something, probably something funny or nice, maybe a joke she remembered, or to say that she hoped he would have a good day, and as she moved behind the big wheel, he had popped the tractor into reverse, and that fat tractor tire, a foot or two higher than Clair was, that tire had just rolled right over her, catching her feet first, and pushing her back, then up over her legs and her hips, as she twisted and shook. He saw it happen, and ran back, seeing the tractor roll over her chest, pressing her into the mud a little, but mostly just pressing her out, breaking her jeans and her tee-shirt as well as her body, her book bag untouched on the ground beside her.

His father had stopped the tractor, the tire still on her, and Ames remembered a great moment of silence with the diesel engine off and the screaming not yet started. Ames had looked into her eyes and found her confused and scared, and then, as she saw him for a moment, he saw her shift, first into understanding, and acceptance, then, in a second, she was gone. Her eyes stayed open, but he could see that she was gone, gone away from this sudden wreck of a body, and gone on, he knew, to somewhere else.

Tina had come by then, screaming. His mother had come from the trailer, screaming, and his father had started screaming, and when Ames saw that it was done, he had run, of course, run and run across the fields and into the woods, seeking higher ground and climbing to a bit of ledge, where he shook and cried and moaned. And when he came back, cold and hollow and alone, a few hours later, Clair was gone, and her bookbag, too. The tractor back was in the shed, and his family was gone, first to the hospital, behind the ambulance, rolling down the road without even a siren to pretend there was hope, then, when they returned that night, it was as if they had all died along with her, cold and silent, and drawn into themselves.

When Clair had died, his parents had never asked for help at all. A few folks came. Church folks came, for a few days, with casseroles that sat untouched on the counter until they were thrown away, Corning Ware and all, and a neighbor or two who knocked, said they were sorry, then, in the long silence that followed, went away. His teacher had asked how he was doing and seemed relieved when he answered that he was doing fine.

But Laura Woods had showed up, first at school, then at home, day after day, bringing some snacks, or a bucket of chicken, or a pizza, a bottle of root beer, and she had sat at the kitchen table, while his parents refused to speak with her, and refused the food she brought, playing games with Tina and him, doing the dishes in the sink, or helping with homework, straightening up their rooms, catching the laundry up, even helping with parts of the funeral. Never asking how they were. Just being there.

Ames thought about that. He couldn't see any way that Laura had all that as a part of her job. She was hired at that time as a school counselor, spread out over the district schools, coming in one afternoon a week to the East Street School, taking a class and working on bullying issues, or personal safety, while the teacher took the hour to catch up on grading papers. She had turned up at the trailer after school, or early in the evenings. On weekends, taking the kids on shopping trips for groceries or clothes. Ames wondered if Laura had done all that, for over a year, on her own time, and with her own money, and he guessed, at last, that she probably had. Laura had been the only real anchor he had ever had, and she had tried to be that for Tina as well.

Ames wanted to be that kind of anchor for Betts. He saw her, so worried and alone on the couch, hiding behind her book, not wanting to make a fuss, and not wanting to be a problem, and he poured out a cup of tea for her, and gently tapped at the back of her book. Betts lowered the book an inch or so, and looked at Ames with her scared brown eyes. "Your tea," he said. "Let's go make a bonfire and sit outside some tonight." He moved to the little green woodstove, opened the door, and carefully raked out a pile of red coals into the lid of the tin ash bucket. "You'll want your sweatshirt," he said, "and you can bring the marshmallows."

Betts stared at him for a bit, then took the bookmark from the back of her book, and put it in place, and put her book down on the table, getting up slowly. She followed Ames out to the fire pit, where he had stacked the coals on a split of birch, and then covered them with three more splits. He bent over the wood, blowing carefully until the smoke came, and the smallest yellow flames licked at the paper bark. Betts sat down, the bag of marshmallows in one hand, and her tea and the roasting sticks in her other. "It's nice out here," she said.

Ames saw that the fire was good, and set back into his chair, his teacup steaming in the cool spring night, and looked up at the stars. "I love it out here," he said. As the fire licked up, the smoke twisting one way and another in the light breeze, he thought about the day, and the school, and Mr. Bowman, and how much Betts had been hurt over the past year and a half. And he thought how little he could do to protect her or make things right. But he could offer tea, and a fire, and marshmallows, and company. Because there's not too much, you can do about the big stuff. In the end, all you can offer is love, and sometimes, that can make all the difference.

CHAPTER TEN

Starting School Again

Zoey and Laura went back to the office, neither saying a word as they drove. Laura tended to be quiet, and Zoey was trying to master her feelings a bit. She was furious that Mr. Bowman, Mrs. Eddy, and of course, Ellen Jensen, couldn't just leave Betts alone. Why go out of their way to make a hurt kid even more hurt?

She posed this question to Laura, who said, "It's not about Betts. They don't even know her." Zoey stewed on this. She could see it was true, on the surface. Bowman might remember Betts from her first two years at the school, but there was nothing there that would make him want to hurt her. Zoey doubted that Mrs. Eddy had ever even noticed Betts, and Ellen had struggled to remember Betts' name in the discharge meeting. Yet all three were going out of their way to make Betts' life even harder. She was irritated at Laura for sounding like she understood all of this, but suspected that somehow, she did.

"Ok," said Zoey. "So, if they don't know Betts, why are they trying to hurt her?" Laura looked at the irritated young social worker riding beside her. She smiled, making Zoey even more irritated.

"They're not. It starts with Ellen, of course. Ellen doesn't want to lose, especially publicly. And she lost big up at the hospital when we took Betts out of there. She had a plan to put Betts in Waterbury, not because she wanted to hurt Betts, but because it was the easiest thing for her to do. State transportation, no follow up, and little chance of ever having to see the case again. Ellen doesn't want to hurt Betts. She just doesn't care if she does. Because Betts isn't her. But she would like to hurt us and get back at us for what happened at the hospital. And she likes to gossip at church, so people will pay attention to her."

"And Mrs. Eddy wants to look like a good parent, even though she knows in her heart that she isn't and that her son is a monster that no one likes. Roaring into school playing mama bear is a lot easier than keeping an eye on him, or spending time with him, or trying to like him. And she doesn't care if she hurts Betts, because Betts isn't her. And Bowman might remember Betts, but she's too young for him to be interested in her, and I don't think he wants to hurt Betts either. But he likes being principal, and he wants to keep on being principal, even though he isn't very good at it. So, he tries to keep the people in power happy, and Mrs. Eddy is one of those." Laura kept on driving, and Zoey sat and stewed. Laura was right, of course, but there was something pretty irritating about someone being right all the time.

Zoey was still mad. "Fine," she said.

"Well," said Laura. "It's not fine. I wish that we all loved each other. But for today I guess I'll settle for good pizza, and getting Betts back into school on Monday."

When they got back to the agency, a much more focused Zoey had a yellow legal pad in front of her, and she and Laura were working out the plans for tomorrow. They debated inviting the district Special Education coordinator, and, since she was an old friend of Laura's, they decided that Laura would call her and ask for a favor. They waited until three-thirty, and then called Mr. Bowman at the school, just before he left, and set a meeting for 9:00 the next morning, "before he has a chance to talk to anybody smarter than he is," chuckled Laura. Laura paused. "I haven't been to war in a long time," she said at last. "I'd forgotten how exciting it is." She looked at Zoey. "Let's not make a habit of it."

Laura and Zoey were at the office at 7:30, a half-hour before the agency opened its doors, and about ten minutes before Laura usually got there. They went back over the legal pad, adding a bit here, and crossing a bit out there. They were in the van by 8:40, leaving just enough time for each of them to pick up a cup of coffee, "something to hold on to," as Laura explained. They arrived at the East Street School a few minutes before 9:00.

Mr. Bowman looked distressed to see Laura with Zoey and said, "Why, Laura, I didn't know that you did active casework any more. Is this a case of yours?"

"Oh, I'm sort of a Jill of all trades these days," said Laura. "I just do whatever needs to be done."

As they walked toward the door, a friendly shout came from the parking lot. "Laura Woods!" Laura turned and saw her friend, Linda Frost, the director of Special Education for the district, getting out of her car.

They waited for her, as Mr. Bowman looked more distressed. "Linda?" he asked. "Why are you here?"

Linda smiled and said, "Laura invited me. I understand that there are some special education issues in this case." Linda and Laura hugged, and the three women walked in together, while Mr. Bowman brought up the rear, following them into the school, and down the hallway to the conference room.

The conference room was the only quiet space in the school. The room had windows that faced the schoolyard, away from town, which was empty of children at this time of day. There was a large Formica conference table in the center of the room, and black folding chairs providing seating for fourteen, with six on a side, and one at each end. A smudgy dry-wipe board covered another wall, and a corkboard, filled with the required staff notices and schedules filled a wall as well. The remaining wall held the door, a clock, a small window out into the hall, topped with blinds, and a table set up for coffee or tea.

Linda Frost asked to see Betts' records, which rattled Mr. Bowman even more. After looking through the record of Betts' first and second years at the school, she handed the record back. "I don't see anything here about prior services, or a disability. Has something changed?"

The question hung in the air for a bit, as Mr. Bowman struggled with how to answer it. His information from Mrs. Eddy and the call from Ellen Jensen were off the record at best, and a clear violation of HIPPA regulations as well. Yet refusing Betts admission to the school, and his hope for a referral to the Alternative School up in Montpelier clearly needed some justification.

Laura laughed. "I'll get us some coffee while you work on that, Mr. Bowman." She rose from the table and proceeded to pour three coffees, bringing them back to the table with a handful of sugars and creamers. Laura drank her coffee and sat and watched Mr. Bowman.

Finally, Mr. Bowman said, "Betts has been away for over a year, missing her education here, and that I understand that she may have had some mental health treatment issues during that time." He paused, trying to think how this might work. "I was concerned, as were some parents, about how appropriate it might be for Betts to come back into a regular population, after ... " He searched for the right words. "After all of that," he finished.

Zoey spoke up. "I'm Zoey Simmons, and I have Betts in my foster care caseload. I'm not sure how the information about Betts last year has come to your attention since I only brought her history to this meeting today. And haven't shared it yet. I'm eager for Betts to have a positive experience back in school, but I'd like to know how you heard about her history, what exactly you heard, and then what your concerns are." Zoey sipped her coffee and looked directly at Mr. Bowman, who looked down into the pile of papers he had brought with him.

Mr. Bowman looked back at Zoey, then back at the papers on the table in front of him. He suddenly stood up and said, "I must have left something in my office. I'll be right back," and hurried out of the room. Laura looked at Zoey, and said, "Right about now, he's calling Ellen. Who, right about now, will tell him not to use what she told him. Since she had no release to talk about Betts, anyway," Laura grinned. "So, what's he going to do?"

Linda Frost looked at Laura over her coffee. "I'm glad we always managed to be on the same side, Laura. You're not all that nice." Laura smiled.

Mr. Bowman came back into the room, looking like it was the last place he wanted to be. "We've had some concerns from the parents," he said. "I can't recall the specifics. I know there was some concern that Betts might not do well here, or that she might be a risk for the other children. We only want what's best for her," he finished.

"Well," said Laura, "that puts us all on the same team. Zoey, would you start out with how Betts is doing these days, and what you think she might need from the school?" Zoey did just that, working from the legal pad in front of her, describing a child who failed to benefit from the special structures and supports of hospitalization, possibly because she never needed to be hospitalized in the first place, but who managed very well in the community, and was thriving in her current placement with her uncle. With the support of Linda Frost, a plan was drawn up offering Betts some quiet time during recess and after lunch, helping in the cafeteria or the library, access to enriched programming in reading and science, where Betts clearly excelled, and setting another meeting up in a month to see how Betts was doing, and modify the plan if needed. Betts would start on Monday, in the third grade. Linda had taken notes and produced a suitable document, handwritten, and this was passed around for signatures, with copies made for the visiting parties to take back to their offices. The three women rose and thanked Mr. Bowman for his hospitality, and went out to the parking lot together. After thanking Linda and walking her to her car, Laura returned and got into the van with Zoey.

Zoey was giddy and offered a high five to Laura, who weakly returned the gesture, then said, "That's only the first skirmish, with more battles to come, I'm afraid. Mr. Bowman is now on the list of people who really want Betts to fail, and I won't be surprised when he tries to make sure she does so. It's the best we could do, but this will come back at us, for sure. Enjoy today, and let Betts know she starts on Monday, but tell her and Ames that Bowman will be looking for the slightest reason to boot her out. You better have Ames ask the teacher - Mrs. Cook, I think? - to send home a behavior checklist every day, with her signature on it. Tell Betts to not leave until she has it in her hand, and have Ames keep them safe." Laura looked out at the farms they were driving past. "As if life wasn't hard enough," she said to herself.

Zoey drove up to the cabin that afternoon, giving Ames the good news, as well as the worries that she and Laura had. Betts thanked Zoey but didn't look happy at all. "I got along with pretty much everybody when I was there before, but now, 'cause I've been gone for more than a year, being in the hospital, the kids will feel funny about me. And the bigger kids grab you and push you around, and say stuff. I'm afraid that if that happens, I'll get all angry again, and get in trouble." Betts rubbed at her eyes. "Maybe I should just go to that school in Montpelier." She looked up at Zoey and Ames, looking sad and worried. "But I can try it if you want me to," said Betts.

The next morning, Ames found Betts already awake, and dressed, wearing her favorite pair of "boy jeans," a pair of black Keds, and a black hoodie. Her hair was brushed back, and she looked clean and nice. Ames thought she looked a little like a tiny ninja warrior going into battle in this outfit, but he had allowed Betts to pick her own clothes since she had first come that summer. Ames had asked Betts about the "boy jeans" when they were first shopping in the thrift store. Betts had unloaded on him. "Boy jeans have real pockets, not fake ones, and they're thicker and don't get holes as easy, and they're looser, and not stretchy. I hate girl jeans. I had one pair of boy jeans at my mom's, but she wouldn't let me wear them much. All the rest were girl jeans." Today's jeans were indeed loose, with real pockets, and thick enough to be warm on this cool spring day. Her backpack, provided by Zoey and the agency, was a nice L.L. Bean, new, that was dark blue and brown. Betts had been thrilled with it.

"Up early?" Ames asked.

"School today," she answered, and then turned to stare back out the window, and down the valley. The mist had not yet cleared, and the view was indistinct, with the grey morning sky blending into the fog. The far mountains were hidden, and the trees were slick with dew. "It's pretty out today," Betts said.

"Yeah," said Ames. "Spring is one of my four favorite seasons."

Betts grinned a bit. "You like all of them," she said.

"I do," he answered. "And by the time you get a little tired of one, the next one is knocking at the door."

"How much more school this year?" asked Betts.

Ames thought for a bit. "I think about seven weeks, a little less than two months," he said.

Betts looked out the window. "I want it to be summer today," she said. Ames said nothing, and Betts asked, "I thought about doing the fire this morning, but I thought I'd better ask first. I could do it right. I've watched you a lot. Would that be OK?"

"Sure," said Ames. "I'll make tea."

Betts went to the little green woodstove, and laid a quick touch to the top of the stove, finding it just a bit too warm to keep her hand in place. A good sign, she knew, there would be enough coals in the back to make starting a new fire easy. She got the galvanized ashcan from behind the stove, and set it in front of the stove. She took off the lid, which was a tight fit, the heavy gauge steel providing a safe place for ashes that might still have a coal or two hidden in them. She set the lid off to the side, and slid the ashcan under the front lip of the stove, and opened the door just a crack, clearing any smoke that might be in the box. She then opened the door and looked in. There was an even layer of soft grey ash, all that was left in the stove from the splits of birch fed in the day before. All that sunshine had been set loose, warming the cabin and boiling the kettle, and drying her mittens, and now all that was left were the minerals, soaked up with the water through the roots, the carbon back with its oxygen buddy, and drifted out the stove pipe.

Betts looked in and could see, at the very back of the stove, just a hint of a glow beneath the ash, where the morning's coals waited for fresh air to breathe them back to life. Betts loved that and forgot about school for the moment, excited to be doing the stove herself. She took the tin shovel and scooped the ash from the front, the shovel scraping along the cast iron just a bit, the sound muffled by all the ash. She dug the ash out a shovel at a time, bringing the ash out and sliding it into the bucket, not wanting to set a cloud of ash into the air of the cabin, making dusting a gritty job later in the day.

Betts worked her way back to the back half of the stove, and then she turned the shovel over, raking the coals out from the back pile of ash, coals the size of marbles, a few as big as walnuts. She raked these to the front of the stove and made a neat mound of them, and they began to glow and even spark a bit with the breeze of the open door moving over them. Betts shoveled out the last of the ash, her hand now hot as she passed over the stack of glowing coals in the front of the stove. When the back of the stove was clean, she set the shovel beneath the stove and used the little broom to sweep the small amount of ash from the lip of the stove into the ashcan. She fitted the lid back on, and pressed it down, and set the ashcan behind the little green stove.

The coals now burned brightly inside the open door, and Betts took up two splits of birch, laying first one and then the other bark side down, side by side, with about an inch between them, and pressed them down onto the pile of coals. Curls of smoke began to come, and Betts took a third split, and laid it across the two, bark side down as well, and angled just enough to let the flames rise around it. She looked at her work, and smiled, and then closed the door, setting the latch, and opened the spinner until she heard the whistle of the fresh air over the coals, and the crackle and pop of the wood going to flame. She looked at Ames. "Did I do it right?" she asked.

"What do you think?" he answered, pushing her to approve of her own work, as he always did.

Betts thought and smiled. "I think I did it just right," she said.

"I think you did, too," said Ames. "Tea's ready."

"Can I do the fire in the mornings, now?" she asked.

Ames thought about that. "I guess if you get up before me." Betts looked happy and took her tea to the table.

Ames drove her in, bouncing just a bit on the little ruts made by the melting snow. Ames drove slowly, as always, easing the truck down the hill, picking the best path between the ruts and rocks and loose gravel, so the ride was smoother, and the truck had less work to do. Betts sat beside him, watching him drive, and listening to the engine and the gears as the old truck worked its way down the hill, toward the East Street School. She thought of the bus rides she had had before, with the bus rocking and shaking and sliding on the dirt roads, the hard grey plastic seats sticky with somebody's peanut butter and jelly sandwich eaten too soon, the noise of the kids, and sometimes the driver, all around her, and the comments and pokes and pulls of the bigger kids, picking on the littler ones. She felt lucky to be in the truck beside Ames, proud to have made the fire so well this morning, and pleased to be in clothing that she had picked out herself. She began to think that the day might go OK, after all.

At the bottom of the hill, Ames stopped, and then pulled onto the pavement, working through the gears and moving smoothly down the road. "How are you doing?" he asked.

"I'm good," Betts replied.

At the school, Betts had Ames drop her off, just like the few other kids who didn't ride the bus. "I'll see you at 2:30," he said. "Have a good day."

"You, too," she said, as Ames looked over his shoulder, and pulled the truck back onto the road, driving off to the cabin. Betts wished that she was still in the truck with him, or up at the cabin, reading, or tending the stove, or having some tea. She turned and faced the school, and walked up to the crowd of kids who were waiting to be let inside, most of whom were staring at her. Betts stood off a bit to one side and reminded herself that it might take a while before the kids were comfortable with her. She thought about Ames driving back home, having another cup of tea, shutting the woodstove down just a bit, and starting his morning chores, without her. She swallowed back her feelings. "2:30 is coming," she told herself and moved with the herd of children into the school building, and down the familiar halls toward her classroom.

Mrs. Cook stood by the door, looking nervous and somehow ashamed, Betts thought. She motioned to Betts, with a thin smile on her face, and showed Betts to a student desk that had been placed in the front of the room, right next to Mrs. Cook's desk. There was a square of red duct tape pressed to the carpet, a barrier around the desk, giving Betts a visual reminder of where she should be. Betts stopped and stared at the desk and the tape around it. "This is where you will sit, Betts, right up by me." Mrs. Cook tried again to smile. "I can help you catch up when you need it." Betts could see the lie in Mrs. Cook, and she could see the other kids looking at her, and the desk, and the boundary of red duct tape. As if she had already been bad, and was now being shamed, and punished. One of the kids snickered and pointed at her and the desk, and said something, and some other kids laughed.

Betts moved to the desk, set her new backpack on the floor, inside the red tape, and slid into the desk, her back to the class, facing the empty front board. She rubbed her eyes for just a bit, and worked to get her breathing back in control, then thought about the morning, and the fire she had built, and how well she had built it, doing it all just right. And she thought about how Ames had seen her do it just right, and how he had said she could do the fire in the mornings if she got up early enough. She had done a perfect job. As good as Ames had done. Betts sat a bit and tried to breathe, and thought about these good things, then turned back to Mrs. Cook, who was still standing beside her, between her and the rest of the class, and said, "OK."

Betts made it through this first day of school. Her seat placement and the red tape had sent a clear message to the rest of the kids that she should be seen as a target, and they wasted no time in taking advantage of this. Betts had no idea of the politics behind this special desk placement, and the red tape, but noticed that Heath, who had been a bully back when she had been here before, kept saying, "Watch out! She bites!" For the rest of the day, this theme of biting was played out over and over, with kids holding their hands out toward her, and then snatching them away, making jokes about mad dogs, zombies, and werewolves, and shoving each other toward her as if she might bite someone.

Betts would have felt completely alone had not Rebekah, her hidden friend from the trailer and the hospital, unseen to the others in the school, come and stood beside her from time to time, offering support. "They're just being mean. It'll get better," Rebekah said. Betts traveled in her mind, loosely moored, back to the cabin time and again, and Mrs. Cook saw only a girl who seemed to drift throughout the day, a girl distracted and unable to focus. "I wonder if she's on medication?" thought Mrs. Cook.

The school work itself proved simple enough when Betts focused on the task at hand, and she finished her papers before the rest of the class. Mrs. Cook was surprised to find Betts' answers correct, her handwriting neat, and her willingness to work in such a trying situation impressive. "Do you mind if I read since I finished?" Betts had asked, and when given permission, she had pulled a copy of *The Lion, The Witch, and The Wardrobe* out of her backpack, and read while the rest of the class tried to finish.

Betts was to help the lunch ladies with serving and cleaning up, rather than eating with the rest of the kids in the lunchroom and then to have lunch by herself while the other kids were at recess. This was a part of the plan Laura and Zoey had made, trying to give Betts some relief from the noise and pressure of the other kids during her first days back at school. This was fine with Betts, who felt some quiet adult company would be a relief. She did her work well, and the initially hesitant lunch ladies were pleased with their new helper. Once, when Betts was scrubbing off a table, and

Heath moved behind her, saying in a loud voice, "Careful! Careful! She bites!" Mrs. Findly, the older lunch lady, grabbed him hard by the shoulder, making him squeak, and sent him off to the office for being a disruption.

While Betts was wiping the tables, Cara Eldridge, a little girl Betts had known from the years before, came up and asked Mrs. Findly if she could help, like Betts was. Mrs. Findly found her a bucket and a rag, and the two girls worked together, as the rest of the school finished lunch and headed out to recess. Betts and Cara sat together as Betts had her lunch. Today there was a steamed piece of breaded chicken, some green beans, a square of red Jell-O, with some grapes in it, tater tots, and two cookies, small, but not bad. Betts had the strawberry milk and was surprised at how sweet the milk tasted, too sweet to drink, really. Cara had been a quiet friend to Betts back when they were little, and now she sat quietly while Betts ate. Cara was one of the kids who never got things from the Scholastic Book Club either, and so the two of them had bonded back in Kindergarten and first grade. "I'm glad you're back," said Cara.

Betts thought about that. "I'm glad you're still here," said Betts. "I hope the other kids aren't mean to you for sitting with me."

Cara smiled back at Betts. "Hey, it's not like they were ever nice to me, anyway."

When Ames picked Betts up at 2:30, she was able to say that she had had a good day, without needing to lie. She had two worksheets, each with a big "A+" on them at the top, and some stories to share about seeing Cara again and having lunch with her. She had decided to not mention the seat, or the red tape, or the teasing. At home there was tea, some homework to do, and some work in the woodlot, stacking splits while Ames ran the splitter. That night, Betts tended the woodstove while Ames made dinner. He tacked her two worksheets, with the red A+s on them, onto the wall, over the counter. "Nice job, Betts," he said.

CHAPTER ELEVEN

Art Supplies, Firewood, and Zoey Gets Her Own Cup

Betts continued to ride to school each morning in the Ford truck with Ames, as the days grew a little longer, and the sun just a little stronger, and the ice began to work its way out of the road. The snows had disappeared from all but the deepest north-facing crevices in the woods, where some snow might remain well into the summer, and the bright song of water moving on the mountain became a noisy chorus, with the winter's water breaking free and cutting its path down to the sea, running at times brown and frothy, up over the road, sometimes taking culverts, driveways, and hauled-in gravel down the side of the mountain with it. Ames' truck, with the tall, deeply treaded tires, the front axle locked in, and Ames at the wheel, made its way down the road, regardless. Betts had been late only twice, and then only because Ames had taken a few moments to pull out a neighbor stuck beside the muddy road.

 Betts woke early enough to tend the little green stove most mornings but was a good sport when she found Ames already awake, and the stove done. Ames liked tending to the stove as well. Neither said much during these morning tasks, but they would talk over breakfast, sitting across the table from each other. Betts would check over her homework, and talk about her schoolwork and her time with Cara at school, and her developing interest in the wildlife on the mountain.

Betts had begun sketching what she found in the woods, and pictures of ferns, maple seeds, wheel bugs, frogs and salamanders now were pinned to the walls of the cabin. Ames surprised her one day with a bag of art supplies. He had gone to the art store in Montpelier and asked the woman behind the counter for a set of drawing materials for an artist. She had selected a stack of colored pencils, black drawing pencils, charcoals, pastels, smoothers, erasers, sketch pads, and even a tray of fine watercolors and brushes. She had meant for him to pick through the stack, but Ames had bought the lot.

When she had run the total, and Ames had unflinchingly paid the bill, as she was bagging up the supplies in two brown paper bags decorated with cats, she asked how old the artist was. When Ames replied, "She's nine," he could tell that she was questioning the purchase. "It's OK," he said. "She takes real good care of her things. And she draws nice, too." Betts had been thrilled with the supplies, nervous at first about using them, but quickly learning to put them to use, and keeping them all in a wooden box she had found down at the thrift store, under the table in front of her couch bed.

Two weeks went by, with Betts going to school every day, sitting inside the red tape lines in the desk in the front of the room. The comments from most of the children were fewer now, although Heath continued to try to start that game up again on a daily basis. Rebekah was more in the background now. Betts' favorite part of the day was working with the lunch ladies, who had become loyal friends of hers, and Cara, who shared her lunch chores and lunch, and some of the meanness from the other children. Betts had felt bad about Cara being teased and had told her so. "I'm way happier with you here than I was before," Cara had said with a smile.

And Mrs. Cook was being won over as well, with Betts' quiet, hard work, and her polite tone, even in the face of the seat and tape that Mr. Bowman had insisted on. So, things had settled into a quiet routine, when Zoey thought to take a trip up to the school and see for herself how Betts was settling in. She stopped at the office, said hello to Mr. Bowman's secretary, and went on down the hallway to Mrs. Cook's room. She peeked through the window in the door and saw the children busy at writing. She looked for Betts and was unable to find her. She opened the door, and stepped in, seeing Betts turn around in her desk. Zoey sucked in a quick breath and felt her temper rise as she took in the desk, the red tape, and Betts' nervous look at Zoey.

Mrs. Cook greeted her. "Why, hello. The kids are all at writing. You work with Betts, don't you?"

Zoey walked past Mrs. Cook and went to Betts. "It's OK," whispered Betts. "I don't mind sitting up here. And Mrs. Cook helps me when I need it."

This blatant lie reminded Zoey that once again that Betts was trying to take care of her, rather than the other way around, and she struggled to pull her feelings together. "I'm just surprised, that's all. Why are you here? Are you in trouble?"

Mrs. Cook came near and looked distressed. Zoey turned to her, but before she could ask, Mrs. Cook said, "You'd better ask Mr. Bowman. It's his idea, not mine. I don't like it either," she added.

Zoey tried to put on a happier face and turned to Betts. "I just wanted to drop in and say hi. I'll see you later at home." She started out the door, walking past Mrs. Cook, who said, "I'm sorry." As Zoey walked by Mr. Bowman's office, the door closed, she considered opening the door and walking in. Then she thought better of it, and walked on past, getting into her van and driving back to the agency, hoping to find Laura at her desk.

Back in town, Zoey had found Laura in her back office, and sat across from her, eating the proffered chocolate, still angry, and struggling with why Betts had never told her about the seat and the tape. Then she stopped and realized that she had never heard Betts complain about anything, or anyone, ever. She thought about her own anger about the seat and the red tape, and she thought of Betts, quietly going in every day, sitting there, up in front of the class, inside the tape boundary, and doing her work, and coming home happy with the grades she got, and the time she had spent with Cara. "Start with where the client is" was one of the guidelines for good practice, but Zoey felt that Betts was so far ahead of her in this area she couldn't even catch up.

Laura looked at Zoey, unwrapping here fifth chocolate, and said, "Ok. So how is Betts?"

Zoey took another piece and said, "Betts is fine. All A+s in school, a new friend, Cara, who she has lunch with, and who helps her with her lunch job, loved by the lunch ladies, doing great with Ames, including taking on a piece of his tree work business, and stashing her pay away in a metal lockbox. She's lost most of the extra weight, seems clear, happy, and sleeps well through the night. She has been off any medication for the past three weeks and shows no need to go back on it. Betts is not the problem."

Zoey took another bite of chocolate, and said, "I went in today, just to see her in class, on my way back from the intake up in Williamstown. The class was reading, and I couldn't see her from the window, so I opened the door and went in. Betts has been sitting every day in a desk set right next to the teacher's desk, with a red duct tape boundary marked around her desk. And that's where she's sat since her first day, up alone and on display, like some dangerous freak, and she's never complained, or even told me about it. I felt like going in and kicking the crap out of Mr. Bowman."

"Betts saw that I was upset, because I was, and now she's going to worry about me and my feelings. I gave her another problem by showing up and getting mad today." Zoey got up from the chair and walked to the window.

Laura thought for a moment, and then said, "Did you say anything?"

Zoey looked back at Laura. "I asked if she was in trouble, and she explained the whole thing to me. I never even knew about it until today, and she's been sitting there for three weeks, even though I asked her over and over how things were going at school."

Laura thought about this for a bit, and then said, "You're upset about where Betts sits, and that she never told you that she has to sit up there, and you're upset that you're not helping her enough because you don't know what's going on, and you're upset that then when you do find out, you get angry, and that scares her, rather than helps her." Zoey thought about this and nodded.

Laura smiled and said, "That's a lot to figure out. Why don't you go up to the cabin and let Betts know that you're OK? I'll bet she worries about all the adults in her life, and she'll be happy to know that you're not still upset. Give her a quick visit, focus on how great she is, and ask her what she wants to do about the seating thing."

Zoey nodded again and then looked at the pile of wrappers on the desk in front of her. "Thank you," she said. "And thanks for the chocolate. I'll head up there this evening."

Ames picked up Betts that afternoon, still dusted with sawdust from making firewood out of a spring-felled maple, the bed of the truck stacked with green rounds, the truck springs riding low under all the weight. He pulled up next to the school, and slid the truck into neutral, seeing Betts was waiting by the door, her book bag in her hand. Ames stepped on the parking brake, then got out and let Betts slid across the seat, and then got back in himself. He let the brake off, set the truck back into gear, and eased on down the road toward the mountain, and home. After a mile or so, he said, "Are you OK? You seem kind of quiet."

Betts told him. "Zoey came into school today, just to visit. She got angry about where I'm sitting, and then she left, looking mad."

Ames drove for another mile or two, trying to sort this out. "Where are you sitting?," he asked.

"I sit up front, with Mrs. Cook, with my desk right up by hers. And they marked out around my desk with red tape, on the floor." Betts teared up, and Ames pulled the truck over to the side of the road and put his hand on her shoulder. Betts sobbed, finally able to cry about the shame and embarrassment of where she had been made to sit. "But it's been OK. I get my work done, and I do have a friend, Cara, and I don't really mind anymore. But Zoey's mad, and now you're mad, too." Betts cried all over again and snuggled next to Ames, who held her while she sobbed and shook.

After a few minutes, Betts had cried herself out and snuffled back in some of her hurt, and Ames had held her, quietly, the whole time. "You OK?" he asked.

"Yeah," said Betts. "Sorry about your shirt. I got you all wet."

"That's OK," said Ames, and he slid the truck back into gear and headed on back to the cabin. The truck rode low, the maple rounds heavy and wet in the bed, smelling green and a little sour, stacked up just a bit higher than the edge of the truck. "Boy," said Ames. "You can sure feel that weight going up the hill. I'll unload this as soon as we get home. Make the truck happy."

"Can I help you?" asked Betts.

"Nope. It's all big rounds and green maple at that. Each one of those weighs more than you do. You can clean out the truck, though. And then stack while I split."

"OK," said Betts.

They could see a faint line of smoke, light grey, from the stovepipe. Betts rolled the window down to see if she could smell the sharp scent of birch over the heavy maple smell in the truck. "Why do we burn birch?" she asked.

"Birch has always been my favorite," said Ames. "A lot of people won't burn it, and complain if there's even a stick or two of it in their load. They want maple or oak, 'cause there's more heat in the wood. And that's true. There's more heat in a cord of oak than there is in a cord and a half of birch." Ames got out of the truck, and Betts slid out behind him. "But even if I could sell the birch for the same money as the maple and oak, I'd still burn birch myself. I love birch trees. They're pretty. Nothing's as pretty as a grove of birch trees with some new leaves on. The wood splits easy and straight. It takes just a tap to knock a split off. The bark sets fire quick. I love the way a stack of birch splits looks if it's stacked right and you've got winter coming on. And it smells good when it burns. Like nothing else."

Ames had parked the truck at the edge of the wood lot, and he dropped the tailgate and began lifting the rounds out, heavy and slow, stacking them beside the splitter. Betts went to work on the cab, sweeping the sawdust out with the short broom, and dusting off the dash with the same rag Ames used to check the oil, and then stood and watched as Ames got the last rounds out of the truck bed and set beside the splitter. She took the big broom from behind the truck seat, and climbed up into the truck bed, and swept the bed from the back corners, out.

The splitter was old, a heavy home-made job, built on a twelve-inch-wide I-beam, and powered by an eight horsepower, cast iron Kohler engine. The splitter stayed under a heavy brown tarp, which had stretched over the years under the weight of snow to take on the shape of the old gas engine, the long steel beam, and the sharp wedge at the far end. Ames took off the tarp and folded it, laying it on the worktable beside the truck. He checked the oil level in the Kohler, looking at the small dipstick that showed a line of clean oil just a hair below the full line. He screwed the dipstick back into place and took the cap off the big square gas tank that hung on the engine. He peered inside, then reached for the red plastic gas can, took the rubber stopper from the spout, and tipped the can, pouring gasoline into the tank, watching as the gas climbed toward the top, and easing the red can back when the gas level came up. He replaced the rubber stopper, and set the can back beneath the splitter. He turned the brass petcock on the base of the gas tank and gave the engine a moment for the gas to fill the bowl of the carburetor. He set the switch to on, closed the choke, and pulled the starter rope slowly, feeling the compression as the engine turned over, stopping when the pull became light again. He then fed the rope back into the starter cover, and holding his left hand on the engine, gave the rope a stout pull. The old engine sparked to life.

Ames let the motor warm up for a bit, feeling the fins on the cylinder head, and then eased the choke off as they became warm, and the motor settled into a smooth rumble. Betts had put the broom back behind the seat, and sat on the tailgate of the truck, watching Ames at the splitter. Ames hefted the first round up onto the beam, using his knees as much as his arms and back, and set it where the sharp wedge could take a few inches off one side. He held the round in place with one hand, and pulled the short lever with the other, driving the log along the beam, onto the wedge, splitting off the first slice of maple. Ames slid the round back on the polished steel beam, shifted it slightly, and took off another slice, working his way, pass after pass, until the two-foot diameter round had become a dozen similar sized splits.

Betts hopped off the tailgate, and moved to the other side of the splitter, putting on her little leather gloves, and began to pick up the splits, stacking them neatly in a row beside where more of the sell wood was stacked. They both worked steadily, without hurry, but also without slowing down, and in two hours the truck rode a little higher, the load of rounds now a neat stack of splits, a little more than half a cord, already starting to dry in the light breeze. The smell of the gasoline engine and the green maple filled the wood lot. The roar of the engine deepened with each pass and quieted a bit after. The rhythm of the work, the sound of the old Kohler, and the smell of the fresh maple, sour and rich, like the woods themselves, opened up, filled Betts with a calm that drove the worry about Zoey and the school from her mind. The hot exhaust filled the air as well, mixing with the birch smoke from the cabin. The roar of the engine was loud enough to prevent conversation, but she and Ames never talked much while they worked, anyway. The work was enough.

When the last round had become the last set of splits, Ames let the engine idle down, closing the petcock below the big square gas tank, and then let the engine run until the carb ran dry and the engine shut down. He brushed off the chips and bark from the steel beam, and set the tarp over the beam, to be pulled over the engine later, once it had cooled down. He looked at the stack of maple splits that Betts had made. "That looks nice," he said.

Betts, bark chips and soil on her arms and shirt, and a bit of sweat on her face, even in the cool night, smiled. "It's all even and sturdy," she said.

Zoey drove up as Ames was putting the tarp over the cooled engine, and Betts was making some final adjustments to the long stack of fresh maple. The line of wood ran from east to west, allowing the southern sun full access to the drying wood. Betts looked happy and relaxed, and tired, and Ames smiled when he saw Zoey climb out of her Subaru. "Who stacked all that wood?" Zoey asked. Betts grinned and admitted that she had, and that Ames had cut it this morning, and split it this afternoon. Zoey moved to the stack of wood, looking down the even line, holding the top of the stack, and walking around to the backside. "Looks like you're a good worker," said Zoey, and Ames agreed.

"I used to have to stop when I was splitting, and clear the splits out, and then I had all of that wood to stack when I was done, but now I just stay on the splitter, and Betts does the rest. She's a big help."

Betts smiled and looked down at the wood. "It's just stacking wood. But Ames showed me how to lay it, so the stack stays level and strong, so it doesn't tip over. This is a good stack," she said, pushing against the wood, which didn't move at all. Zoey thought about Betts at school and Betts at the cabin, and she understood how right Betts was to have wanted to come back here.

The three of them headed up to the cabin, where Ames put on the kettle. Betts went to the little green woodstove, and opened the door just a crack, letting the smoke clear from the firebox, and then opened the door all the way and looked in. The remains of a single split, now mostly coals, lay on the grey ash, with blue flames licking out of the remains like ghosts. She turned to Ames. "Do you want another split on the fire?"

Ames looked up for the teapot, and said, "Do what you think is right." She took a split off the stack behind the stove, and opened the door again, setting the split carefully on the bed of coals, watching as the bark lit and flamed into yellow brightness. Betts closed the door but opened the spinner just a bit. Zoey watched, fascinated. Betts stood by the stove, listening to the soft clicks as the cast iron heated back up.

"Maybe I should get a woodstove," Zoey said. "My gas bill just about kills me every winter."

"You should," said Ames. "The gas you pay for could have stayed buried in the ground, and never brought all that carbon back into the air. The tree takes the carbon out when it grows, and gives it back when it dies, whether it lays and rots in the forest, or you cut it up and burn it for heat in the winter. Wood heat is carbon neutral, and helps to keep CO_2 levels down, saves you money, gives me another customer, and lets you be a little closer to taking care of yourself."

Betts chimed in. "And it helps you not drown the polar bears." She gave what Zoey thought must be a drowning polar bear gasp and then tightened the air down just a bit on the little green stove. "I think everybody in Vermont should heat with wood." Betts added. "It's kind of like the water cycle, where the rain falls out of the clouds, runs down to the sea, and rises back up in the clouds again. The tree makes itself out of carbon from the air, with the energy of sunlight to help. When we cut the tree and burn it, that sunlight comes back out of the wood, heating the house, and the carbon goes back into the air, ready to build another tree. It's like magic, only better, 'cause it's real."

Zoey noticed that Ames had poured her tea into the same cup she had had last time, the tall brown mug with a green stripe at the top. Ames saw

Zoey looking at the cup of tea. "It's the same cup I had last time," said Zoey, feeling a little bit silly.

"Yeah," said Ames. "That's your cup."

Zoey felt so happy at this that she blushed. "I think that's nice," she said. Ames smiled and sipped his tea.

Betts looked over at Zoey. "It's a nice cup," she said.

CHAPTER TWELVE

Sugaring

The week went by, and the weekend came. And on Sunday, the sap began to run. Ames always tapped a few trees, the bigger maples on his property, which, being on the southern slope of the mountain, did pretty well. Betts had grown up seeing the buckets and the lines, and visited a local sugarhouse during a school field trip in the first grade, but had never had the chance to make syrup herself. Ames took out his old carpenter's hand drill, called a brace and bit, a coffee can full of taps, and three stacks of galvanized buckets, with clip-on galvanized lids. All these sugaring supplies had come with the cabin and had been stored under the eaves when he bought the place.

Betts was excited, asking more questions this morning than she usually did in a month, running back and forth, carrying the can full of taps, spilling the can full of taps, gathering them all up and then spilling them out again so she could count them, finding sixty-five, and two more that were badly bent. "How many taps do we have, Ames?" she asked.

"I have no idea," laughed Ames. "I guess we have sixty-five now." Betts ran to count the buckets and came back with sixty-three. "I think that's right," said Ames.

"So, we still have enough taps for the buckets?" she asked.

"Sounds like we do," said Ames.

Betts found the scars from the last year's taps on the first tree they came to, the old wolf maple that shaded the back half of the woodlot in the summer. Betts had to stand on tiptoe to see them, and Ames decided then to tap a little lower this year, so Betts could check the buckets, and maybe drill some of the taps if she could handle the brace. The top of Betts' head came about to the bottom of Ames rib cage, so he drilled the first hole about waist high, bending awkwardly as he turned the drill and pressed the bit into the bark, and the hard maple underneath.

Ames had set a mark on the bit, with a file, showing the depth each hole should be drilled. He showed the mark to Betts, and then pulled out the bit, and blew into the hole, clearing the chips that had stayed behind. He held out his hand for a tap, and Betts fished one out of the can and handed it to him. He set the tap into the hole, and then had Betts look at it. He tapped it in tight with the hammer that hung from his carpenter's belt. He moved a few feet to one side, and drilled another hole, set the tap, and drove it in.

"You ready?" he asked Betts.

"I think so," she replied. He handed her the drill, and she turned it back and forth in her hands, trying to understand how it worked. "This is cool," she said. She set the bit to the tree, the tip of her pink tongue showing between her teeth, her forehead wrinkled with concentration, and twisted the brace, first in the wrong direction, then the right, pulling out chips of bark, and then wood, as the sharp bit found its purchase and moved into the tree. She stopped when the mark reached the bark, unscrewed the brace a little, and pulled out the bit, blowing into the hole as Ames had done. She set the tap in, pulled it out and set it back in a little straighter, and tapped it in with the hammer. She looked up at Ames.

He looked back at her and said, "So. What do you think? Did you do that one right?"

"I think so," she said. "Do you think so?"

"Looks good to me," said Ames. "Look here," he said, pointing to the first tap he had set. Drips of clear sap were rolling off the spout, about one every two seconds or so. "Taste it," he said.

Betts laid her head against the tree and stuck her tongue out under the spout. "It's sweet!" she cried and then ran to get some buckets. Ames showed her how to hang them, and how to clip the lids on to keep the trash out. She hung three buckets, and the two of them stood and listened to the plink ... plink ... plink of the sweet sap dropping into the buckets. "This is so cool!" said Betts. "More taps on this tree?"

"Maybe two more," said Ames. "The others are smaller and will only get two or maybe three buckets. Do you want to do these?"

"Yes!" said Betts, and then measured with her eyes and set the bit to the tree again. Betts hung and set about half of the taps, growing tired from time to time and letting Ames do some, and then asking for the brace again, and she hung and capped each bucket. When all the buckets were hung, and the coffee can had two good taps left. Ames sat in the chair beside the fire pit, and Betts tried to sit as well, her tea growing cold as she kept jumping up to check buckets here and there, finding the old wolf maple with its buckets now covered in fresh sap, and a few trees, those more in the shade, it seemed, were as yet bone dry.

"You think maybe you're making those trees a little nervous?" asked Ames.

Betts grinned. "No, I think they like my interest."

Ames dragged a small, galvanized stock tank out from beneath the eaves, left over like the buckets and the taps from the prior owner. The tank held about a hundred gallons and stayed upside down on a pair of cinderblocks, which Ames carried out as well. He set the blocks over by the fire pit, brought out a pitcher of water and a cloth from the cabin, and scrubbed out the tank, and then set it on the concrete blocks. He kicked some more gravel under one block, so the tank seemed about level, and then went back to the eaves of the cabin. Betts watched as he carried out a half of a steel drum. A door had been cut with a torch in one side; the door hung back in place with welded hinges, and a latch was bolted in place to keep the door closed. Along the top of the barrel piece were holes, maybe an inch or so in diameter, also cut, it seemed, with a torch.

Betts watched mystified as Ames set the contraption into their fire pit, again shifting it until it was sturdy and level. He then walked back to the eaves of the cabin and brought out a giant metal kettle, large enough to sit over the barrel, with a few inches hanging out over the sides. The kettle had a round bottom and a spout for pouring. Ames went once again to the cabin and brought out two pieces of plywood, which he set as lids on both the stock tank and the kettle.

He smiled at Betts, who was obviously trying to sort the whole thing out. "The man I bought this cabin from made sugar every year, too. This is his rig, left under the eaves. You know about the taps and buckets. We'll gather the sap from the buckets in a couple of plastic pails, carry them to the stock tank, and pour them in. We'll use a pitcher to fill the kettle. Which I think used to belong to the National Guard. I understand they made oatmeal in it."

Betts made a face. "That's a lot of oatmeal," she said.

Ames nodded. "We put a fire under the kettle, and boil the sap, turning most of the water in it to steam, leaving all the sugar behind, and making syrup. While it's still hot, we'll use a ladle to fill the jars, cap them, and sell them at the farmer's market in town. We'll keep maybe ten jars or so for pancakes, and give away another ten, maybe to Zoey and your team."

"Do we do it tonight?" asked Betts.

Ames shook his head. "Maybe tomorrow, or Tuesday, when the first buckets fill up, and there's enough to boil. It takes all night, and you'll be tired in the morning. But it's fun, sitting around the fire every night. Sugaring is my favorite season."

Betts looked at Ames. "You say that every season is your favorite."

"They are," he said. "You'll have to be careful. We boil until the sap is about 216 degrees, really hot. There was a girl in my school who was helping her folks make sugar, and they spilled hot syrup into her barn boot, and pretty much ruined her foot."

Betts looked at Ames, a little offended. "I will," she said.

"I know you will," he replied. "I just worry, is all."

Betts checked the buckets in the morning and was disappointed that there was so little sap. "It runs in the day when the sun is pumping the water up from the ground," Ames explained. "You don't get hardly anything at night. Check it again when you're back from school."

At breakfast - tea, eggs, and toast - Ames asked about Zoey and the desk at school. Betts said, "It's fine. She asked me what my plan was, and I told her I'm just going to keep doing a good job every day, and eventually Mrs. Cook will move me back to the rest of the class. She's already on my side, but she's afraid of Mr. Bowman, and he's afraid of Heath's mother, and Heath has hated me ever since we were little kids. I don't know why."

"Hmmmmm," said Ames. "So, you're OK with that? Waiting?"

"Oh, yeah," said Betts. "It's really not that hard. I like school."

After school, Betts' first words as she slid into the truck were, "Did you look in the buckets?" Ames had not, and suggested that Betts do that when they got back home. As usual, the ride was a slow one, and Betts was champing at the bit when they parked the truck. She ran to the first bucket that she had hung on the old wolf maple, and tipped the lid back. "It's almost full!" she shouted. Ames looked at Betts, running from bucket to bucket, excited, and almost tripping over herself in her eagerness to see the beauty and wonder in the world. He thought of the vague, swollen little girl who had come back to him and thought that in just a little over a month, Betts had sprung back real good.

He brought two plastic, five-gallon buckets from the porch, like the one they used for water, and pried the lids off them, setting them on the work table in the wood lot. Betts came to him and reported that a few of the buckets were almost empty, but most were half full or better, and the ones on the wolf maple were almost ready to overflow. Ames picked up a plastic bucket and handed the other to Betts. He walked to the wolf maple and popped the lid off the first bucket. The sap was an inch or so from the hole where the spout came in, and he lifted the bucket off the tap and poured it into the plastic bucket. Betts watched the clear liquid flow into the pail and then watched as Ames put the bucket back in place, over the tap, and snapped the lid back on it. "The full ones are going to be heavy, and you probably need to let me do them," he said. "Don't try to do more than you can with this."

Betts nodded but looked anxious to try. She popped the lid off another bucket on the tree, and finding it as full as the first, looked at Ames and asked, "Can I try it, maybe?"

"Sure," said Ames. "Use both hands, and watch to see that it comes off the tap OK." Betts struggled a bit but managed to get the bucket off and poured it into the plastic pail without spilling any sap. She put the bucket back in place and looked up at Ames. "You can do the full ones. I'll do the others."

"OK," said Ames.

Betts took her plastic pail and went to another tree. A gallon of water weighs about eight pounds, while maple sap weighs about eight and a half. The syrup, all boiled down, weighs about eleven. Bets weighed about fifty pounds at this point, and she soon found that she could only fill the plastic pail half full before it became too heavy for her to haul it back to the stock tank, where Ames had already dumped one bucket in and was getting ready to dump a second. Betts looked at Ames, annoyed, and said: "You're getting ahead of me."

Ames looked back at her. "It's not a race. And, we're on the same team. What are you worried about?"

Betts thought about the question. "I wish I was stronger, and I don't want you to do all the buckets and me not have any to do."

Ames thought about that. "You're pretty strong for a little kid, but you're not a grown-up."

Betts struggled with being pleased with "pretty strong" and being annoyed at "little kid." "So, can you just do the full ones? And then go make tea or read or something?" she asked.

Ames smiled at her. "Sure. You do the ones you can, and I'll go get a book and sit out here in the sun. I'll do what you leave behind."

And so, the sap came in, and the stock tank became more than half full of sap, waiting to be boiled. Betts did all but seven of the sixty-three buckets, and Ames had read some thirty pages on the impact of glaciers on the boreal forests, made tea and finished his first cup. Betts had thought she might somehow do all the buckets, but her arms were growing tired and shaky toward the end, she had almost spilled a bucket, and decided that fifty-six would be enough. Ames did the remaining buckets and then fished through the sap in the tank with the fine net he used to clean the spring, taking out bits of wood and bark that had found their way into the sap. He set the plywood top in place and offered Betts some tea.

"Can we boil it tonight?" asked Betts.

Ames thought about that. "Usually I wait until the stock tank's full, pretty much," he said. "But I guess we could boil what we have tonight. We don't boil every day, though, so next time we can wait 'til the tanks full." Betts accepted this compromise cheerfully, and brought an armload of birch splits to the fire pit, and Ames lay three of them inside the door to the half-barrel. He then sent Betts into the cabin to bring out a shovel of coals from the stove, and to tend the stove while she was there. He settled back in his chair and returned to reading about the boreal forests.

In a bit, Betts returned, carrying the tin shovel in front of her, with a stack of glowing and sparking coals inside it. Ames could see the smoke from the fresh fire coming out the stovepipe. Ames had Betts slide the coals out onto the layer of splits he had made in the barrel, and then put three more splits on top of the pile of coals, bark side down and set across at an angle from the splits below, and then three splits more on top of those. The white bark had already taken to flames when Ames blew, long and slow, in through the tin door, and the fire sprang up under the kettle. "Let's get some sap in there before we burn the kettle," said Ames. Betts carried pitcher after pitcher of sap from the stock tank, pouring each into the kettle, which soon started to steam. Ames tipped the tank so that Betts could scoop out the last of the sap with her plastic pitcher, and then covered the empty tank with the plywood.

Betts sat down hard in her chair. "I'm pooped," she said.

"That's the hard part," said Ames. "Now we just sit by the fire, put in some wood from time to time and keep it boiling. Why don't you go get a book, and a lantern or two, and we'll read while we wait?" Betts came back with her book, number 32 of the Nancy Drew series she had borrowed from school, and two lanterns, which she had lit in the cabin. Ames set one lantern on the work table by the boiling syrup, and the other on the small table between the two chairs, where the light would help them to read as the day continued to fade. Ames looked over at Betts, who was sitting in her chair, her book on her chest, fast asleep.

Ames tended the fire and read, looking at Betts from time to time. He learned that the glaciers had extended all the way into what was now Vermont, and had left behind the giant rounded rocks he sometimes saw. "Carried all the way down here by glaciers," he thought.

The kettle, once almost full, had boiled down to about seven inches and boiled now with a different sound, the bubbles making their way to the surface through thicker fluid. He spoke Betts' name until she awoke, and then gave her a minute to remember where she was and what they were doing. "I fell asleep?" she asked.

"I think so," said Ames. "Let's check the temperature and see how we're doing." Ames had a glass-tubed thermometer on a stick, and with Betts holding the lantern, he set the base of the tube into the boiling liquid.

"It looks different," said Betts.

Ames pulled the thermometer up and studied it in the light from the lantern. He showed it to Betts, and pointed, saying "214. That's getting close. It goes kinda quick at the end." Betts looked at him, and he said, "Water, plain water, boils at 212 degrees Fahrenheit if you're down at sea level. Up here, it boils at about 210, since we're maybe 1700 feet above sea level. The higher you are, the easier it is to get water to boil, so it boils at a lower temperature. The syrup would be done at 218, if you boiled it at sea level, which you don't since I don't think they even have maple trees at sea level. Maybe they do. We can look that up tomorrow. For tonight, we look for 216, which means the syrup is done, and we shut it off a hair early, since it boils for a bit even after the fire is out. Let's stop feeding the fire at 215 or so, and see how we do. Sometimes you can keep a pitcher of sap back to cool the boil. If you stop too soon, the syrup pours like water and will go sour in the jar. If you boil it too long, it'll turn to sugar, which is OK, but not what we're making."

Betts looked like she was having a hard time following this. Ames grinned at her, and she said, "I just woke up." Ames put two more splits in the fire, and the two of them sat and watched the steam up against the stars in the sky. The sound of the boil continued to change just a little, and Betts asked twice, "Should we check it yet?"

Ames finally dipped the thermometer in again, and then read it at 215. He showed it to Betts, and then said, "OK, we're close. Let's let it burn down a bit, and keep an eye on it."

The wood turned to coals, and the coals were about grey when the thermometer finally showed 216. Betts was still awake, but just barely. Ames had brought out the jars and the lids while she had been asleep, and the long ladle they would use. Ames dipped the ladle in, the lantern on the table showing the syrup to be darker and thicker than the sap. He carefully poured the syrup into the jar, a ladle at a time, until the jar was close to full, and then screwed the lid on tight, using a cloth to hold the hot glass. He tipped the jar back and forth, coating the inside of the lid with hot syrup, and set the jar aside, then began to fill another.

Betts watched with sleepy eyes, content to have Ames do this work. She had dozed off again by the time he had the last jar done, and had covered the kettle and the stock tank up with their plywood. He woke her gently, and said, "I think we're pretty much done for tonight. I need to carry the syrup in, so we don't get a bear wanting to share our syrup." He carried Betts to her couch bed and brought her bedding from her porch room. She stayed awake just long enough to take a trip back out to the outhouse, with the lantern from the worktable, as Ames brought the last jars onto the porch in a wooden box. "Good night, Betts," Ames called from the loft. But Betts was already asleep again.

CHAPTER THIRTEEN

Faith

The next morning, Ames heard Betts up first, gathering the bedding off the couch and carrying it to her official bedroom on the porch. He lay in the loft, listening to her tend to the little green woodstove, then heard the door as she went for her morning visit to the outhouse, and then the top rock. Ames got out of bed, slipped on fresh boxers and a tee-shirt, and put on the jeans from yesterday, smelling of wood smoke. Ames always tried to get two or three days out of a pair of pants. Today the pants just barely passed, the smoke not a problem at all, but there was a little stickiness over one pocket where he had wiped his hands after filling the jars last night.

Betts came back in, excited. "There's just a little sap in a few of the buckets, and the rest are pretty much empty. I counted eleven quarts on the porch. Is that all we got?"

Ames smiled at her and said, "Good morning."

"Good morning!" she grinned. "Can we have pancakes today? With the syrup?"

"Boy! You're full of pizzazz this morning," said Ames. "Yes, we can have pancakes, and I have a peanut butter jar with some syrup from last night. It's up by the tea."

Betts found the jar, opened it, and stuck her finger in. She looked at Ames, the syrup still dripping back off her finger into the jar, and said, "I washed my hands."

"Good." said Ames.

Betts stuck her finger in her mouth. "Oooh! This is great!"

Ames put the teakettle on to boil and watched Betts stick her finger back into the syrup, and lick that off as well. He reached for the Assam tea jar, and breathed the simple prayer he said quietly at least once every day. "Thank you."

Ames faith had been an odd and twisted journey, naive and untended in his childhood. His grandmother, his mother's mother, was a large countrywoman, trapped in the nursing home, who angrily missed her chickens, her garden, and her own home, having lost a foot and her mobility to diabetes, with the other foot soon to go, and her eyesight fading as well. GranMa had never gotten along with their mother, Cora. Cora would drop the kids off for a visit after the tractor accident when she needed to run a few errands, or just drive the car down by the river and think long and hard about drowning herself. She had always come back and picked Ames and his sister up, although once she was wet up to her knees.

His grandmother had lain in the cranked-up hospital bed, a rail raised on one side, a small table filled with medicines, creams, and patches for the places where she was wearing out. The room smelled of urine and decay, and perhaps the dead flowers in the tall vase in the window, where the water had gone thick and sour. She remembered their names, and was quick to call out sharply "Ames"! "Tina!" before she spoke to either of them. She would ask questions, not the general questions you might expect, but odd things like, "Are you learning about the American Revolution yet?" Or, "What did you have for dinner last night? Did you eat all of it?" Sometimes there were questions about their mother. "Is your mother still smoking cigarettes? How many a day?"

Tina and Ames answered as best they could, knowing that the questions would only stop after she had her answers and that then she would move on to talking about her life, her childhood, how polite she and her six brothers and sisters had all been, about their mother as a child, and how difficult she had been, and her life on the farm with her husband, who had died of cancer some eight years before, and who neither Ames or Tina could remember. She sometimes talked about Clair, making it clear that Clair had been her favorite, and noting that Clair had been taken because she was more loved than the other two. "God wanted her. You're supposed to love all your kids the same, but I know your mother just loved Clair more than she did you two. She loves you, she just loved Clair more. I did, too."

Tina and Ames had no idea how to respond to this, so Ames said, "We loved her, too." Tina said nothing at all but went to pull at the few remaining petals on the dried-up flowers.

"I'm going to be dead pretty quick, and I'm going to go see Clair. First thing. I always loved that girl." There was a long uncomfortable silence after that, with their grandmother's labored breathing and the sound of the wind outside filling in the space. "Well," she said, "I am."

Ames went back home after that visit, thinking hard about his dead sister and his dead grandmother sitting together up in heaven, having the kind of pointed conversation that he and Tina had with her. He wondered if Clair had kept growing, or if she would remain a child forever. They had buried her in a beautiful borrowed dress, a pink silky party dress, in a small white coffin lined with pink satin, and piled a few stuffed animals, with paperback books, her favorites, and a few that they just found in her room, and even a few checked out from the library, which ran up some real fines until the elderly librarian heard from a neighbor where the books were and marked them off as "lost." Ames wondered if she read the same books over and over, or if there was a library in heaven, and if she checked out new ones every Saturday.

Ames mother had never taken the children to church. The funeral was held graveside, at the edge of the "Our Loved Ones at Rest" cemetery between Brookfield and Randolph. Ames remembered nothing of what had been said. He was dressed in a loose suit with the cuffs tucked up with pins, borrowed from a distant cousin, and wore a tie, clipped under his chin. The adults were all crying, even his father. A big yellow backhoe had dug a hole in the ground, and now was waiting off to the side, while the words were said, and the little white coffin was lowered into the ground, and the flowers and dirt tossed in after. When they left, Ames had seen the man who ran the backhoe starting it up. When the school bus rolled past the cemetery the next day, he could see the fresh earth all mounded up where the hole had been.

The only thing that had made any of this bearable was his memory of standing over Clair as she died. Ames knew the moment she slipped away, and the peace she seemed to have at this transition. It was as if he had felt her leave, and knew, absolutely knew, that she had not disappeared, but had gone on to some other place, and was still Clair. This fact was solid and real, like a rock in his pocket, and he knew the funeral was just about putting the body in the ground and everyone being sad together. He tried to explain this to Tina, but Tina had not been there to see when Clair had died, and she wouldn't listen to him now.

While Clair's death was the first he was to see, Ames saw many more people die, over and over, people he knew and ate with, and strangers, men, women, and children, some younger than Clair had been, dying in the desert, in the Sand Wars. And when he saw them die, he knew that they had gone on to somewhere else and that the somewhere else was OK. This was his faith, that life was a part of it, but not all of it, and that what came after was OK, too. He expected little and was grateful for the blessings that came his way, and in this way, too, he was a lot like Betts.

CHAPTER FOURTEEN

A Shower, More Syrup, and a Really Big Tree

At Zoey's suggestion, Ames had looked into getting a better shower set up for the cabin. The sprayer, with water heated on the stove, had worked for him since he had moved in, and Betts could use it as well, but he agreed that it was time for something a little nicer. Betts was pretty shaky around showers, anyway, and he hoped that she might feel more comfortable with a better system. He had studied his options down at the library, looking in some homesteader magazines, and going online to see what was available. He thought about adding a traditional propane water heater, but lacked the water flow to make that make sense, and even looked at a wood-fired water heater popular in Mexico, but couldn't find one that would ship to Vermont. He settled on a propane-fired portable tankless heater, designed for long-term campers, and a twelve-volt pump that was designed for use in motor homes. The twelve volts would be available from a couple of solar panels mounted on the porch roof, and a deep cell battery, and could power a light on the porch and in the cabin, as well. He used the computer at the library to order the parts necessary, sent off something like eight hundred dollars to Amazon, and waited for the parts to come in. When the packages did arrive, he took them up to the loft, and stored them behind his bed, hoping to surprise Betts with a working shower.

The pump was the last item to arrive, and this set Ames to a night of drawing, measuring, and drafting up the system. He bought a few more supplies at the hardware store down in Randolph and got to work, right after he dropped Betts off at school. He climbed the porch roof, lugging the two solar panels behind him, and then went back down to get the hardware, the brace and bit, and a set of tools. He had mounted the brackets to the panels the night before after Betts was asleep, and now set them on bits of butyl rubber tape, setting them side by side on the tin roof of the porch. He drove self-tapping screws, each fitted with a rubber washer, through the brackets and deep into the roof. He gathered the wires from the panels, and took them over the side of the roof, drilling a hole in the side of the wall, feeding the wires through, and then filling in the rest of the hole with butyl calk. He had set the big deep cell battery on the table below where the wires came in, and mounted a tiny control panel on the wall, hooking the panel wires and the battery wires up. By ten o'clock, Ames had twelve volts of electricity in place at the cabin. He set a voltage meter on the wall as well and enjoyed seeing the voltage climb as the sun shone into the panels on the roof. He unrolled the half-inch black plastic pipe, one hundred feet of it, and walked one end back toward the spring. He tapped into the overflow pipe, allowing the spring water to run down the pipe, and installed a valve to control the flow. When the valve was shut, the spring continued to flow out onto the splash rock. Betts would like that.

He followed the pipe back down toward the porch, and ran the pipe beside the cabin, to another hole he drilled, bringing the pipe inside. There he set another valve, a tee that would let them draw water here instead of at the spring, and hooked the whole thing into a float valve made for a livestock tank, like the hundred-gallon plastic tank he set on the floor. He had about twenty feet of the black plastic pipe left, and he ran it through the floor beside the tank, and out to the side of the cabin, back to the little stream that ran from the spring. Here, in the winter, he could set the pipe to flow just enough all the time to keep it from freezing.

He mounted the little rubber-footed twelve-volt pump onto the plywood lid he had made for the plastic tank and set a feed line from the pump down to the bottom of the tank. He ran a supply line up the wall and clamped it onto the propane water heater, which hung on the wall. It was about the size of a large shoebox and would fire itself when it sensed water flowing. He took the hot supply and ran it to the shower valve now on the wall, where he also hooked a cold-water supply, hooked directly to the pump. The old shower base and curtain would work fine, a black pipe carrying the water off below the cabin. He finished up the project by hooking a thirty-pound propane tank to the heater and reached for the cold-water knob on the shower.

As he turned it, the pump kicked on, driving cold water out the nozzle. He turned off the cold and turned the hot water on. This time, the pump kicked on, but the water heater lit as well, with a soft roar, and within a few seconds, warm, and then hot water was spraying out. Ames played with the knobs until a comfortable stream came out, then marked the knobs with a Sharpie, turned them off, and set the Sharpie lines in with a file. As soon as the water was off, the propane heater shut down, and the pump quit as well. There was a bit of hissing as the spring water ran to fill the stock tank back up, then that stopped also. Good system, Ames thought.

Betts was already outside when Ames pulled the truck up at the side of the school parking lot. He climbed out, and she slid in beside her book bag. "Sorry, I'm a little late. I've been working on a project at home."

"Did you already do the buckets?" asked Betts. Ames assured her that the buckets were waiting for her and that he had been working on something else. When they got home, he led Betts toward the porch. "Can I check the buckets first?" she asked. Ames nodded, and Betts ran from tree to tree, announcing with horror that three buckets were already spilling over. Ames agreed to help Betts with the bucket run first, and then show her the surprise after.

She was right about the buckets. Three had started to overflow, and most of the rest were close to the top. Ames did about half of the buckets, their weight just being too much for Betts, and the two of them worked steadily until the stock tank was almost full. The sap still flowed, and Betts asked if they could empty them again after starting the boil. Ames agreed, and Betts brought a shovel full of coals out from the little green woodstove, while Ames cleared the ashes out of the barrel stove beneath the giant kettle. Ames let Betts make the fire, and was pleased to see her set the wood exactly right, without hesitation, blowing the fire into life, while he tipped sap in from the tank with a pitcher. When the kettle was filled to within a few inches of the top, he set the pitcher back on the worktable and put the plywood cover over the tank, which still had several inches of sap in it.

Betts was exhausted and made a move to sit in the chair by the fire pit. Ames said, "Why don't you go check out the porch, and I'll watch the sap." Betts looked at him with confusion, but walked to the porch and looked in.

"Oh! What is it? How does it work? We have a real shower now?"

Ames sat in the chair and answered, "Yep. See if you can figure it out."

Betts scurried around in the porch, then under the porch, then up to the spring, and then back down. "Where does the electricity come from?" she asked. "Go up to the top rock and look down at the porch roof," Ames said. She ran up, and then ran back down. "Solar panels! You put solar panels on the roof!" Betts went back into the porch, and Ames heard the pump kick on, and then off and then on again, with the muffled hiss of the propane water heater starting up. "And the water's hot!" He heard the pump turn off, and then on again.

Betts came running out and stood in front of him. "That's so cool!" she said. "How does the pump and the heater know to come on when you turn on the water?" Ames thought about it and then said, "I think the pump turns off when the water pressure builds up, and when you open the faucet the water pressure drops and turns on the pump. When you shut the faucet, the pressure can build up, since the water can't go anywhere, and the pressure shuts off the pump. And I think the heater knows when water is flowing through it and turns on when the water moves, and off when it stops. It lights the gas itself with an electrical spark, because it needs a wire from the battery, too. And we can fill the kitchen bucket right on the porch. And we can have a twelve-volt light in the porch, and in the cabin, too. All from those two panels and the battery."

Ames looked at Betts. "Do you like it?"

She thought for a bit and said. "I like it a lot. But I like the way we did it before, too. Does having the lights mean we can't use the lanterns anymore?"

"No, we can use the lanterns any time. And the lights maybe when we first get home and don't want to stumble around trying to get a lantern lit. Go take a shower and see how it works. The knobs have a line filed on them that should be at the top for the water to be about right. Adjust it how you want, though."

Betts went back up to the porch, and Ames sat and watched the kettle of sap, just starting to steam, and the fire flicker around the steel door and out the holes at the top of the barrel stove beneath it. He thought about the worry that Betts had, worrying that the shower and the battery might mean that things could get worse, as well as better. He guessed that that was true. Change was a mixed bag, sometimes.

"Ames! This thing works great!" he heard from the porch. The pump hummed and the water heater roared. Progress. Ames thought of all the ways his life had changed since Betts first came, and since she had returned. Ames smiled into the night and said his prayer. "Thank you."

Betts came back out, wearing a fresh shirt and looking clean and happy. The night was coming on, and Betts had brought out a sweatshirt for herself, and one for Ames, as well. She checked the buckets and was able to bring in another five gallons or so of sap, which Ames poured right into the boiling kettle. The boil stopped, and then slowly started up again as the fire heated up the new sap. Betts sat in the chair, looking sleepy, and watching the fire and the steam. "I wish we could do this every night," said Betts.

Ames looked at Betts in the chair, her head back and her eyes closed. "Did you fall asleep in school today?" he asked.

"Almost," said Betts.

"Why don't you just nap in the chair, and I'll wake you up when the syrup is ready?" But Betts was already asleep.

Later that night, after Ames had tried to wake Betts up, after the syrup had been put into the jars, sealed, and brought into the porch, and after the fire had burned itself out, Ames lifted a sleeping Betts from her chair and moved toward the porch. Halfway there, Betts woke up, screaming, scratching and hitting at Ames, who carefully set her down on the ground and said to her, "You're OK, Betts. I tried to carry you in, and you got scared. It's OK." She glared at him, her arms tucked in close to her sides, but her hands up in fists, and her eyes bright with hatred. Slowly she came back, opening her hands and looking at Ames, confused and then ashamed. "It's OK, Betts. I scared you. I shouldn't have tried to carry you in while you were asleep. I should have woken you up first. I'll wake you up first next time." Betts began to cry, and moved toward Ames, hugging him and burying her face in his shirt. He held her lightly, stroking her hair a bit, and saying over and over, "It's Ok. It's OK."

They walked together to the cabin, only to have Betts remember her trip to the outhouse. He waited for her while she took the lantern, and then the two of them went inside, Ames to his loft and Betts to her couch bed. After a few minutes, he heard, "I'm sorry." Ames answered, "I'm sorry, Betts. Next time I'll wake you up."

"But you shouldn't have to," she said. "Parents carry their kids to bed all the time in the books I read. And it's nice. I'm tired of everything feeling scary and bad when it ought to feel nice."

Ames thought about that. "You're right," he said. "I think it will get better." Ames thought some more. "I love you, Betts."

Betts was quiet, and then said, "I love you, too."

Ames had a hard time sleeping that night, although Betts dropped off like a rock, and awoke the next morning still tired. Ames had stewed on

Betts' troubles the night before but had also been kept awake by a storm that blew through the hills, a real wind, he could tell. The cabin as tight and snug, and even the whistle of the wind in the trees could only make a bit of noise through the winter windows Ames had caulked in, but the force of the wind shook the cabin itself, and Ames wondered what the morning would show.

Early the next morning, while the tea was still steeping, the phone rang, and a neighbor down the hill begged Ames to bring his saw and clear a tree out that had fallen during the night. Ames promised to come right after he dropped Betts off at school, and loaded his tree working tools into the truck before then went on down the mountain.

Near the base of the mountain, about a half-mile from the paved road, Betts whistled, a new skill she had been working on, and pointed to a giant maple tree, tipped over the night before. It had torn up a rock wall on the left side of a driveway, crashing across onto the wall on the other side, blocking the drive as if an angry giant had slammed a gate. The roots now stretched into the air some thirty feet, and the trunk was at least four feet at the base. Other trees lay smashed beneath it, and the crown of the tree was still thirty-five feet in the air, as tall as many of the trees around it.

Ames pulled the truck over and stared at the monster, silent, and Betts stared as well. "Is that the tree you're supposed to cut up?" she asked.

Ames said nothing for a long time. "Yep," he finally said. "That's a big one."

"You sound worried," said Betts.

Ames thought about that. "Yeah, it is worrying. There's no easy way to do it. And I'll have to buy a longer bar even if I saw from both sides. Probably a thirty-six-inch bar, and chains for it. And I'll have to cut the rounds up before I can get them in the truck. There must be four or five cords of wood in that tree."

"It looks dangerous," said Betts.

"Yeah. It could be." Ames stared at the tree. "I'll have to figure out how to do it."

"Can I help?" asked Betts.

"Yeah," said Ames.

"Can I skip school, just today, and help you?" she asked.

Ames thought about that. "OK. We need to go to town and get a bigger bar, though. And I guess we need to stop by the school and let them know."

After stopping by the school and telling the secretary, Betts would be out for the day, and picking up a long bar and two chains for the saw, as well as an extra-long tow rope, Ames and Betts headed back up the road and parked some distance away from the giant tree. The property owner was standing by the tree, looking very upset. He was a perfectly nice gentleman from Manhattan who had bought and remodeled the old farmhouse, and a hundred acres of lovely pasture land that was currently going to brush. "I can't believe this!" he said. "This was my favorite tree!" Ames thought about that, wondered how many trees were on the hundred acres of land, and finally guessed that this was possible. "Can you get it gone today?" the man asked.

Ames laughed just a little bit, then said, "Probably have most of it done in a week or so. I can get one of your cars out through the pasture to this side, though, so you can get into town."

"A week? Why so long?" the man asked.

Ames looked at the man and finally said, "It's a big tree."

"That it is," said the man, resignedly. "How much will it cost me?"

Ames thought for a bit. "Hard to say. If I keep the wood, it'll cost you less. There might be four or five cords of wood in it. But that whole trunk is likely half-rotted on the inside, and the rounds are going to need to be quartered to get them on the splitter. Some folks just roll them off into the woods and let 'em rot."

The owner thought about that. "What would you do?"

"I'd quarter them up and split 'em," said Ames. "It won't be any fun, but I hate to leave firewood to rot away. You're also going to have four, maybe five brush piles after. Betts here will stack them right, and it's good for the wildlife. Then there's the other trees that are broken underneath, and they'll need some work. I'll save as much as I can, and clean out the rest. And somebody will have to fix your walls there, I guess."

"Do you do stone walls?" the man asked.

"Nope," said Ames. "Never have. I guess I could try."

"So, how much, do you think?" the man asked.

"I try to get $200 a day, with Betts helping some," Ames said. "I'd need at least that, 'cause this tree looks pretty tough. Maybe five days, but it might be six or seven. And that's just the trees, not the wall. I've got no idea how long that wall might take."

"That sounds fine," said the owner, reaching for his wallet.

"Pay me when we're done," said Ames. "And that may be awhile. Want me to bring your car around through the pasture?" Ames offered. The owner handed Ames the keys, and Betts followed him to where the Lexus SUV was parked. Ames looked at the controls for a few minutes, then got back out and asked the owner about putting it in four-wheel drive. After some consultation with the manual, Ames decided that it was always in four-wheel drive, somehow, and started it up.

Betts put on her seat belt, a broad smile on her face. "I love this!" she said. Ames got the car out and through a gate, and into the pasture, rolling slowly across the grass, picking a line through the rocks, and coming up to a gate in the fence. Betts hopped out and got the gate, and Ames rolled on through, parking the car back on the side of the driveway, away from the tree. He handed the keys back to the owner, and he and Betts got to work.

Ames kept his original bar on the saw. At sixteen inches, it would be fine for the limbing work he was going to do first. He moved to the crown of the tree and started taking off the easy stuff, nipping the small branches off first, which Betts trucked away, building her first brush pile back a little way into the woods. The two of them had worked for a couple of hours when Ames called a break. Betts needed her gloves from up at the house, and this job was close enough that a drive home would only take a few minutes. They drove up in silence, took time for tea, and sat at the table, looking out at the valley below them. "I don't see how you're going to get that tree down," said Betts.

"I need to trim all the stuff I can reach, then top what I can, then climb up on it, and take off the branches on one side, the side toward the road, and then tug it over on that side with the truck."

"When does it stop being dangerous?" asked Betts, still worried.

"Probably when I get it over. Most of the tree will be on the ground at that point, and then it's just regular work." Ames made sandwiches, and Betts checked the buckets, pouring a few into the tank.

When Ames got back to the tree, Betts at least had an idea of how the work would go, and she seemed less worried about him. Ames thought about that, and how dependent Betts was on him at this point and decided to go extra slow and be careful with the job. They skinned off the easy cuts, with Betts still working on the top of her brush pile, happy to have her leather gloves on. Ames tied a rope to his saw, laid it on the ground beneath the tree, then climbed up the roots until he was on top of the main trunk. He pulled the saw up, took off the rope, and made a neat coil of it, looping it over one shoulder.

Carrying the saw, he moved along the trunk, some sixteen feet or more above the ground. The tree was wide, but the bark was loose in spots, showing rot beneath, and Ames worked his way slowly, kicking at the bark to find spots that might be loose enough to be a problem. About thirty feet along the trunk, he stopped and fired up the saw, balancing himself with a large vertical branch, then carefully bending to one side and sawing off two good-sized branches that stood straight off to the side. These were a foot and a half thick, and heavy enough to shake the tree when they fell, with Ames holding on to the top branch with one hand, and the saw with the other.

Betts stood below, and watched, holding her breath as the tree shook, and then again as Ames moved further out on the trunk, doing the same thing three more times before he got to the crown. Ames moved slowly, close to twenty feet above the ground, while Betts watched from the truck. He moved from one big branch to the next, finding a place he could lean in against something sturdy while he started the saw and made the cut. After an hour, he moved slowly back down the massive trunk, the tree topped, and a mess of limbs filling the ground under the tree. He lowered his saw once again and climbed down the roots to the ground. Betts ran to meet him.

"What happens next?" she asked.

Ames took several slow, deep breaths. "First, I take a minute to be thankful that I'm back on the ground. I hate that kind of work." Ames walked around the tree, making a plan. "We need to clear this stuff out first, then we'll see if we can pull the thing over to this side. That will put the trunk on the ground, and I can do the rest of the job without being up in the air. You can do the brush." Ames fired the saw back up and went to blocking and limbing what he had dropped onto the ground. Betts started a second brush pile a little ways from the first.

After another couple of hours, the ground beneath the tree was clear, and a second brush pile was solid and high. "You're going to get thank-you letters from all the animals in these woods," Ames said. Betts smiled at the idea. Ames walked to the truck, and brought out the long tow rope he had bought in town, and tossed one hook in the air, over the tree. He took that end and hooked it to the rope, and then stretched the rope toward the truck. "Too close," he said, and got his regular tow rope out from behind the truck seat, and hooked the two together. Betts watched, fascinated, and very glad that Ames was back on the ground again.

Ames laid the rope out toward the road and then backed the truck over to the end. Betts rode in the bed, her favorite spot, and peered over the tailgate, shouting, "Good!" when his bumper was a bit past the rope. Ames climbed out and hooked the rope onto his tow bar, and had Betts get into the cab of the truck. "I think that rope's long enough, but there may be a lot of stuff in the air when that things goes over, and you might as well be inside. You can look out the window." Ames walked around to the front wheels, and locked each hub into four-wheel drive, then got back in the truck, and shifted the truck into low range. Betts pressed her face against the back window of the truck, and Ames eased the clutch out, and the truck moved forward slowly until the slack in the rope was gone, and the rope rose up from the ground, twisting a bit, and pulling tight.

Ames set in the clutch, and the tension on the rope moved the truck back just a few feet, and then he let the clutch out, and the truck moved forward again, stretching and tightening the rope, spinning first one tire and then another just a bit, as Ames worked to keep the truck pulling. The tree rocked forward, then the tires spun, and Ames backed off, letting the truck once again move back. This time he added some speed, and when the rope was tight, the tree shuddered and began to rock forward, toward the truck. Ames looked back and then said, "Here we go," and gave the truck just a little more gas. The truck spun a bit sideways, and Betts grabbed at the seat, trying to not be pitched over. The tree continued to roll toward them, huge and creaking and cracking as branches broke and splintered under the shifting load. Ames gunned the truck, just as the tree rolled over toward them, smashing into the ground where the truck had been only a moment before. Ames stopped, then backed up a bit, and shut off the engine. "Let's not do that again for a while," he laughed, and Betts, still white-faced, nodded, unable to make a noise.

Ames loosened the tow ropes from the truck, and then from around the tree, and coiled them both, putting them back behind the truck seat. "Let's head up for lunch and take a break. My heart's still pounding," said Ames. He gathered up his saw, helped Betts into the truck, and the two of them headed up the road toward the cabin.

As they pulled into the drive, they saw Zoey's van pull in behind them. "You should see the giant tree that's down there!" she said. Betts filled her in, while Ames made an extra sandwich.

CHAPTER FIFTEEN

Coffee and Donuts

Zoey looked at Betts and Ames. "I drove up to the school, just to try for a better visit than I did last time, and they told me that Betts was home today, working with you. I thought I'd come up and see how you two were."

Ames laid a chicken sandwich in front of Zoey, and of course, her mug of tea. He sat down across from her and Betts. "I think Betts was worried about me and wanted to make sure I didn't get hurt."

Betts nodded, her mouth full of peanut butter and jelly. "It's a big tree, but we got a good piece of it done this morning. The rest of it should just be a lot of regular work, without the up in the air stuff." Betts had finished swallowing and took a sip of tea. "I was scared. I'm glad I missed school today."

Zoey asked about the sap buckets, and Betts gave her a tour, finishing up by dumping a few more buckets into the tank. She also showed Zoey the shower, turning it on and off, with the system working perfectly. "I took a really long shower yesterday, and the water never got cold," said Betts.

"I'm glad I got it done yesterday," said Ames. "I think the rest of the week is going to be pretty busy, and a shower will feel good." Ames poured himself another cup. "We'll go back after lunch, and clean off the rest of the brush that we can reach, and maybe tomorrow I can cut a chunk out to open up the driveway. The owner said that that was his favorite tree."

Zoey smiled. "It might be. It's about the biggest tree I've seen around here. How old do you think it is?"

Ames thought about that. "Lots of these old maples are three hundred years old. That one might be four hundred or so. We can count the rings once we get it down. I'm going to try to get a nice section slice for the owner. He'll like that, I'll bet. Figure that that tree was a seedling back when Champlain first sailed into the lake, claiming Vermont for France. First European in the state, I guess. Mostly Iroquois around then. No roads, only footpaths, and the whole state was forest. The Indians used to set fires pretty often to burn out the brush, so I guess the land looked like great big parks, huge trees, with lots of grass below, full of deer, turkeys, and rabbits. Easy hunting and easy to walk through. It must have been like the Garden of Eden."

Betts looked thoughtful. "I would have liked to lived back then," she said.

"Maybe," said Ames. "There's a book upstairs that talks about the Indians living here before the white men came. You could read it, and maybe look for another book when we go to the library this Saturday. One thing I liked was the idea that none of the Indians tried to get rich. They all shared with each other. And they all took care of each other's kids."

The sandwiches were gone, and so was the tea. Ames gathered the dishes and cups, and he and Betts did a quick washing up while Zoey sat by the window. "Back to work," said Ames. Zoey asked if she could stop for a bit and watch them on her way back to town, so her Subaru followed Ames's truck on down the mountain. Ames parked his truck and pulled the saw out and some extra chains. He used the tailgate as a workbench, swapping this morning's chain out for a fresh one, and refilled both the gas and the bar oil tanks. Betts had her gloves on and was waiting for Ames to make some brush for her to haul away.

Ames started the saw, and walked to the trunk, and began limbing what he could reach, with Betts following along, hauling the small stuff and stacking it in her third brush pile of the day. Zoey sat on the hood of her car, the heat coming up from below a welcome thing on the cold spring day. She tried to make sense of the girl hauling out and stacking the smallest branches that Ames took off the tree, comparing her to the girl by the Plexiglas window in the hospital. Not quite two months had gone by, and this was the girl who had emerged. And Ames had changed as well, more open, cheerful, even making jokes from time to time.

What medicine was this? Zoey pondered the question and felt she was on the edge of understanding something important. Regardless, she knew she would forever see the children in front of her with a memory of Betts transformed, and the painful knowledge that the care Betts had been given, the foster homes, the hospitals, and the medication, had likely done as much damage to her as whatever abuse must have occurred before. Zoey wished Laura was here on the hood of the Subaru, watching Ames and Betts working together, and that Laura could somehow help her to make sense of it.

Ames moved on to the tops of the tree he had cut and began limbing them as well. As the brush was cleared, he began to block the smaller rounds, branches maybe three to five inches wide, which he cut at sixteen-inch lengths, measuring as he went with the bar on his saw. Betts picked these up as well, moving them to the truck, stacking them into the truck bed. After an hour, Ames took a moment out and walked back over to Zoey. Betts kept on working, moving between the truck and the tree. Ames laid the saw on the tailgate, and taking a tool from his pocket, tightened up the chain just a bit.

"You work well together," said Zoey.

Ames grinned. "Betts is a good worker, steady, and she does a good job, once she knows what to do. Well, back to it." Ames turned and fired up his saw and went back to blocking the smaller limbs. Zoey watched, wishing he had chosen to stay and talk some more. She got in her Subaru, waved, and drove back to the agency, planning on talking with Laura.

Laura was not in her office when Zoey got in, so she went to the park across from the agency, and found Laura sitting at her picnic table, watching the empty swing set. She had a cup of coffee steaming in front of her, and she sat motionless, staring at the empty swings. Zoey approached and sat down beside her. Laura turned and smiled at her, then went back to the swings. "I like your outdoor office," Zoey said. The table was known to be Laura's favorite place, for paperwork that did not require a computer, and time that did not need a phone. Laura had once drawn a map, and posted it on the door, referring to the table as "The East Office," and directing people out to the picnic table.

Laura nodded. "It's a good spot for me. Out to pasture, in a way." Zoey heard a catch in Laura's voice and looked to see a bit of shininess in her eyes. Laura caught her looking and said, "I'm having one of those 'think about my life' sort of days. Never a good idea, and I don't let myself do it very often. It never turns out well, and really, it gets nothing done." She wiped at her eyes, and then looked down at her hands, the skin papery and wrinkled, a few brown spots like melted freckles on the backs. She pulled up a flap of skin and watched as the tent hung in midair, then slowly sank back to level. "Getting old, bitter, and morose, at times."

She laughed, without much humor, and turned to Zoey. "So, what brings you to the hinterland?" Zoey stopped, thinking she ought to say something about Laura's obvious sadness, to offer comfort or questions. Laura saw the hesitation. "I'm fine. I do this occasionally. Wonder what my life would be like if I had done things differently. Weep a bit, and then go back to doing the same damn things I always have. Tell me about your favorite case."

"I went up the mountain today and found Betts and Ames. They're working on this enormous old tree that fell over in the wind last night. Huge, as wide as this table is long and big as a barn. Betts skipped school today to be with him. The first time, and I think it was because she was worried about him. We had lunch, then the two of them were back to working away, Ames cutting off the smaller branches, and Betts hauling the sticks off into the woods and making big piles of them, or taking the little logs and stacking them in the back of the truck. She had on leather gloves, like his, and they worked like a team. And she seemed so steady and so happy. And so did he." Zoey stopped, wondering where this was going.

Laura said, "And were you happy, too?"

"I felt kind of left out, actually. But I had a question. How does this work? Why is Betts doing great now, with no meds, no therapy yet, no nothing, except tea and books and living in the cabin? I mean, she's doing better than anyone could think, with no services at all." Zoey paused. "Is that why?"

"There's the question," said Laura. "Do we do anything at all that's helpful, or do we only take hurt kids from hurt families and then make them both worse?" Laura looked out at the empty swing set and shifted on the bench seat. "It's not that simple, of course. We, you and I, and even Ellen Jensen, from time to time, do a lot of good. Our clients will tell us that. And it's true. We can stop the abuse, sometimes, and we bring in support and direction for families that are overwhelmed or lost. We can separate children from predators, and help a mom and her kids with housing, food, and safety. It's good work."

"But we need to ask that question of yours every day. Because a lot of what we do is not helpful, a lot of what we do is harmful, as a matter of fact, and Betts' case is a good one to study. You see Betts doing so well, being Betts, as it turns out, without all the drugs, or the hospital, or the restraints, or the staff. You put her there, remember, you brought her up to the cabin, and you gave her Ames, against all better judgment. Pretty much told your supervisor how it was going to work, is the way I heard it, and then made it happen. You did good. I'm proud of you, and you should be, too.

"But the rest of it deserves a good look. You know, Eddy Roberts, one of the night staff on the Children's Retreat, was caught Monday night tapping a little girl on the unit. A seven-year-old, I think. One of the nurses walked in on it, got into a fight with him, kicks and punches, the whole nine yards, and he got hauled off to jail with a broken nose, I heard. Where I hope he rots for all eternity." Laura looked back out at the swings. "Betts was there for a year. He worked on her unit five nights a week. And we put her there."

Zoey started to argue but stopped. Laura reached out and put her hand on Zoey's. "Let's go to Dunkin' Donuts. Then come back and drink coffee and eat donuts. And try to figure the world out." They took Zoey's car and were back at the picnic table in ten minutes, six chocolate frosted donuts and two large coffees now sitting on the table in front of them. Zoey opened the box. "I feel better, and we haven't even started on the donuts yet."

"Yeah," said Laura. "Amazing how that works. But to get back to your conversation, Betts is better because her world is safe, and she gets to do the things that she needs to do. Be safe. Be helpful. Be outside. Be loved. Read and explore. Kid life, in all its glory. And if we could have gotten her to Ames fresh from Tina's, she'd be in better shape, still. The good news is that she's not in the state hospital, where I'm sure some other version of Eddy Roberts is working tonight. Betts gets to spend today working with Ames, then go home and boil syrup, read a bit, and then sleep safe on her couch, up in the mountains. And that is 100% your doing."

Laura picked up her coffee and made a toast, donut in her other hand. "Let's drink to our successes, remember our failures, and go forth into battle with a kind and very humble, questioning heart." Zoey tapped her coffee cup against Laura' and took a sip. Laura looked back out at the swings. "Usually I come out here after school lets out, or in the mornings in the summer, when the kids are here, and the moms are pushing them on the swings or watching them play. Then I get to remember that the world can be happy, and kids can be safe, and moms can do a good job. But today, I'm remembering all the kids who aren't here to play, kids like the kid Betts was, before you got her case, and kids like the seven-year-old who took her spot up at the Children's Retreat. Grieving a bit, I guess. Feels like it."

They sipped their coffee in silence, working their way through the donuts, watching the empty swings, and trying to make sense of the world, and their place in it. Laura said, "We do what we believe in, but we grow to believe in what we do, and once that kind of belief takes root, we stop questioning. If we stop and ask, we risk tumbling the whole house of cards. Try having this conversation in a staff meeting. If you point out to an investment banker or hedge fund manager that his work harms others, he will grin and shrug, and tell you, 'Hey, so what? I do it for the money. And the money's good.' If you tell the same thing to a social worker, they'll fight you tooth and nail. Because there is no money, really, and the kindness of the work is its only justification. Take that away, and you have nothing left."

Zoey could think of nothing to say to that, and Laura was happy enough with the coffee and the silence. "So, why do we do all the hospitals, and treatment foster homes, and medications, and therapy, if what kids really need is to be safe, and outdoors, and useful, and loved?"

Laura looked at Zoey with a bitter smile. "Follow the money. There are a few kids with real psychiatric issues, who need and benefit from all that stuff. I've worked forty-five years in the field, and I've met maybe three or four of them. The rest are kids who are healthy, but unsafe where they are, or kids with trauma. Shitty parenting is an aberration. Almost every parent wants to be a good parent, and if they fail, it mostly comes from poverty, drug and alcohol addiction, and trauma. Some of it's taught, like the "Raise Up A Child" crowd, or learned, when kids grow up with shitty parenting, and think that's the way the world works.

"If we really focused on teaching kids about how to be good parents, then supported new parents to make sure that they're on track, and addressed the poverty and the drug and alcohol issues, our kids would be healthy and grow up to raise healthy kids. That's happened in lots of countries where families and kids are a priority. Finland, Norway. France. Here, poverty, addiction, child abuse and neglect, even jail, are business opportunities, and we have a whole industry built up around believing kids are mentally ill and need drugs and hospitals and all this crap. Rich people get richer. And the front-line people, like you and me, we do the work, because we want to be helpful. And kids like Betts end up in the hospital for a year, getting worse and worse. And the kids of the poor get it the worst because their folks don't have the supports or education to fight back."

Zoey thought about that and thought about Betts. "I wish I was helping Ames with that tree." "Yeah," said Laura. "That looks pretty good, compared to sitting here. So why aren't you?"

Zoey thought about this. "He hasn't asked me."

"You like that boy?" asked Laura with the first real smile of the day.

"I do. I mean, he's a client, I guess, but I do like him. A lot. If he adopts Betts, which he will if he can, then Sarah or somebody in adoptions will take the case, and Betts won't be my client anymore. Right?" Zoey had thought about this but had never put it to words before.

Laura perked up. "You mean we get to talk about happiness? Oh, goodie! I would so much rather talk about that." She turned away from the swing sets and looked at Zoey. "Ames is a good man. And cute, I suppose, in a stretched out, lumberjack sort of way. I still see him as an eight-year-old, eager to do the right thing. The client thing is a little awkward, but it sort of goes away once it's not your case anymore. And if people talk, so what? Let 'em find their own stretched out lumberjack."

"I don't know," began Zoey. "I just feel happy up there. The cabin, or sitting outside. Ames fits it so well. And so does Betts. And I do, too, I think. It feels like I'm back where I should be, somehow. I think about spending the day outside, cutting wood, or walking around. I think I could fit in, too, with them," she added.

"I can see that," said Laura. "How much of this is about Ames, do you think?"

Zoey thought about the question. "I want Ames," she said, working it out. "But I want Betts, too. I love her, I think." Zoey set her cup down. "And I want that life, I think. I like my job, but I don't want to work forty hours a week for the rest of my life. When I was in school, I was outside all the time. Hiking, reading, walking with friends. Camping! We used to go camping up by the lake, swim, build a fire, talk about our lives. I don't really read much anymore, and the only time I'm outside is walking from my car to work or home. I want that outside kind of life back."

Zoey looked at Laura, who was looking back toward the Agency, the parking lot half full, three of the minivans off on calls, the office windows shut and sealed in support of the air system. She knew the phones were busy, the computers busy, too, as cases were documented and contacts made. "Does that make me lazy?" Zoey asked.

"No," answered Laura. "I think that makes you smart."

Laura turned back to Zoey. "Ames grew up watching his parents work all day, every day, on that dairy farm. Cows are a full-time gig, and these were someone else's cows, to boot. That little trailer, parked right by the barn, smelling of manure inside and out. I visited there for a while, maybe a year or so after Clair died, and I used to shower and wash my clothes right when I got home. And all the misery on a dairy farm. It's not like the picture on the milk carton. No happy cows.

"I think Ames saw all that and decided he just wasn't going to play. Some of it, his life in the cabin, is from coming back from the war, but I'll bet most of it is just not wanting to live like his parents did, working their whole lives on other people's cows, just to make the owner money. And maybe the only way out is to not play at all. Give up the job, the house, the car, the vacations, and all of it. Get a cabin out in the woods, and spend some time every day taking care of what you really need, and have the rest of the day free to live. I don't think that's lazy. I think it's smart and brave."

CHAPTER SIXTEEN

Springtime in Vermont and Taking a Risk

Sugaring is the first hint of spring in Vermont. Well, maybe an earlier hint is that first flirty day when the sun is bright and hot enough to melt a few bits of snow and ice. The silence of the winter is broken by the quietest hint of a sound, water running. That sound, muffled and small, shouts to anyone who has spent the last six months in the chill silence of snow, muffling the rivers and the creeks, the insects, the frogs, and most of the birds. The flow of water is like the flow of life itself, and when the rivers ice over, and the rain stops falling, and only ice and snow are on the ground, silent, and thick and unmoving, it feels as if the world has died.

Winter in Vermont is a full six months long. Children trick or treating wear long underwear under their costumes, and winter boots and gloves. Winter comes early, and hard, and stays a long, long time. April is the beginning of spring, but spring sports are a chilly affair, and many soccer games are played on a stiff-grassed field dotted still with snow.

Spring is a gift for everyone in Vermont, a rescue, grace, and hope, arriving after so many long hard days and nights. Spring arrives with that first hint of moisture in the air, the hard crunch of your steps on the snow becoming a softer, duller sound, and then your feet sinking in as the ice fails and the snow becomes heavy and wet. Spring comes with the sound - Oh!

That sound! - the sound of water, liquid water, whispering, trickling, oozing, and running, freed from its long winter prison, running like any sensible person would for the far-off beaches and seas. The water at first grows still again at night, trapped again in crystals, but when the first faint sun reaches out onto the snow in the morning, the water runs free once again.

When the sun finally wins, and the snow and ice are broken, the water rushes down the streams and rivers in such a torrent that banks are torn away. The trees ripped from beside the river, and the mad water becoming a thick, brown flood, thundering through the small towns and taking with it any who stand too close to the banks. After six months of winter, I can understand the hurry.

Betts was used to the long, cold winter of the poor since she had always been poor, as were her parents, and her parent's parents before them. Poverty tends to stick with the family, as does wealth. Betts would have been confused or even offended if you had been uncouth enough to suggest her poverty to her. She lived as her parents did, and her friends at school, and thought no more about it than to wish and pray when her mother bought the occasional lottery ticket down at the gas station.

The surest way to wealth and comfort is to have the foresight to choose wealthy parents, or better yet, a long line of bankers and stockbrokers and other moneymen from which to descend. Betts had only Tina and Peter, both raised in poverty, and inured with a life paid for day to day, working full time on minimum wage jobs and living in rented housing. Always a little short, always a bit behind. The stress of angry phone calls and pink-tinted letters, the choices of what could be bought and what would not, food or gas. The spectacle of furniture, whose payments could not be kept up, being carried back out of the trailer by strangers and hauled away back to the Renter Center, leaving the family to sit on the floor, or sleep on piled blankets. And the grim realization that the next day would be the same. This stress sometimes drove people against each other, trying to pin the fault on why life had failed. And so, the fights and the recriminations.

Life with Ames, on $826 a month, plus what could be earned by cutting wood, was different. It wsn't fancy. The cabin and the hillside scrap of land had been bought for a mere $8,300. The toilet sat over a hole in the ground. The cabin itself was just a tad over 350 square feet, not counting the porch, and the truck in the yard had been made in 1982, some thirty-three years before, with a patina of rust covering the body, deepening to an almost lace around the fenders and door sills. But Ames was somehow not poor at all. Oddly, when he walked away from full-time work, he walked away from poverty as well. When he decided to meet his needs directly, instead of through the middlemen of landlords, employers, and the credit hawkers at the bank, Ames found himself set. His life was a more successful model of the life attempted by his flatlander neighbors, who struggled to maintain their life in the country with constant infusions of cash.

Ames kept the cabin neat, tidy, dusted and swept, in perfect repair, his window clear, the furniture smooth and oiled, and he luxuriated in that most precious commodity, time. He worked only as much as he wanted, the cash income being more than sufficient for his simple needs, and his money gathered in the bank, a few hundred more, every month. The old Ford truck started easily and ran beautifully, making it up and down the mountain. Ames' life in the cabin was filled with books and a decent pot of tea, and his windows and woodlot offering a view down the valley that was still breathtakingly beautiful after the years. Ames had crafted a life that fit his needs and abilities to a tee, and he had crafted it from scratch, without any of it being handed to him, or modeled in any way. There was no shouting, no clutter, no resentment, no conflict, no pressure, and lots of time to walk and swim and think and read. Quiet, peaceful, and predictable from day to day.

Betts soaked up this new life like a sponge. Her homework, busy work, really, was done in the truck on the way home from school, somehow keeping her handwriting neat over the dirt road, stacked on the table by the couch, and checked again in the morning over breakfast. A longer assignment, a book report perhaps, would be done on the table by the couch, while Ames read in his chair by the window, with Betts asking from time to time for the spelling of a word, or perhaps reading a bit to Ames that she was proud of and wanted to share. The cabin would be warm, the tea hot and fresh and good, the dishes done and the floors swept, the cabin as neat and tidy and snug as any that could be imagined.

The end of Winter, and the first start of Spring in the cabin, living with Ames, had been a time of peace and beauty, with some outside tree work, some wood delivered, trips to town once a week, and hikes and bonfires. Sugaring had been lovely as well, and Ames had allowed Betts to make the labels for the quart Mason jars. She had drawn several sketches, settling at last on a picture of a maple tree with buckets hung around it, snow on the ground freckled with tiny boot prints, and a steaming kettle of sap boiling over a fire. "Betts' Best" was written proudly across the top, and "100% Vermont Maple Syrup" on the bottom. She copied this drawing at the library sixty-eight times, and then hand-colored each one with her fine pencil set, trimming them, and taping them onto the jars with clear packing tape. On the lid, there was a price tag of $15, and the librarian, who loved Betts as a reader, sold forty-eight of them out in a week from her desk at the library. Ames had Betts keep the money, saying that she had done most of the work anyway, which was true, and he still had her good syrup for his pancakes. Betts put the money into a metal toolbox, along with the money she had earned from helping with the firewood, banded into nine stacks of one hundred dollars each, and some loose bills and change. Betts kept the rest of the syrup at home, giving two to Zoey, and saving two for her mother, as well.

Even as nice as the winter had been for Betts, her first nice winter, six months is six months, and the excitement of spring captured Betts' heart. "The gully is roaring!" she said, as she came back into the cabin from a trip to the outhouse. Ames looked up from his book and smiled at the excited little girl in front of him.

"Yeah. You can hear it from inside if you listen. I'll bet the river is up over the road today, or maybe tomorrow. This is a big one." Ames was reading a red cloth bound book from the library, which looked more like a hymnal than the South American fiction that it was. He looked up over his book. "I'm glad our cabin is up where it is. I'd hate to be streamside, or down where you had to worry about flooding every year. We're staked pretty sturdy up here on the side of the mountain."

Betts saw that Ames was deep in his book and did not try to continue the conversation. She thought about their life here in the cabin, here on the mountain, and saw that the life she had had before had been unsafe and uncertain, set as it was stream-side, in a way, where every current of jealousy and anger would flood through the trailer, sweeping up the people inside and carrying them away. If Peter had got in trouble at work, he would come home angry and belligerent, looking for a fight, one he could be sure to win. If Peter came home late, Tina would be afraid as she waited, and eager to turn that fear into anger and pour that out on the one little person who was available. Betts caught it, either way, her face and her backside the target for all the adult chaos in the trailer. Life in the cabin, life with Ames, did not include these turbulent, dangerous, and hurtful floods. She felt snug here, staked up pretty sturdy, as Ames would say, here in the cabin on the mountain.

Zoey had spent the next two days catching up on her caseload, thinking, and resisting the urge to drive up the mountain to see Betts and Ames. She thought a lot about her conversation with Laura at the playground and listened to the conversations in the staff room regarding Eddy Roberts at the Children's Retreat. The nurse who had indeed broken his nose was something of a hero, and the staff took up a collection, sending her a hundred-dollar gift certificate to a nice clothing store in Montpelier.

On the third day, Zoey made the drive up the mountain, late in the afternoon, planning on catching Ames and Betts at work on the giant tree. She found them just finishing up for the day. The tree had been reduced to four stacks of brush, each about six feet tall, and maybe ten feet in diameter, stacked tight and level - Betts work. The trunk still lay in giant sections, the largest of which Ames had been unable to cut, even with the thirty-six-inch bar, working from both sides. The driveway had been cleared, and most of the wood was gone, stacked up at Ames's woodlot in front of the cabin. Ames dusted off his hands, and walked over to her car, a big smile on his face. "Nice to see you!" he said. "I've missed you the past couple of days."

Zoey beamed, inside and out. "I brought pizza," she said. "I thought we might have dinner up at your place."

Zoey had a large pizza and a medium pizza in her Subaru, and a watermelon from the grocery store in town. The smaller pizza was cheese and pineapple, Betts' favorite, and the larger one was a chicken and garlic, Zoey's favorite, which she hoped Ames would like. She had a big bottle of root beer as well. She followed the old Ford truck up the road, pulling in after Ames, and parking beside his truck. Ames took the watermelon, and Zoey brought the pizza and the root beer, while Betts got plates and cups from the kitchen. They set it up at the picnic table, and Betts checked the sap buckets and began bringing in the day's haul.

The sugar run had slowed a bit, and the sap was darker, with a richer taste that Ames loved. Betts asked if she could set the fire, and then did so, while Zoey and Ames sat across from each other and talked. Zoey watched Betts work, stacking the birch splits, and bringing in the shovel of coals from the cabin, and blowing the flames to life. Ames poured the sap into the kettle as Betts brought more buckets, and soon the fire was roaring, the kettle steaming, and the empty buckets hung back on the trees for what Ames thought might be the last day of the season.

"Last run?" Zoey asked. "Is that a good thing, or a bad thing?"

Betts answered first. "Both. I love making syrup every night, with the fire and the stars and staying up late. But I'm tired in the day, and almost fell asleep in school a couple of times. I'm ready for summer, anyway. Last time I was here we swam down at the Floating Bridge almost every afternoon. I want to do that again."

Ames nodded. "Every good thing in its season. It's been a pretty good run, and Betts has done most of the work. She'll get the income to add to her toolbox. I've sat here by the fire and looked at the stars, but I do that pretty often anyway even without boiling sap. And summer will be nice. Betts can swim pretty good now, and I won't have to keep watching her all the time, and maybe get some swimming in myself."

Zoey thought about that. Nights by the fire, swimming by the bridge and cutting enough wood to keep the bills paid. Zoey took another piece of pizza. "Sounds nice," she said. She thought about her summer, so much the same as her spring, winter, and fall. She had two weeks of vacation at this point, and would for the next three years if she stayed on with the agency. She could move up to three weeks at that point. But three out of fifty-two seemed a poor bargain, and two even worse. She had loved her apartment when she first moved in, but the rent and the utilities took up a bit more than half of her paycheck, and with car repair and what she spent on cable and her phone, there was little enough left at the end of the month.

And the work seemed to take all that was good out of her. Her nights and her weekends seemed to be spent in recovery, healing up from the week before, and getting ready for the week to come. She thought of her time in school. Busy, sure, but somehow always able to travel on the breaks, go camping, hikes with her friends, and nights out under the stars, talking forever, it seemed. Now she worked and watched TV when she wasn't working, and spent her precious vacation time back at her parents' house.

Ames put his hand on her arm. Zoey startled a bit at the warm touch. "Kind of quiet," he said. "You OK?"

"I'm OK," she said. "I just want more of this sort of thing in my life. I was talking to Laura earlier, and now seeing you and Betts out here again, it makes my day seem kind of bleak."

Ames nodded. "I couldn't do what you do, with the hurt kids and all. And I don't think I could do forty hours a week of anything at this point. I'm getting pretty resentful of that big maple, taking up most of every day. We'll finish it up, but I'm ready for some reading, and maybe just looking down the mountain."

They sat in silence for a bit, the last of the pizza gone. Betts had gone in to get the flashlight to check the temperature of the boil. "I like being up here," said Zoey.

"I like you being up here, too," said Ames.

"I like you being up here, too," said Betts, arriving with the flashlight. She looked at Ames and Zoey, leaning toward each other beside the fire, and handed Ames the flashlight. "I'm kind of tired. I think I'll go get a shower and go to bed. If you don't mind finishing up without me." She grinned at Ames, not looking tired at all, and then faked a yawn. "See you guys later." She turned and walked back up to the cabin. They heard the hum of the water pump in a moment.

Zoey turned to Ames. "What was that about?" she asked.

"I think Betts is giving us a little time alone." There was a long silence, then Ames moved his chair closer to Zoey. "You warm enough?" he asked? Zoey leaned closer, and said, "Mmmmmmmmm."

CHAPTER SEVENTEEN

Some Horrible History That You Might Not Want to Read, and Rebekah.

Betts often thought of her new life, as she pictured it, high up on the side of Bear Mountain, living in the cabin with Ames, and the little green woodstove and the spring, and her old life, living with her mother and Peter, in the trailer in Williamstown. Betts was a thoughtful child anyway, prone to paying attention to the things around her and wanting to make sense of the world she was in. She paid attention to details, and remembered both the events and the ripples around the events, and worked hard to stitch together a reasonable, predictable model for the world.

At first, Betts seldom hoped to either control these events, or even predict what might happen next, although these goals motivate a good many people who hope for power, or at least, safety. Betts had pretty much given up on both safety and predictability and had accepted her life before as one in which she was the recipient of a series of random, often hurtful events over which she had no control at all. Things happened, often things she would not have wished for, and they happened for reasons that were as yet beyond her understanding.

The fights between her mother and Peter took place often, but without any discernible pattern, and could go from bad to even worse, or from thrown dishes to loud lovemaking, without apparent rhyme or reason. If she were witness, the fury would turn on her. If she hid, they would find her. Betts got the belt, the slaps, and the cursing, regardless of her behavior or location. And there was nothing she could find to do that could change that.

Things took a turn for the much worse when her mother was given the late shift at the sock factory, and now worked from three to eleven in the evening. Peter came home around six. Betts had been home from school since about twenty minutes after three, doing her homework, drawing, and maybe fixing herself a package of Ramen noodles or a can of soup. Betts was in her room by the time Peter came home, reading, or trying to.

Peter had long been one of those men who enjoyed what was easy and available, and he seemed to like a slice of fear served up on the side. With Tina gone to work, he sought out Betts, one night knocking her door open to her little room and telling her to go take a shower. Betts had showered when she got home, but quietly got up from her bed, put her book down, and walked down the narrow hallway to the bathroom. Once she had the water on, her clothes folded on the counter, and had stepped once again into the shower, the bathroom door was pushed open, and, not surprisingly, Peter walked in. He said a few disparaging things about Betts hygiene and her ability to keep herself clean. Betts said nothing, and Peter said little else, both of them knowing that Peter had little practical need to justify anything he wished to do.

This disgusting, painful, gasping and intrusive attention became a regular part of Betts evenings without her mother. Betts learned that the best she could hope for in these five evenings each week was to do nothing to provoke more of a response, unless a response was demanded, such as crying or an apology, in which case compliance was the best path. Betts' fear and discomfort seemed a spice of sorts for Peter, and as he became used to sending Betts into the shower as he came home, he added to the drama that would follow.

There are animals in Vermont, possums, perhaps, who when under threat, and as a last resort, feign death. Like the advice often offered in bear country - play dead, and the bear will leave you alone. It's hard to imagine someone who could actually do that, and play dead while a bear bit into your ribs, or your leg. But if Betts were the one being chewed on by a bear, she could have easily lay still, while bits of her were torn off and swallowed, pretending to feel nothing, keeping her eyes closed and her voice quiet, giving the bear, at least, no satisfaction that she knew she was indeed being eaten alive.

This astonishing skillset, so often found in the children of trauma, comes at a significant personal cost. That doorway between "here" and "not here" is at first torn open, as the child who must escape and cannot, finally finds a way. Then, with repeated events and escapes, that tear becomes stretched and jagged, the psychic tissue scarred and deadened, and an opening forms that seldom heals closed again. Soon such children find themselves falling from here to there, with little choice, or will. They drift, unmoored, between here and somewhere else.

The second night in the shower, or perhaps the third, with Peter emboldened by his undetected success the nights before, and aroused by his anticipation during the day, things got even worse. Betts had panicked, both from the physical pain and technical impossibility of the situation she was in, and from the awareness that this would go on and on, night after night, as long as her mother worked the late shift. She could neither fight, nor flee, and so, instead, something in her simply broke, the silky barrier that had held her soul tight as "Betts" since birth now ruptured. Betts drifted away, leaving her prior self, bent over on the tiny bathroom floor, gasping for air, the shower still running away.

All such drifting children seek safety, and some describe disturbingly similar landscapes of peace and comfort. Some find friends in this vague world, companions of a sort, guides or protectors, who shield this little part of the child that has escaped. Betts found Rebekah.

***

The second time Peter came in, followed her in, actually, and demanded that she get in the shower, and then he proceeded to do his version of "getting her clean," her brain had screamed, "Run! Run! Run!" But there was no place to run. "Hide! Hide! Hide!" her heart had shouted, but there was no place to hide. Fight? She had pushed back once and been slapped so hard, over and over, that she had almost lost the ability to stand. It was then, while she was still reeling from the blows, that Rebekah had first come. Rebekah was about Betts' age and size, a little heavier, with blond hair and a round, open face. She had come into the shower, that first night, dressed in a fancy satin dress, a party dress, her hair combed out and beautiful, and somehow strangely dry under the spray. She had smiled a sad smile and said, "Let's go to the cabin."

She took Betts' hand, and Betts then found herself by the spring, the blond girl beside her, and Betts saw that she was somehow now dressed in jeans and a tee-shirt, and her black Keds, and Peter, and the shower, and the trailer, all of that, was nowhere to be seen.

The two of them had sat there, on the splash rock, the night warm and soft even though there were the first bits of snow on the ground back at the trailer, with the water from the spring bubbling up from the earth, and washing out the shame and terror and dirtiness that had been all over Betts, washing her clean, and carrying her tears downstream, into the creek, into the river, and on into the great salty ocean. Rebekah sat beside her, silent and calm, but crying a bit with Betts, their tears falling together into the water on the splash rock and being washed away.

And somehow, from the splash rock, there was the view from the top rock, and Betts could see all the way down the valley, but the view was different, and she could see the red taillights of her mother's car winding up the road to the trailer, and she knew that it was time to go back again. "I need to go home," she said, and she was there, in her bed, sore and defiled, her pillow wet from her hair and her tears, and her mother's voice in the hallway, trying to stir some interest from Peter, who was already spent. The something turned into a fight, and she could hear Tina's voice rising, complaining that Peter was never interested in her anymore, and then a slap, and then the crying, and then more yelling.

Betts put the pillow over her head and tried to drown out the words. Tina yelling, "Who is she? Who is she?" over and over, then another slap, a table being tossed, and the front door slamming, as Peter gunned his Camaro and spun off down the road. Her mother crying, and then the sound of a few more things breaking, and then silence. Betts waited for her mother to come slamming into her room, turning her rage toward her, but the night was quiet, and Betts eventually fell asleep.

Rebekah came again, as needed at first, as Peter continued his assaults, and then, Rebekah came at times that were calm as well, sometimes at school, sometimes on the bus, not just keeping Betts safe, but wanting, it seemed, Betts' company. For Rebekah seemed a sad and lonely little girl with her own story to tell. Rebekah was there when Betts was removed by the social workers, and hovered helplessly while Betts went through the foster care whirlwind, and took her in hand again during the night shift visits by that one aid, Eddy, who seemed to have been cast from the same mold as Peter.

Rebekah seemed to take pleasure in the same things as Betts, the quiet time in the cabin, the books and the tea, and Betts would sometimes see Rebekah watching Ames, smiling, watching him with love. Rebekah coming to her, and sometimes taking her away, this was the part that Betts could not yet talk about. Both because it still made no sense to her, and because she worried that were she to tell, Rebekah would disappear.

CHAPTER EIGHTEEN

A Visit to Ames' Mother

Ames' father, Jim, had died of a heart attack while Ames had been in the Sand Wars. Jim had been found in the barn, sitting on the concrete, still gasping for breath, when he failed to come for lunch. He had died strapped to a gurney, beneath the flashing lights, while riding in an ambulance from the trailer down to the Randolph hospital. Ames missed the funeral, being across the world, and Tina had refused to go. With Jim's death, the trailer was needed for the new hired hand and his family, and Cora found herself in a small Section 8 apartment in Randolph. She worked for a short time at the grocery store. But her diabetes made her legs swell, and standing all day proved impossible. A series of small strokes settled the matter, taking away what mobility Cora had, and clouding her speech as well.

Ames' and Tina's mother now lived in the Green Mountain Village, a combination retirement community and nursing home. It was a nice enough place, clean, with lots of activities, conversations, and a kind and competent staff. The facility was up North, a few miles past Burlington, and the back of the building had a view of Lake Champlain. Cora took advantage of very little of what the Village offered, staying in her room, refusing friendship and conversation and activities, and ignoring Ames' regular visits as well. She had a single room, after two attempts at finding a compatible roommate had failed, and Cora now spent her days alone, in bed, watching TV, or napping.

Tina had not seen her mother for two years before the nursing home placement and had not visited since, at all. They had not spoken more than a hundred words since Clair's death, anyway, and neither would have admitted to missing the other. Ames went for a brief visit every two weeks. The visits were always the same, and worried Ames beforehand, and depressed him a bit afterward. Ames would leave the cabin after Betts had been delivered to school, drive up Interstate 89, taking Exit 16, and arrive at the Village around ten o'clock. He would check in with the nurses, who loved him, and then walk back to his mother's room, #151, past the woman in the wheelchair who yelled out, "Help me! Help me!" all day long. He could hear the TV as he opened the door and would see his mother propped up, with the electric bed holding her almost like a chair, the TV as loud as was permitted, and a game show holding his mother's attention. She would turn as he walked in, recognize him, and then go back to the television, without saying a word.

Ames had thought on the first visit that either she was angry with him for something, or that, with the strokes, she no longer recognized him. But as he thought about it, this was the pattern that had been established with Clair's death, back when he was eight, and he was pretty sure that Tina had received the same treatment, at age eleven. Perhaps Cora thought that acknowledging Tina or Ames would be giving her consent for Clair's death, or that if she refused the children she still had, God might recognize his mistake and bring Clair back, taking one of the others. Or both.

Ames had tried gently breaking through, asking his mother why she was mad, even bending over to block her view of the TV. She shut her eyes until she knew he had moved away. His pattern for visits now was to sit in the chair and hold a one-sided conversation about the events in his life, and what he had seen in Brookfield, and on the way up to Burlington. He tried to be in by ten, and out just a tad before eleven. Sometimes the nurses would come in for a moment, and watch for a bit, but they had no answers either, only sympathy for Ames' reception, and admiration for his willingness to come so regularly for such a sad result.

Ames brought bits of news but had chosen to not tell his mother about Betts. He felt that somehow Tina's business was bound up with Betts in such a way that he felt unable to sort out what was about him, and what was about Tina. So, he said nothing. And he had told Betts nothing about his mother, her grandmother, until one day in late spring. Ames had brought the staff a few jars of syrup, and they had thanked him, and asked about the new label, "Betts' Best." Ames explained that he now had his sister's girl living with him and that she had done most of the syrup making this year. The staff insisted on meeting Betts and thanking her for the syrup, and so Ames promised to bring Betts up for a visit the following Saturday.

Betts had been to Burlington before, once, for a ten-day evaluation at the University hospital, a visit that she did not even remember, and several times with Ames, shopping at the Old Crow Bookstore in the open street mall. Betts loved the trips to Burlington. She liked both the shops and the people, most of them looking like college students. She even enjoyed the long drive up, with Ames driving around sixty miles per hour while the rest of the cars whizzed past at seventy-five or eighty. Betts had asked him why everyone was passing them, and he explained that the truck was geared for heavy loads and back roads. This set Betts off on a silly country western song she made up on the spot. She sang in a twangy Texas voice, using every "ode" rhyming word she could think of, including "horned toads," skies that "snowed," tires that "blowed," creeks that "flowed." Betts cracked herself up to the point of gasping for air, giggling, and then saying, "Wait! I have more!!" Ames wiped the tears from his eyes in order to see the cars whizzing past, while Betts choked out something about "corn that's hoed." She gathered herself together for a moment, looked at Ames, dead serious, then said, "I have a gift..." then cracked herself back up again, giggling on and off for the next ten minutes.

They had talked about the trip the night before, with Ames careful to explain that his mother was unlikely to say anything to Betts since she had said nothing to Ames for the past year and a half. Betts remembered asking her mother about her grandparents but had gotten little in terms of a response, other than a clear picture that her mother and grandmother did not get along. Ames explained about the staff liking her syrup, the old woman in the wheelchair who yelled, and the hospital bed and possible tubes of medication and drainage that he thought Betts might find worrisome.

Ames planned for lunch and some quick shopping in the Church Street Mall, including a trip to the Old Crow, then to drive on up to the Village, and introduce Betts to the staff, and to her grandmother. This way, they could arrive after lunch had been served, and noon medications were over. Ames thought how awful he usually felt after the visits, and hoped that Betts would not feel the same way.

Ames took Exit 14W and headed down toward the lake, shimmering and huge to the west. He found a two-hour parking space, and the two of them headed off to the Old Crow. Betts had packed a twenty-dollar bill for books, and another twenty just in case. The Old Crow was one of two remaining independent book stores in Burlington after what had once been a lively assortment had been decimated by the arrival of both a Borders and a Barnes and Nobel.

The Old Crow was everything a book shop should be, smelling of books and reading, with rooms and rooms of overflowing bookshelves, labels over the doorways leading you to *Mystery!*, *Poetry!*, *Literature!*, or several other sections, a large young adult room, and a delightful children's room, with shelf after shelf of beautiful children's books. There were creaky oak floors that tipped this way and that, mismatched paint and furnishings, and colored stars on some to the books to indicate a staff favorite. There were worn couches and armchairs, coffee tables, newspapers, and even a tea station, with a big vessel of hot water, old chipped cups and boxes, and boxes of tea bags. There was a coffee can for tea donations, and Betts always brought some change to clink in. And the staff read constantly, even at work, and they knew the convoluted rooms and where each book might be.

Betts spent her time in the Young Adult and the Children's rooms, torn between the stories in the YA section, and the pictures in the children's room. Ames took the occasional tour through the Lit section but mostly spent time in the large Sciences room, carefully sorting through the college texts and field guides for something that increases his understanding of how the natural world worked. He had discovered that the Environmental Sciences section was a good fit, and had been bringing home books on watersheds, the weather, and most recently, the impact of beavers on the habitat of North American mammals.

Ames always picked one book, the cabin being pretty full as it was, and Betts always dragged a stack of ten or fifteen around the store with her, finally laying them out on a table, and painfully selecting the best four or five books her twenty dollars could buy. Ames had asked her why she didn't just spend a little more, and she had looked at him, reprovingly. "Twenty dollars is a lot to spend on anything."

After the bookstore, with Betts clutching her books to her chest as they walked, they bought two large slices of pizza from a shop with a wood-fired oven, and then stopped at the Ben and Jerry's for a small cone. They looked in at Old Gold, an exotic vintage clothing and costume shop, where Betts had bought a few favored things, including an extra small black leather motorcycle vest that she wore on the cooler days. Ames was a bit nervous in the store, with the collared and fetish clad manikins seeming so wrong for a child, but Betts was unperturbed. "Grownups like that stuff," she had said.

"I'm not looking." There was a tea and coffee shop next door, called Muddy Waters, that he and Betts had tried and liked before, but time was short, and a visit to the Village was coming up.

They found the truck with fifteen minutes still on the meter, and Betts tossed in another quarter, a gift to the imagined next parker that Betts could see being so pleased to have found a meter with some time still on it. Ames found the way back to the Interstate, with Betts eyeing the college and the students as they drove past the campus. "You think I might go here?" she asked.

"Yeah," said Ames. "You might. Unless you want to go somewhere else. Montpelier has a college, and there's a couple down south. Randolph has a community college for nursing and welding and stuff." Betts thought about it, looking out the window, and said nothing.

Ames pointed out the lake on the left and suggested that the next trip they take, they ride the ferry over to New York, and get lunch there. Betts came out of her college reverie long enough to think about this. She smiled and suggested that they take Zoey with them and come up the following Saturday. "She'd like that, too," said Betts. Ames was unsure, but Betts wasn't. "She likes us, not for work, but for real people. And we like her." Betts paused. "You guys kissed the last time she was up." Ames colored up and glanced at Betts. "I was looking out the window." Ames looked at her. "Just a little," she said. "Then I went to bed." Ames said nothing until they got to the Village, and took the turn in to the parking lot.

Ames signed them both in at the front desk, where an elderly volunteer eyed them as they walked in the door. "151," the older woman said. "She stays in her room."

When they passed the nursing station, one of the nurses saw Ames with Betts and gathered up the other staff to meet the "syrup girl." Betts was a bit shy, but pleased, and went over for them how the syrup had been made, and her role in it, including the labels on the jars. As Ames led her down the hallway to her grandmother's room, Betts became quiet and moved a bit slower. Ames worried that she was scared, but when he asked if she was OK, Betts just said, "Yeah, I want to see her."

Ames knocked on the door, decorated by the staff with artificial flowers and a calendar for the month of May. He opened the door and ushered Betts in. Cora lay on her bed, flat now, the rails up, and a tube back in her arm, and another appearing from underneath the sheets disappearing somewhere under the bed. Her face was drawn and pale, and her eyes were focused on the TV, still lit with action, the sound turned off by the nursing staff, hoping for Cora to take a nap.

Her eyes flicked over to the doorway, to Ames, and then, on to Betts. Ames watched his mother's eyes widen, and then soften, and shine, and her voice, unheard for so long, croak out, "You're here!"

Betts smiled and moved toward his mother's bed, taking the chair where Ames usually sat. "I'm here," Betts said. His mother said little else, her voice hoarse and unsure, but she clasped Betts hand through the bed rails, and leaned up from the pillow, her face radiant, and her eyes eager. Betts sat by her, quietly talking, first about their trip up, then softer, about something Ames could not hear, his mother listening closely and nodding her head and gripping Betts' hand.

Ames stood near the doorway, watching this happen with little understanding. His mother greeted Betts as if a long-lost child. And then he saw it. Betts's face was blurred, her eyes warm and open, her voice soft and low, her smile encouraging, hopeful, wanting Cora only to be happy. Ames saw his sister, Clair, beside his mother's bed, Betts' thin small body, her long black hair, but somehow, Clair was there, holding his mother's hand, and bringing her the comfort that only she could give.

He moved closer, and Betts turned to him, shining with his sister's face, and Cora saw him as well, and said, "Look at you! You're all grown up!"

Ames felt his eyes tear up, confused, but feeling for the first time that his mother saw him, and was glad that he was there. He moved to the bed and lay his hand on her shoulder. "Yeah, Mom. All grown up, pretty much."

"Do you have a girl?" she asked.

Ames was confused, and then said, "Yeah, I think I do."

His mother smiled. "That's nice. You were always so shy."

"How's Tina?" asked his mother, some worry in her voice.

Betts said, "Tina's fine. She has a little girl, named Betts, and works full time at the sock factory. She'd be here today, but she has to work. She sends her love." His mother's eyes brimmed over, the tears moving down her cheeks in a tiny path, dripping onto the pillow beneath her head.

"I am so happy to know all my little chicks are safe!" she said. With Betts drying her eyes, Cora fell asleep, her breathing shallow and irregular. Ames turned to see a nurse at the door, her face as startled as his own. She entered the room and moved beside the bed.

Betts turned up, her own face and voice back, somehow, and said, "She's sleeping."

"I haven't ever heard her say anything before," said the nurse.

shaking and sobbing and unable to drive. After a few minutes, his breathing settled, and he wiped his eyes on his sleeve and pulled the truck back onto the highway. It felt odd for him to be crying out in loss, for he and his mother had never been close. It had been Clair she was close to, and Clair she missed, and Clair who he was sure she had gone on to see.

He and Tina had been the odd ones out, somehow. Ames accepting it, pretty much, and running when it got to be too much. Tina fighting it, demanding that she be seen and loved and held, with no more success than he had had from running. But something had woke his mother up, this last weekend visit with Betts. Something that, down deep, he had hoped would give him, and maybe Tina, a second chance to have their mom. Maybe that was what he grieved: the lost last chance for reconciliation, for love. And he wondered if Betts' visit had somehow given his mother the contact she had somehow needed to move on.

Ames worked through the gears, keeping an eye on the road, and the traffic that was moving past him. The truck ran at a smooth rumble, sixty-three being a speed at which the engine settled into a comfortable lope, without the stress of the higher speeds. The rough tires whirred on the smooth pavement, and the wind whistled around the dried-out weather-strip on the doors and windows. Ames watched as Exit 14W came and went, and remembered the ice cream he and Betts had shared on the Church Street Mall. He thought about next Saturday when he had made plans with an excited Zoey to travel with him and Betts up for a ferry ride to New York for lunch.

He found himself at the exit for the Village, and took the truck around the loop and then into the parking lot. He parked in his usual space, at the far side of the lot, and looked up to the window he thought must be to his mother's room. It was hard to know for certain, with all the curtains and blinds looking the same, but he had counted once, from the wide windows of the day room, and was pretty sure this was it.

He thought of the dead, of Clair, so scared, so surprised, and then, so calm, and of the dead in the Sand Wars, some dead by his own hand, fighting to stay alive, even when it was clear to anyone else that they could not. All the dead, taken without their consent, and gone, gone somewhere that Ames could not yet go. He wondered if his mother had felt ready, or if she had chosen in some way to move on, having made peace with Betts, and with Clair, and with him, and maybe even with Tina. "All my chicks," she had said. And Ames felt his heart tear again, and he sat in the truck and cried and cried.

Ames got out of the truck, his second wave of loss ridden out, and walked up to the door of the nursing home. He could feel that it was now only a place where his mother used to live, and he wondered if he had come for a visit without the call if he could have still felt her absence so completely. He signed in at the front desk, and the nurse there looked at him with so much kindness that he felt his breath catch again. He turned away, toward his mother's room, and the nurse behind him said, "I'm so sorry."

He opened the door and found her, grayer and smaller, it seemed, the bed flat, the sheets neat and tidy, her arms smooth and straight beside her, her eyes closed, and her hair brushed back. Someone had done this kindness, on her behalf and his. And he could tell that she was no longer here. Behind him, he heard another nurse come in. She put her hand on his shoulder, and he felt again the shocking burn of compassion, that oh- so-needed! And yet so painful contact with the kindness of others. "She went really well," the nurse said. "After your visit, she woke up that evening and talked with the chaplain, and Mary, her night nurse. She made out this note for you. Mary wrote it, but Cora signed it, and the chaplain signed it too, as a witness. She also wanted the little girl that was here with you to have her ring," she said, handing him a small plastic bag with his mother's name written on the frosted label part, a plain gold wedding band inside. "She called her Clair, but she must have meant Betts, right?" Ames nodded. The nurse went on. "She went to sleep, deep sleep, on Tuesday, only waking up a bit from time to time, then less, and then this morning she just slipped away. It's about the best you could hope for."

Ames sat with his mother for this one last time, her body already close to room temperature, her features setting and losing any sign of the animation she had once had. Ames sat beside her, his hand on hers, and he could see the last parts of the transition from here to not here up close. As was his habit, he spoke from time to time, not expecting an answer in return. He lay his hand on his mother's cold arm and let the tears fall for a bit. The room seemed different with the TV off, silent, and large. And Ames realized that he was alone, an orphan, in fact, this time, rather than simply feeling abandoned. His father dead, and now his mother. Ames felt the strange shift of generations, as he moved up in line, giving up on ever having what he had missed in childhood, and taking on the lonely role of adult. His thoughts went to Betts, his responsibility now, and probably from now on if things went well.

Ames had spent much of his childhood aware that things were not as he wished, and he had responded by running away from the bad. The fights, the yelling, even his own feelings of loneliness and need. He had run from home all the way to the Sand Wars and had run from the war all the way back to Vermont, to the cabin on Bear Mountain. Ames remembered a book, maybe from the thrift shop, on Celtic history and religion. Ames was French/Irish, and he found the book intriguing. He remembered that in some rituals, people moved counterclockwise, or widdershins, they called it, the direction of undoing and unmaking. His running had been like that, all an effort to undo, to escape. Now he looked to stop and turn in the circle, and move clockwise, the direction of doing and making. Making a home for Betts, for one thing. And maybe making a relationship with Zoey.

He took the ring from his pocket and took it out of the little plastic bag. He remembered this ring on his mother's hand, always, tiny and tight, the one piece of jewelry she wore. She scoffed at the idea that it was jewelry, and always said instead that it was a commitment. Sometimes her voice had been angry when she said that, but sometimes it was not. Ames thought of commitment, and of making and doing, and of moving into the head of the line, no longer sheltered by a parent, even one who had been so wounded as to lose her will to be much of a parent at all. And so, with acceptance, and forgiveness, Ames held his mother's arm one last time, then got up, walked out and closed the door.

The note his mother had left expressed her love for her kids, and named them, Tina, Clair and Ames. She also shared her decision to have Tina sort out her few belongings, and asked that what money might be in her checking account be divided between Tina and Ames, and that her body be buried in the little cemetery where Clair, her husband, and her parents were. It had been a small life, lived within a few miles of where she had been born. The work that she had done was not the lasting kind, and her friendships had been precious few. Her faith had been lost with the death of her child, and it was hard to see her life as anything more than a series of hardships, losses, and failures. But the tone of the letter was hopeful and loving, and full of grace. Ames drove home at his usual slow pace, thinking about the future, about his sister, Tina, and looking forward to picking Betts up from school.

Tina was now without a mother, and so without any hope of reconciliation or redress, without her daughter, and with only Peter for company. Although much of Tina's loneliness was self-imposed, she felt herself abandoned, and could only feel anger at her parents and her brother for the lack of relationship. She saw herself as tied to Peter, simply because she believed no one else would have her.

These feelings came early for Tina, probably with the birth of Clair. Tina was born when her mother was seventeen. Cora had discovered she was pregnant and had sought out direction from her own mother, who promptly slapped her and sent her packing. Cora walked the three miles or so to Robert's house, the twenty-year-old boy who was responsible. Robert lived with his parents as well, who were only slightly more supportive, allowing Cora a place on the couch up until Robert and she could arrange to be married.

Life with Robert's parents was less than ideal, showing a side of her future husband that looked remarkably different than the handsome young man she had met in town. Robert's mother and father missed few opportunities to comment on the sluttish behavior which had snared their son, although his father frequently managed to walk in on Cora while she was changing, taking the time to stare at the tall, thin young woman who suddenly shared his home.

A town hall marriage was arranged, and Cora and Robert were wed before Tina arrived, and they moved to the first of three single wide trailers, set into a barnyard, so work was never more than a few seconds away. Robert resented the sudden shift in his life from a handsome young man with change in his pocket to an exhausted husband smelling of cows, but at least he stayed, complaining only a few nights a week.

Cora grew larger and more exhausted, and her discomfort seemed a fitting punishment for having thought she might be loved. Tina was born with little difficulty, though, and Cora gave it her best. Tina was soon seen to be colicky and cried without stopping much of the day. Robert took to spending his little amount of free time sitting in the truck in the yard, smoking, or having a beer or two, while Cora alternately tried to soothe the baby, or screamed back at her.

In spite of these circumstances, Cora became pregnant again and found this second pregnancy, perhaps because of the status of marriage, easier to bear. Clair came easily, too, and proved to be a pleasing child, round and blond and happy, asking little other than to be held from time to time. Cora took what Clair had to give, and found herself feeling loved for what might have been the first time in her life. Tina, at age two, was not at all pleased to have her mother's lap filled with this little cherub and pinched and slapped at the baby whenever she could. This did little to improve Tina's already rocky standing in the family. Tina withdrew to sulk, making occasional attempts to demand her mother's attention, which usually resulted in the wooden spoon being brought out, and more time behind the door of the tiny room she slept in.

A year later, Ames was born, after much struggle that left Cora unable to have more children. Ames was dark and thin like his oldest sister, but quiet, and willing to take what was leftover from the attention Cora gave to Clair. All three children were as different from each other as you can imagine, sharing only the same bedroom in the trailer, the same worn clothing passed down from older and more fortunate cousins, and the same inescapable odor of the dairy farm on which they lived.

When Clair died beneath the tractor wheel, Ames was eight, and Tina eleven. Cora gave up on her life, her husband and her remaining two children, sinking into black despair that she would never fully recover from. Robert, who had put the tractor into reverse and rolled the big International up and onto his favorite little girl, cried most of that day, and then never again. He withdrew, as a murderer must, from those around him, doing the jobs on the farm, and even climbing back into that tractor seat the following day, taking what comfort he could in seeing the work done, and a six-pack or two of PBRs at the end of the long day.

Ames and Tina found themselves with the run of the house, as their mother stayed each day in her bedroom, and their father took his meals in his truck, eating what they could find, bathing when their skin began to itch, and sleeping in their clothes, in front of the TV, which now stayed on throughout the day and night. School provided some reprieve, although Ames was shy and had few friends, and Tina so angry that the other children shied away. The smell of the barn, always a curse on their school life, now also carried the smell of unwashed children, their teeth scumming over until the individual teeth became a blur of yellow fuzz.

The school called in social services, and Laura, already middle-aged and experienced in the ways of families and loss, came into their lives. She took the children home from school that first day, in an agency car, knocking first on the door of the trailer. Tina pushed past her and sat down before the TV. Laura knocked again on the bedroom door, where she found a sleepy Cora, irritated at the interruption, not interested in what Laura had to say, but willing to have Laura in, if that's what she wanted. Laura started with the dishes, worked her way through the counters, and then found a vacuum, with a filled bag, in the closet. She carefully emptied the bag into an already overflowing trash bag on the kitchen floor, taped the bag back up again, and vacuumed the trailer, picking things up off the floor as she went. Ames followed her around and began to pick up as well, while Tina complained about the noise.

After a few hours, the trailer looked better, and Ames was suggesting projects around the house. Laura demanded that each child take a shower and brush their teeth, offering dinner out at McDonalds should clean children present themselves. Ames promptly disappeared, then reappeared scrubbed red and shiny. Tina stayed on the couch until it became clear that Laura and Ames would go without her, then reluctantly got up and washed, being sent back twice for further cleaning. After their meal, they stopped at Wal-Mart for clothing and pajamas for each child, some cleaning supplies, and some basic groceries.

They were home by seven-thirty, Laura aware that these interventions were well outside of her pay scale. She offered to read the kids a book, and Tina was willing to turn off the TV and listen, while Ames shyly sat on the couch with his shoulder brushing Laura from time to time as he leaned in to see the pictures. Teeth were brushed again, with gums bleeding from this unexpected attention, and both children were put to bed, with Laura noting the need for new sheets. After they heard the door close, Ames whispered to Tina, "I like her." Tina snorted and turned over, saying, "Don't be stupid."

Laura regularly came, daily at first, then several times a week, then a couple of times a week, for over a year. Ames and Tina arrived at school looking more presentable, and their schoolwork was now passable as well. Cora remained in the bedroom, but Robert came in from time to time, watching Laura work with his children, and taking on some of the household chores, even reading haltingly to the kids in the evening. Laura watched to see that her presence encouraged him as a parent but tapered her involvement as he began to show some interest in her.

After a year, it seemed her work was done. Cora remained in the bedroom most of the afternoon, emerging to help with farm chores when Robert had his hand stepped on by a cow. Robert's hand healed up, pretty much, after a few weeks, but Cora continued to work by his side, saying little, but ready for something to do other than to question and grieve. Ames missed Laura but was grateful for his father's slight involvement. Tina kept her anger and would pound on her mother's locked door, demanding a signature for a school event, or money for school fees, and neither the shouts or slaps from her mother and father seemed to discourage her.

The fighting distressed Ames. He begged Tina to stop and then began to leave the trailer when the conflicts started up. Ames spent hours on his bike, a heavy two speed Schwinn, dark green and blessed with two heavy canvas ammo bags wired on the back. Laura had found the bike at a garage sale in town and had a friend fix it up before she hauled it out to the farm in the back of an agency minivan. Ames loved it, even though it was a bit too big for him, and quickly mastered how to ride, as well as how to keep the bike in good condition. He rode along the highway, into Williamstown, and Laura would sometimes see the bike parked and chained in front of the town library or the grocery store. Ames began asking for odd jobs from the neighbors, stacking wood, helping with haying, and doing yard work as requested. He saved his money, having nothing he wished to buy, and hiding it under the cover of a broken bailer after Tina cleaned his savings out twice.

CHAPTER TWENTY

About Tina

Ames knew little of the details, but he knew that Tina was less lucky than he had been, out seeking some affection at age twelve from those who might offer it. She found a series of predatory, older boys and men willing to take the tiny risk of trouble in exchange for the pleasures Tina struggled to offer. This list of players included a minister from Randolph, an older man at the Williamstown feed store, and some high school boys who Tina first saw on the school bus.

One of these older boys was Peter. Peter was nineteen when Tina turned fourteen. He had graduated the year before and worked at the granite shed in town. Tina remembered him as one of the boys who called her to sit in the back of the bus with the big kids. She had been almost eleven, and the boys in the back of the bus were all in high school. She had tried that, once, rising from her seat, but the sometimes open eyes of the driver saw her in the big mirror, and he sharply called her back to the front where the younger kids had to sit. At the next stop, he pulled the bus over, and walked past Tina, all the way to the back, and had a hissed one-way conversation with the boys in the back, who must have believed he was serious since the back crowd stayed quiet for the rest of the ride into school. Tina could feel the heat rolling off the driver as he made his way back to his seat, and felt a bit scared herself. The boys never called her to the back again, but Peter would look at her and grin, and move his fingers and his tongue, grinning at her.

By fourteen, Tina knew what to expect, and went with the boys and men anyway. The girls in her class were aware of her situation and were unkind as a result, and she had no one at home that she could talk to. Laura had tracked her down as often as she could, but Tina had rebuffed her attempts at connection, seeing in Laura nothing but the doorway to foster care. So it went, with Tina finding Peter, and Peter finding Tina to be both pliable and available. Peter liked easy, and his mean streak liked a little bit of nervous in his dates, and Tina, at fourteen, provided both.

Her grades had slipped, falling from the C's she had gotten since letter grades began in the fifth grade to a series of F's, reflecting classes missed, work not turned in, and tests refused in class. While Cora had once kept an eye on the two report cards that came each year, offering a dollar for A's, and the wooden spoon for anything under a C, she no longer looked at the mail, and Tina tossed all school communication into the burn barrel in the front yard.

By fifteen, Tina was seen as something of Peter's, a designation she encouraged. Peter had some scrapes with the law, some fistfights, and Tina could smell bad all over him. Nothing could have suited her more, finding the kind of boy she felt she deserved. In ninth grade, only by the grace of the Orange County school systems "pass 'em on" policy, Tina struggled going to school at all. Peter worked at the granite shed most days, and would sometimes pick Tina up after work, to drive around a bit, and then go park on a back road for a while. Tina cursed her age, living in her parents' trailer, and the other things she believed got in the way of her having a real, full-time relationship with Peter. In reality, Peter took his afternoon pleasures with Tina, then delivered Tina back to her trailer and her parents, and then went back out again, hitting the beer joints along the valley, and seldom leaving alone.

While she was still sixteen, Tina found herself sick in the mornings, throwing up all over her sheets, and had the realization that she felt different. She bought a pregnancy test kit, peed carefully, and watched as the little plus sign turned blue. She sat back down on her bed, the unchanged sheets stiff and sour, and thought about what to do next. She kept the pregnancy to herself and tried to start eating a little healthier, reading what she could find on the internet, and trying to think of how to make this work with Peter. He continued to come by a few times every week, but their time together was spent in some variant of automotive coitus, and very little was ever said.

One afternoon, with Tina stretched out on the back set of Peter's rusty Olds, commanded to hold on to the door handle while he moved his hands over her, he found the hard, new lump on her tiny flat stomach. "What's that?" he asked. Tina explained, through tears, still gripping the door handle as she had been told, and Peter said, "You're shitting me," then grinned. "Guess that makes me a dad," he added, casually pinching her twice, first one side and then the other, hard enough each time to make her cry out.

So, this is the star that Tina hooked her wagon to. The birth of Betts changed Peter very little, but it changed life for Tina. When her pregnancy became obvious to Cora, there was a fight, including some name-calling, and several slaps to Tina's face. Tina walked down the road, already leaning a bit back under the weight of her baby, walking a few miles toward town until a neighbor saw her on the road, picked her up, and drove her to the home of Peter's mother.

Peter's mother was not much better, calling Tina the same names, and accusing her of trying to trap her son. Tina stood her ground, until Peter's rusty Camero rolled into the driveway. Peter and his mother took over the fight, until Peter tipped over a table, and then left with Tina, spinning his tires in the dirt driveway, and then parking the car in one of the side roads he had used before. After some more unpleasant time in the back seat, Peter drove to an uncle's farmhouse and got permission for Tina and himself to camp for a bit in the old RV in the yard.

Tina's new life of nausea, back pain, and remembering to lock the door of the RV against Peter's uncle was worse even than her life with her mother and father. School was no longer an option, and she was now hungry most days, with Peter having the only transportation and money, and seldom remembering to bring anything home except chips and soda and beer. Tina refused a series of deals for food that the uncle suggested to her through the locked door. She worried about her pregnancy, both because of her hunger, and because of the rough treatment, she experienced from Peter. It wasn't easy.

A few months later, Betts was born at the hospital down in Randolph, while Tina and Peter were still living in that RV, where Betts spent her first cold winter with a constant cough and a runny nose. Betts was an easy baby, having learned that making noise was seldom a good idea. Peter showed little interest in her and left things up to Tina. They moved to a single wide trailer in the spring, and Tina found herself pretty isolated, but at least away from Peter's uncle.

Betts grew into a quiet and easy child. Peter was out of the trailer much of the time, keeping up his old pattern of spending some time doing things to Tina, then heading out "for a drive," and not coming back until late, or not at all. Tina tried to keep the trailer neat, and Betts clean, and her temper in control, but often failed at all three. Most days were spent in front of the TV, but there were walks down to the river on the nicer days, with Betts thrilled to be let down onto the leaves and grass.

Betts made it to kindergarten with no apparent damage. She was small for her age, thin and dark and quiet, but there was an eagerness in her eyes that her teacher found could be encouraged by learning. Betts did well in school, blossoming in an environment where her obedience was rewarded, and where books and stories could be found.

As Betts moved from her diapered, milk-scented toddlerhood into the lean body of a young child, Tina saw herself in her daughter. While Betts temperament was nothing like that of her mother, her dark hair and her face, thin, with the almost black eyes and the sharp cheekbones that might have belonged to an Apache, her long thin legs and tiny feet reminded Tina of the unhappy and unlucky child that she had been. Tina had never learned to love herself and struggled to love Betts, with a dread that Betts would grow up to be like her mother.

It was when Betts was seven, that late spring morning when Tina walked into Betts room and had noticed the pinch bruises on Betts flat chest, and then discovered more of the same on her legs and backside. She was intimately familiar with these marks and panicked at the thought that Peter was now getting at Betts. Tina remembered the young Peter on the bus, sitting in the back rows, smirking at her and making crude gestures with his tongue and fingers. She had probably been ten or eleven at the time. She understood that the foundation of her relationship with Peter had always been her willingness to do what she was told, take what was done, and to make herself available. But this was something else.

She looked at Betts, her shirt still off, and tugging her pants back up, her dark eyes trying to see if she was in trouble. Tina said nothing but slapped Betts hard across her face, then stopped, crying angrily while a silent and confused Betts rubbed her hot cheek. Tina then got up and packed a few quick armloads of Betts things into a trash bag. That was the day she drove Betts up Bear Mountain at such speed, handing her young daughter off to her surprised brother. I don't know how Tina explained Betts' absence to Peter that night if Peter came home. I don't know what Peter did when he got home. Tina handled it, somehow, and gave Betts some safety, for that summer, at least.

CHAPTER TWENTY-ONE

Comfort

Tina took the news of her mother's death hard. Ames had stopped by the trailer, on his way back from the Village. He had not seen Tina since she had picked Betts up in the fall, a year and a half ago. Tina came to the door, after a bit of a wait, wearing flannel pajamas and holding a cigarette. "Why are you here?" she asked. Ames said nothing, but stood on the porch, looking troubled. Tina swung the door open and moved toward her brother, her face angry, and she shouted, "Is she OK? What happened to Betts?"

"Betts is fine," he said. "Mom died." His eyes teared up again, and he reached for the porch rail, feeling himself beginning to drift a bit.

Tina leaned into the doorway, took in the breath she had been missing, then let the air out, swore, and then swiped at her eyes. Ames looked up at his sister. She was still furious, as she had been since he had known her. He thought of the years since Clair's death, and the years before, with Tina so angry and always drawn back from those around her. He thought of his family, graveside, at Clair's funeral, while the minister murmured vague comfort, and the neighbors wept and held each other, his family stood apart, not even leaning on each other, not touching even shoulders, but alone.

He saw Tina, crying hot tears that she swiped away before they could wet her cheeks, breathing as if she was choking, and he leaned toward her, reaching to her arm with his hand. She recoiled from his touch as if burned, looked at him with a flash of anger, and the turned back inside the trailer. "I need some time by myself," she said. She closed the door, and he heard the click of the lock.

He stood for a moment, hugged himself against the sudden cold, and then turned, walked down the metal steps and back to his truck. He stood beside the old Ford, laid his hand on the cool steel of the door, feeling the familiar comfort of the things around him, well-kept, and cared for, cleaned and oiled and maintained. And as the cold from the metal settled into his hand, he realized that what he needed was the warm touch of a person who cared that he was sad. He realized how alone he was, and how alone he had been since he could remember, since forever. He looked at his watch, opened the truck door, and headed off to pick Betts up from school.

Inside the trailer, Tina wept hot angry tears as she rubbed her face. The salt and the rough scrape of her hands hurt her face, and so she rubbed all the harder. She was furious at Ames, and said out loud, "Who the hell does he think he is?" She swore, and said this again, slamming her plate off the table, where her toast and broken pottery slid against the far wall. She pulled at the top of her pajamas, wiping her smarting face dry, and said "As if … " ending without either finishing the thought or the words. "As if … " she tried again.

She lit another cigarette, sucked in the smoke, and then looked at the glowing red tip. "Damn!" she said. She wandered through the trailer, kicking at the shoes, magazines, and trash on the floor, arriving in the bathroom, where she saw her red face sputtering in the mirror. She punched the wall beside the mirror, over and over, the mirror and her reflection jumping with every blow, breaking bits of drywall out, and finally leaving some red on the crumbled plaster as her knuckles split. "Fuck!" she said. She sat down hard on the toilet. "Another funeral."

Ames drove back toward town, listening to the faint hum of the snow tires on the wet, patched pavement. The engine purred along, third gear and forty-five being one of the 351's happy spots, and he could hear just the beginnings of a hiss from an exhaust manifold, something he could fix this weekend. Third gear kept the engine up a little higher than a fourth would have, but he loved the rumble of the V-8 as he drove down the road. A bit of wind whistled around the side vent window, and he reached up and moved the latch just enough to pull the window tight. Ames thought of how comforting driving had always been for him, even riding his bike back when he was just a kid.

He thought of how he had avoided going home as a child, staying late at school, at neighborhood jobs, at the river, putting off going home as long as possible, waiting until bedtime before entering the dark and dreary trailer, so filled with anger and grief, and guilt and blame, and isolation. Getting out of the house had been important, getting away from the yelling and the fights as Tina raged against their sullen parents, thinking perhaps that she could force them to see her, to think about her, maybe to care about her. Such fights never ended well, with Tina yelling until she was hit, then yelling at a higher pitch as the blows fell, or the belt whistled down on her. Silence only came when they were all exhausted, with Tina sobbing and swearing on her bed, their father back out in the barnyard, and their mother washing dishes with the crack and bang of plates and pots slapped together in the sink.

Ames had seen it enough and learned to leave before the blows began. He would be out the door and pedaling furiously down the road, even in the dark sometimes. He rode past the farmyards of the neighbors, their quiet houses lit by soft light from inside, down toward town, or down to the river. Ames would pull his bike off the road, lay it beneath the bridge, and sit and watch the dark and powerful water surge and run across the rocks, and around the concrete pillars, moving ever downward toward the sea. Watching the water beneath him was somehow both soothing and scary. In the Spring, when the snow and ice were melting, the flood was strong enough that the bridge itself vibrated from the impact of the rushing water. The roar was so loud that any thoughts he had of the fight at home were washed away, leaving him empty and clean, free of his anger and shame, and ready for a careful ride home in the dark, waiting in the yard to be sure that the fighting had ended.

He saw that Tina was still reacting to loss with anger and that he had continued to run from his feelings, hoping to find solace in being outdoors and in being alone. When he began to fall apart in the Sand Wars, all he could think of was the quiet and peace of the river and the mountains in Vermont, and he rushed back, when he could, with the urgency of a man who had dived too deep, and had run out of air, fighting for the surface. He thought about Tina and wondered where she could find relief. He pulled into the parking lot of Betts' school, and waited for the bell.

Betts picked up on Ames' distress before she had even slid into the truck, of course. She ignored his usual question of, "How was your day?" and asked, "Are you OK?"

Ames slid in beside her but didn't start the truck. "Yeah," he said. "Your grandmother died this morning. I just came back from seeing her. She had a good night," he went on. "She slept a lot the last couple of days, and then they just couldn't wake her up this morning. They called me as soon as I got home." He fished in his pocket for the ring. "She gave you this. It's her wedding ring."

Betts's eyes widened, and she took the ring, taking it out of the little plastic bag and slipping it on her finger, where it was too loose. She moved it to her middle finger, where it seemed to fit well enough. She leaned against him, tipping her face into his chest, crying, and she said, "I'm sorry. You must feel really sad."

"Yeah," Ames said. "I wish I had taken you to see her sooner. She really liked you."

"She loved me," said Betts. "And she loved you, too. And my mom. She just didn't tell anybody." Betts lifted her head. "She's OK now," she said, sounding sure of this.

Ames wondered again at Betts and felt his eyes filling up, and the tears running down his cheeks. "Yeah," he said. "I know." And he did.

The funeral was again graveside, at the same cemetery, with the cast iron arch over the entry that spelled out "Our Loved Ones at Rest." The grass was still wet with the recent rain, and a cool breeze and the few people gathered around the grave shivered and wished they had thought to bring something warmer. Betts stood next to Ames, with Zoey on his other side. Betts leaned into Ames, reaching up to his hand, her other hand in the pocket of her hoodie. Zoey stood close to Ames on the other side, prompting some questioning looks from the neighbors, wondering who this young woman was. Tina stood alone, after rebuffing Betts' attempt, then Ames', saying only, "We're not here for that!" in an angry whisper.

The minister, an old fellow who might well have been the same man who presided over Clair's service, had spoken briefly with Ames and Tina before the service, trying to get a picture of the woman he was about to eulogize. They had little to offer, with Ames saying, "She was our mom, and she worked pretty much all the time. We lived on a dairy farm, and she and my dad took care of the cows. She liked her TV shows. Our sister died when she was only a kid, and mom took that real hard. My dad's already dead. We weren't real close." Tina snorted at that but had nothing to add.

Out of this thin soup, the minister managed quite well, painting a picture of a hard-working farm wife, a busy mother of three who still found time for her children and some of the joys in life. He touched on the difficulties of family life, including hurt feelings and disappointments, and the challenge of balancing work and family. But he spoke of love: the dedication and the daily desire to do the best you can for those you love, of work and caring being love perhaps unspoken, but love being made visible. And he spoke of the ability of grief and loss to bring families together, not just tear them apart. He talked a lot about love, the frightened love hidden in the heart, and love that became brave, and reached out to others. And he spoke of Cora, now loving best, being with the Lord, and with her beloved daughter and husband.

It was a good service, spoken well before such a little crowd, in the cold and damp. Ames felt the truth in the minister's words of comfort, Zoey held Ames' hand and thought about the frightened love that hid in her heart, Betts cried and squeezed his other hand, and Tina wiped at her eyes, with an angry and hurt look on her face. When the service was over, Ames, Betts, and Tina had taken a red rose and a handful of dirt from beside the grave, tossing them both in the hole, on the grey metal casket. When the Minister came to speak with Ames and Tina, Ames thanked him, and shared a hug with this stranger, but Tina had turned away and walked quickly to her car. Betts broke from Ames and ran after her mother, catching her beside the car, where Ames saw Betts reaching out to her mother. Tina pushed Betts hand away, slipped into her car, and drove away. Zoey went toward Betts, but Betts wandered away toward the back wall of the cemetery and sat in the wet grass beside a small concrete lamb marking a child's grave. Zoey returned to Ames and thanked the minister. The neighbors shook Ames' hand, while Zoey stood back, away from the flow, watching the handshakes and brief hugs of the older people who had known this family, so slightly, for so long.

When the last hand was let go, and the last words of care were heard, Ames and Zoey went to where Betts sat. Ames was somehow not surprised to see that Betts sat on the top of a grave marked only with a charity stone, a numbered concrete lamb, worn a bit by the string trimmer after these past sixteen years. This was where Clair was buried. "You OK?" Ames asked.

Betts looked up, her face still wet and a little red. "Yeah," she said. "I wish my mom felt better, though. She's always alone." She stood up and looked at the minister, who was walking toward his car. "He did a good job," she said. "I liked what he said."

"Me, too," said Ames.

"That's where Clair is buried," said Ames.

Betts nodded. "I know." The wind picked up, and a bit of drizzle started to fall. Betts pulled up her hood and took Ames hand. "Can we go back to the cabin, and make some tea? I'll make lunch for us. And put a fire in the little green woodstove."

"That sounds good," said Ames. Ames and Betts took the truck back up the mountain, where Betts sat warm and tight next to Ames all the way. Zoey followed in her Subaru, thinking about all the minister had said, and wondered how brave or how frightened her love would be. Ames thought of how alone Tina was, and how alone he had been, for so long, and how sad it was to have had so many years go by without the warm comfort of human touch.

CHAPTER TWENTY-TWO

Across the Lake

Mrs. Cook, Betts' teacher, drove into school early that Monday morning. She had stewed on Betts all weekend long and had made the decision Sunday night. "Enough is enough," she, and tugged Betts' desk back into line, setting it behind the desk that Cara used, so that the two friends could sit together. She got down on the carpet, and angrily pulled up the red tape, digging with her fingernails to get under the bits of tape that had been stepped into the carpet for the past month. While she was tugging away at the tape, she thought of Mr. Bowman. "To hell with him," she thought. "Asshole." She stood up, happier to be in the classroom than she had been since Betts arrived.

Betts arrived a half-hour later, just before school was to start, and stopped at the door, confused. Her first thought was that she had been thrown out of school. Mrs. Cook stood up and said, "Good morning, Betts. Your desk is behind Cara's. You girls try to not get into trouble by talking." Betts' broad smile replaced the worried look she had, and Mrs. Cook said, loud enough for the class to hear, "I'm sorry, Betts. I should never have had your desk up here. It was a mistake, and I was wrong to go along with it." Betts moved down the aisle to her desk, walking past Cara, who sat looking as if it might be Christmas morning. As Betts sat down, she put her hand on Cara's shoulder, and Cara folded her hand over Betts', for a moment, then the girls got ready for work.

When Ames came to pick Betts up, she was still beaming. He smiled back, and stood beside the door of the truck, letting her slide in first. "Good day?" he asked.

Betts nodded. "Mrs. Cook moved my desk, right behind Cara. I get to sit there for the rest of the year!"

Ames said, "That's good. Zoey will be happy, too." He slipped the truck into gear and pulled out onto the road. "I think we need a celebration," said Ames. "What would you like to do?"

Betts thought about it while the truck drove down the road. "Can we go to Burlington, and invite Zoey, too?" Betts asked.

Ames grinned. "I think that would be great. Let's do it Saturday. How about we take the ferry across the lake into New York, and have lunch there?"

Betts was excited, having never been on a boat at all, or even been out of the state of Vermont. "That will be so cool," she said, grinning out the window.

Zoey came by that evening. Her visit was not a surprise to either Betts or Ames. Zoey had been more and more of a regular guest at the cabin, often showing up with a pizza or two, or a couple of tubs of take-out Chinese food from down in Randolph. Betts was busy building one of the elaborate fairies houses she had begun to construct all over the woods, this one with a waterfront view down by the spring. Ames was under the hood of his truck, checking out the exhaust leak he had fixed earlier, and seeing that the fix was good. "Go tell her," said Ames, as Zoey's car came into view.

Betts ran up, standing beside the door, hopping up and down, saying, "Guess what?"

Zoey had to roll down her window since Betts was standing so close, she couldn't open her door. "What?" she asked.

"Mrs. Cook moved my desk back with the others, right behind Cara's so I get to sit right behind her every day. And we're going to celebrate by going to Burlington this Saturday, with you, for the day, and go over the lake on the boat, and have lunch in New York. And lunch is my treat, 'cause it's my celebration."

Betts was breathless when she finished all of that, and Zoey leaned out of the car and gave Betts a kiss on her cheek. "Congratulations, sweetie! It couldn't happen to a nicer girl."

Betts yelled back to Ames, who was standing a few feet away, "She's coming!" and then danced back to her fairy house.

Zoey climbed out of the car, holding a plastic bag with some ice cream and a box of cones. "Dessert is on me," she said. Ames gave her a hug, something that had been happening since the funeral a couple of weeks before, and Zoey responded by stretching up on her toes and giving him a kiss, something that was still new. This lasted a bit, with Betts looking up at the silence, and watching the two of them kiss. Betts stared for a bit, then blushed and looked back down at her fairy house, glancing up from time to time to see when they might be done. "I feel like I just had dessert," said Ames, after a bit, and Zoey said, "Me, too." Betts stood up and said, "Well, I still want ice cream."

On Saturday, after a glorious week of sitting behind Cara and not getting in trouble once, Betts got up early and took out the toolbox where she kept her syrup money and her woodcutting wages, and the $10 per week she was to get as an allowance. Betts had clipped the bills into stacks worth $100 each, and there were several stacks in the box, as well as some loose bills that did not yet add up to being clipped. She took out a twenty, her book money, and then turned to Ames, who was tending the fire. "How much money should I bring for lunch?" she asked.

Ames thought about it. "I've never been there, so I don't really know. Stuff might be expensive in New York. Fifty would do it, for sure, even if we only found a fancy place." Betts took out three more twenties and tucked them into the back of her wallet, a recent find at the thrift store down in town. It was brown leather; whip stitched along the sides and featured a horse on one side, and a horseshoe on the other, carved into the leather. Betts loved it and had carefully made out an "owner's card" that she carefully filled in with her name and phone number. Ames put the kettle on for tea, and Betts made a trip to the outhouse, and then the top rock, on the lookout for Zoey's car.

She spotted the Subaru a few minutes later and ran down just as Zoey was getting out of her car. Ames came out to greet her as well, with yet another kiss and hug. Betts started counting out loud, "One. Two. Three. Four."

Zoey laughed and broke away from Ames. "Are we bothering you?" she asked.

Betts said, "No, not really. I just don't know what to do while you guys are kissing."

Zoey squatted down a bit, getting on eye level with Betts. "Tell you what. You count in your head, and if it gets to ten, start counting out loud. That sound OK?" Betts thought about it and agreed that that would be fine.

Ames looked embarrassed and followed them into the cabin. "Ten?" he asked. "Why ten?"

Betts made a breakfast of pancakes, and then eggs, using the bigger cast iron skillet. Betts stood beside the little green stove, pouring the batter into the oiled pan, watching the bubbles rise and firm up, then flipping the pancake with the thin metal spatula without hesitation. She fried the eggs as well, asking how Zoey liked hers, then delivering up the "over medium" request perfectly. When six pancakes were done, and six eggs as well, Betts ran some of "Betts Best" through the hot skillet, and then poured the hot syrup into a glass measuring cup, which she placed on the table. The three of them sat down to eat, each with their own mug of tea. The windows were polished the day before, and the whole valley stretched out in a thousand greens, all the way to the mountains in the far distance. "This is pretty perfect," said Ames. "Thank you."

"You're welcome," said Betts. "I want to take the truck," said Betts. "I like it better when we all sit together."

Ames nodded. "Me, too."

Zoey said, "Sounds good. I'll move my car." Betts hated being in the back seat, and when the three of them were in the old Ford, they sat nice and close across the bench seat, all together. Betts liked to keep her hand on Ames' hand while he shifted, and had learned the moves well enough that he sometimes let her shift the truck herself while he drove. She would have her hand on the shifter, and Ames would push in the clutch, and say "second" or "third," and Betts would glide the truck into the next gear. Zoey had dutifully delivered a car seat to the cabin, when Betts had first arrived, since Betts, even at age nine, was still small enough to officially need one. But Zoey ignored the fact that the car seat had stayed on the porch, and that Betts rode without it, sitting on her knees much of the time, in order to see out the windshield. "Car seats make me feel like a baby," she had said. Ames had agreed. "She doesn't ask for much," he'd said.

Ames had cleaned the bed of the truck out the night before, and Betts had done the cab, sweeping out the dirt and sawdust carefully, then doing the glass, inside and out with Windex, and then using the moist rag to dust off the dash. Betts slid into the middle seat, her spot, with Zoey getting in the passenger seat, and Ames sliding in behind the wheel. Betts looked down at the six legs sitting side by side across the worn seat. All dressed in blue denim, her boy jeans not as faded as the loose pair that Ames had on, and not as stylish at the lady's jeans that Zoey wore. Betts liked the look of all those legs there, together, and thought that it would be a nice picture to draw.

Betts always looked for boy jeans now at the Randolph thrift store. Ames pretty much gave her permission to shop as she liked, while he went through the books, after grabbing a couple of tee shirts, or another pair of heavy denim pants. Betts loved this, having never had any say about her clothing before. She had always gotten her clothing from some second cousins, girls never seen, but prone to frilly, fancy and Disney themed outfits. Betts was tired of the thin, tight, stretchy fake denim girl pants, with no usable pockets, pants that were cut so low as to render the zipper barely longer than an inch.

Today, Betts had on her favorite pair of boy jeans, loose and heavy, and gathered at the waist with a beaded leather belt she had recently found, stamped "Texas" on the inside. She wore a faded yellow tee-shirt, with a white and blue sailboat on the front, with the words "No Bad Days at The Lake" written below the boat, a perfect choice, she thought, for this particular trip. The shirt was one of her favorites, anyway, and Betts often put it on, thinking "No Bad Days at The Cabin," an amazing thought that seemed to be true. Black Keds, with low white socks, covered her feet, and a Red Sox cap sat on her head, her dark hair hanging in two braids down the sides. She had her brown leather wallet in her left front pocket, and her pocketknife and some change in her right pocket, and Betts felt that she looked just right. "I look like who I am," she thought.

They parked in a small lot in downtown Burlington, leaving the truck unlocked. Ames could have parked closer to the Old Crow, but both he and Betts enjoyed the walk down the Church Street Mall, where it seemed that everyone in Burlington had gathered. There were tons of college students, lots of families, some with kids around Betts' age, old people, police officers on bicycles, dogs on leashes, musicians playing and singing, their cases open to the hearts of the crowd. There were kiosks selling pizza, ice cream, earrings, tee shirts, wool hats, buttons, and shoes. A carnival atmosphere hung over the mall, and the occasional magician or juggler seemed right at home.

When they came to the Old Crow, Betts went straight to the YA section. Zoey and Ames found her there, her head tipped sideways, her fingers running along the spines of the books, both to mark the place as she looked, and to feel the hardcover cloth and paper slide beneath her fingers, searching for the new books. Ames went to the section on natural history and had pulled out a book named *Owls of New England*. Zoey came and stood beside him, taking his hand in hers. "I love this place!" she said. "I can see why it's a favorite for you and Betts." She eyed the couches and chairs, and the tea station, with the electric kettle of hot water steaming, and the basket of tea bags set out for free. "I didn't know there were any of these places left," she said.

Ames nodded. "There used to be a nice bookstore down in Randolph, but they closed up a few years ago. Not enough people buying books, I guess, and the big chains have pretty much killed off the little guys." He looked at Betts. "She always brings a twenty and spends all of it but some change. If we had more kids like Betts, these shops would do OK."

Zoey looked at the book Ames had. "Owls?" she asked.

"Yeah," said Ames. "We have four different kinds of them up at the cabin. You can see a barred owl pretty easy, but the others are pretty shy. That one we hear at night is the barred owl. And the pellets Betts showed you, with all the little bones buried in the hair? That was from a barn owl that has a nest in that old sugar shack."

Zoey looked at Ames, a man unaware of the World Cup, NASCAR, or the NFL, but he knew his birds, and trees and how things on the mountain lived and worked. She handed him back the book. "Maybe I can borrow it when you're done?" she asked.

"You can read it first if you like," he answered. "I already have a big one on hawks and owls that should take me a while to get through."

Betts came up with a stack of books in her arms, which she again laid out on the table and began to pick through, carefully returning the less favorites to the shelves they came from. The sorting process was slow and painful, and Zoey could see Betts struggle between two books. "Let me buy one for you," suggested Zoey.

Betts looked up. "No, thanks," she said. "I don't need to buy everything I want. Lots of folks can't even buy one book." She put the books she planned to buy off to the side and returned the others. Betts then looked at the prices and added them up as she went along, to make sure she stayed under her twenty-dollar limit.

Ames paid for his book on owls, Zoey bought a book on wildflowers, and Betts paid for her six books, having a little over fifty cents in change. Betts took the offered brown paper bag for her books and carried the owl book and the wildflower book in the bag as well. On the way back to the truck, they passed the bakery kiosk, and Betts offered everyone a snack if they would like. Ames offered to pay, but Betts countered with something from *The Hobbit*, in which Hobbits give presents to the guests on their own birthday. "This is kind of my party," she said. "And I have the money." Betts ordered a bagel, with butter, Ames got a muffin, and Zoey simply had coffee, although she nibbled at Ames' muffin, and got a bite of Betts' bagel as well.

When they got back to the truck, with just a bit of Zoey's coffee remaining, they got in, with Betts taking the top book out of the bag and carefully opening it up on her lap. She was gentle with the book, trying not to open it too wide, and Zoey commented on this. "I love books," Betts said. "I try to look after mine. Getting them wet is the worst. Cara dropped a schoolbook into the bathtub once, and her family had to buy the school a new one. She kept the old one, but it stayed all swelled up, even when it dried." Ames watched her with one eye, reading, and turning the pages, smoothing them out beneath her hand.

"Sometimes you remind me of Clair," he said. "She was real careful with her books, too."

Betts stopped reading. "Tell me about Clair," she said.

Ames paused, then started in. "Everyone else in our family fought. Well, not me, really, but never Clair. Your mom got in fights all the time with our folks, trying to get them to pay attention to us, I guess or buy us stuff she thought we should have. And mom and dad fought, too, over money, mostly. I always ran out and hid somewhere, or rode my bike down to the river. I hated the fights. But Clair would always stay and try to make things better. She brought home funny stories from school, and told jokes, and tried to fix whatever she thought was making people unhappy. In some way, I guess she was able to make it so the family was able to get from one day to the next. When she died, it all pretty much fell apart. Partially 'cause we were all so sad, but mostly because nobody else tried to make things better like she had." Ames said, "Third gear," and Betts shifted the knob up, across, and to the right.

Zoey stared at Betts, and she giggled. "He lets me shift sometimes," she said.

"She slept on the couch a lot, too," Ames continued. "She read all the time, and Tina would get mad about the light being on when she wanted to sleep, so Clair would go back out to the living room, after the folks were in bed, and lay on the couch to read. Sometimes she'd get in trouble if she fell asleep and mom found her out there. But mostly she just read 'til she was sleepy, then came back into our room." Ames thought a little and looked over at Betts. "She didn't look like you, but you and her do a lot of the same things. And her eyes looked like yours, too, sometimes. Not the color, but the caring, or something. I don't know. Kind of deep."

Ames finished up lamely, but Betts nodded. "I understand," she said.

Ames pulled up to where the line of cars waited for the ferry. Zoey had steamed her glasses holding her coffee up too close, and took them off and rubbed them on her tee-shirt. Ames dug for his wallet, and Betts said, "Do you think I can get out of the truck and walk around on the boat?"

Ames said, "Probably. You can ask." There was a woman who had hopped off the ferry, collecting money from each car, and handing each driver a ticket. Ames already had his window down, and when she came to the window, she looked in and gave them a price for one way, and a little less than twice that for a round trip. "Round trip," said Ames, offering her a twenty. She gave him back two dollar bills, which he slipped back into his wallet.

The woman stuck her head in the window a bit, smiling at Betts. "First ride, sweetie?" she asked.

Betts nodded. "Yes, Ma'am. Can I get out and walk around once we're on?"

"Sure," said the woman. "Look me up. I'll give you a little tour."

At the front of the long line of cars, the ferry had unloaded the cars from New York, and they rolled off, heading back toward Burlington. The line they were in began to move forward as cars drove onto the ferry, and as Ames pulled up to the edge of the boat, another woman was directing traffic. She showed Ames where to park his truck, off to the left side, where he would have a perfect view out the window. Once all the cars were on board, the first woman closed the chain across the road, then turned a handle, raising the metal ramp they had driven over and cast off the two giant ropes that held the ferry in place. She motioned to the captain, who was somewhere up in the wheelhouse above the cars, and the ferry began to move out onto the water.

Betts was squirming, so Ames got out, letting her slide past and out onto the steel deck of the ferry. She turned to Ames. "Can I wander a bit?" she asked.

"Sure," said Ames. "Don't fall in." Betts headed off to see the woman who had sold them the ticket, and Zoey slid over next to Ames. "Well, hi there," he said grinning.

During the ride over, Betts managed to have a conversation with both women working the deck of the ferry and a third woman who was up in the wheelhouse, captaining the ship. Betts was invited in, where she had a view of the lake, and the cars and people they were shepherding over the water. The women agreed that working on the ferry in the summer was the best thing and that in the winter, you could at least count on some excitement. The captain let Betts take the wheel for a bit, and one of the blasts on the horn was Betts' work as well, warning off a small boat from the path of the ferry.

As the ferry slowed, nearing the dock on the New York side of the lake, Betts went back down to the truck. Zoey was in Betts' seat, next to Ames. Betts felt a brief flash of jealousy, then smiled. Ames was lonely and needed a grown-up in his life. And Zoey was nice. Betts tapped at the door, and Ames, startled, popped the door open and hopped out to let her in. As Betts took her place, she said, "Oh! My seat's all warm." She then proceeded to tell them all about the women who ran the ferry, the wheelhouse, and the feeling of steering the giant ship.

Port Kent, NY, the little town across the lake from Burlington, proved to be a nice destination. As the ferry docked and was tied in place, and the steel ramp lowered onto New York pavement, Ames started up the old Ford, and moved onto dry land, then up the hill, and on into town. Huge stone houses lined the shore, but up on top, Fort Kent looked a lot like Randolph or Montpelier. Smaller houses were behind the main street strip of shops and cafes, a few gas stations, and one big grocery store. Ames tucked their return ticket into the ashtray, which was half-filled with quarters and a few dollar bills. They found the town parking lot, inserted quarters into a machine until they had bought two hours of parking, then set the little ticket on the dash of the truck, as instructed, locked the truck, and walked back to the main street.

They first spotted a pizza place, then a seedy bar and grill named "Billy's Hot Spot," neither of which seemed suitable. On the next block, they found "Pearl's, A Famous Cafe Devoted to Good Food, Good People, And Pie," the sign proclaimed. "This looks great!" Betts said.

Ames agreed. "Can't go wrong with pie," he said and held the door while they all went in. They took a booth by the window, sliding across the cracked but clean vinyl from the fifties, and were greeted by an older woman in an apron, her hair pinned under a cap, bearing a tray with three glasses of ice water and menus.

"Welcome!" she beamed. "I'm Dot." She set the menus and water out, and then asked, "Did you come across on the ferry?" Betts nodded and told her about driving the ship and blowing the horn. "And it's all women!" she added.

"That sounds wonderful," Dot said. "I thought I hadn't seen you here before. Well, take your time. The soup is broccoli cheese, or black bean and rice. I like the broccoli. We have a delicious spinach pie, and the fish is freshly caught as of this morning. Still kicking when it came in. I'll be back," she promised. She walked away but then turned back. "You have a beautiful family!" she said.

No one said anything. Ames looked a little embarrassed, and Betts was all shiny-eyed. Zoey looked at Betts and said, "You do look like your uncle. You both have a sort of serious beauty." She stopped, as Ames colored up some more.

He laughed. "Well, I can see the beauty in Betts," he said.

Betts smiled but looked down at the menu. "Well, I think that's nice," Betts said. "We feel like a family, and I like that." She looked up. "And I think we're beautiful, 'cause we're nice," she finished.

Zoey got the fish, in spite of Betts comment, "Still kicking? I think that's gross. And fish can't kick, anyways." Ames got a stack of sliced turkey with mashed potatoes and gravy, and Betts had the mac and cheese, not off the kid's menu, but the real one, with a hot roll and some coleslaw. Pie followed, with apple and peach slices being shared back and forth. Their waitress was attentive and wished them well as they left. "That was great!" said Betts. "I like this place. We should come back," she said.

CHAPTER TWENTY-THREE

Three Chairs by The Fire

The ride back from New York was uneventful. Betts sat with her stack of books, looking up from time to time, and thinking about the day, and the possibility of working on the ferry when she grew up. Ames drove easily along the interstate, being passed by every other car on the road, listening to the old Ford purr. And Zoey was quiet. It had been a good day, and she tried to sort out her feelings and thoughts.

She wanted very much to be a part of the beautiful family the waitress had seen. And she thought of the frightened love hidden in her heart, the love that the minister had told her to help be brave, and she thought about her work, this job and the roles she now played. Her time with Ames and Betts no longer felt like work. She had talked with Laura about it, and then with her supervisor. The consensus from these good women had been that the case was going well. Zoey had managed to save Betts after all, and that with Betts freed for adoption, the case would move out of casework and into adoptions, freeing Zoey up from this irregular mix of professional and personal roles.

While her relationship with Ames moved slowly, it was clear that they were now more than friends. Ames lit up when he saw Zoey, and he seemed willing to take the risk of allowing her into his life, bit by bit. And Zoey, so burned in her last relationship, which was really her first, was cautious as well. Betts seemed to bless their relationship as well, sometimes insisting on her place between them, like a cat Zoey had once had, she thought, but Betts also now gave them time to be alone, taking an early shower and bed, or sometimes reading in her porch bedroom, giving Ames and Zoey the cabin or the fire pit, for privacy.

On this evening, when the truck pulled in after the long trip to Burlington, and then Fort Kent, and back home, it was already dark. They had stopped in town for some pizza, which had been eaten in the cab, and Betts took her bag of books and announced plans for a shower and then time to read. "I had a great day," she said, giving Ames a kiss, and then Zoey one as well. "I'm going to go read *The Ghost Girl*." She bounded up to the cabin, leaving Ames and Zoey out under a thousand stars. They stood by the truck, Ames gathering the pizza boxes and cups for the fire, and Zoey with her head tipped up, taking in the brilliant spray of stars across the night sky.

Sometimes there was enough of a moon to read by, but tonight there was only the thinnest sliver, trying to follow where the sun had disappeared behind the mountains to the West. Ames lit the fire with the paper from the truck, and the acrid smell of burning pizza box gave way to the sharp, clean smell of birch, as the white bark lit and licked the wood into flames as well. "Pretty nice day," said Zoey. "Betts is doing so well, it makes up for the rest of my week. I loved seeing her on the boat, running around and talking with the ladies. And I loved being with you, too," she said.

Ames smiled. "It's hard to remember what she was like before when she first came back," he said.

There were now three Adirondack chairs gathered around the fire pit. He had built the first one, three years before, having sat in one while waiting for payment on a local land owner's place. The chair was on the crest of a hill and looked out toward the same valley that Ames saw from his cabin. Ames had worked all day, and was hot and sweaty and very tired, and took up the man on his offer of a jar of ice water and a place to sit for a moment. The chair seemed perfect for doing nothing, and fit Ames to a tee. It leaned back at too much of an angle for Ames to feel attentive, but not so far back as he would fall asleep. The wide, flat arms were just right for a book or his jar of cold water, and when the man returned with the money, Ames surprised himself by asking to borrow the chair for a day, so that he could make a copy of it.

He brought it back to the cabin that night, and in the morning, after tending the stove and making a pot of tea, proceeded to take the chair apart, using the pieces as a pattern to make himself a copy. While the borrowed chair, which had come from the hardware store down in town, was made of pressure-treated wood, with a heavy, two by four frame, Ames chose to make his copy out of yellow pine, a strong and light wood he thought would do well against the elements. He didn't trust the chemicals in PT wood and wanted something he could sand silky smooth, anyway. He bolted his chair together with stove bolts, rather than using screws like the borrowed chair, and when the sanding was done, and the hardware tightened, his copy was solid as a rock, smooth as butter, and light enough that he could carry it with one hand.

He had made a smaller version, in the same way, almost half-sized, when Betts had come up that first summer. Two days after his mother's funeral, the minister's words still echoing in his mind, Ames had built a third chair, sized a bit smaller than his own, for Zoey. He had tapered the top slats just a bit, to give it a more finished look, and to take off a bit of weight, and matched the grain of the southern pines as carefully as he could. It was sanded silky smooth, and set beside his. Zoey had come up, the next night, and Betts had shown her the third chair sitting beside the fire pit, with Ames smiling, and admitting that he had made it for her. She had cried, surprising them both, and given him a hug. She thought it the nicest gift she had ever received, and when she was at work, especially when the work was hard, she thought of her chair, and her mug, waiting for her up on the mountain, rather than her apartment in town.

They sat, side by side, watching the fire, and the stars overhead. Betts emerged, still dressed, but sleepy, holding the lantern and making for the outhouse. The lantern laid a pool of yellow light out on the ground around her, and kept the light out of her eyes, letting her see the beautiful stars as well. She stood beside them for a moment, looking up, and then sighed in contentment. "*The Ghost Girl* is really good," she said. "Kind of gripping, really." She headed off to the outhouse, and the yellow light from the lantern disappeared into the little cedar house.

When she came back out, Ames asked her, "Did you flush?"

Betts laughed and stood behind him and tapped his head. "You're starting to make jokes," she said. "That's something new!" She said goodnight, and wandered back to the cabin, looking up at the stars as she went.

The stars were a million points of clean, white light, spread across the perfect black velvet of a Vermont country sky. High above, a single jet had moved silently across, and was just disappearing in the west as the faint roar of its engines came up in the east. "I like that," said Ames. "How fast do you have to be going to be already gone by the time your sound comes along?"

They sat, holding hands, listening to the sounds of the jets pass overhead. Zoey pointed out a satellite, moving across the sky, looking just like a star gone adrift. Ames thought of the melt out in the spring when the first bits of ice began to go, and the soft trickles of liquid water were first heard after the long-frozen winter. That first trickle, letting the world know that spring was on its way, regardless of how many disappointing and freezing nights might interfere, that spring would come, and the world would again come to life and become green. Zoey's hand on his gave a warmth that moved up his arm, and into his heart, bringing feeling back into his body and spirit, thickening his breath, and awakening his heart with hope.

They were startled by a series of shrieks from the cabin, with Ames springing up, knocking his chair over, and stumbling through the dark to the cabin door. Zoey followed as quickly as she could. Betts had left a lantern on the porch, and in that glow, Ames found Betts on her couch bed, crying and curled up in the comforter, which she clutched with both hands. He moved slowly now, sitting on the edge of the table, and reaching for her shoulder, touching it just a bit. "Betts?" he asked. "Are you OK?"

Betts shivered away from his touch, then opened her eyes and looked at him, slowly coming back to the world. Her breathing was quick and shallow, and she looked pale and tiny in the faint light. "I had a dream," she said. Zoey had come into the cabin and sat down beside Ames. Her first instinct had been to rush to Betts and hold her in a big hug, but she watched Ames keeping his distance, and remembered that Betts didn't do too well with a lot of physical contact. Betts gave an embarrassed smile. "Sorry," she whispered. "I had a dream that felt so real...and I woke up and yelled before I knew it was a dream."

Ames sat quietly beside her and waited. Finally, he said, "What would you like?" Betts said nothing. Ames said, "Would you like to come outside with us and look at the stars? You could just bring your blanket."

Betts thought about that, but said, "No, I'll stay in. Could I have some tea, though?" Ames got up and filled the kettle, then set it on the gas stove. He lit it with a wooden match, and the sharp smell filled the cabin.

Zoey watched him work, steady and quiet, and then turned and saw Betts watching her. Zoey smiled. "What were you reading?" she asked.

Zoey saw the stack of books beside the table, and Betts picked up the one on the top. "I'm almost done," Betts said. "I read pretty quick, but if it's a book I really like, I go back and read it over again. Three times, maybe." She handed the book to Zoey, who looked at the covers, front and back. The cover showed a young girl from the back, looking down on a log cabin, far below.

There was a large dog beside her, and they seemed to watch a family who was outside the cabin.

"The girl," started Betts, "she's Sarah, and the Indians killed her family, and she's the only one who got away, and she got lost in the woods, with her dog, Jack. She lives alone out in the woods for a long time, catching fish, and Jack is killing rabbits that he brings back, and she cooks them over a campfire, and they eat apples and roots and things. And she makes a little shelter out of branches that's all hidden, and dry, and she has a few things from her family in there, like a picture of her mother and father when they got married. And then she finds this other family, but she worries that they won't like her, or they won't like Jack, and so she stays away but keeps watching them, 'cause she's lonely sometimes and misses having a family.

"And one time, when she was watching, she saw Amy, she's like three or four, go down by the river and fall in, and so she has to run down and save her. When Amy gets back to her family, she tells them about the girl that saved her, and the dad goes down to the river, to look. But since Sarah stayed in the water, he can only see Amy's footprints. So the family think that Sarah is an angel who looks after them. Amy tries to tell them that it's a real girl, but they don't believe her." Betts paused, looking a little embarrassed.

"It sounds like a good book," Zoey said. "Do you think Sarah will go down and join them, or keep living by herself?"

Betts nodded. "That's what I wondered. She wants to, because she's lonely, sometimes, but it's hard, 'cause she's been off by herself for so long. I think maybe it's too late for her to go back to being somebody's little girl."

Betts looked so sad as she said this that Zoey wished she hadn't asked the question. "Let me know when you find out how it ends," she said.

Ames had made a pot of Sleepy Time tea, from the green box with the sleeping bear on the cover. He and Betts called it Bear Tea, which had confused Zoey when she first came. Ames poured a cup for Betts, and handed a steaming cup to Zoey as well, then poured one for himself. Zoey took the cup and held it close, in front of her face, letting the steam drift up into her nose. She smiled. "This smells like flowers in the woods. And mint."

Ames nodded. "You're right," he said. "It's chamomile, spearmint and rose hips, all of which you can find in the woods. We like it for bedtime, and the chamomile is kind of relaxing, if you've had, like, a nightmare or something. We usually have a pot every night, just before bed, while we read." Zoey tried to picture the quiet nights at the cabin, with Betts on the couch and Ames in his chair, both of them reading, with the scent of Sleepy Time in the air.

Zoey was tempted to ask about the dream but chose to follow Ames lead, and she said nothing. "Now I need to pee," laughed Betts. "This tea does that to you." She took a lantern from the porch and walked back out to the outhouse.

Zoey turned to Ames and said, "You're really good with her. You seem to know just what to do when she's upset."

Ames looked confused. "I don't really do much of anything. She doesn't like to be touched a whole lot, and I figure she'll talk about stuff when she feels ready. She kind of likes to be on her own, somehow, as she figures this stuff out."

Zoey looked down at the book on the table, and the girl hidden on the top of the mountain, watching the family below. "I'm glad she has you," Zoey said.

"Me, too," said Ames.

CHAPTER TWENTY-FOUR

Emma Green and Toby

Zoey made it in early to work the next day, and worked her way back, to Laura's office, carrying a bag of bite-sized Hershey's bars as an offering. She knocked on the open door and entered. "Uh, oh," said Laura. "You're bringing me a bag of chocolate. That must mean something's up."

Zoey grinned. "I figured I must owe you at least a bag at this point," she laughed. "I was up at Ames' place last night, and Betts had a nightmare. I wondered about getting her back into therapy. What do you think?"

Laura opened the bag and selected a crunchy little chocolate bar. She unwrapped it, and bit off half, closing her eyes and chewing slowly. "I love these little things," she said. "Therapy. All kids in treatment foster care are supposed to have it. Betts, too, of course. The problem is that in this whole area, there are only two therapists worth spit for most kids, and they're booked way out in advance. She's doing well, and I can understand your reluctance to get her in with someone who might just make her upset." Laura ate the other half of the chocolate. When it was gone, she looked up at Zoey. "What was the dream about?" Zoey explained that she had not asked, and Betts had not volunteered.

Laura thought about that. "Sounds like Ames knows what he's doing. So. You sleeping up there or something?" Laura had a twinkle in her eye, but Zoey blushed and looked uncomfortable. "Not that it's any of my business," added Laura.

"No," replied Zoey. "I was just up there for the evening, sitting out by the fire. Betts had gone to bed inside, and she woke up screaming. We had a nice day, though. We went up to Burlington, then took the ferry across the lake and had lunch in the little town on the other side. Betts was great and set herself up for a job later on running the ferry. Did you know that it's all women running that thing?"

Laura nodded. "I heard that after a lot of "boys will be boys" crap, the women all got on the same ferry, and things have been fine ever since." Laura pulled a card out of her desk and handed it to Zoey. "Emma Green, Family Services, on River Street. She's good, not pushy, and has a good handle on the trauma thing. She's always booked, but she might work Betts in for cancelations if you brought her a big bag of chocolate. She keeps a cat in her office. Big old striped thing, kinda spooky, I think. They only let her do it because she's so good with the kids." Zoey put the card in her purse and took another piece of chocolate.

"You liking this Ames boy?" said Laura, with a wicked grin.

"Arrrggh! You sound like my mom. Only in a good way," Zoey laughed. "Yes, I am liking this Ames boy. I thought I was about done in that department. But he's quiet and nice, and I don't know, he feels safe and real and solid, somehow. I love watching him with Betts. He's perfect with her, not really doing much of anything, but being there, sturdy, and quiet, and she knows he's there, and that helps her. It's hard to describe, but it works. For her. And for me."

Laura smiled. "I've liked Ames since he was a little boy. I'm glad for you two. You three, actually. How's Tina doing?" Laura asked.

Zoey looked up. "She's angry, defensive, and pretty clear that she doesn't want Betts back. She no-shows her appointments, and won't even come to the door when I go out. I think she'll go for the termination without fighting it. But somehow, I wish she'd fight a little bit more. She's giving in so easy, it's like she doesn't care anything about Betts at all."

"Maybe," said Laura. "I'll bet there's more to it than that. Where does Peter figure in all of this?"

Zoey stopped to think about it. "I don't know," she said. "I'd fight harder than that to keep a kid like Betts. And if it were Betts or Peter, I'd never choose Peter."

Laura looked at Zoey. "Yeah. But you're not Tina. She's been with Peter since she was about fourteen, I think, and he was maybe twenty or so. She pretty much anchored herself to him and has been with him ever since. She probably thinks that he's all she'll ever have. I don't get it, but then, I'm not Tina, either."

"The court date is coming up," said Zoey. "I need to talk with Betts about it. And Ames."

"That's another good reason to get her in to see Emma," said Laura, "and then maybe the three of you can work out what Betts wants to happen. We always see these things from our point of view, and we usually miss the kid's take on things. Let's not do that this time. Emma will be great for Betts."

As Zoey got up to go, Laura offered her the bag of chocolate back, but Zoey declined. "You keep it. That way I won't feel so guilty when I come back down for another visit. Thank you," she said.

Laura took the bag back and put it in her desk. "My pleasure," she said. "Try to spend some time with Emma. You'll like her." Zoey smiled and walked out the door, back down the hall, and to her own office and desk. She looked outside, and the sky was grey. It looked like more rain.

Betts' first appointment with Emma Green happened the following week. Betts was less than enthusiastic, arguing at first that she had already had therapy at the hospital, and at Children's Retreat, the yearlong program she had been in. "Group therapy. Individual Therapy. Family Therapy. Recreational Therapy. Movement Therapy. Stuff I never heard of. I already had them." When this didn't work, she suggested that she didn't need therapy, because she would just stop having the nightmares. "I didn't even have one last night!"

"Give her three sessions," said Zoey. "If you don't like it, then you don't have to go back."

Family Services was housed in a small Victorian house, near Randolph's downtown. There were three therapists there, their names and initials hanging below the main sign in the yard. The waiting room was tiny, in what might have been the parlor of the house, holding a desk, three file cabinets, a large fish tank, and some folding chairs along one wall. Magazines, including some for kids, were spilled across the low table in front of the chairs. While Zoey and Ames went to the desk, and began filling out the paperwork, Betts wandered to the fish tank and pressed her face against the glass, first on one side, and then the others. After a few minutes, she announced, "There are no fish," loudly enough that the man at the desk could hear her.

"You're just not looking hard enough," he replied, not looking up from his work on a computer.

Betts was annoyed by this, embarrassed to have her words for Ames and Zoey intercepted by the man at the desk, and irritated to be told she wasn't looking hard enough. She returned to the tank, looking again into every corner of the empty tank, the clean water, and spotless glass giving her no reason to believe she had missed something. Then out of a plaster castle in one corner, a snake-like creature came gliding out, black and white, about the size of a pencil, taking two passes in front of Betts as if to make sure she saw it. Then a second one emerged as well, swimming around in the tank for a bit, then the two of them disappeared back into the castle. Betts turned back to find the man at the desk smiling at her as if he had successfully played a trick. "What are those?" she asked.

"Fish," he replied.

Before Betts could come back at that, Emma Green walked in, going to Betts and extending her hand. "Did you find our boys?" she asked.

Betts nodded. "Are there only two?"

"As far as I know," said Emma. She turned to Betts. "I'm Emma Green." Betts took the hand, and introduced herself as well, and then Emma went to Ames and Zoey, finding Ames with a book he had brought on aquatic insects, and Zoey looking through the magazines. "Hi. I'm Emma Green. I'd like to meet with Betts today, and then have you in for a few minutes during our next session." Ames and Zoey introduced themselves, and Betts and Emma went back down the hallway, disappearing behind a door with Emma's name on it.

Emma's room had most of the therapy stuff that Betts had seen before, including a table with a flat tub of sand, and about a thousand little people and creatures and tools and houses and trees and fish and weapons and animals of every kind, all stored on a wall of narrow shelves a few inches apart. Betts had seen this kind of set up before, as well as the basket of puppets, the dollhouse, the family of dolls, sometimes with a nasty surprise, and an art station, with paper on a big roll, and paints, crayons, and pencils all neatly arranged. Betts was tempted by the art station, but then, she saw the cat. Huge, the size of a medium dog, grey and black striped, with great golden eyes and a thick, twisting tail. He was sitting on the desk, looking right at her, right into her, really, and his mouth opened just a bit as if he had whispered, "Hi." Betts stood in the doorway, staring at the cat, until Emma finally said, "You can come in. His name is Toby, and he seems to want to meet you."

Betts had almost no experience with pets, with the exception of having spent some time sitting in the dirt next to the board fence beside the trailer, talking to the unseen dog on the other side. She had read about pets, of course, most recently the dog in *Ghost Girl*. She had been around cats and dogs in the flurry of foster homes she had blown through, but the pets had shied away from the angry whirlwind that Betts was back then. This cat seemed really different. He stared at her with his great gold eyes, and seemed somehow to know her or maybe understand her. He stayed rock steady as she approached, her hand out, his tail the only moving part, his eyes focused intently on her, and his mouth open just the tiniest bit. "Hi," he said. Betts stopped and stared, and then looked at Emma, who was at her desk, doing something to the phone. "Hi," he said again.

Betts turned to look at Emma, who was at her desk. Betts turned back to the cat, who continued to look at her with his huge, gold eyes. Emma came from her desk and stood beside Betts, and gave Toby a soft scratch behind the ears, eliciting a soft purr. He leaned up against Emma's hand. "Your cat," started Betts.

"His name's Toby," Emma said. "Find a seat you like, and then tell me why you're here."

Betts looked back at the cat, who was now purring softly and looking right back at her. He seemed to be smirking, somehow. Betts doubted herself, thinking she might have imagined the cat's voice, and sat down on an old wing chair, a little like the one Ames had back in the cabin. She looked at Emma, sitting on the couch across from her. "Your cat ... talks?" asked Betts.

Emma looked at Betts and then shook her head. "I don't think so," said Emma. "He purrs nicely, though." Toby closed one eye slowly at Betts, giving her the feeling he was winking at her.

Betts leaned back in the chair, feeling irritated at the cat, who seemed intent on bothering her. "I live with my uncle," she started. Betts told the story of her first summer with Ames, her time back at her mother's house. She told about the belt marks the teacher had found on her arms in school, and the school nurse and the social worker having her take her clothes off in the nurse's office, then about the police car, and the foster homes. She made sure to tell about biting the foster mom, and the nurse, and her being scared, and then the hospitals, and then being back with Ames. She talked some about the cabin, the woodstove and the spring, and the work with Ames, and the trip to Burlington and New York.

Betts told this version of her story clearly, and without much drama. This life was the only life Betts had known, first hand, and it seemed a normal life to her. The lives of the children in the books she read were often more dramatic than her own, with wonderful things, and often terrible things, happening to them that made her own history seem unspectacular and maybe even plain. Emma listened to the story without a sound, her eyes on Betts most of the time, drifting down to her cup of tea from time to time, or even out the window, but listening sharply, the whole time. Toby listened as well, his eyes half-closed, but his attention focused on her.

Betts stopped, surprised at how much of her story had come out, and that Emma had listened the whole time, and now knew these things about her. She had said nothing about the secret stuff, partially because she really had no words or ways to explain what had happened, even to herself. She also stopped to think that nothing she had told Emma was especially interesting or exciting, except maybe the part about biting the foster mom, and then the nurse. And she felt ashamed of it, not proud at all.

Emma had listened without a sound, and said nothing at this point, either. She sat and sipped her tea, not waiting, but simply being there. Toby lay on the desk, his eyes closed, except for one eye that seemed to be open just the tiniest sliver, watching her across the room. She felt he had listened to her story, and was only waiting for the rest of it. As the silence grew, Betts felt a bit at home, with the quiet and the cups of tea, and the sense that you could be with someone without saying a word. And she felt that Emma was with her, somehow. And Toby, too.

Emma rose and refilled her cup, rubbed Toby's shoulders for a bit, and then looked out the window again. "What do you like to do?" she asked.

Betts took a moment to get her attention off the cat and think about the question. "I like to read," she said. "I like to be outside. Ames does most of his work outside, and I like to work with him. We cut trees and stuff. Firewood. We made syrup this past spring. The cabin is on the side of a mountain, on Bear Mountain, in Brookfield, and there's a spring that feeds into a little stream." As Betts fell into the familiar memories of her current life, her shame and embarrassment about her story began to fall away. Betts told Emma about Zoey, about the Old Crow Bookstore, the trip on the ferry, and all the books she now had, her school, and her desk being moved, and Cara, and the little green woodstove, and making tea, and her cup with the moose on it, and sleeping on the couch every night, and even the outhouse. As Betts described her life, now, she realized that this life sounded pretty nice and that she sounded like the sort of kid people would like. Which maybe she was.

Betts finished for a bit, and Emma looked up, and then said, "It sounds like when you first went into foster care, you were really upset, and that now, you're only upset sometimes, mostly when you have bad dreams or get frightened about stuff that used to happen." Betts nodded and waited. "What do you think is different now?" Emma asked.

Betts thought that the easy answer would be about going to live with Ames. That answer would be true, but not completely true, because before she had lived with Ames the second time, there had been something else that had helped her to be OK when she no longer felt trapped and alone. Betts tried to explain this, starting with Ames and the cabin, when she was first there for the summer, and then when she went back, but she realized that some of the comfort she had found came not from Ames, but from Rebekah. She stopped, panicked at the idea of revealing the blond girl who had become her companion and her guide to safety.

Emma, who it seemed had been paying only casual attention, picked up the sudden tension in Betts voice and breathing, and waited. When Betts said nothing, Emma said, "So something happened, but you don't know if you want to talk about it, yet?" Betts nodded. "That's OK," said Emma. "No rush and not everything needs to be said. You'll know what you want to say and do for each time you're here. Just trust your own instincts about it. You did a wonderful job today. I feel like I'm getting to know a little bit about you. I'll find you a slot for next week, and call your uncle and let him know when to come back. I'll get you a regular slot as soon as I can, but for now, you'll come in when there's an opening. But I will get you in every week, regardless."

Emma got up for the couch, and Betts rose from the chair. Even Toby got up, stretching on the desk, his claws clicking on the slick top. He was staring at Betts again, and she could feel his eyes on her. She moved toward him, and he lowered his head as an invitation. Betts rubbed his neck and shoulders while Toby purred. Betts said, "Bye, Toby." When Toby said, "Bye, Betts," she wasn't even surprised.

Ames and Zoey were in the waiting room, getting up as Betts and Emma came in. "How'd it go?" asked Zoey.

"Good," said Betts.

Emma turned to Ames. "I'll call you for a slot next week," she said, smiling, and then walked back to her office.

Betts looked at the fish tank, which appeared empty again. As she went through the door, which Ames held, she said, "I really like her cat."

Betts was quiet on the ride home, and both Ames and Zoey were quiet as well. Betts was thinking a lot about the session. That cat had her stumped. When you had been locked up on the children's psychiatric unit for over a year and treated as if you were certified crazy by everyone around you, and you had a little friend who came and whisked you away from time to time, and you're only nine years old, you might question your own sanity. But Betts somehow knew she was OK. And if the cat seemed to be talking to her, he probably was. The thing that was hard to sort out was the thing she couldn't talk about.

Betts experience with Rebekah, which both comforted her, and disturbed her, was never spoken of. It was one of the two big secrets, along with her abuse by Peter, and later, a night shift staff named Eddy at the Retreat. As the events of trauma no longer occurred in Betts' life, her new life, and only the scars of trauma remained, Betts no longer needed the safety of Rebekah, standing by that magic door, brushing the curtains aside and inviting Betts away, to the cabin, to the sea, to the great library. But Rebekah came, anyway, seeming to enjoy her time with Betts, and maybe even to need it as well.

Betts had had Rebekah in her life for over two years at this point, and Rebekah seemed to age along with Betts, seldom wearing the satin dress she had first appeared in, but now wearing the same jeans and tee shirts that Betts wore herself. Rebekah was interested in Ames and spoke as if she knew him. She was also interested in Betts' mother, Tina, and shared Betts' worry about Tina's safety in living with Peter in the trailer. Sometimes Rebekah would comfort Betts when she worried, saying, "Tina's fine. Peter's not even home now," as if she knew.

Betts thought that her experience of Rebekah might be the best evidence that she was crazy, a terrifying idea she had resisted even in the face of five diagnoses, regular medication from the fingers of nurses, and the locked steel doors she had spent over a year behind. She had wondered if her mother was crazy, and wondered if Peter was crazy, or just evil. Out of all the crazy that filled her first house, how could she be otherwise?

There were more nights like that, with Tina at work and Peter at home, and Betts finding Rebekah and going to the cabin. This was a comfort, a safety, a hiding place, and a secret friend. But it was a worry as well, for Betts found this girl at the door more and more often, and travel with her more easy. Betts found herself somewhere away more and more often. By the time Betts was in the Children's Retreat, the door was propped open wide, and Betts' hands had merely to brush aside the torn curtains between what was real and what was something else, and be gone.

Often Often Betts went to the cabin, and tea, and the little green woodstove, but sometimes she traveled to the deep and cushioned seats of a great library, where Betts' tea cup with the moose sat waiting for her. Sometimes there was a great striped cat in the library, who spoke softly to Betts, and came and went as he pleased. And after a while, Betts could feel some bits of Rebekah with her, and in her, even when life was calm and good, even after she had returned, for real, to live with Ames in his cabin on the mountain. She feared that telling about Rebekah would break the spell, and the blond girl who had somehow kept her safe, and as sane as she was, would disappear. Life with Rebekah was puzzling, worrisome at times. But the idea of life without Rebekah seemed hard, too.

CHAPTER TWENTY-FIVE

Summer in Vermont

Summer might be the best time of year for those trapped in school for nine months, and Vermont might well be the best place to have summer happen. Summer is so much more democratic than the winter is. Camping, in Maine, if you have money, and in the back yard if you don't, swimming in the ponds and lakes and rivers, canoeing, fishing, biking and hiking, three months of outside frenzy for the kids, and even the grown-ups sneak out in the evenings and on the weekends. Summer here in the Green Mountains is short, lining up pretty close to the very days the kids have off from school, so there is a healthy sense of urgency about it. People start swimming when the water is still cold enough for happy trout, and reluctantly put away their suits when the first of the fall colors are seen, and the chilling water makes breathing almost impossible. Even the folks who retire down to Florida tend to come sneaking back in the summertime.

Betts started her second summer at the cabin, still in the glow of successfully having completed third grade with all "A"s, and having won back her place in the class. Although nothing was yet promised, Betts felt secure at the cabin and assumed she would live here with Ames for the foreseeable future. Betts rose early, one of the benefits of her couch bed being under two east-facing windows that brought the morning sun onto her face, at just a bit after five in the morning on those lovely, longest days of the season. The little green woodstove was cleaned out, dusted off and oiled, waiting for September, and tea was made on the gas stove, an easy enough affair.

Ames and Betts took a weekly trip to the town library, and she had talked the librarian into allowing her to exceed the limit of five books at a time, and so there was plenty of reading material, and several places to read, including Betts morning favorite, the top rock. The view extends some eighty miles to the south if the fog in the valley was not painting a seascape where there should be green fields and trees. Betts could see the small towns gathered along Rt. 12, Randolph, their home base, then Bethel, then South Royalton, then on down to White River Junction, where the White spilled into the great Connecticut. To the east lay New Hampshire, and the White Mountains, tall peaks that earned their name by holding their snow long into the summer. Far to the south lay Killington and Pico, cut with downhill ski trails, and a bit off to the east, on a very clear day, the top of Mount Monadnock, which had called the poets out of Boston a hundred years ago. Betts had been to the White Mountains, visited Killington on a school ski trip, and climbed Mount Monadnock with Ames, so the view from the top rock was familiar in the best way.

Betts brought a cup of tea, and a faded green metal thermos filled with the rest of the pot, and could comfortably camp out here for hours at a time. Ames would rise by six usually, but he was content to make another pot of tea, and start his day alone, leaving Betts to her hilltop reveries. When she was ready, Betts would descend, breakfast would be made, and they would eat together at the table, planning the day. Summer meant summer people, with their park-like expectations for their large, unproductive tracts of land, calling Ames for his services in clearing out the casualties of winter, old trees, often huge and rotten to the core, falling back onto the ground from which they had sprung three hundred years ago. These jobs paid well, and Ames' reputation as an artist, who left only low stumps and neat brush piles behind, made him desirable for those who wished their land to look perfect, and who were used to paying well for what they desired. This kind of work was dangerous, and Ames had little competition from the other loggers in the area, who preferred steadier and less risky work.

Ames was already a rich man, in that he spent less than he earned, and he was able to choose between jobs, selecting those closest to home, with a preference to being near the cabin, and a sense of loyalty to those who were his neighbors. Betts went along on the jobs, at first reading in the truck, or staying within calling distance and staying out of the fall line while Ames worked, then exploring the woods. Betts watched Ames work, and soon joined him, handling much of the smaller material that came off of Ames' saw, building sturdy brush piles, or stacking the truck with the smaller rounds that she could lift.

Her work on the job site was steady and solid. She had asked for a set of leather gloves, like the ones that Ames wore, and he had finally found them in her size on the Internet down at the library and ordered them for her. They were soon stained and worn, just like his. One of her tasks was to gather the small branches that Ames cut from a fallen tree, wood too small to be of use for man, and to build a tight, rounded stack along the edges of the woods, providing a shelter for the animals from the weather, and from those that might see them as prey.

Ames showed her how to make the stack, the cuts all to the inside, the fine end branches interlaced around the outside, locking the stack, and shedding some rain and snow from a dryer protected center. These brush piles were a sign of Ames work, and he had shown her some he had made a few years before, still tall and sturdy, with tracks around them showing the value they had for the wildlife. The smaller rounds she carried and stacked in the truck, allowing Ames to keep on with the saw. She wore cutoff jeans, a tee-shirt, her gloves, of course, her Red Sox cap, and a pair of decent leather hiking boots that Ames had had to order as well. She and Ames looked like a team, working steadily and silently in the woods, both thin and dark, and both covered with dirt and chips of wood. Betts smiled when she thought about that.

When Ames was working with the big rounds, and there was no work for her to do, Betts took off to explore, looking for birds, animals, and plants that she had not seen before, and seeking the springs that dotted the Vermont hillsides. This desire to find the beginnings, tracking the small streams back to their source, the spot where Earth gave back her water that she had held for so long, was almost a religious quest for Betts. When she would find the spring, often hidden under leaves and branches, she would clear the debris with her hands, clearing the water and opening a clean flow down the hillside. She would turn a nondescript boggy place in the woods into a thing of magic and beauty, a tiny pool of clear water, edged with stones, and icy cold, ready for those who might thirst in the woods.

She had once placed a mug over a sharpened stick she drove into the ground at the side of a pool, an invitation for visitors of the human variety to her spring. She liked the idea of this well enough to have bought mug after mug at the thrift store, for ten cents apiece, and had placed several in the woods where Ames worked, a gift for strangers who might chance upon her work, and that of God. She knew that the woodland animals would seek the spring as well, and had been pleased to find several sets of tracks showing her springs to be important to mice, chipmunks, birds, woodchucks, and foxes.

Ames was paid well for this work, taking in two hundred dollars or more for a full day, and he shared out a third of that to Betts, in addition to the ten dollars per week allowance that the State of Vermont provided for her. Betts now kept her money in a heavy metal toolbox she had found at the thrift store, stacking the bills at first by twenty dollars, then giving up and making one-hundred-dollar stacks, binding the stacks with a rubber band, and laying them side by side in the bottom of the toolbox. Change and bills less than enough for a stack stayed in the tray on top, and Betts locked the toolbox with a padlock from the hardware store. She tied a string to one key, and tucked it into a pocket of her backpack, and gave the other to Ames, both so that he would not feel she had locked the box against him, and in fear that she might lose her key and have to ruin the lock with a saw.

By the middle of the summer, Betts had earned and saved almost a thousand dollars, the stacks of bills filling a third of the bottom of the toolbox. She decided to go shopping for a present for her mother. Betts brought up the idea when Zoey was there for a visit, during dinner. Zoey had brought a brown paper bag half-filled with ears of corn she had picked on the way up to the cabin. She had called from the farm, telling Ames to put on a big pot of water to boil, and had rushed from her car, holding the paper bag in front of her, calling to Betts to help her with shucking the corn. She showed Betts how to tear back the leaves and strip the silks from the fresh yellow and white kernels.

Betts had made brownies earlier in the day, and Ames had cut up a chicken, dusting the pieces in flour and pepper and a bit of garlic salt, frying them in a cast-iron skillet half-filled with oil. Betts brought in a watermelon that she had put to cool by the spring, and the three of them had quite the feast on the picnic table near the fire pit. They filled their plates, and set to eating, with the only sound chewing and their slight noises of pleasure. After Betts had finished her first piece of chicken, and her first ear of corn, she looked up and spoke to Zoey. "I want to buy my mother a present. I have the money saved up, and I have an idea of what she would like. I know I can't go see her, but I thought that maybe you would take it to her when you go for a visit."

Zoey chewed on the chicken in her mouth, took a sip of tea, and then swallowed, wiping her mouth and fingers with a piece of paper towel. "Well," she started, and then quit. She took another drink of tea, and then said, "What would you like to get her?"

"I want to get her a music box, kind of like the one in the book I just read. The mother has a music box with a song on it from her wedding, and she plays it whenever she feels sad. And she feels better. She winds it up on the bottom, then opens the lid, and it plays music. I want to get her something like that."

Zoey was quiet, thinking before she said anything, and Betts, quick to pick up on anyone's worries, got nervous. "Is that OK?" she asked. "Can I get her something? I know she doesn't come to the visits, but I'd still like to get her a present, and I think she'd like a music box." Betts was a quiet kid who seldom asked for anything. Ames was used to simply saying, "Sure," if she did ask, and they would go shopping for what she wanted, once a magnifying glass, some paper for drawing, and once a journal, which she wrote in from time to time, and kept in the bottom of her toolbox.

Zoey had been the one Betts had asked, but she looked stuck, so Ames said, "Sure. You can do that. I don't know where to get a music box, though."

Zoey found her voice. "There's a store down in West Leb that sells music boxes, but I think they cost quite a bit."

She hesitated, and Betts said, "I have a bunch of money from the syrup, and the tree work, and I hardly ever spend anything. So, do you think that would be OK?" It was clear that Betts wanted Zoey's approval on this, even after getting permission from Ames. Betts was afraid that her reaching out to her mom would hurt Zoey somehow, and now that seemed to her to be the case. Zoey, however, worried that Betts might be the one getting hurt, if the music box was an attempt to get her mom to show up for the visits, after all this time. Betts was just a few weeks away from getting freed up for adoption, and Zoey had already made the referral for Betts' case to be transferred to the adoption worker.

Zoey spoke. "I'm worried that your mom might think that a gift like that meant that you wanted her back in your life."

Betts looked surprised. "I do want her back in my life. She's my mom. I don't want to live with her anymore. I want to live with Ames. But I don't want her to disappear, either. I want to keep seeing her, and if she knows that, she'll want that, too." Zoey said nothing, and Betts continued. "I want to give her the music box. And it's my money." There was an edge now to Betts's voice, and she set her hands on the table.

Zoey stared. "OK," she said. "It's fine by me. I just don't want you to get hurt."

Betts saw how unhappy Zoey was. "I'm sorry," she said. "I don't want to be mean. But I thought about this a lot, and I think it's the right thing to do."

Ames smiled at her. "I think it's fine. I bet she'd love a music box." Zoey said nothing.

After Betts had gone to bed, and Ames and Zoey were sitting by the fire pit, watching the fire and the stars overhead, Zoey brought up Betts plans for the present again. "We're just about to do a termination of parental rights, and move Betts from foster care into adoption. It seems an odd time for Betts to be reaching out to Tina. And Tina's done nothing to try to be with Betts."

Zoey was trying to talk in a whisper, and Ames looked at her, surprised. "Tell me about this "termination" thing. What does that mean?" Zoey realized that she had not yet explained the whole adoption process, although Ames and Betts were clear on their desire for Betts to continue to live with him and be adopted. Zoey realized that she had failed to keep up her role as Betts' social worker, in this whirlwind of campfires, corn on the cob and kisses. She started in again.

"In order for Betts to be adopted, her birth mother and father need to either permit that, by signing away their role as parents, or the court needs to do that for them. That's a "termination of parental rights." The first parents step aside or are moved aside by the court so that the court can appoint new ones, by adoption. It's supposed to be a clean break, so the child can make solid connections with their new parents." Zoey heard herself quoting her training on the adoption process, and at the same time, questioning it, as she was sure Ames was. She could see Ames face in the flickering light of the fire, and he looked troubled.

"Betts and I want for me to be her dad," he started. "But I know she wants to keep Tina as her mom, even if she doesn't live with her. She wants to visit with her, and have her come for lunch and things, like school stuff, and maybe some trips or something. I'd keep her safe, and she'd live with me, and I'd make sure that Peter was never around her. She's clear about that, but I know she wants to keep in touch with her mom." Ames stirred the fire, and a flash of sparks flew up into the night sky. Zoey tried again.

"I know that Tina's your sister," but Ames interrupted her, his voice louder.

"That's not it. She's Betts' mother, and Betts isn't about to give that up. I know Tina doesn't look like a good mom to you or the folks down at the agency, but she's Betts mom. That's forever. Peter lost his dad role with Betts, but Tina hasn't. And we need to respect that. Not for Tina's sake, or because she's my sister, but because that's what Betts wants. And needs." Ames took in a slow breath, trying to stay calm, with all of this, and failing.

Ames suddenly lost the calm thing. "You probably wouldn't have liked my mom and dad much, either. They used the belt a lot, slapped Tina around, and got drunk sometimes. They never ever came to school stuff. Dad ran over Clair with the tractor. And then they both just gave up on us, and let me and Tina run wild. But we loved them because they were our mom and dad. I can count the things that they did right on the fingers of one hand, but they did the best they could, and we're a family. That counts." Ames finished up louder than he had hoped, and he was clearly angry.

Zoey felt her own anger well up, feeling that Ames had attacked her work, her friends, and her own lack of family connection. She thought of how little Ames had received growing up, and how loyal he had remained, visiting his mother in spite of her unwillingness to even speak with him. And she thought of her own parents, distant, who she might visit once a year or so, with no drama, but with not much connection, either. The value stressed at work, and at school, for that matter, had been all about independence, not family. But it seemed that Ames and Betts had a different feeling, and she couldn't help but wish she had that kind of blind loyalty and connection, too.

Zoey needed to go home. She rose and made her way to the car. Ames stayed by the fire pit, trying to think of what to do or say. She turned to him as she opened her car door, the sudden light spilling out and ruining the night sky. "You're probably right, and I'm probably wrong. I'll talk to Laura tomorrow and see how Betts can keep her mom and still be adopted. I'm sorry." She slipped inside, started the engine, and flipped on the headlights.

Ames got out of his chair, and moved toward the car, but she put it into gear and was already rolling down the road. "Shit!" he said and turned back to the fire.

Later, as he was climbing up into the loft to go to sleep, he heard Betts from her couch bed. "I'm sorry you had a fight. But you're right about my mom and me. And Zoey will figure it out. It'll be OK. Thank you for being on my side," she added.

"Goodnight, Betts," Ames said, climbing up the ladder. "Sweet dreams." He lay awake, replaying the events of the evening, trying to see where things went wrong.

The next morning, a tired and worn looking Zoey made her way into work, going directly to Laura's office in the very back of the hallway. She found Laura at her desk, finishing up a home study, a cup of coffee steaming beside the papers. Laura no longer needed a checklist and seemed to have the format of the thirty-one page document memorized. In fact, Laura had added a bit to the standard document, with additional documentation of a potential foster family's income, debt, and job stability, as well as personal interviews with five references. Her reports were long, but the families she approved served the agency and the children year after year with few problems. She smiled and put the papers away as Zoey came in. "Long night?" she asked. "You look like you just got back from a bad vacation."

Zoey was too tired to be offended by Laura's assessment. "I'm beat," she said. "Last night Betts told me she wants to stay involved with her mom, and Ames backed her up, and I think Ames saw me as a flatlander do-gooder with no real clue about family, and I drove home thinking he might be right. And he's angry, and I feel like shit." Zoey poured herself a cup of coffee and sat down in the chair across Laura's desk.

"Hmmmm," said Laura, pouring herself another cup.

Zoey went on. "I mean, I assumed we would do the termination, since Tina's done literally nothing, and Peter's done probably worse, and then Ames would adopt Betts, and we'd have a happy ending. But Betts wants to buy her mother a music box. She read a book with a mother that has one, and I thought it meant that she was trying to win her mom back, or something, and that it wouldn't work, and Betts would get hurt. But I thought about it, and Betts doesn't seem to feel hurt at all by her mom, somehow. Her mom won't even visit her, much less fight for her, and Betts doesn't seem hurt at all. I don't understand it. I hate Tina for what she's done to Betts, and Betts isn't even angry. And she wants to buy her a music box, and I think Betts is more right than I am. And that Ames is more right, too, and that I really don't have a clue about what family is, or how it works. And I'm supposed to be the professional, and really Betts is a better daughter than I have ever been." Zoey began to silently cry, setting her shaking coffee down on the desk and holding her face in her hands.

Laura sat quietly for a bit, then pushed a box of Kleenex across the desk to Zoey, who dried her face and hands, and then looked up a little angrily at Laura. "Do you think she's right? Are we wrong about how we do all this?"

Laura took a slow breath and then said, "I have no doubt that Betts is right for Betts' situation. We need to hear her and respect her as the expert on Betts, and let her call the shots regarding her mom." Laura paused. "Are we wrong, in general? Do we do more harm than good, sometimes, or maybe, often, because we forget to listen to the client and let them lead in their own healing? Betts is smart, and there's something sort of Buddha about her, so I think she's an especially good kid to listen to. But I think we ought to listen to all of them, and that if we did, we would do better work, and less harm. If we listened, our work with troubled families and their kids would be different than the way it is.

"Part of the problem is that we're expected to make kids safe, and if we don't, if they get raped again, or beat again, then it's our fault. And it happens over and over, if we leave the kids with their families, or even if we place them in foster care with other families. We fail at the keeping them safe thing, and we get into the newspaper, or we get fired, and we feel like shit. So, we try to do what we think is safest, most of the time, safest for us, really, and not necessarily what's best for the kids, and hardly ever what the kids are asking for. We shoot for "best practices," so we can defend what we did. And I don't know that most of that ever makes kids much safer, anyway.

"What are the long-term outcome studies on kids we place in foster care, or help get adopted? We know they're not good, and we comfort ourselves with the idea that, well, it would have been worse if we had left them alone, but we can't know that. And the work is hard, so hard that if you question it, if you question whether we help much at all anyway, you might as well just quit. Which I have done, over and over," she said, laughing. She got out the bag of chocolate that Zoey had left before.

"I know a couple of things," Laura said. "I know that we need to listen, carefully, every day, to what our clients say, and learn how they see their world, and what they feel they want and need. I know we don't do that enough. And I know that we need to understand ourselves enough to know what we bring to the table, our own history, our past and current relationships with our parents and family. How many social workers do you know who have positive relationships with their parents and siblings? Any? It's pretty rare, and folks who go into the job hoping to fix their own history can do a lot of damage. And we do that. We do a lot of damage." She smiled again and reached for a piece of chocolate. "Now you know why they don't have me do trainings anymore."

Zoey sat, sad and tired and confused, thinking about why she had come to work in this field, and about her work with Betts and Ames. "Well," she said, "I was hoping you could make me feel better, but I guess I need to do some thinking. Maybe Betts can help me figure this out."

"That's where I'd start," said Laura.

Zoey felt battered and resentful driving up Bear Mountain, missing the beauty of the road that usually enthralled her. Full summer was on, and the old maples at the side of the road were heavy with leaves, and leaned ponderously in, making a deep green tunnel all the way up the mountain. The gravel road had been kicked loose by the recent heavy rains, and the agency van Zoey drove skittered from side to side, sometimes sliding dramatically around the turns. The van bounced up and down and rattled over the washboard in a way that would have horrified Ames, who was so careful to baby his old Ford. But Zoey was oblivious, keeping the van on the road by a combination of luck and muscle memory, having driven up and down this particular road several times a week for the past year.

When she arrived at the turn for Ames' cabin, she slowed just a bit and came rolling into the yard at twice the speed she usually did, sliding a bit as she hit the brakes, then clanking the van into park, and opening the door. Ames was standing with the new splits, the wood splitter still uncovered, with heat waves rising from the cast iron engine. He smiled when he saw the van, then looked a bit worried as Zoey slid a bit past her usual parking place, and opened the door, her face dark and cloudy. He waited while Zoey got out of the van, and closed the door, and then said, "Still upset? I'm sorry about last night. I shouldn't have said all of that. You do a good job, and your work is really important."

She stopped him. "No. You brought up some stuff I needed to hear. I've been off track, and you helped me to see that. Sorry about driving up here like a maniac. I was just thinking on the way up." She gave him a lingering kiss. "And I'm not mad. It's just hard for me to see that I'm off track sometimes. I want to do everything perfect."

Ames kissed her again. "Practically perfect is just fine for me," he said.

Betts came tumbling down the trail, from, the top rock where she had been reading. She ran to Zoey and gave her a big hug. "Just like Mary Poppins!" she said. "Are we still going shopping for the music box today?"

Zoey hugged Betts back for a bit, then kissed the top of her head. "Sure thing, Betts," she said. "Let me settle just a bit, and then we can head out."

Ames looked up at the sky and left the splitter uncovered. "I want a shower before we go. Betts, see if Zoey wants a drink or something."

In ten minutes, a cleaned-up Ames, a much happier Zoey, and Betts, carrying a drawstring bag filled with money, were all ready to go. "Let's take the truck!" said Betts. "I like it when we all sit together."

Ames laughed, looking at the marks the sliding van had left in the yard. "I'm up for that," he said.

On the way to West Lebanon, Betts explained to Zoey how she hoped that things would go with her mom. Betts started out with the plan for living with Ames. She stopped and looked over at him. "You are going to adopt me, aren't you?"

Ames smiled and said, "Yep."

Betts continued. "I want that. And I want to see my mom, like every week or so, when she can, for, like, lunch, or maybe dinner or something. Or maybe have breakfast down in town, like pancakes, and she can tell me how she's doing, and I can show her my pictures and stuff from school. And I want her to go to my school stuff, and she can sit with Ames. And I don't want Peter there. Ever." Betts got quieter, thinking. "I don't ever want to see Peter again. Even in court. Not ever."

The truck was quiet. Zoey said, "I think we can keep you away from Peter. And once Ames has adopted you, he gets to decide who you see and who you spend time with. There's no court order preventing you from seeing your mom, and if she wants to do that, you and Ames can set it up."

"She will," said Betts.

They pulled into the West Lebanon Plaza, a strip mall that included a gift store that specialized in music boxes. The inside was air-conditioned to the point of being chilly, and one wall was filled with shelves of music boxes. Some were as small as a ring box, and a few were so large they stood on legs like a small desk or table. Betts stood before them, a bit overwhelmed by the huge selection. Betts walked toward them, as a man moved to her side, offering his help. They spoke a bit, then he began to take some of the smaller boxes and wind them up, setting them back on the shelf while they played. Ames and Zoey still stood by the door, with Ames saying, "This could take a while. Betts is pretty picky."

Betts walked down the shelf, taking a few of the larger music boxes in her hands, tipping them over to see the price, and then handing them to the man to wind up and play. Ames held Zoey's hand, and said, "Betts knows what she wants. She never says much, but when she does, she's pretty clear."

"I'm beginning to understand that," said Zoey. "She was right about her mom."

Ames nodded. "Yeah. So, is that kind of unusual, having a kid go with someone else, but stay in touch with their family?"

Zoey nodded. "It is. I was talking with Laura this morning. She thinks we need to listen a whole lot more to the kids we have. Laura's amazing."

Betts came over to them and asked that they come and listen to a few music boxes. "They play different tunes, and they all sound a little different. Louder, or clearer, or something. And the box is different, too. It's hard to pick the right one."

The man, who seemed worried, or even annoyed at first, was smiling and introduced himself. "She has a good ear," he said. Betts had narrowed the field down to five different boxes, all about the same size, and when the second one was played, it struck both Ames and Zoey.

"That second one is really different, but I like it," Betts said. "It sounds really sad, but it sounds nice, too." Zoey agreed. They played it again, and then again, with Betts listening carefully, then holding the box and looking at it, inside and out.

The salesman spoke up. "That one is odd. These boxes all have fifty notes and play two or three different tunes. This one plays three movements to the same piece. *Kindertotenlieder*. They all have a maple box, with different inlays, and a spruce bottom for the sound, and a Thorens movement. That's the best you can buy," he added. "I've never seen that tune before in a music box. Most folks want something a little more peppy, I guess. But it is pretty."

Betts had him wind it up again, and they all listened to it play the music, terribly sad, but beautiful, at first, then somehow finding a bit of resolution and meaning, even, maybe in the last movement. "This is it," said Betts. She picked it up and carried it to the front desk and set it on the table. The man began to wrap it up in tissue, newspaper and then bubble wrap, while Betts counted out a thick stack of bills on the table.

Betts looked a little nervous and looked at Ames. "You like it?" she asked. "You think my mom will like it?"

Ames nodded. "I think it's perfect," he said. The salesman placed the well-wrapped box into a sturdy paper bag, and handed it to Betts, along with some change.

Betts held the bag with both hands, tight to her chest, smiling. "I think she's really going to like this. We need to wrap it up pretty when we get home, and I'll make a card for it."

Betts leaned into Ames, who had his arm over her shoulder. Zoey looked at the tall weathered man, and the small dark girl at his side, so similar. She thought again of the vague little girl by the plastic window and wondered at how she had changed.

Zoey moved beside Ames and took his hand. "We do make a beautiful family," she thought.

They stopped for lunch at the burger and ice cream place down by the river. Tasty Cone was a cinder block building that had once served as a garage. Picnic tables were set beneath the shade of an old wolf maple, close enough to the river to hear the flow of the water over the rocks. Ames and Betts loved the ice cream, and the river, with Betts wading through the shallows in her underwear and tee shirt while Ames read on the bank. Today, Betts attention was on the music box. She sat at the picnic table, the paper bag in front of her, while Ames and Zoey brought back the food in plastic baskets. Betts had agonized over whether she should open the careful wrappings and again look at the music box, obviously tempted, but wanting to keep the box safe on the way home. She finally decided she could wrap it back up again and took the box out of its protective layers.

Betts had asked the man about winding it, and he had shown her to turn the key until she felt some real resistance and to then stop. She did this, and set the box on the table, and opened the lid, letting the tune play. The tune was slower at first, a thin solo it seemed, gradually joined by other notes, and finishing, at last, with chorded harmonies that brought the sadness to a resolution of sorts. They all ate quietly and listened to the music. Betts thought that the music sounded like her mom's life, Ames heard the loss of his sister in it, and Zoey found the music to be about the sorrows and joys of her work. After the third play, Betts closed the lid and thought for a bit.

"I never heard a music box before. With my mom, we had the radio, and the TV and they were on all the time, and Peter played really loud music in his car. He bought these really big speakers that shook the whole car and made everything rattle. But I hated that. The words were awful, and the music was stupid, and sitting in a car that was shaking and rattling was embarrassing. When I read about music boxes, it seemed cool to have a song that meant something to you, that you could hear by just winding it up, quiet and pretty. I think my mom is really going to love it."

"I love the quiet," Betts said suddenly. "The quiet in the truck, where all you can hear are the tires whirring, or the quiet up at the cabin, with just a little whistle coming from the woodstove, or the coyotes at night. I like this music box music, because it seems to sort of fit in with the quiet, somehow."

"I can see that," said Ames.

Betts looked at the massive trunk standing beside the table, then up, with a woodsman's eye, seeing the splits and the possible rot, and then on to the distant green branches at the top. "I'll bet you'd hate to cut that one," she said to Ames.

He nodded. "Looks like it would go just above that first big branch. See all those woodpecker holes in there? That's where the bugs are."

Zoey and Betts walked back up to the building after Betts carefully set the music box, now carefully wrapped up again, into Ames' keeping. "I thought about what you said about your mom," Zoey started. "You were right, and I'm sorry I didn't listen better. I'll try to do better next time. I want to listen more to the other kids I see, too, and not just think I always know what I'm doing."

Betts smiled. "That's OK. I needed to get away from Peter, and so I needed to get away from my mom, too, since she can't really do anything about Peter. She thinks about him all the time, worrying that he's going to leave her, or that he's with somebody else. She can't think about anything else, like me, even, or herself. And I don't think he cares about her, at all."

Zoey nodded, and Betts continued. "I think this music box might help her to think about herself, and about me, and about her mom, and maybe her sister. It's really sad, but the music sort of tells you that sad is OK some times, and that things can be sad and still be alright." Betts looked frustrated. "I'm not saying it right," she said, but Zoey disagreed.

"You're saying it just fine," she said. "Some stuff is hard to say, hard to find the right words for. That's why people like music and pictures, because sometimes there's stuff you can't say too well with words. I like the music box you got. It makes me think of the hard stuff at work, and it makes me feel sad, but I feel better, at the same time. I think your mom will like it." They took the cones back to the picnic table, where Ames sat looking out at the river.

After their ice cream, Ames suggested a trip to the co-op, but Betts declined, not wanting to either bring her music box in with her or leave it behind. She was apologetic and offered to stay in the truck by herself, but Ames said that home looked pretty good to him at this point, and they headed back up the mountain. Betts cushioned the box in her lap as they drove, and handed it to Ames when they arrived, then took it back after she climbed out of the truck, and carried it into the cabin.

Ames and Zoey stayed outside for a bit, talking. "She sure likes that thing," Ames said. "I wonder what Tina will think about it. She was sort of stand-offish toward Betts at the funeral, and you'd think that would have been an easy time for her to reach out a little. I know she loves Betts, but I'm not sure that loving has ever been something that Tina has been comfortable with. We didn't do it a whole lot as kids. I mean, I know my parents loved us, but no one ever said it, or hugged or anything like that. I'm still no good at it. I wanted to reach out and put my arm around Tina, but she looked so angry I just didn't. Tina and my mom never did get along. Mom saved all her good stuff for Clair, and then, when Clair died, there just wasn't any good stuff left. In her, or my dad."

"Families aren't the easiest thing," said Zoey. "My dad was all hugs, but when he drank, it got to be more than hugs. He and my mom divorced when

I was fourteen, and I only saw him a couple of times after that. And my mom married a guy that hated me, and then she blamed me for it, of course. Not a whole lot of happy there, either." She sighed. "That music box really brings stuff up."

"Never too late for happy, I guess," said Ames. "I never thought about having a family at all, before. I figured that my best bet was to come up here to the cabin, cut enough wood to pay the bills and put back a little extra, for when I couldn't cut wood anymore, and keep to myself. That worked out fine until Tina dropped Betts off that first summer. I'd always just gotten up and gone to work, but suddenly, I was kind of happy to get up, and looked forward to chatting with her over breakfast, and then taking her to the job. When Tina came and took her back, it was like all the color had drained out of my life. When she came back, I felt like I found my breath again. Then you started coming up, not just for work, but to be with us, and I felt like my life was this beautiful thing that I wasn't supposed to have, but I had it, anyway. And I worry every day that I'll do something wrong, and it will all disappear." Ames and Zoey sat in the dark, without talking, while Betts was in the cabin, making a card for her mother.

CHAPTER TWENTY-SIX

Termination

Betts was halfway done with the card for her mother when she discovered that she needed some new pencils. Ames had bought her quite the collection of art supplies several months ago, but Betts had been sketching every new thing she found in the woods, and her pencil set had gotten shorter and shorter. A few of the colors that were most in demand for her natural history sketches had become such nubs that they disappeared into the sharpener and could be used no more. Ames suggested a trip up to May's, the art supply store in Montpelier where he had gotten her supplies the first time.

They drove up to Montpelier the next morning, having tea at the cabin, and planning breakfast at the Coffee Corner, a favorite spot with a giant table in the front window, where strangers met as they ate breakfast. The cafe was decorated with about a hundred colorful chef's hats, each for sale, hanging from the ceiling. Betts loved Coffee Corner, and always wanted to sit in the front table, where she could listen in and sometimes join in on the conversations of the people around her. In the summer, there would be families visiting Vermont, as well as the usual businessmen and local characters.

Betts had brought some of her money for pencils, and after breakfast, they headed over to May's, across the street and up a little more than a block. There was a bench in front, where Ames plunked himself down, announcing his intention of watching the people walk past. "If May is in there, introduce yourself. I've known her since I was a kid, and I told her about you. She'll want to meet you." Betts was used to being cut loose like this, going on by herself while Ames read or sat outside. He wasn't much of a shopper and understood that Betts sometimes liked to do things on her own.

Betts pushed open the heavy door and stepped onto the worn old oak floor, filled with shelves and cabinets, tight together, with the high ceiling disappearing into the dark. On the left was a counter, and behind the counter was an older woman, wearing a loose cotton dress, her long grey hair braided down her back. She sat drawing something on the brown paper bags with an old-fashioned ink pen, dipping the pen from time to time in a bottle of black ink that sat on the counter beside her. She looked up and nodded at Betts. "Let me know if you need help. You're Betts, I believe?" Betts nodded, surprised that this woman would recognize her, and wandered off down the narrow aisles, staring at the hundreds of fine things, many of which she had never seen before.

She stopped beside a lot of small boards, backed with a soft grey rubber, sets of sharp knives for carving, rollers for ink, and tubes of the ink itself. There were a few carved blocks and some prints that had been made by these blocks. Betts was enchanted. She picked up the carved block and tried to imagine carving the design, a shore scene, with cattails, two ducks, and a snapping turtle moving through the water. The sheets of heavy paper bore the design, printed in several different colors, and some prints with the colors mixed. This was something she wanted very much to try.

She remembered her mission and set the block down and went off in search of pencils. She found the wall where drawing materials were displayed and saw tin after tin of colored pencils, including a tin of thirty-six pencils that was an exact match for the first ones Ames had bought her. She picked them up and gasped at the price tag, which she figured out meant that the pencils were well over a dollar apiece. While she was looking, Ames came in and went to her side. "Those are the ones I got last time. You liked them?" he asked.

Betts nodded. "They cost a lot," she said. "Who buys these things?"

"Artists, I guess," said Ames. "That's pretty much who shops here. They're good pencils, and you got a lot of use out of the last set." Ames handed the tin back to her.

"Is it OK to spend that much?" Betts asked.

Ames looked at her. "Well, it's your money, so I guess you can spend it however you want. I don't spend much, but sometimes I spend a lot on something that's important to me. These boots cost over three hundred dollars, three or four years ago. There's a guy up in Burlington who makes them. He measures your feet every which way, and you tell him what you need the boots for, and in two or three months, he calls you up and tells you they're ready. I've had them up to him twice for new soles, and the tops still look pretty much brand new. I keep them oiled and let them dry out slowly, away from the heat, so I figure I'll have them for a long time. I think I got a bargain.

"You take good care of your stuff, and you're serious about your drawing. I think good pencils make sense for you." Ames picked up a small brass sharpener from the shelf, turned on a lathe, with a knurled grip and a small razor-sharp blade screwed on to one side. He handed it to her. It felt heavy and fine in her hand. "That's a nice little thing," he said. "You wouldn't need the extra blades. I think I can keep an edge on that one with my Arkansas stone. You needed a new pad, too, didn't you?" Ames asked, pointing to the drawing pads at the base of the shelf. "Come out when you're done, and we'll get Italian ice. The guy with the stand just opened up."

Betts watched Ames head back out the door, stopping first to chat a bit with May, then heading on out the door. Betts sighed, and took the tin of pencils, the brass sharpener, a new pad, and a gum eraser, and headed up to the desk at the side of the store. May looked up with a smile. "You and your uncle sure were cut from the same cloth," she said.

Betts smiled. "Is that how you knew me?" she asked.

May nodded. "I've known Ames since he was about your age," she said. "I had a book store down in Randolph back then, and his sister Clair used to come in and clean for me, in exchange for books. That girl loved books!" she said.

"I do, too," said Betts. She looked at the bag that May had been working on. "When Ames bought me my art stuff, last year, it came in a bag like that, with the cat drawn on it. I didn't know you drew the cats yourself. I cut the cat part out and put it on my wall."

May smiled. "Every bag gets a cat or two. I still like to draw, and I've always liked cats." She looked at the cat she was finishing up. The cat lay on its back in a beach chair, a drink with an umbrella in one paw, and a book in the other, while a large pair of sunglasses with tipped up points gave the cat a glamorous look. A red bikini, with three tops, finished the cat off. "I wanted a bathing suit, but the top thing kind of threw me. I settled on three. Which I think is right. Should it be four?"

She looked questioningly at Betts, who said, uncertainly, "I don't know. I never had a cat."

May sketched in a palm tree, and put its shade over the picture below, and then added a sailboat in the distance, and a dark shark fin slicing the water behind it. "I like the details," May said. She blew the ink dry and opened the bag up. "You want this one?" she asked.

"Thank you!" said Betts.

Ames was out in front on the bench, his long legs tucked under him to keep them out of the traffic. He was reading from a small book he must have had in his pocket. "You have a chance to talk with May?" he asked.

Betts nodded. "She's really nice. She drew the cat on the bag."

She showed him the cat, and Ames smiled. "I like her," he said. "She tried to get Tina to work for her in the book shop after Clair died. Tina wouldn't do it, though. I think working for May would have been a help to her."

Zoey arrived that evening, while Betts was using her new pencils to finish the card for her mom, bearing gifts of pizza and news that a court hearing had been set for the following Monday. Ames was excited to have the date, but he was careful to not show that to Betts. Betts was quiet with the news, wrestling with her mixed feelings about the process. "That's good," she had said cautiously when given the date. "I'm ready. Will my mom be there?"

"I don't know," said Zoey. "She got notice of the hearing, and I tried to see her at her home today, but she wouldn't come to the door."

"She goes to the bathroom and locks the door," said Betts. "Like, when someone comes that she doesn't want to see, like the guy for the electric bill, she goes in there and runs the shower. Sometimes she took me in there with her. We just sat there, hiding." Betts looked sad, and Zoey tried to shift her irritation at Tina, and see her instead through Betts's eyes, hiding, frightened and alone.

On the morning of the hearing, Ames put on his newest pair of jeans, a collared shirt and a thin jacket that Betts had never seen. His boots were shined up as well, and he looked younger and more handsome than he usually did. Betts wore her regular clothes, jeans, a tee-shirt and her black sneakers, but she took some time to brush her hair and then asked Ames to braid it for her, in a single thick strand down her back. He did this, pulling the strands of hair tight as worked down the braid.

Having Ames braid her hair had been a struggle for Betts. She loved the feeling of being cared for, but she had felt a real terror at having someone behind her, telling her to stand still or move this way or that. Several times she had had to stop and tell him she would just let it hang today, leaving him seated, with the brush in hand, while she quickly went outside. But with time, and lots of trying, Betts was usually able to sit while Ames did her hair. Ames may have suspected some of the battle that Betts was fighting, but he never said anything, other than "OK," one way or another.

"Looks good," Ames said, handing her back the hairbrush.

"Maybe my mom will be there," said Betts. She felt at the tight braid.

"Maybe," said Ames. They drove down the road into town, quieter than usual, and stopped by the agency to pick up Zoey. Zoey introduced Heather, the adoption worker who would be taking over Betts' case after the hearing, as Betts case moved from one of foster care to pre-adoption.

Ames parked the truck in the shade of an old maple along the town square, across from the courthouse, and the three of them got out. Betts reached for Ames's hand, and then took Zoey's hand as well, and the three of them entered the great heavy doors. Heather chatted quietly with Zoey, and the four of them sat on one of the long benches outside the courtroom. Betts looked around the hallway, trying to find her mother. At last, they were called in, and the judge read from a file of papers that sat on the desk in front of her. She read a brief history of how Betts came into the custody of the state, including a medical description of the belt marks Betts had carried into school that day. The judge noted the attempts to bring Tina and Peter into the treatment team, and the number of failed appointments they had racked up.

The judge asked a few questions to Zoey, regarding the licensure of Ames' home for foster care and his training as a foster parent, and then asked for Zoey's assessment of Ames' relationship with Betts. The judge then turned to Betts, and asked her directly, "How are things going, young lady?"

Betts took a moment to realize the question was really as brief as it sounded, and simply answered, "Good."

The judge nodded and went on. "It is hereby ordered on this day, August 12th, 2013, that Rebekah Grace Townsend shall be freed for adoption, and the parental rights of Tina Marie Townsend and Peter James Townsend be terminated as permitted by Vermont Statute 15A.1-105."

Betts was startled. "Rebekah?" she asked, out loud. No one answered, and the Judge rose, as did all the people in the courtroom. Betts found herself back in the hallway, with Ames and Zoey on either side. "Rebekah?" she asked again. "My name's Rebekah?"

"They have to use your full legal name in court," said Zoey.

Ames understood, though. "Your mom named you after our sister, Clair. Her real name was Rebekah, too. Her middle name was Clair, and we all called her that, maybe because 'Rebekah' is too much of a handful. Your mom called you 'Betts' for that reason, too, I guess. My dad's mother was named Rebekah. Somehow that name got passed down for the girls. She was Jewish, I think and came from a big family up in the Hudson Valley. My dad's father was a Bennet, from right here in Vermont. I think there was an 'Ames' back on his side, maybe his grandfather."

Ames's voice trailed off as he found Betts crying into his chest. He held her tightly and swayed a little bit from side to side. "It's OK," he said, over and over.

"I'm ruining your nice shirt," Betts sobbed. "Again."

"That's OK," he said.

They decided to get a drink at the little cafe across from the town square. Betts and Ames ordered root beers, while Zoey got a black coffee. Betts was quiet, mulling over the name she had carried since her birth and this evidence that Rebekah and Clair were somehow one and the same. Betts' eyes kept going out to the square, thinking she might see her mother, coming in late, as was often the case. But she saw no one. Zoey tried to interest her in a sweet roll, but Betts didn't even want the root beer Ames had ordered.

Ames paid the bill and left a tip on the table, and they headed back out onto the sidewalk. "She didn't come," said Betts.

"I guess not," said Ames. They walked along the old broken sidewalk, the cement buckled and broken and tossed up here and there in great slabs which were patched in a few places, as the town crew tried to make the sidewalk walkable. Betts tripped on an edge, and Ames caught her. "Glad I wore my boots," he said. "Looks like the roots are winning the battle around here. Folks love the maples, and the shade, but they forget that those great big trees have great big roots, pushing and searching underground. The roots are as big as the tree, and a whole lot stronger than cement." Betts remembered the old wolf maple she and Ames had cut up and the giant roots that had been pulled into the air when the tree fell over.

Betts pointed at the truck, still a hundred feet away. "What's that?" she asked.

Ames looked and saw something in the bed of the truck. When they got closer, they saw two black trash bags, knotted at the top, set up toward the cab. There was an envelope taped to one of the bags, which Ames opened. "It's from your mom," he said. "She says she loves you, and that she wanted you to have some of your stuff. Some of it she wants back. There's a list," he added.

Betts climbed into the bed of the truck, and unknotted one of the bags, looking through folded baby clothes, toddler clothing, tiny shoes, a few looking brand new, and an assortment of stuffed animals. Everything was washed, and a few of the animals had nametags her mother had made and taped on. There were books as well, worn picture books, mostly, and a large baby book, with Betts's handprints and footprints inked in the first pages, some pictures from the hospital of a very young mother looking tired and scared, holding a very tiny, black-haired baby, looking tired and scared as well. The book had a list of "firsts," including first solid food, first steps, first word (mama), and even first pee in a potty. Betts cried into a stuffed rabbit, with a name tag that read "Pinky," and Ames and Zoey cried as well, holding each other and reaching out to touch Betts.

Betts took the rabbit into the cab, and Ames put the bags back together and tied them shut. They rode back up to the cabin, with Betts snuffling a little, and Ames trying to comfort her. "She isn't throwing you away. She just wanted to remind you that she loves you, and took care of you as best she could. She wants the baby book, and some of the shoes, and the stuffed puppy back. You can give her the music box at the same time, and let her know you want to keep seeing her."

Zoey sat on her side of the bench seat and thought about her work. She watched as Ames did just the right thing with Betts. She had thought of the day in court as a goal of sorts, achieved through careful documentation and doing all the required work, "freeing the child up for adoption," as this phase was known. She thought of Laura's bitter assessment of their work as necessary, but terribly flawed, and often harmful. Zoey wondered how long it might take her to get to that same tired and dismal place. She wondered if she could continue to do this work, now that she better understood the real nature and impact of taking families apart on behalf of the children at risk of abuse and neglect.

She thought of her brief attempt to work with Tina, and her lack of compassion for her, the mother who had once been the exhausted young girl looking so scared and alone as she held her new baby stiffly at the hospital. Why was it so easy to be on Tina's side in that picture, and so hard a few years later, when things had gone the way you knew they would? There was no family in the picture, no flowers, no balloons, and Zoey guessed that the nurse had taken the picture as a kindness. She realized that had Betts been less strong and clear, had Ames offered her less support, and had Zoey been quicker and less involved in her work with Betts, today's court hearing would have been just another termination, forever severing the child from her mother, in the name of safety, expediency, and best practice.

"I can get pictures of the baby book, and put them together so you can have a copy to keep," she said. "You might like to make a book for your mom, sometime, with some pictures of you and Ames, and your new home, and your drawings and stuff. She might like that, too."

Betts looked at Zoey and saw tears in her eyes. "Are you OK?" Betts asked.

"Yeah, I'm OK," Zoey replied. "I'm just sad, that's all."

"Me, too," said Betts.

CHAPTER TWENTY-SEVEN

Therapy

Betts had a therapy appointment the following Tuesday with Emma and looked toward the visit with mixed feelings. So much seemed to be going on, with the court hearing, the bags of things from her mother, the music box, and of course, Rebekah. Rebekah continued to come and go, less like a guardian angel, and more like a neighbor child or a cousin, sometimes wanting to talk, sometimes just sitting in the background, present, but quiet. Sorting all this out seemed like something that Emma could help with, but Betts was afraid to share too much, and she had no idea how much too much was. And then there was Toby, the cat. Toby had been present, paying attention, but silent, except for his greeting and saying good-bye. He seemed to know what was in her heart, and in her history, and Betts had panicked a few weeks before, fearing that Toby was telling Emma everything that Betts had kept secret.

Secrets. A word that might hint of close friendships and giggles for some girls, but for Betts, it meant something else. There had always been noise in the trailer, with the TV and the radio and the scanner going non-stop, and the constant and meaningless conversations between her mother and Peter, accusatory, threatening, flirty, demeaning and worrying, with most of what was said unheard and unremembered a moment later. Most of what was said had little meaning, but there were a few powerful exceptions, whispered from the tight lips of Peter to the cowering girl, tiny bits of words that still stayed with Betts, years later.

Secrets, visions of things done and things threatened, bits of sound and taste and sight and feeling. The menace of a quick look, the sudden betrayal of her own shuddering body, a hot flash of pain or shame, a laugh or a curse, these bits of the past came unannounced and unwanted, like a quick blow to the stomach, folding her up with pain, driving her breath from her. Bits and pieces, that if she gave them the power of speech, if she brought them to the light of day, they might string themselves into a truth that could end her once and for all. Her story. Emma had said that everyone had one and that sometimes, by telling it, people could become more free of their past, able to step aside and say, "Yes. This happened to me. And I will go on." Toby had watched her carefully while Emma explained this, and had said sadly to her, in a whisper, "It's true."

Ames never asked about the therapy. He would be waiting in the truck when she came out of the building, often tinkering under the hood, or sometimes just admiring the old V-8 351, with its fading blue paint, and the hoses and wires all neat and clean, the coolant and oil fresh and at just the right level. Ames liked to just look at the engine, even if nothing needed to be done.

"Hi," Betts would say, and Ames would turn to greet her, then close the hood, tucking a shop rag into his pocket, and open the door for her to slide in.

"How'd it go?" he would always ask, and Betts would always say, "OK," and that was a far as it went. Betts got to pick a destination after her therapy every week, with Ames willing to drive to a local cafe, a favorite swim hole, or even back up to Montpelier. Some days Betts just said, "Let's go home," and was quiet for the ride up the mountain, walking up to the top rock, or curling up on the couch with a book.

Ames said nothing, but he made tea, and went along with his chores, giving Betts the space to work out what she might need. Sometimes she would come to him with a question, usually sharp and well defined, such as "How long does it take to forget things?" or, "Do you think I'm a lot like my mom?" She asked him a few times about nightmares, and if dreams meant that things were going to come true. Sometimes Ames didn't know the answer, but he would say that, and then think about it for a while, and he might come up with an idea or an answer a day or two later.

She once asked if animals could talk, and he said that he thought they could, some of them, anyway, like asking for food, or warning others away.

Betts pushed on with, "No, I mean, talk like us. In words." Ames thought about that and remembered that there were birds who could be trained to speak in human language, but added that he didn't think they really knew what they were saying. "But maybe they can?" asked Betts. Ames thought about that and finally said, maybe they could, but that he had never heard of it. He never asked her questions back, and Betts came to trust that he would always try to help her, but never push her in any way. She liked that.

Emma was much the same way, mostly quiet, sometimes making a small comment, like, "That sounds scary," or, "That must have been hard." Emma looked right at her some of the time, but might look out the window, down at her cup of tea or the floor, and might draw some when Betts was drawing something herself. She kept a cup of tea at her desk, and held onto it through much of the session, slowly drinking it from time to time. Betts had a cup there, as well, one of the several that hung on a set of pegs over the electric kettle, always the same cup, which Emma admitted to not washing in between sessions. Betts had picked it out that first day and Emma told her she could take it with her at the end of her last session when she was finished with therapy. Betts liked the idea of a part of herself remaining in the office, claiming space, there with the other mugs, and liked the reminder that therapy was not forever, that one day, she would be finished, and take her mug home.

And Toby. The cat always seemed happy to see her, and sad with her when she was sad, comforting when she was scared, and angry, sometimes, on her behalf. He seemed to know her, and to believe in her when she doubted herself and looked at her with that smirk of his when she was wasting time or letting her fear keep her from being honest. While Emma seemed content to only know what Betts was able to share, Toby seemed to know Betts inside and out, to understand her story before she had found a way to tell it, even to herself, and to be on her side, anyway.

He mostly kept to his space on the desk, facing her with at least a half of an eye open. Sometimes, when Betts had begun to cry, he had come from the desk, landing lightly on the floor, and then leaping onto her lap, his heavy weight settling on to her and his quiet purring filling the empty space she had found. Sometimes he would whisper, "It's OK," and once, "It's not your fault. At all." She cried onto his back, leaving his grey and black fur slippery with her tears, and when Betts had grown calm and wiped her face and the cat with tissues, Toby returned to his spot on the desk, grooming himself until he was once again shiny and fluffy and perfect.

Emma seemed sad with her from time to time as well, sometimes taking a Kleenex from the box for herself after passing one to Betts. Crying seemed OK here, and sadness had stopped being scary, and even shame seemed to lose its power over her.

Betts had asked, in her first or second session, "What am I supposed to do here?" and Emma had answered that Betts was here to tell her story, not to Emma, but rather to herself. Drawing, playing with the countless tiny creatures that could inhabit the worlds made in the sand tray, drama with the puppets and dolls, even making up songs and singing them along to the guitar in the corner, all of this could be a part of telling her story. Betts drew pictures and talked some, at first about her life with Ames, the cabin and the little green woodstove, and the Ford truck, and the firewood and the top rock and her couch bed, and the books and the tea. This was easy, and important, too, to show that there was comfort and love and stability in her story.

But after a while, Toby would start to roll his eyes, and Betts would know that it was time to work on something a little more difficult. She talked about being taken from her mother, about the bruises and welts on her back and legs from the belt, and the little bruises from Peter's fingers, and the sad looks from the teacher and the school nurse that had made her feel so ashamed. She talked about her foster homes, and about going a little bit crazy, and biting the woman who had tried to get her in the shower, although she knew only about this from what she had been told, having little direct memory of the event.

She talked about the days, and the nights, in first one hospital, and then the other, and the dull, puffy deadness that replaced her real feelings, and about the window in the dayroom, thick and greasy and plastic, but with the whole world locked outside, including the spring and the cabin on the mountain. Betts couldn't yet talk about the evenings when Peter had used her, or about the man on the night shift at Children's Retreat. A sense of panic rushed over her when these thoughts came to her mind, and she was no longer able to speak, and sometimes even breathing was very hard. But even without yet being able to talk about these things, Betts began to see the connections between the events in her life and her thoughts and feelings, and she felt a little less crazy every week.

Emma sat outside of this, taking some notes or sketching something, but listening, and being there, somehow, as Betts journeyed back in time. Toby rode with her as well, sitting on the desk, his eye on her, and his ears twitching, and his tail flicking back and forth as if it had a life of its own.

Toby, in her lap, when it seemed she had gone too far in her memories, in her quest to tell her story, Toby who was suddenly and quietly there, purring and rubbing his face against her, his broad back soaking up her hot shame and tears. As time went by, as weeks came and went, and as the hour-long sessions began to be stacked behind her, the story, her story, began to unfold, and the power it had to control and define her life began to wane.

And as Betts did the work of healing, the nightmares had come. Betts would bolt awake, crying out against something that would vanish into the night, leaving her racked with sobs and tears, filled with cold fear and clutching her comforter with both hands, shaking with the anger and shame that had come from nowhere, it seemed. Ames would hear her, and come quickly down the ladder from the loft, speaking softly, but standing a little bit away, until Betts had found her way back into the cabin, back into this night, and then, he would come forward and carefully put a hand on her shoulder, and tell her, over and over, "It's OK."

Betts had had these nightmares three of the past five nights when it was time for her next therapy session. The nightmares had worn her down, not only for the sleep lost, and the energy lost in her gradual recovery. Betts had found herself afraid to fall asleep, and ended up drawing or reading late into the night, in a sad effort to avoid, or at least, put off the next terror. Ames was exhausted as well, both from his own sleep loss in waking up for Betts, but also from trying to sleep lightly enough that he could be quick to respond should Betts get into trouble. He had had nightmares of his own, on coming back from the Sand Wars, at first a vague terror that woke him up, and then a slow parade of the faces and bodies he had watched suffer and die. Betts' cries brought back some buried memories of his own, and there were nights in which he struggled to stay enough in the present to be there for Betts, fighting back his own horrors in order to be there for her.

Emma saw a worn and tired out Betts come into the waiting room, as she chatted with Bill, the young man who minded the desk. Emma smiled and turned back toward her office. "After you," she said, and followed Betts until the two of them had joined Toby in the familiar space, and closed the door. "Rough week, it looks like," offered Emma.

Betts took her cup off the peg and filled it with hot water from the kettle, and dropped in a tea bag from the basket. She sat down on her chair, pulled her shoes off, and tucked her feet up, and her knees under her chin. Toby hopped off the desk and came onto the seat where Betts' narrow figure left just enough room for a very large cat. He oozed a bit over her feet and rested his head against her legs. "Oh, Toby!" Betts said, and then began to tell Emma about the nightmares. Slowly, with lots of silence, Betts explained. "I wake up really scared, and then I realize that I've died and that I've let everyone who depends on me down, by dying. There's nothing I can do, and what hurts worse is that I know everyone I'm leaving behind will be hurt as bad as I am, or worse, and it's all my fault." Betts took a sip of the tea and freed a hand to rub Toby's face for a moment. Emma said nothing, but sat with her tea, as well, and leaned forward a bit toward Betts, and waiting. Betts was done and said nothing.

"Same dream? Each time?" Emma asked.

Betts nodded. "Same dream, and once I wake up, I feel so sad I almost can't breathe. It still hurts. In my stomach."

"Hmmm ..." said Emma. "Have you drawn it, or tried to?"

"No," Betts said. "It doesn't make any sense. All I can see is sky, and Ames is leaning over me, only he's a little kid. And he looks so scared. And then that fades away, and Ames is there, only he's a grown-up and we're in the cabin, and he's saying, "It's OK," and he's standing off to the side, not over me anymore. It still hurts when I wake up, and I feel really bad for letting everyone down."

"Everyone?" asked Emma. "Who is everyone?" she quietly asked.

Betts looked wildly at Emma and opened her mouth, but no words came. Finally, she said, "My mom and my dad, and my brother and sister." Emma looked puzzled. "I know it doesn't make any sense. But it seems so real. And I can't hardly sleep anymore. I don't want to be crazy," Betts added.

Emma smiled just a little. "I don't think you're crazy. At all. Even a little." She looked at Betts. "But it is hard to understand. Do you worry about your mom, without you being home with her?" Betts thought about that. "Yeah, I worry about her. But I couldn't stay with her anymore. I think she did what she did to get me safe. Away from Peter," she added, looking down at the wet cat's head on the chair beside her. Emma heard but chose to keep the Peter conversation for later.

"You're planning on seeing your mom regularly after you're adopted by Ames, I think?" asked Emma. Betts nodded. "And you feel good about that?"

Betts looked up. "Yeah. I got her a music box, a nice one, and we're going to have her out to the cabin, and give it to her, and show her my drawings and stuff. I want to tell her that I want to keep seeing her after the adoption, like every week, maybe, because after I'm adopted, it's up to Ames, not the state, and he's OK with it, and so is Zoey."

Betts took some more tea, a signal of sorts that it was time for a bit of a break. "Do you want to work on the sand tray a bit?" asked Emma. "I know you're a talker, but some folks like to work things out on the sand tray. I added some new things."

Betts shook her head. "We're all comfortable here," she said, indicating Toby in her lap. But her eyes traveled to the lines of small figures, animals, and people, and all the things they might use, plants, trees, rocks, cars, motorcycles, boats. And a new red tractor. Betts eyes fell on the tractor and came to a halt. She took in a sharp breath and drew back, startling Toby, who drew up in alarm, digging his claws into the seat of the chair so as to not be tossed off onto the floor. Betts's eyes widened and stared, and Emma followed her eyes to the place where the farm, animals, and implements were arranged.

Emma got up and moved to stand between Betts and the sand tray things, blocking her view. "You OK?" she asked. Betts's eyes came up to Emma, and the look of sheer terror seemed to fade a bit, and she sank back into the chair, breathing quickly, almost panting. Toby reached up with one paw, and placed it firmly on her shoulder, and eased out just enough claws to get Betts' attention. She looked down at him, and her face softened. He looked at her, and mouthed a quiet, "It's OK," and held her eyes until her breathing calmed down and became more regular.

"Ouch," Betts said, lifting his paw off her shoulder, and kissing the top of his head. She reached for the box of tissue and began wiping the cat dry. "I don't know why he likes me," she said. "I get him all soggy."

Emma laughed. "He does like you. I see a different kind of Toby when you're here. He seems to focus on you." She waited a bit and then said, "If there's something up there that bothers you, I can take it down and keep in in my desk. Some folks need an item gone."

"No. I'm OK," said Betts, looking at the cat.

She petted the now drier cat and shifted her weight a bit in the chair. Emma remained standing and said, "We're about out of time for today. Maybe next week you can tell me about the music box and your mom?"

"OK," said Betts, as Toby sensed the time and hopped onto the floor. Emma walked Betts to the door and then down the hallway to where Ames was reading in the waiting room. "Thank you," said Betts, and as she and Ames walked out to the truck, Emma returned to her office, trying to think about how to write this session up. On the floor was a small red tractor, with Toby standing over it, his tail twitching and his eyes wide and wild.

"How'd it go?" asked Ames.

"OK," said Betts, looking tired. "I cried all over Toby again. That cat is something."

Ames hated the idea of Betts crying but remembered his own slow recovery from the Sand Wars. "I wish I had a cat to cry on, sometimes," he said.

Betts looked at him, seeming to work something over in her mind, and then said, "Can we get a cat?" Ames was a bit taken aback, having never had pets as a child, and having not considered getting a pet at the cabin. "We don't have to," said Betts sensing his discomfort.

"No, I'm just thinking about it," he said. He thought some more. "Yeah, I think that would be fine," he said. Betts let out a small shriek, then muffled herself with her hand.

"So," he asked, "Where do you get a cat?"

CHAPTER TWENTY-EIGHT

Filling In The Gaps

Where to find a cat? Betts first thought of a pet store, but Zoey suggested the White River Animal Shelter. They had a reputation as a good, no-kill shelter, Zoey explained, and the animals there were well taken care of. Betts told her that Toby had just showed up one day, standing at the door to Family Services, and had come in when the door was opened, walking straight to Emma's office, and had been there ever since. "Would you like a cat like Toby?" asked Zoey.

Betts shook her head. "Toby's great in Emma's office, but I want a cat that's just a regular cat. You know, plays with squeaky mice, purrs when you pet it. Regular cat stuff."

"What does Toby do, then?" asked Zoey.

Betts grinned back at her. "That's therapy stuff. 'What happens in therapy, stays in therapy.' You said so yourself."

Zoey noticed the slightly sassy voice of the young girl who was starting to trust herself, and the people around her. "Right," she said, smiling.

They drove out to the shelter the next Saturday and found the long, cinderblock building with no difficulty, due both to the nice sign out in front, and the cacophony of barks and howls they could hear a half-mile away. Betts was so eager to get into the building that she bolted as soon as Ames slid out of the truck. He and Zoey watched the child run up the path to the building, her black Keds slapping the pavement, her braid swinging back and forth below her Red Sox cap. "She's turning into a regular kid," said Zoey. "Happy, sassy, funny, eager, running off. Can you picture her doing that a year ago?"

Ames nodded. "She's still having trouble with the nightmares, but it's getting better. She's sketching them and bringing the pictures into Emma. This cat thing is just like any other kid. 'I want a cat. Can I have a cat? Please?' I love that."

Ames held the door for Zoey, and then followed her in. The barking was somehow quieter inside. There was a row of chairs, and a woman sitting behind a desk, working with papers, reading them, clipping some together, and sorting them out. She smiled as Ames and Zoey came in. "Are you with the little girl who just came in? Betsey, I think?"

Ames nodded. "It's Betts. She's looking for a cat."

"That's what she said," said the woman, rising, and leading them to the right, through a door marked with a large cartoon picture of a dog. "She heard the dogs, and went off to see them first, I guess."

They could see Betts, sitting in the aisle, her hand up to the chain-link gate, reaching to something on the other side. There, on the concrete floor, beside a large, dented water dish, stood a huge grey dog. His loose skin was covered with wrinkles, and his head and neck covered with deep scars. His massive head was pressed against the chain-link gate, his eyes closed while Betts rubbed him and spoke softly. As Ames moved into view, the dog startled, drawing back from Betts, the hair along his battered spine bristling in a sharp line, his lips curling back over long, broken yellow teeth. He gave a deep and powerful growl, enough to stop every other bark in the room. He looked right at Ames and then threw himself right at the chain-link gate, which bowed back under the impact, the dog cutting his lips on the wire, snapping toward Ames as though he might bite through the gate. Betts fell back, and when Ames put his hand out to her, the dog went wild, throwing himself at the gate over and over, bending the steel catch, and leaving the gate loose on its steel hinges.

The woman from the desk came running toward them, a large can of pepper spray in her hands. Betts stood in front of the dog, blocking the woman, who yelled for Betts to get out of the way. Ames spoke to the woman, and said, "I think it's OK. He was fine until I came along. Maybe he just doesn't like men." The dog settled back into a low rumble, the hair on his neck still up about halfway. He watched Ames. Betts stepped back to the gate and put her fingers through to pet the dog again.

"Didn't you see the sign?" said the woman, upset and out of breath. She pointed to a hand-lettered sign on the top of the gate. The sign said "Not available for adoption. Please keep back." Betts was ignoring the conversation, trying to calm the dog down. "He's not even supposed to be here," the woman said, "but they can't move him until they have more staff."

Betts looked up at Ames. "I want to take him home. We have to. He's just like me."

Ames looked at the tiny girl, fresh and clean, her hair braided and her eyes pleading. He saw what she meant. And he knew the dog was just like him, as well. "We need to do this," he told Zoey.

Zoey took her budding bureaucratic skills back into the office with the woman and after several phone calls, the two of them returned, with another woman, who was only a little older than Zoey. The three of them looked at Betts, who had slipped her hand through the gap in the loosened gate, and was petting the huge dog on his broad and scared neck. Ames stood nearby, beside Betts, and the dog did little other than keep a sharp eye on him. "See?" said Ames. "Better already. I think he's going to be fine." Betts turned to the young woman, and said, "I thought you were here to save dogs. That's what we want to do." Zoey was persuasive, painting a picture of Ames and Betts as a solid team that could provide a safe home for the giant dog. The young woman asked Ames a few questions about his home, confirming that there was only Betts and him in the house and no other pets. She produced a series of forms, which allowed Ames to foster this dog, prior to another evaluation, to see if he could be adoptable.

In the end, when a stack of papers was signed, and an appointment was made for the shelter staff to come to the cabin for a review, Betts was allowed to lead the dog out of the tiny pen, down the corridor, and out into the sunlight. He bristled up just a bit as he walked past Ames, and Betts spoke to him. "That's Ames. He's nice, so you be nice, too."

The ride home was a series of slow back roads, with Betts riding in the back of the truck, holding onto a leash with one hand, and petting the giant dog with the other. Zoey sat next to Ames, keeping one eye on Betts, and the other on the lookout for the law. "I have become such a bad social worker," she said. They took a stealthy detour behind the grocery store in town, where Zoey brought out a fifty-pound sack of dog food, "the first of many," as she said. When they got home, it was getting dark. Ames lowered the tailgate, and Betts climbed out of the back of the truck, leading the dog, who jumped down and sniffed the ground. Betts took him on a tour of the area, which he marked as he went. He was polite on the leash, and Betts, still weighing a good deal less than fifty pounds, led the dog who weighed more than three times that. Zoey watched, standing with Ames still beside the truck. She laughed. "Mastiff and pitbull, they said. Biggest cat I ever saw."

Ames nodded. "Betts is right, though. He is like her, and like me, too. It doesn't always work out the way you planned. Sometimes it works out better."

The next day, while Betts was at school, and the huge dog slept uneasily on Betts' couch, waiting for her to return, Ames stood on the steps outside Tina's trailer, knocking on the door from time to time. He could hear her footsteps inside and was annoyed that she didn't at least tiptoe. He stopped knocking but still stood on the porch, waiting. He knocked again, and Tina opened the door, her face red and angry, her lower lip swollen and sore. She stood breathing as if she had just climbed a flight of stairs and looked at him as if she were a stranger. "What do you want?" she asked. Ames spoke as evenly as he could, thinking of Betts. "Betts, and me, too, wanted to have you come to the cabin and see her. She wants to keep seeing you, and I want that for her, too. She wants to show you her drawings and stuff, and the dog, and she has a present for you. I can come over and give you a ride if that would help."

"You got her a dog?" Tina asked.

Ames nodded. "Will you come?" asked Ames. He tried to not look at her lip.

Tina looked confused, but said, "I'll think about it. Give me your number, and I'll call you. Don't call me or come by here again. Peter wouldn't like it." She went back into the trailer for a moment and came back with an envelope and a pen. She wrote down the number Ames gave her, and then closed the door without saying anything else. Ames stood there for a bit, uncertain if she was coming back out, but then gave up and headed back to the truck. He was glad he had not brought Betts with him but wondered if things would have gone better with her along. He drove slowly home, trying to think of how to tell Betts that her mother might come to the cabin. Or that she might not.

Ames thought about Tina on his drive back to the cabin. He was angry and frustrated that Tina could not see the chance that Betts was offering her. He found that being angry at his older sister was a comfortable and familiar feeling and that he had lived with that anger and judgment since he was younger than Betts. He remembered Tina standing up to his parents, demanding new clothes for the start of the school year, getting slapped hard enough to leave a bright handprint across her face, and her coming back for more, making the same demand over and over. He remembered his desperate prayers that she would just shut up and stop making problems. She kept coming back, yelling through split lips, demanding what she thought she should have. Ames could not have cared less what he wore to school, but he wondered if Tina had been fighting for him and Clair as well. She fought almost every day, always losing in the end. And Ames wondered now, for the first time, if maybe her fighting wasn't a better thing than his running away.

Clair had always tried to stay and get the family to not fight, trying to please first one, and then the other, and having as little luck as Tina. Clair, promising to make it right, somehow, Tina demanding what she thought they should have, and himself, running away. Three kids, all having to live with the poverty, the exhausted parents, the unwashed stacks of laundry and dishes, the spoiled food served for dinner, the curses, the slaps and the belt, the permeating smell of the cows, the cold and leaky trailer, and the general unhappiness that all of them felt. Tina fought, Clair tried to please, and he ran. Each doing what they could, not able to change things, but only being who they were.

Tina could no more run than he could have stood up to his parents and demanded new clothes. Clair could only try to please. Was one role better than another? Or were they just three unhappy kids, being who they were, and doing only what they knew to do? Ames sighed, feeling, for the first time, some admiration for Tina and her scrappiness, but also feeling a sense of powerlessness as he thought how little choice any of them had. That powerlessness felt like giving up, but the compassion for Tina, for himself, for Clair, and for his poor, struggling parents felt like forgiveness. It was a complicated world.

Betts and Zoey were both deep in a book when Ames arrived at the cabin, Betts on her couch, and Zoey curled up in his chair. Neither had heard him come in, although the dog, whom Betts had named Magnus, had his huge head up, looking at the door as Ames opened it. He recognized Ames, and set his jaws back down on the arm of the couch, and even gave his knotted tail a slight wag of recognition. Ames was in, as far as Magnus was concerned. Ames stood in the doorway and took the time to appreciate the scene before him, remembering the empty cabin he had always returned to before. Somehow this lack of greeting felt the best of all. Everyone belonged and trusted that they belonged, and he was no longer alone.

He took a deep breath, gave his thanks, and then went to Betts, bending over and kissing the top of her head, under the still watchful eyes of the dog.

She looked up, smiled, and said, "Sorry. This is a really good book!" and then went back to reading.

He moved to his chair, where Zoey had gotten up and waited for him with a different kind of smile. "Maybe we need to get another chair?" she asked.

Ames took her in his arms, swung around and sat, pulling her into his lap. "I don't know why," he said. "This seems to work pretty well to me."

"How'd it go?" she asked.

Ames shifted in the chair, pulling her up tight against him. "OK, I guess. She said she's going to think about it, but I think she'll come over. Her lip looked like she'd been slapped. She's angry, hurt, and still wanting to fight, the same as she was back when we were kids. It got me thinking. She was the fighter, Clair was the peacemaker, and I just ran away. I think we all just were who we could be. Tina's still mad, and I'm still hiding. And Clair would still be trying to make things better if she could. And maybe that's all OK," he said.

"It feels OK to me," Zoey said. "In fact, it feels a whole lot better than OK."

Tina called the next day, and Betts answered the phone. Ames was reading a slim book on travel to Costa Rica, which he had found at the thrift store. Tea had been made, and the pot was nearly empty, the day having started a couple of hours before, with a breakfast of eggs and toast already made, consumed, and washed up. Ames heard the surprise in Betts' voice and stopped reading, watching her face as she spoke with her mother on the phone. When she hung up, she turned to Ames with an excited smile on her face. "My mom's coming over here at ten o'clock! We need to clean up!"

Ames looked around at the spotless cabin, swept out and dusted that very morning, the windows washed the day before, Betts' couch bed made up, and her bedding carried back to the bed on the porch. Even Magnus had been brushed that morning and looked as lovely as a retired 160-pound fighting dog could look. He said, "Clean up what?"

Betts grinned, and said, "I don't know, we just need to get ready!" She got up and walked around the cabin, straightening a book here, and taking the silverware off the dishtowel, and putting them in the drawer. The music box sat on the table, the beautiful card propped up beside it. She stopped and grinned at Ames. "I'm just nervous, I guess. Ten o'clock. Everything looks pretty good." She stood and flexed her hands, then smoothed her hair, and then petted Magnus. "Maybe I'll go up on the top rock and sit for a bit. Or wander around some. If she comes early and I'm not here, honk the truck for me."

Betts slipped on her sneakers and headed toward the door. Magnus stepped off the couch and followed her out, glad to have all this nervous energy going somewhere. Ames put his book down, and poured himself another cup of tea, emptying the pot. He looked out the window, and watched the dark little girl and the enormous dog head up the trail until they were out of sight. He turned back to his book but first took a moment out to say thank you.

Tina did indeed come early, at around nine-thirty. Ames heard the rattle of the stones on the path as Tina's Chevy once again slid up next to Ames truck. As she stayed in the car, Ames walked out to see his sister. Tina had driven up to the cabin twice before, to drop Betts off for her first summer, and then to take her back again. Those times she had stayed in the car, refusing Ames' invitation to come in, just sitting in the car, smoking cigarettes one after another, and pitching the still burning butts out onto the ground. Ames was almost to his sister's car when Betts came bounding down the hill, followed by a protective Magnus. Betts stopped at the car window, and quickly leaned in, putting a kiss on her mother's cheek before the startled Tina had a chance to pull away.

"Come on!" plead Betts. "I want you to see my room. Come on!" She jiggled the door handle, and Tina opened the door and stepped out, looking crossly at Magnus, who looked crossly back.

Tina turned to Ames. "Is that dog OK?" she asked. Ames held up his hands.

"I guess," he said.

She turned back toward Magnus and flicked her cigarette butt at him. "Shoo!" she said. Magnus lifted up a few hairs on his neck and stared at her.

"That's Magnus, and he's mine!" said Betts, gleefully. "Let's go inside. I want to show you my present!" Betts tugged her mother up the walk, followed closely by Magnus, and Ames stopped to pick up the still-smoldering butt in the gravel beside the car. He ground it out with his fingers and then carried it to the fire pit.

Betts held the door for her mother, pointing out the porch bedroom, the new shower, and her books and the little museum of found things she had gathered from the woods. She explained about her pictures and showed her mother her set of art supplies, now housed in an old leather briefcase from the thrift store. Ames went to the counter, making a fresh pot of tea, and Betts drew her mother around the small room, pointing out the books she had read, the drawings she had made, and then, the music box. Betts had her mother sit down and then handed the box to her with the card perched on top. Tina set the box in her lap, and read the card. She turned to Betts. "Did you draw this?" she asked. Betts nodded.

She took up the box, admiring the fine inlay and the smooth maple, then opened the lid and looked at the movement inside. "What is it?" she asked. Betts wound it up, and then set it on the wooden table, and lifted the lid to make it play. The chiming song, so sad and so beautiful, rolled out and filled the cabin. Tina stared at the box in awe, leaning over to watch it play, and touching it lightly with one finger, then looked back at Betts. "I know that song. Or something like it. I don't know the name." She wiped at her eyes.

"It's sad, isn't it?" said Betts, proudly.

Tina nodded. "It's beautiful," she said.

"Do you like it?" asked Betts. Tina nodded without saying anything. "She likes it," Betts informed Ames.

Ames poured the tea, handing Tina a steaming cup, and then putting Betts' cup and his on the table. Betts leaned forward and asked her mom, "Do you like your cup? I picked it out for you. I knew you liked horses, and this can be your cup for when you visit up here."

Tina looked at the cup, which had a mare and a filly standing in a green field behind a fence. Tina set the cup down on the table and looked suddenly nervous. "I can't stay. I better go back. Peter might get home early and find me gone. Since he got sick, he doesn't like for me to go out much. And he doesn't know about this. I'll come back on Tuesday morning, early, if I can."

She turned to Ames. "Don't call, or come to the house. Peter won't like it." She rose to go, dabbling a bit at her eyes. Betts moved to her and got in a quick hug before Tina could get away. Magnus stood as well, watching Tina slide out of Betts arms and head to the door. Tina turned to Betts. "Thank you," she said. "I love this," she said, holding out the music box. "I'll come back." She turned and hurried out the door.

Betts stood in the doorway and called out, "I love you, Mom."

Tina opened the Chevy door and turned back. "I love you, too, Betts."

Betts stood on the porch, Ames' unfelt hand on her shoulder, as Tina backed the Chevy out and spun on down the drive. Ames looked at Betts and saw that she was crying. "That went good," she said.

Tina cried too, all the way home, angry at every tear, of course, and had to pull over twice to wipe her face and eyes, so that she could see to drive little more. She cursed herself for losing her daughter, cursed her brother for taking Betts in, and cursed Peter for giving her no choice. She cursed her parents for having three kids with little or nothing to give them, and the world for making her life so hard. And she cursed the prostate cancer that had hollowed Peter's identity, leaving him as impotent and shamed as she had felt her whole life.

This cancer, and the botched surgery done by med students half trained by the University had left Peter limp and leaking. Adult diapers were now on a man who used to admire his abs in the mirror every morning; a vain man who used to pride himself on his ability to have a woman now could have nothing at all. Tina had known about the others and had finally known about Betts. It was easy to see the cancer as something deserved, and Tina wondered if her own rage at Peter after sending Betts away had somehow caused his disease.

Tina had been with Peter since she was fourteen. She saw Peter as a chance to escape the silent trailer on the dairy farm and felt like Peter was what she deserved. Tina was careful to ask for nothing more than a place in his trailer and had kept that promise over the years, accepting his neglect and abuse, his infidelities and gross cruelty, with every year adding to the investment she had made in this life, a life as the one who stayed. And Betts, who looked so much like Tina herself that Tina found her hard to love, Betts asked so little as well, accepting her role with little or no complaint. Uncomplaining, even when Peter had turned on her as if she were another woman.

Tina thought again of the happy Betts who had showed her her new life at the cabin, the pictures, the plants and stones, the enormous dog, the comfortable and safe life she had made with little Ames, and the unreasonable love that Betts still had in her loyal heart for her sad excuse of a mother. Tina touched the music box, this odd and beautifully crafted thing of such sadness and sweetness, which carried what she now understood to be the song of her life, full of grief and sorrow, full of terrible loss, and perhaps, at the end, a bit of redemption.

"I'll bet my mom is listening to that music box right now," Betts said, later on that evening. She had taken her shower, drawn a full-page portrait of Magnus, managing to catch the deep pools of his eyes, and was now sitting on the couch, the bedding brought in from the porch and laid out, a cup of tea in her hand. She had a book open on her lap, but a careful observer might have noted that she had not turned a page in the past twenty minutes. Magnus was on his end of the small couch, looking quite asleep, except for the single eye that was open just the tiniest bit, watching Betts as she thought about the visit with her mother. Betts referred to this as "his dragon eye," a reference to Smaug setting a less protective eye on poor little Bilbo.

Magnus had become an easy part of the household, having taken on the job of protecting Betts from all dangers, real or imagined. He stayed with her on walks, stood on the porch while she showered, and took his own end of the couch every night. Betts' nightmares had slowly disappeared, having lost much of their power the moment she was able to share them with Emma. Her eyes began to have a relaxed, open look, so different than the child she had been that, were one of the hospital staff to meet her on the street, they would pass her by without a clue. Betts' eyes that evening were sparkling as she thought about her mother's visit, and her promise to try and come every week for "tea and conversation," as Betts had put it.

Ames was pleased with the visit as well, relieved, perhaps, but he was worried about how all of this might work out. His anger for his sister was gone, replaced with an affection and a grudging admiration for her pluck and determination. But Ames worried that something would somehow go amiss and that the happiness that Betts now had would again be snatched away from her. Peter had been at the rotten center of Tina's life for these past ten years, and Ames worried that his ability to cause harm was not yet finished. "Maybe I just worry too much," he told himself. But he doubted it.

Betts put the drawing of Magnus on the counter, holding it with one hand and comparing it with the sleepy face of her companion. "I think drawing Magnus is going to be good for me," she said. "He holds still really well, and his wrinkles are almost like he's wearing a robe or something. I think this one is pretty good." She turned the page to Ames, who looked at it carefully.

"I like that," he said. Betts put the picture down on the counter and took up the kerosene lantern.

She raised the globe, then struck a wooden match, and held the flame out, and then on to the moist wick exposed on the lamp. The flame spread and Betts lowered the globe, and took the match away, blew it out, and put the match into the resting little green woodstove. She adjusted the wick down just a bit to stop the smoke and turned back to her uncle. "We're going out to answer Nature's call," she announced. The big dog got off the couch and followed her out the front door. She had almost closed the door, but pushed it open again, calling to her uncle. "The stars are great. You should come see."

Ames set down his book and got up from his chair and followed her outside. He watched Betts and Magnus head down the gravel path to the outhouse, their walk lit up by the yellow pool of light that swayed from side to side as she walked. There was a hook inside for the lantern, and Ames saw the pool of light disappear into the little house, with a bit showing at the cracks around the door. He looked up at the stars and took in a breath. Living on the mountain had its challenges, but the blessings were well worth it. Thousands of tiny white lights, spread across the black sky, with a sliver of a moon rising up in the east, just visible through the trees. He looked at the beauty before him, and above him, and prayed again, "Thank you. Thank you."

CHAPTER TWENTY-NINE

Letting It Out

Betts was back for her next appointment with Emma two days after her visit with her mother. Betts was still glowing about it, and she was excited to tell Emma. She left Ames in the waiting room, where he pulled out a book he had found on building saunas in Finland and walked back with Emma. Betts was so excited that she almost forgot the session from two weeks before, up until she tried to enter the office, and something held her back. Betts stood in the doorway, leaning against the doorframe. Emma turned back to her and said, "You OK?" Toby lay on the desk, his golden eyes staring into hers. He winked at her and gave her just a bit of a cat smile. "Yeah, I'm OK," she said.

Betts's eyes went to the shelf of tiny figures for the sand tray. "Did you take down the tractor?" she asked.

"Very observant," said Emma. "Toby knocked it off the shelf, and when I put it back up, he knocked it down again. I just put it in my desk." Betts looked at the desk, with its closed drawers, and then at the big cat stretched out on top, looking like a lion standing over his prey. He purred as she walked into the room, lying on top of the desk. Betts took her chair and tried to think of what she could say. Toby moved off the desk and sat beside her, his claws out just a bit into the arm of the chair, purring steadily with his eyes closed. Betts reached out a hand to rub his head.

Emma sat on the couch, after getting herself a cup of tea and pouring one for Betts. She waited. The only sound in the office with the steady purring of the cat, and the faint sound of cars driving past outside. Betts took up her tea and took a sip. "I was all excited to tell you about my visit with my mom, and then I just kind of felt weird when I came in." Emma sipped her tea and waited. Toby purred. "My mom came up to the cabin for a visit, and she saw my room, and the pictures I made, and I gave her the music box. She really liked it." Betts paused for a breath. "I told her that I wanted to live with Ames. He's adopting me. But that I wanted to keep seeing her, too, like for visits, at the cabin, or maybe out for breakfast down in town or something. And she could come to my stuff at school, like plays and things. Ames is OK with that, and once he adopts me, it's up to him if I can see my mom. So, I can. I told her I loved her, and she said she loved me. I think she was planning for me to live with Ames, so she could get me away from Peter." Betts stopped, aware that she had brought up Peter again.

Emma sat quietly, listening. She smiled at Betts and said, "I'm glad you can still see your mom. And I'm glad she liked the music box."

Toby purred, and Emma waited, and Betts relaxed a little. She took a breath and started. "Last time I was here, I saw the tractor on the shelf, the little red one. I saw it, and I just felt awful, like I was going to be sick." She waited. So did Emma. "I thought about it when I got home. I don't think the tractor bothered me. I mean, there's no reason it should. I've never even been around a tractor." She waited again. So did Emma. "But I thought about it, and there's this girl, she's about my age, named Rebekah, and she was afraid of that tractor. Really scared, and kind of sick about it, too. I had dreams where I was dying on the ground, and Ames was over me, only he was a kid? I think those are Rebekah's dreams, not mine."

Betts stopped and looked at Emma, who looked back. They both sipped their tea. Emma said, "Tell me a little about Rebekah."

Toby purred in her lap, and said, "It's not crazy. Emma will know that."

"Rebekah has been kind of with me, kind of inside me since Peter hurt me." She stopped and then started again. "Peter raped me and did worse stuff than rape me, and Rebekah came, and she took me away." Betts stopped, her breathing so hard it was as if she was underwater. She made a low moaning sound, and then gagged, and threw up onto her lap, narrowly missing Toby, who leapt to the chair's arm. Betts sat there sobbing, struggling to breathe, with tears streaking her face, and the vomit dripping down her chin onto the pool in her lap.

Emma was suddenly up and with Betts, taking her own sweatshirt off and wiping Betts face first, and then her lap. Betts moaned and sobbed, and Emma squatted beside her, saying, "It's OK. You're safe now. It's OK."

"I'm sorry," Betts wailed. "I'm sorry."

Emma leaned close to Betts and spoke quietly to her. "It's not your fault, Betts. None of it was your fault at all. You're OK." Toby climbed up on Betts, kneading his paws against her shoulders, his claws neatly tucked in, and he rubbed his face against hers. Betts cried, and cried, and her breathing settled some, and then she snuffed in a great breath, and let it out in a slow sigh.

"Oh," she cried, "I threw up all over your chair. And your sweatshirt!"

"It happens," said Emma. She tucked the sweatshirt into the closet and brought out a roll of paper towels and some wet wipes. "Sometimes feelings come out all at once, bringing a little lunch or dinner with them," she said, with a smile.

Betts smiled back and finished cleaning herself up as best she could. "I stink now," she said.

"That's OK," said Emma. "Do you feel better?" she asked.

Betts thought about it. "I think so. I have been wanting to tell you, and I couldn't do it. Rebekah came and helped me kind of get away, not my real self, but just my mind or something. Like she and I just left. We went up to the cabin, where I live now. And ever since then we're kind of blended sometimes, although I don't see her as much anymore. She's Ames' sister, the one that got killed by a tractor when she was nine. And we're both named Rebekah." Betts stopped and looked at Emma, still wiping at her hair with a wet wipe. "Do you think I'm crazy?" she asked.

Emma smiled and worked a bit at the vomit in Betts hair on the other side. "Not at all. Lots of times when sturdy kids are stuck in a situation where they just can't stay, but they can't get away either, like if someone is hurting them, they find ways to be OK. It sounds like Rebekah found you just when you needed her, and that she helped to keep you as safe as she could. That sounds like a good thing, to me."

Betts cleaned one of Toby's paws, which he tolerated with an irritated look on his face. "You've heard of stuff like this before?" Betts asked.

"People find a way to be OK. There's a lot of good in this world." Emma answered.

Betts thought about that for a bit. "Rebekah is my real name. They called me Betts 'cause it's easier. And my mom named me after her sister, Clair, who was really named Rebekah, too. Clair was just her middle name. Her dad killed her with a tractor, by accident, when she was nine. The dreams I had about dying are really her dreams, not mine. She was really nice, and Ames said she always tried to make everyone else feel better. When I went up to visit my grandmother, in the nursing home, Rebekah was there with me, and she and my grandmother talked, while I just kind of watched. She showed me her grave when I was at my grandmother's funeral. She's not here so much anymore, like today, even though I got really scared, she wasn't here at all." Betts looked scared again, but she went on. "I think she came to help me, but I think she needed my help, too, to see her mom, and to help my mom get better. I think she wants Ames and my mom and me to be OK." Betts came to a stop and just sat petting Toby. She looked at Emma. "So, you don't think this is crazy?"

Emma looked at Betts. "Crazy is when something breaks, and a part you need doesn't work right anymore. You have something that came along and helped you to stay in one piece. Kind of the opposite of crazy. I guess it's a someone, rather than a something, although I don't understand all of that. But you work just fine. You think for yourself, you're kind, you help other people, you love people, you're funny and brave. I think you're in great shape. And maybe Rebekah helped you to stay that way when some hard things were happening."

Betts thought about that and looked up at Emma. "Did you know your cat talks"?" she asked.

Emma looked at Toby, curled up on the arm of the chair, grooming himself, still purring faintly. "That wouldn't surprise me a bit," she said.

"Can we talk about the Peter stuff next week?" Betts asked. "I'm pretty done for today, and I want to go home and take a shower and change."

"Sure," said Emma. "You talk about it when you feel ready. I think the hardest part was today. And that's already behind you. I'll see you next week. And I'm glad about your visit with your mom. I think that's a good thing."

Betts walked out of the office to find Ames sitting by the fish tank, now reading a book about handmade knives from Finland. He looked up and smiled. "How'd it go?" he asked.

"Good," said Betts.

"Ice cream?" asked Ames.

"Nope," said Betts. "I want a shower." Emma waved, and then went back to her office, to write this session up, somehow.

CHAPTER THIRTY

Tina Gets Free

Tina got home way before Peter was due back from the doctor. She now saw the trailer a little differently, having just come from the spotless cabin where her brother was raising her daughter. The kitchen sink was loaded with unwashed dishes, and more dirty dishes crowded the counters. The kitchen smelled of cigarette smoke and old chicken, due to the overflowing ashtray and last week's KFC bucket, half-filled with bones. She knew the fridge would smell as well. She opened the window and cleared the stack of dishes from the sink, ran the water until it was hot, pushed in the plug, and squirted in a good-sized dose of detergent. She let the hot water run until the sink was half full, then scraped the dishes, and slid them into the steaming water.

She thought about Betts, safe and happy with Ames, and thought about the visit she had just had, and how happy Betts was to see her. "I love you!" Betts had said, and she waved from the porch. She was packing the trashcan down with a paper towel, and thinking about the other times she had heard, "I love you." From Ames and Clair, back when Tina would be crying in her bed, after losing another fight with her parents. Maybe not once from her mother and father, but maybe their love was spoken in the long work and the food in the fridge, and the occasional new set of clothes for school. She added another squirt of dish soap into the water and kept working her way through the dishes. When the counter was empty, she wandered through the trailer, collecting two loads of plates and dishes, scraped them, and then, drew a new sink of water, and slid them in.

She thought about the life Betts had had with her and Peter, and the almost two years Betts had suffered between that life and the one she now had with Ames. Her tears slid down into the soapy water. "I love you." Tina thought about the happy, cheerful face she had left behind at the cabin. She thought about the music box, playing the music of her life, now hidden in the trunk of her car, hidden from Peter, who would smash the thing in a minute. Shame and regret made it hard for Tina to breath, and she moved from the sink, opening windows, and trying to clear the air.

She washed the glasses and cups next, then did the silverware. Most of the cooking had been done in the aluminum foil tubs the food had been bought in, but there were a few pots and pans crusted with food, that she put in to soak. She dried her eyes over and over, but the tears continued to come, and in that blurry, watery world, she changed the bag on the vacuum, and went over the floors, under the furniture, and then changed the bag out again. She moved to the bathroom, gathering up clothes and towels from the floor and sink, scrubbing out the toilet, then doing the sink and shower with one of the towels. She looked at her face in the mirror, red and raw from the salty tears still running down her face, her lip still swollen and a little split from the night before.

She moved to the bedroom, and took a few favorite things, tucking them into a trash bag, and then carrying it to the front door. She walked through the trailer, straightened the furniture from where she had vacuumed, left the windows open, then went in to look at the fridge. She took out a few gone south baggies of leftovers, noted the beer and pickles contents, and then closed the door, taking in the kitchen, and giving it a final nod of approval. She went to the door and stood for a moment, and thought about leaving a note. What could she possibly say? She walked out the door, got the music box out of the trunk, and set it on the seat beside her, tossing her bag of clothes in the back seat. She started her car up, and drove away, to the north. To a new start.

When Betts and Ames returned to the cabin, they found Zoey and Magnus out by the fire pit, Zoey reading a book and Magnus snapping at the gnats that buzzed by. Betts said, "Hi," but declined a hug and headed to the shower.

Ames sat down beside Zoey. "Has she been sick?" asked Zoey.

"I think she threw up with Emma today, but she seemed to feel it was a good session. She never talks much about it," Ames said. Ames stretched out with a bit of a moan. "I'm still sore from all that green maple yesterday," he explained.

"You're just fishing for a back rub," Zoey laughed.

Ames nodded, "Maybe so," he said.

They could hear the increasing roar and rattle of a car coming up the road, and before they could say anything, the car burst into the drive, and a drunken Peter threw open the door and tried to get out. He had one leg on the ground, and his hand on the door, just trying to rise up from the low Camaro, when Magnus struck him square in the chest, knocking him back, his head slamming against the top of the doorframe. Magnus had his teeth dripping and bare, his lips curled back, and a deep growl came from his belly, or maybe the pits of Hell. Ames rose and laid a hand on Magnum's collar, and slowly drew the dog back, with some effort. Peter gasped for breath, his eyes red and his breathing ragged. "Where's Tina?" he demanded.

"Not here," said Ames, holding the dog with some difficulty. Magnus still growled and leaned in toward Peter, and Ames stood beside the door, looking down.

The effort that Ames had made over the past years to keep himself in check was paying off, but just barely. "I think you need to get out of here," Ames said quietly. "I'm getting tired of holding back the dogs. They want to kill you." Peter looked up through his bleary haze and saw the cold fire in Ames' eyes looking hungrily into his, and he suddenly felt afraid. Ames stepped back, pulling Magnus with him, and closed the car door, still looking at Peter through the open window. Peter started to say something, but he looked up at Ames, and his voice ran dry, and he shifted the car into reverse and spun the balding tires back out the drive.

Ames turned back to the fire pit and Zoey, seeing a side of Ames she had not yet seen, was quiet, scared by Peter, and a bit by Ames as well. "Sorry," he said, still breathing carefully. "Peter ought not to come up here."

Betts stood in the door of the cabin, draped in a towel and crying. Ames moved toward her. "He's going to hurt my mom," she said.

Tina had driven, without a plan, heading north up the Interstate, past Montpelier, then past Waterbury, and on up, past the statues of whales' tails so oddly placed by a cornfield, and up to Burlington, taking the main exit into the city. She drove down toward the lake, toward the downtown, and saw a parking garage, where she thought she might hide the car for a bit. Since her crying had stopped, around Montpelier, she had begun to think about Peter, returning to a clean and empty house, and the rage he would have for her. Some instinct, or perhaps just the years of drunken threats, had let Tina know that she might run, but she could never hide, and that Peter would track her down and make her sorry she ever left.

So far, she was not sorry at all, but she needed to think. She drove up three floors in the parking garage, before picking a spot somewhat hidden behind an elevator and the stairwell. She backed the car in, hoping to hide the bumper stickers that Peter had put on. She took a change of clothing from the garbage bag, picked up the music box, and took the elevator down to the ground level, and walked out onto the street.

As she walked through Burlington, she felt lighter and freer than she ever had before. She had come to Burlington once as a kid, to take a big boat out on the lake, and had been up a few times since for shopping at the Best Buy. She had always felt that Burlington was a little magic, with all the college kids, the long slope down to the lake, the shops, the musicians, the feel of the place so different from Williamstown or Randolph.

Today felt good. She had cleaned the trailer, one last time, and done a good job. Betts was safe and happy and on the way to having Ames take care of her from now on. Even if Peter came and killed her now, Tina felt that that might be OK. But she wanted a chance for more days like this, exploring, thinking of possibilities, and watching Betts grow up. She realized that Peter was probably on the road right now, with enough beer in him to make him reckless, driving up to the cabin, maybe, then off to her job in town. Burlington would come eventually, but not tonight.

She walked into an old hippie coffee shop, Muddy Waters, carrying her music box in one hand, and her purse and some clothes in the other. She had been in this place before and loved the shabby couches, the stacks of magazines, and the groups of people sitting together, laughing, talking, touching each other, and being friends. When she had been in Burlington as a kid, she had seen the city as a different world from the dirty strip malls and predatory guys she found around home. Today, it looked like a new life.

She relaxed a bit, and ordered a black coffee and a turnover, and took a seat at a tiny table in the corner. The place was filling up, and Tina felt a stab of the old loneliness as she looked from table to table, feeling like she was ten years old and back in the small school gym, the lunch tables folded down, and everyone there sat with friends, except her. Happy people, safe and easy lives, open and friendly with each other, listening, laughing, telling jokes and stories.

A woman about her age, carrying a cup of tea and a slice of banana bread came and stood beside her table, then leaned over and said, "Mind if I sit with you? This place is pretty full."

Tina drew back but then said, "Sure. OK." Tina moved the pile of clothes to her lap and shifted the music box off to one side.

The young woman sat down and smiled, holding her hand out to Tina. "Hi. My name's Mary," she said. Tina offered her own hand back and felt the shock of another person's touch. Mary smiled and said, "Do you live here?"

"No," said Tina, "I've been living down in Williamstown, but I moved today."

"Are you moving here?" asked Mary.

Tina smiled, a little embarrassed. "I don't know," she laughed. "I don't know what I'm going to do yet."

"There must be a story in that," said Mary.

Tina said there was, and amazingly, began to tell her story, there, over coffee and tea and a turnover and some banana bread, like all the other people in the room, laughing, and crying some, while Mary listened and laughed with her, and cried a bit, too, holding her hand from time to time. Tina told about Peter, and then Betts, and Ames, and then Clair, and then about the music box, which she wound and played for Mary. Tina realized that if a person walked into Muddy Waters, right then, she would see Tina and Mary, laughing and talking, and assume that they were friends, just like everybody else. And then Tina realized that maybe she and Mary could be friends.

They refilled their drinks, and ordered another piece of banana bread to share, and talked, and as the evening came on and the streets became dark, plans were made for Tina to move into the guest room at Mary's house until her plans firmed up. Mary rented the upstairs of an old house on the Northside, where the rents were lower, and the residents "more interesting," as Mary said. They walked together to retrieve Tina's car, drove it to Mary's, and slipped it into the garage, pulling the door down, and leaving Mary's Subaru on the street. Tina began to relax a little and to imagine that there was a chance that Peter wouldn't find her, after all.

Tina called into her job and explained that she would not be coming in. "We can find you something around here," said Mary. "Lakeside Pizza had a card up in the window, and the India Palace has one, too." Mary showed Tina the tiny bedroom, already made up with clean sheets and a few books by the bed. Tina went through her trash bag of clothes, and hung them in the closet, or folded them in the drawers. She put the music box on top of the small dresser and wound it up. They listened to it, and this time the song sounded a little less sad.

Ames got a call from Tina the next morning, telling him that she was in Burlington, living with a new friend. Although Tina tried to sound nonchalant, Ames could hear the excitement in her voice. He told her that Peter had come by the cabin, and then put Betts on, who was tugging at his sleeve the whole time. "Are you OK?" Betts asked, then listened to Tina, her face relaxing as her mother described the new apartment, looking for jobs and living with Mary, who wanted to meet Betts. When Tina told Betts that she was no longer going to live with Peter, Betts' face darkened. "I still want to live with Ames," she said. "I still want Ames to adopt me, even if you aren't living with Peter anymore."

There was a pause as Betts listened to Tina's response, and Ames walked away a little bit, wanting to give her some space to work this out with her mom. Betts nodded a couple of times, then her face began to brighten up, and she turned to Ames. "Can we go up to Burlington and meet my mom and Mary this Saturday? She wants to show me her new place. We can meet at Battery Park, at eleven?"

Ames smiled and nodded. "That would be fine," he said. He went to his chair by the window and opened his book, a study of the life cycle of a pond.

When Betts hung up, she looked relieved and went to stand by Ames chair. "She says she's not going to go back to Peter, but she's said that before, and gone back a lot. She gets lonely and scared, and then feels that she needs Peter somehow, or even that I need Peter somehow, which is crazy. Peter is the last thing anybody needs."

"Did that go OK?" asked Ames.

Betts thought about it. "I guess so," she said. "It's weird, though. Mom never goes anywhere, and she went all the way to Burlington. And she never makes friends. And now she has this friend named Mary that she moved in with. And she seems happy. She never sounds happy. It's just weird."

Betts sat back down on the couch, and Magnus scooted around, trying to make room for her. She picked up her book, and then put it back down again. "If I were going to wish something for my mom, I'd wish that she would leave Peter, not go back, make friends, be happy, want me to be adopted by you, and see me for visits and come to my school stuff. And I would want her to be happy. But I never thought any of those things would happen. She ran away from Peter before, but she always came back. I don't know," finished up Betts, not sounding happy at all.

"You worried that it won't work out?" asked Ames.

Betts nodded. "She might go back to him, or he might find her and hurt her. Or maybe she'll change her mind and not want me to live with you, and be angry when I do and not want to visit me." Betts looked a little teary as she broke off, and Magnus shifted his weight, laying his massive head on her lap.

Ames nodded and got up. "Would you like some tea?" he asked. Betts nodded and kept rubbing Magnus's head. The dog stretched out, his huge feet hanging off one end of the couch. She rubbed his belly, and he closed his eyes. Ames picked up Betts' moose mug from the table, and took it and his mug to the counter, where the big teapot sat beneath the cozy. He filled both mugs, and brought Betts' mug back to her, putting it on the table. Ames leaned over and kissed the top of her head. "I guess there's nothing you can do but wait and see how it works out," he said. "I can take you to Burlington on Saturday, and you can see how your mom's doing.

"Yeah. It's just hard," she said.

"Yeah," said Ames. "Sometimes, it is hard."

CHAPTER THIRTY-ONE

Making Plans

While Peter was alternately drinking and breaking things in the trailer back in Williamstown, Tina had arrived with Mary at her apartment in the north end of Burlington. Narrow clapboard houses, painted vivid colors, stood in tight rows along the narrow street. Tibetan prayer flags hung on the porches, and bicycles cluttered the yards. The North end was a student neighborhood, with the University of Vermont and two smaller colleges in town, the most affordable housing in this wonderful city on the lake. Mary's house was painted a deep blue, with coral trim, and sported a bright yellow door.

Mary had found Burlington as a student, blowing through her parents' patience and savings at the end of two years, earning only nine credits and a GPA of slightly below a 2.0. The financial tap was turned off, with the expectation that Mary would return to Hartford, CT, move back into her old bedroom, and take classes at the local community college under the watchful eye of her parents. Instead, Mary got a job at a small Vietnamese restaurant, first bussing tables and washing dishes, then prepping endless piles of vegetables in the morning before the restaurant opened, and finally moving on to a sous chef position of sorts, as well as being Jill of all Trades, as is usually the case in a small place.

She worked close to thirty hours a week, just enough for the rent on the top floor of the bright blue house she welcomed Tina too. After a year,

Mary's parents gave up on their daughter returning home and offered enough tuition dollars for Mary to take a few classes each semester, classes she completed with pride and decent grades. Boys came and went, with Mary reluctant to surrender her newfound freedom.

    The apartment was small, clean, and half-filled with a variety of found objects, including some sidewalk furniture, cast out at the end of the semester by students returning home, either graduating or giving up. A couch that was worn threadbare by dogs and cats was vacuumed and dressed in an Indian print tapestry. Tables nicked and scratched celebrated their scars with some sandpaper, steel wool, and a bit of lemon oil. The table in the kitchen was half-filled with books and papers from Mary's current Human Anatomy class, a class Mary described as "kicking my butt." The table had room for two plates and two cups, which Mary filled with cold leftovers from her job, and apple wine. There was a quart jar filled with knives, forks, and spoons, as well as a handful of chopsticks. Mary took chopsticks, and handed some to Tina, showing her how to use them, and the two chop-sticked up the cold rice noodles and veggies over laughter, stories and cups of apple wine.

    Tina sat in wonder. Had this house, this life, existed all along, just a few miles up the interstate? Had laughter, cold Vietnamese food and friendship been there all along, waiting for her to wake up and open the door? Tina found herself dropping half of her food back on the plate, laughing and trying again, amazed at how it felt to have a friend. While Peter was falling over the pieces of furniture in the darkened trailer, having broken out all the lights, Tina was putting away her clothing into a small wood dresser, each drawer painted a different color, and turning on the ceiling fan, cooling off the tiny guest room. She set the music box on top of the dresser and wound it up one more time. The music played out, beautiful and rich, filled with sadness and harmony, healing, and hope.

    Tina was used to sleeping alone since Peter was often out for the night. The bed was comfortable, and the dark tapestry curtains, embroidered with elephants, were pulled shut, promising the chance for sleeping in. Mary checked in on her, and then went back to the table, pulling out the books for a bit of late-night studying. Tina lay awake, her excitement, her fear, and this new feeling of friendship and happiness keeping her awake for a bit. She felt like a balloon, finally released and flying up into the air over the old country, which had held her down for so long.

    She lay in the bed and thought about her life with Peter, that life she had had since she was fourteen, and all the years she had before that on the dairy farm, and tried to find a moment that was anything like this. Tina was twenty-five years old, and now had her first friendship, her first happiness, and her first night without fear or anger. Betts was happy and safe. And now, suddenly, she was happy and safe, too. She lay awake on the small bed, under the cotton quilt, with the ceiling fan turning above her, smiling and feeling somehow new.

The smell of coffee and a soft knock on her door woke Tina in the morning. At first, she startled, then, as she looked around the room and remembered where she was, she smiled again, in wonder. Mary came to the door, holding a steaming cup of coffee for her, which she set beside the bed. Beside the cup, she placed a brass key on a bright yellow ribbon. "I'm heading off to class. You don't need to get up. If you do, explore the place. The bathroom has everything you need: soap, shampoo, conditioner, and I think a new toothbrush, behind the mirror. This," she tapped the brass key, "fits the doorknob lock. We don't have a key to the deadbolt. I'll be back around eleven-thirty, and we can get some lunch if you're here. If you are looking for work, the India Palace, down by Muddy Waters, has a card in the window. I would love cold Indian food to give us a break from the stuff I bring home." She turned to go but looked back. "Did you sleep good?" she asked.

"Yeah, after a while. I just lay there and tried to believe it and all. Thank you," Tina said.

"Nice to have you here," said Mary. "Don't go back to Peter. I'll be back after class." Mary closed the door, and Tina lay still for a bit, smelling the coffee, and thinking about this new life she might have found.

Tina called Betts that morning and set up a meeting on Saturday. The North end of Burlington was a crazy patchwork of one-way streets, and giving Ames directions to the "flat," as Mary liked to call the place, was too hard, so they agreed to meet at Battery Park. Battery Park was a favorite part of the Burlington scene, a long stretch of greenway along the shore of Lake Champlain, with a bike path, picnic tables, and a nice playground that the local children flocked to. It was by the Northside, and an easy walk for Tina, and Mary, who wanted to meet Betts. Betts had been there before with Ames and thought that it would be a perfect place to meet.

After calling Betts, Tina walked to the Royal India Palace, an eight-table lunch and dinner spot near the Church Street Mall. She arrived before they opened and knocked at the door. An elderly woman came to the door, dressed in a sari and high-top sneakers, a Red Sox hat, with her thick, black hair pinned out of the way. She asked Tina for her food service work history, and Tina explained that although she had worked since she was thirteen, house cleaning, doing some retail work and a few factory jobs, she had never worked in a restaurant before. Working at thirteen impressed the women, though, and she hired Tina on the spot, asking her to come in the next day at nine in the morning to start her training. She told Tina to be on time, with "on time" being some fifteen minutes before she was supposed to come in. Tina promised to be there at eight forty-five in the morning, and she and the woman shook hands. As Tina went out the door, the owner removed the help wanted card from the window.

Tina walked down the street, looking in the windows of the shops, and at the people who were already filling the open mall. She walked to the end, and saw the Old Crow bookshop, which Betts had mentioned, and went inside. She pictured Ames and Betts walking the aisles, and sat for a moment in one of the couches. She thought of this new life Betts had, and this new life she might have and thought of them having breakfast at Muddy Waters, then walking down to the Old Crow and watching Betts shop for books.

Ames, all grown up and being a father, Betts, happy and healthy and safe, Clair gone, forever nine years old, laid out on satin in a borrowed dress, surrounded by books and her stuffed animals. Her mother and father, dead. No chance her parents would ever step up to the plate, now. And Tina? Tina, living with a friend in Burlington, working at the Indian Palace, and hanging out with her daughter on the weekend? It all felt OK, and lots of it felt really good. She and Ames had turned out all right, and Clair was all right, too, she somehow knew. Tina could parent herself a little now, taking care that she was safe and happy. And parent Betts some, too, when she could, making regular visits that were about listening to Betts and learning to touch some, and to make a new life that felt safe and good.

Back at the apartment, Tina shared the news about the job. Mary was thrilled at the prospect of adding Indian food to the current Vietnamese fare she had been living on. "Now all we need is a part-time gig at a Mexican place. Then we'd be all set," she said. Mary opened a beer and then opened a second one for Tina. "So," she said, "tell me about Prince Charming." Tina was confused and said nothing. "Like, is he going to show up and pound on the door?" She saw how unhappy Tina looked, and dropped the humor from her voice. "Do we need to worry about that, or do you think it's OK?" she asked.

"I don't know," said Tina. "He came to my brother's place, but the dog knocked him back in the car, and he left. I think he'll look for me. He's never been left before, and he won't like the idea of it. And he's sick now, with cancer, and that makes him crazier. I don't think he'd look in Burlington, but he might. I think he might just keep on looking." Tina looked scared, and her eyes filled up with tears.

"Hey," said Mary. "We'll be OK. We can let Steve, on the first floor, know. Steve's huge, and we can keep the door locked. Maybe we can get a dog?"

Mary had a lot of ideas about what to do with Peter, but most of them came from watching *Thelma and Louise* or singing along to *Earl*, by the Dixie Chicks. Although it was nice to have Mary all angry and dangerous on her behalf, Tina found very little of it helpful. Tina's car would remain tucked out of sight for the time being, with her work and the downtown within walking distance. Trips to visit Betts could be done in Mary's car, which she seldom used, anyway. Steve was indeed informed of the situation, and he was eager to be of use, although Tina thought he must be pretty clueless to be that enthusiastic. There was a battered women's shelter downtown, and Tina planned a visit with them to ask their advice. Mary said, "So many guys turn out to be crazy assholes there must be a system in place for dealing with them."

CHAPTER THIRTY-TWO

Getting Ready

Ames was working on a fallen maple up the hill from the cabin, an easy enough task since the tree was about sixteen inches in diameter at breast height, and lay solidly on the ground. Betts worked with him, hauling the smaller rounds and the brush away, enjoying the rhythm of the work, and the competence she now felt in working with firewood, and the astonishing stack of bills that were accumulating in her toolbox. She was planning on buying two bicycles, one for her, and one for her mother, to be kept at her mom's place in Burlington. Betts saw her mother and herself, gliding along the bike path beside the lake, a picnic lunch packed in the basket on Betts bike. She saw them riding side by side, their strong legs pushing them along together over the smooth pavement, the wind in their faces. Betts had even found a store in Burlington called "The Old Spoke's Home," that carried used bikes, nice ones that were affordable for a girl like Betts, with steady work.

Ames worked his way through the maple, lugging the bigger rounds onto the truck, and stopping from time to time to tend to the chain on his saw, or fill the tiny oil and gas tanks from the red plastic gas can marked "2 Stroke," or the black plastic jug of bar oil. Betts took a break when Ames did and worked steadily when he did, as well. Her stamina had grown over the year, and she was able to do the right thing over and over, building up the same fluffy coating of sweat and sawdust on her arms and legs that covered Ames, wiping her face from time to time with the bandana in her pocket.

Ames was aware that Betts matched his pace but worked at the same rate he always had, careful, no hurry, but steady. The two of them were able to put up a good three cords in a day, leaving the ground behind neatly raked, and the brush piled at the edge of the woods. Landowners sometimes came to check on the work, once bringing a jug of lemonade and a bag of Oreos, and they occasionally commented on Betts' steady output. She shrugged off these comments, a little offended that her work seemed exceptional, just because she was a young girl. She knew she was tough, and tougher, as Emma had said, at the broken places.

The rage and fear and numbness that had pretty much defined her life a year ago was now mostly gone, and her sense of Rebekah had faded as well. She still felt the girl's presence sometimes but found her less clear, less defined, as time went on. While Betts at first missed the other girl, she saw the increasing distance as a vote of confidence for the sturdy new life she was building.

Betts' work with Emma, slow at first, and never clearly directed at the trauma, had none the less brought forth her story, and Betts was beginning to see herself as the brave, strong and resilient girl in the center. Ames had come in twice, prepped by Emma beforehand to keep his own feelings in check and be there as a support for Betts as she shared her story. He did that well, breathing steady and saying things like, "That must have been hard." He had ten minutes in the truck to cry and twist his hands in helpless rage before he met Betts back at the door of the clinic, his face dry and smiling. "Ice Cream?" he suggested.

And so, the story came out, with even some vague sense of the abuse at the Children's Retreat. Emma watched Betts' stability return after each revelation, timing her move to report the abuse to Betts' ability to tolerate that process as well. Emma took in the reality of Betts' early years with a calm and accepting face and a quiet and supportive voice. After Betts left, Emma wrote the sessions up, sometimes crying as she did so. Her supervisor, a grizzled old veteran of the trauma wars, had described Emma's role as a child trama therapist as something like the firefighters at Chernobyl, suiting up to go and do their shift, even as they knew the radioactive fires at the melting core were etching cancer in their bones.

Five years was a good guess for how long a trauma therapist might stay in the field, and many moved on sooner, seeking a lighter work in the schools, or in education. All the good ones carried a burden forever after, taking on, at some level, the injuries, and wounds of their small clients, learning to see the world as capable of great cruelty and evil. The astonishing resilience and ability of their young clients to heal and love even after such a betrayal offered a balm of sorts.

Emma had struggled to make sense of Rebekah, the ghost girl that Betts had described. She recorded it only lightly, referring to Betts' successful use of a positive introject in surviving her trauma. How lively and independent that introject was and how directly connected to the dead aunt of the same name was not recorded, since Emma had decided to let that part of the work remain unexplained. Emma was thankful for more evidence of a positive spirit of healing in the world, and kindness in a world that could be so cruel. In the face of horror and abuse, it was important to have some talisman of good to hang on to. Emma had wondered how Betts had come through her nightmare of abuse at the hands of Peter and the child psychiatric system in such relatively good shape, and Rebekah was clearly an important part of that.

Across the room, as Emma worked, Toby stretched in the chair that Betts usually took. He looked over at Emma and purred. Emma knew that Toby had a role in Betts work as well, and might understand how all this worked better than she ever could. She stood up and walked over to the cat, petting him along his thick neck. "So, Toby," she asked, "What's the deal with Betts and Rebekah?"

Toby rumbled and rubbed against her hand, then looked up at her and opened his mouth just a bit. "Purr," he said.

Saturday morning was bright and clear in Vermont. Betts was up early, checking out the blue sky with the puffy white clouds drifting across, a few wispy strands moving below. Betts could have told you their names, and maybe explained the prevailing winds, as well, having recently gotten into a book on climate and weather that Ames had left out on the table. Saturdays were often a workday in the summer since the summer folks were up, and their acres needed to be brought up to city park standards.

This Saturday was different, though, with Betts up not only early, but showered, and wearing a shirt she found at the thrift shop, featuring a mother horse and a filly, looking a lot like the cup she had found for her mother to keep at the cabin. Betts also had a newish pair of pedal pushers, as the elderly lady at the shop had called them, which, unlike the rest of her shorts, had not taken the wear of the woodlot on.

Ames was just getting up, and Zoey was as well, still a bit shy at waking up in the cabin and climbing down from Ames' sleeping loft. Zoey had that long, super fine hair that puffed like a dandelion in the morning, and Betts smiled at Zoey as she came down the ladder. "Your hair exploded," she said.

"I know," laughed Zoey. "I ought to braid it before I go to bed, but I keep forgetting. It'll take me an hour to get it combed out now."

Betts had put the kettle on for tea and had brought eggs in from the old propane fridge on the porch. "Eggs and toast?" she asked. "And some tea?"

"That would be wonderful," said Zoey, looking with wonder at her hair in the mirror by the door. Betts laid out three plates as Ames came down the ladder, looking sleepy as well, but happy. She broke the eggs, one-handed, and set them to fry in the hot butter in the iron skillet.

"Excited?" Ames asked.

Betts grinned. "Yep. Can we take Magnus up, too? He'd love to see the park, and he's good with other dogs now."

Ames thought about it for a minute. "You can't ride in back with him, but I guess it would be OK. He'll need to behave himself."

Betts petted the giant wrinkled head on the couch with her foot, not wanting to wash her hands again as she was cooking. Magnus yawned and tolerated the foot, keeping his eyes on Betts, as always. "Magnus is the perfect gentleman," she said.

"I don't see how the two of you fit on the couch," said Zoey, looking at the enormous dog.

Betts smiled. "He leaves a little wedge for my legs, and he hangs off the end. He's just taking up the whole thing now because he can." She looked at her dog. "I love you, Magnus," she said in her singsong, mommy voice. Magnus wagged his tail.

Zoey had been sleeping over most nights, and breakfast for the three of them had become a normal thing. Betts enjoyed having Zoey there, and only teased the couple a few times, counting the seconds out loud while they kissed. She had made it to seventeen a few days before. Zoey had been worried that Betts would be angry or jealous, but Ames pointed out, "She likes you, and likes having you here. And I do, too."

"Will you braid my hair?" Betts asked Zoey, who was still trying to find a way to work the brush through her own hair.

"Sure," said Zoey, "If I ever get done with mine."

The phone rang, and Ames took a call from a neighbor down the hill, who had gotten up that morning to find a tree across his driveway, trapping his family at their summerhouse. Ames held the phone and spoke to Zoey. "Would you be willing to take Betts up to Battery Park today? The Meyers have a tree down on their driveway, and need it gone."

"Road trip for the girls!" shouted Zoey, and Betts grinned, meeting her high five, and adding, "The girls, and the faithful Magnus." Ames turned back to the phone and agreed to come for the tree after breakfast if he could get a ride back up to the cabin when he was done.

When Ames hung up the phone, Betts picked it up and called her mother. There was no answer, which seemed a bit odd since it was still early, but she left a message reminding her mother that she would see her at Battery Park that day at eleven in the morning. As she hung up, she said, "Nobody answered. Do you think she's OK?"

Ames nodded and said, "She's probably in the shower or something. She'll see you at eleven. She hasn't forgotten. I'll bet she's as excited as you are."

Breakfast was enjoyed, the pot of tea drained, the eggs and toast perfect, and Zoey and Ames did the washing up while Betts took Magnus out. Betts tied Magnus in the bed of the truck with a piece of baling twine she found in the cab, a slim string for a hundred- and sixty-pound dog, but Magnus was a gentleman, after all. The wind at sixty was enough to keep Magnus up by the cab, anyway, and Betts watched him out the back window, the slider open so she could lay her hand out the back window on his rough head.

Ames had gathered his tools and put them in the back of the truck, under Magnus's watchful eyes, and they rolled out just a tad before nine o'clock. Ames got out at the Meyer place, now blocked by an ash tree lying across the narrow drive, and unloaded his saw and tools. "You two have a good time," he said, kissing Betts in one window, and then moving to the other side to kiss Zoey.

"I guess my mom was sleeping this morning," said Betts, "or maybe she was out for a walk or something," still worrying about the phone call.

Zoey looked over at Betts as she drove down the road. "Third." Betts shifted the truck up. "I'm sure your mom is fine. We'll see her at eleven. I'll bet she was in the shower," Zoey said. Betts nodded but continued to stew. Something about the phone call felt wrong, somehow.

Tina was up early, in fact, excited to see Betts, and even more excited to show Betts her new life in Burlington. Tina felt that she was building something wonderful here for herself, and for Betts when she came to visit. She wanted Betts to see it, and to see the new Tina who she felt was starting to really be a different person than she had ever been. Tina showered, got dressed, and poured a bowl of cereal, while she waited for her coffee. Mary was sleeping late, although she planned to go with Tina to the park to meet Betts before she started work.

The coffee quieted down, and Tina poured herself a cup, heading back to the breakfast table. There was a science museum just off the park that she planned to take Betts to. Mary had said the museum was all about the lake and the things that lived in it. It sounded like a perfect fit for Betts, as much as she loved science and nature. Tina glanced at the answering machine, half expecting a reminder call from Betts, but the machine was silent, with no beep and no blinking light. Betts had always been the one to try and remind her mother of appointments when the two of them had lived together, and a call would have not been surprising. She had given Betts her new number. Tina sat down with her coffee and cereal and thought about the day to come.

While Betts was still having her hair braided by Zoey, and when Tina was just getting out of bed, Peter was waking up, lying in the wreckage of the ruined trailer, his neck stiff from a night on the floor, and his right hand bruised and bloody from punching the walls and furniture the night before. Lots of things in the trailer had been punched and kicked in the past few days, and with the alcohol starting to seep out of his system, Peter could feel his heartbeat pounding in the swollen hand. Peter remembered again that Tina had left him, just walked out after him taking care of her all these years, and he remembered again that he was waking up alone in the wrecked trailer, the TV smashed, the kitchen torn apart. He swore the same two tired words he had spit out a thousand times a day and tried to roll over and sit up. His hand throbbed, and his head throbbed. He gasped, as his head seemed to split open with pain, and swore again.

Just then, he heard the phone ring, faintly from under the couch that had somehow been tipped over on it. It rang six times, then the answering machine clicked on, and he could hear Tina's voice. "I'm not here. Leave a message." Then he heard Betts voice, excited, reminding her mother of the meeting in Battery Park at eleven o'clock that day, by the playground. Betts's voice sang out, "I love you!" and then she hung up.

Peter was awake now, staring at the blinking light on the machine. He forced himself upright, gritting his teeth against the pain. He looked at the clock on the wall. Eight-thirty. Plenty of time to get to Burlington by eleven, he thought. He picked up the Star 9 mm pistol from the floor beside him, checked to confirm that it was loaded, and tucked it into his pants. He found his car keys in his pocket and also discovered that he had wet himself badly enough to soak through the adult diapers he now wore, soaking the front of his pants. He thought of the effort and time required to get on a fresh diaper and clothes and gave it up. "First things, first," he said, heading out the door.

CHAPTER THIRTY-THREE

Battery Park

Tina finished breakfast and sat and chatted with Mary, who came to the table, still sleepy after a date the night before. "They're on the road by now," said Tina. "It takes an hour and a half, or so, to get from Randolph up to Burlington. I'll bet they left early. You can meet my brother, too. He'll be driving them up. He's super quiet and shy."

"Is he cute?" asked Mary grinning.

"I'll introduce you," Tina said, "but I think he's sweet on Betts' social worker."

Zoey pulled into the parking lot of the playground at about ten minutes before eleven. The beautiful weather had filled the park with families eager to get one last warm weekend in by the lake. Betts scanned the crowd for any sign of her mother. "I don't see her," she said.

"We're early," Zoey replied. "She'll be here at eleven, or maybe a little earlier. Do you want to go play while we wait?"

Betts gave Zoey a hard look. "I brought a book," she said, sitting down on the stone wall where she had a good view of the area. Magnus sat in the back of the truck, keeping an eye on Betts, and soaking up the last summer sun on his scarred and wrinkled coat. Zoey sat beside Betts on the wall, watching the children at play, and wondering about their lives.

Tina and Mary had walked a quarter-mile from the apartment to the edge of the park and now walked along the bike path, staying to the side as bikes and kids on skateboards wheeled past. "We had a field trip up here once when I was a kid," Tina said. "A free trip, so I got to go. We took a boat out on the lake. It was fun. And I think we played on the playground where we're going to meet Betts, although I bet it looked different back then."

Mary nodded. "I love this place. We used to hang out at Battery Park when I first came to school. I remember seeing Burlington and the lake, the first time I came up with my parents, and feeling like this was where I wanted to live. I love this place."

"See that old blue truck?" Tina asked. "That's my brother's truck. They must have come up early."

Across the street, in his black Camaro, Peter sat low in his seat, watching the playground as well. He saw the nose of the blue truck, poking out from behind a van parked next to it, and he saw Betts on the stone wall, sitting beside a young woman he didn't know. His pistol was in his hand, and he watched for Tina to come into sight. His head hurt, and hand hurt, and his pants and the car seat were soaked in his sour urine from the night before, and now from the trip up as well. He realized he had no plan to get away if some cop or a brave do-gooder tried to get in his way, but he didn't really care. He thought of the ruined trailer, his ruined health, the job he had failed to show up for the last week, and decided he had no plans to go home, anyway.

He saw Betts stand up, an excited look on her face, pointing down the bike path, and saying something to the woman beside her. He opened the car door, tugged himself up and out of the car, and began to walk across the road toward the crowded parking lot. His hand held the pistol next to his soaked pants, and he darted between the cars that slowed to let him cross.

Tina saw Betts waving, and tugged Mary along with her. She was within a few feet of Betts when the smile on her face changed. Betts saw her mother's face freeze and looked to the side, where she saw Peter, with an ugly grin on his twisted face, a wet stain on his pants, and a gun in his hand, swinging it up toward Tina. Zoey was still on the wall, and Mary had been left behind in the rush. Betts saw with perfect clarity the sun on the lake, the cool shadow of the trees rustling overhead, and the look in her mother's eyes as Peter raised the gun, said those awful words one more time, and pulled the trigger.

Peter's body suddenly flew to one side as the gun exploded with a bright flash of light and sound. The roar of the pistol was like a hard slap to Betts' ears. The people screamed and fell away, as Peter disappeared beneath the silent force of Magnus, who had broken his thin tie and leapt from the truck, understanding that Betts, his girl, was in danger, and seeing in Peter the kind of man he already knew. Magnus did not make a sound, other than the rush of his huge feet across the gravel, and the steady breaths he took as he ran and jumped, taking Peter's head from behind in his great jaws. He tore the skin across the skull, then digging into the bone with his broken yellowed teeth, he threw his whole weight onto Peter, and shaking him back and forth like a rag doll. Peter's neck was broken before he hit the ground, and Magnus stood upon him, his stained jaws still gripping the cracked skull.

Tina came up off the wall, and ran to Betts, as the people screamed and fell away. Tina was on the ground, and Betts was over her, sobbing. "I'm OK," said Tina, holding Betts, and then trying to sit up. She saw the limp body of Peter beneath the huge and gore streaked Magnus. "Is that your dog?" she asked. Zoey moved quickly to Betts, then to Magnus, taking him off Peter, and into the truck, where she wiped his jaws with one of Ames shop rags. Tina and Betts followed, and by the time the police arrived, first on bicycle, then in three cars, Magnus was calmly sitting with his family, looking like the hero he was.

There was a wide circle around Peter's body, and when the ambulance crew shifted him onto the stretcher for the silent trip to the hospital, Betts and Tina and Zoey were being interviewed by two police, who took statements and contact information and then allowed them to go. They drove the truck back to Mary and Tina's apartment, and sat around the dining room table, while Betts insisted on cleaning up Magnus some more. Nobody had much of an appetite, although Mary did bring out some cold Vietnamese and Indian food, and a bottle of juice. She made a pot of coffee, which had more success, and Betts and her mother just hugged and cried together on and off. Later, after a quiet tour of the apartment, after the song of the music box, and more hugs, and after plans were made for the next weekend, Tina and Betts said goodbye, and the three of them headed out to the truck. Magnus was somehow fit into the cab, with Betts leaning on him and still crying from time to time, and in this way, they found their way back to the cabin on the mountain, where Ames had just made a fresh pot of tea. Betts flew from the truck into Ames's arms.

The dust settles. In spite of trauma, in spite of the events that shake our lives, we move on. We sleep, we eat, we drink, we shower and change clothes, and if we are lucky, we have loved ones to hold us close while we recover. Death, especially death right in front of us, is traumatic, and Peter's death meant not only the end of a threat but also the end of any hope that Peter might be redeemed on this side of the grave. Betts thought a lot about her phone call, calling her mother's old number instead of her new one. She wondered if she carried some responsibility for Peter's death and if his death was the only way her mother could be safe. Lots of questions never have an answer, but Betts had good people around her to help her sort it out.

Seasons change. With the color back in the trees, Betts started a new year of school, sitting again next to Cara. Zoey gave up her apartment in town and then gave up her job as well, rolling up her sleeves and putting on a pair of leather gloves and boots to join Ames in his work on the mountain, and to spend time with her new family. The spring flowed its blessings out onto the splash rock, down the mountain and off into the sea. The split wood gave up its store of summer sun in the little green woodstove and kept the cabin warm and snug, and boiled water for a thousand pots of tea. The silence of the long, Vermont winter came, and the cold nights found the four of them safe and warm inside, drawing or reading or talking. Rebekah moved on, seeing that all was well with her family, at last. And Magnus lay on the couch, keeping half an eye on his girl, Betts.

NOTE FROM THE AUTHOR

Word-of-mouth is crucial for any author to succeed. If you enjoyed the book, please leave a review online—anywhere you are able. Even if it's just a sentence or two. It would make all the difference and would be very much appreciated.

    Thanks!
    Gary

ABOUT THE AUTHOR

Gary D. Hillard lives just down the road from Betts, in a cabin of his own. His life as a parent, a child therapist, a school teacher, a foster parent, an adoptive parent and a social worker laid the foundation for this book, a book filled with the kind of truth that can only be told in fiction. Hillard writes every morning and spends the rest of his time drinking tea.

Thank you so much for reading one of our **Coming of Age** novels.

If you enjoyed our book, please check out our recommended title for your next great read!

The Five Wishes by Mr. Murray McBride by Joe Siple

2018 Maxy Award "Book of the Year"

"A sweet...tale of human connection...will feel familiar to fans of Hallmark movies." –*KIRKUS REVIEWS*

"An emotional story that will leave readers meditating on the life-saving magic of kindness." –*Indie Reader*

View other Black Rose Writing titles at www.blackrosewriting.com/books and use promo code **PRINT** to receive a **20% discount** when purchasing.

BLACK ROSE writing

CPSIA information can be obtained
at www.ICGtesting.com
Printed in the USA
FSHW021330170720
71761FS